Accl
THOMAS
Nothing but Blue Skies

"I don't know of another writer who can walk Thomas McGuane's literary highwire. His vaunted dialogue has not been overpraised.... He can describe the sky, a bird, a rock, the dawn, with such grace that you want to go out and see for yourself; then he can zip to a scene so funny that it makes you laugh out loud."
—Beverly Lowry, *The New York Times*

"McGuane's best novel in years....[He] imparts to his slapstick a shivery recognition of human weakness....*Nothing but Blue Skies* explores the scary territory with brio and originality."
—*Newsday*

"Thomas McGuane is the pool shark of our prose. His sentences click with imperious precision....McGuane puts English on his English so the words swerve with fatal charm."
—*Christian Science Monitor*

"Few writers have explored our national malaise as persistently — or as elegantly—as Thomas McGuane...a writer whose command of the language has helped define our American loneliness."
—*Philadelphia Inquirer*

"A master of the contemporary picaresque....His prose is visual, dense, exact; it evokes the look and feel of the landscapes he's in-habited....[McGuane] never belabors a point; even when he's brooding about life, he does it with a wry, ironic grace."
—*Vanity Fair*

Books by

THOMAS McGUANE

The Sporting Club, 1969
The Bushwhacked Piano, 1971
Ninety-two in the Shade, 1973
Panama, 1978
An Outside Chance, 1980
Nobody's Angel, 1982
Something to Be Desired, 1984
To Skin a Cat, 1986
Keep the Change, 1989
Nothing but Blue Skies, 1992

THOMAS McGUANE

Nothing but Blue Skies

Thomas McGuane is the author of several highly acclaimed novels, including *The Sporting Club; The Bushwhacked Piano,* which won the Richard and Hinda Rosenthal Award of the American Academy and Institute of Arts and Letters; *Ninety-two in the Shade,* which was nominated for the National Book Award; *Panama; Nobody's Angel; Something to Be Desired; Keep the Change;* and *Nothing but Blue Skies.* He has also written *To Skin a Cat,* a collection of short stories; and *An Outside Chance,* a collection of essays on sport. His books have been published in ten languages. He was born in Michigan and educated at Michigan State University, earned a Master of Fine Arts degree at the Yale School of Drama and was a Wallace Stegner Fellow at Stanford. An ardent conservationist, he is a director of American Rivers and of the Craighead Wildlife-Wildlands Institute. He lives with his family in McLeod, Montana.

THOMAS McGUANE

Nothing but Blue Skies

VINTAGE CONTEMPORARIES

VINTAGE BOOKS • A DIVISION OF RANDOM HOUSE, INC. • NEW YORK

FIRST VINTAGE CONTEMPORARIES EDITION, FEBRUARY 1994

Copyright © 1992 by Thomas McGuane

Library of Congress Cataloging-in-Publication Data
McGuane, Thomas.
Nothing but blue skies / Thomas McGuane. — 1st Vintage
contemporaries ed.
p.   cm. — (Vintage contemporaries)
ISBN 0-679-74778-8
1. Men—Montana—Fiction.   I. Title.
[PS3563.A3114N65   1994]   813'.54—dc20
93-6330
CIP

Manufactured in the United States of America
10 9 8 7 6 5 4 3 2 1

For Annie, Heather and Maggie with love

"If you come to a fork in the road, take it."

— YOGI BERRA

Nothing but
Blue Skies

1

Frank Copenhaver put his wife Gracie's suitcases in the back of the Electra and held the door for her. She got in. He walked around the front of the car gravely and he got in. He leaned forward over the steering wheel to look up at their house as though it were he, rather than Gracie, who was looking at it for the last time. A magpie flew across his view. It was a clue for Gracie in the event she didn't realize that this was her chance. He didn't want her, halfway to Arizona, to realize she had, in her sadness, forgotten to do this very important thing.

Once they were under way, he said, "We've got a few extra minutes, let me take the scenic route."

"Oh, Frank, oh, please God no, not the scenic route," said Gracie.

He was undeterred. As he drove, he chatted easily about the clash between Kellogg and General Mills over the seven-and-a-half-billion-dollar cereal business, realizing too late that it might seem to be an attempt to prefigure their own impending divorce and settlement. He tried to be almost too specific in fending off this parallel, running on about Cheerios and Wheaties and Rice Krispies and Raisin Bran; and, considering the state of their own lives, making far too much of Tony the Tiger autographing baseballs at Safeway stores.

Gracie was dressed for travel, jeans, a cotton sweater tied around her waist, tennis shoes; her long black hair was braided and wound atop her head. She was at once weathered and pretty, remarkably girlish for the mother of a college student. She was wearing mountaineering glasses with leather side pieces. She didn't seem to see much of the ordinary suburb and barely tightened her focus when Frank stopped in front of his — their —medical clinic on Alder Street and watched in apparent satisfaction as patients wandered in and out of its breezy, modern entryway. They had not owned the clinic long, and the many nursery aspens were still held up by stakes and wires; the beds of annuals had an uncanny uniformity. Frank took one more turn so that he could see the building from the side, then went on to the Kid Royale, his pet project.

The Kid Royale Hotel was a short walk from Deadrock's old Territorial railroad station and was one of the monuments of the Montana frontier. Frank was going to restore it to its original glory, with its carriage bays and hitching racks and vaulted lobby. It was in poor shape now and stood with faded tobacco and soft drink advertisements painted on its side in a neighborhood that was giving way to transience and light industry. The success of this project would probably do more to endear Frank to this small city than anything. And it was only with the mildest of irony that he looked forward to his acceptance.

"Can we skip the mini-storage?" Gracie asked. "It's getting late." Frank was able to include the mini-storage facility in the scenic tour despite Gracie leaning disconsolately against the side of the car.

"You know," he said, "it's hard to believe, but there's some five percent adjustable mortgages out there. Sometimes I think my bank is trying to put me out of business. You can't always absorb these little things just to be courteous, let people nick you when they want. Like today, the Nikkei stock index plunged under the effect of arbitrage-related selling. This crap skids around the Pacific Rim in about four nanoseconds and scares hell out of little guys in Montana like me. Gracie, I hate to see you go. It's been what, exactly?"

"A long time."

"A long time. But Grace, you should have never done what you did. People don't rise above things like that. Their marriages don't."

"I know, Frank." As they reached the airport behind a stream of cars looking for short-term parking, Frank suddenly felt wild and unacknowledged conflicts in his breast. He had not spent enough time thinking about what this moment could mean. There was something spinning loose.

"Gracie, I just know you're going to hit the ground running." The thought that that might actually be true renewed his malice. "I'm going to focus on my business. Our situation has been so anti-synergistic that, to be completely honest, I expect to take off like a rocket as soon as you're gone."

"I bet you're right."

"If you get a chance, I'd like to see you salt a few bucks away in tax-deferred variable annuities, but that's between you and who-ever." "Whoever" was like a drooling new face at Mount Rush-more.

"Thanks."

Frank managed to catch a skycap's eye. The skycap, a boy of about eighteen with long hair falling out of his cap, came to the driver's side window where Frank gave him several bills. "Give the lady a hand with her luggage if you would." Then he turned to Gracie, who was getting out of the car. "Goodbye, Grace. Give my regards to a town of your choice."

"Goodbye, Frank." Her cheeks were wet with tears.

He pulled away with a bizarre, all-knowing expression on his face, his hands parallel on the wheel and feeling, as he glanced in the rearview mirror too late to see Gracie enter the airport, that something inside had come completely undone. There was no chance to analyze her gait and try to determine if she was eager to get on the plane. There was no chance to collapse with grief and, perhaps, start all over again.

He had really thought he was adjusting to a changed Gracie but not an entirely new one. They had two cars but they never went anywhere in two cars before. They picked one and both went in it together, either Gracie's unkillable Plymouth Valiant with its smooth-ticking little slant six or his low, domineering blue-black Electra with the insouciant lag shifts of its fluid-swilling transmission. Often Gracie slid over near him like in high school, elevating slightly on the spheres of her buttocks to touch her hair into place in the rearview mirror or put her hand high on his thigh. The Buick seemed like an old-time sex car, and unlike the light-spirited Japanese cars that had come to dominate things, the Electra still seemed to say, You're going with me and you're going to put out, period. The wanton deep pleats of its velvety upholstery invited stains. Recently, however, Gracie had begun to take the Plymouth for "time to think" on her way to her restaurant, Amazing Grease — sometimes, it seemed to Frank, with plenty of time to think. She had promised she would learn how to fish so that they would have more time together, but that plan went sour. He was quick to notice that things had changed but slow to realize what should be done about it. He reminded himself that he still had his health.

Frank buried himself not in his work but in fantasies of escape. He became a connoisseur of maps. He loved the history of maps and he felt drawn to the theory of the flat earth as the only one that adequately explained the disappearances common to everyone, especially death. He saw a kind of poetry in the spherical projections of the world as devised by Ptolemy. The more insistently the mystery of Gracie's changed patterns intruded upon his thoughts, the more interested he was in the shrinking *terrae incognitae* of the old world; flat or round, what was the difference? Really, he often thought, what is the damn difference? It just seems likely that my parents, like other generations, milled around for sixty-eighty years and fell off the end.

He bought a scale model of a nineteenth-century surveyor's carriage and had booked a trip with Gracie's travel agent friend, Lucy, to visit the Royal Observatory at Greenwich, home of the Greenwich meridian, about the time Gracie hit the road without a map of any kind. By this time, the impending change had elaborated into a full-fledged human by the name of Edward Ballantine, a traveler and breeder of race horses, a resident of Sedona, Arizona, spiritual headquarters for Shirley MacLaine's crystal people. Suddenly, Galileo's discovery of the satellites of Jupiter, Newton's announcement that the earth was flattened at the poles, even his simple pleasure at reading the mileage tables in his gas station, were out the window. He had never really thought about his wife leaving him. She was gone and he would never be the same again. He would never have a single second of time that was in any way continuous with his previous life, even if she came back, which was not likely. What good was his map collection now?

In 1968, a now ancient time full of scathing situations, trying love but preferring lust and, for many, one meretricious *scène à faire,* the flushing of narcotics down the toilet, Frank was banished from the family business by his father. This involved a long autobiographical recitation in which his father told about his early years on the ranch, the formulaic (in Frank's eyes) long walk to a poorly heated country school, the pain of being Catholic in a community of Norwegian Lutherans, the early success in getting calf weights up, the malt barley successes, the highest certifications and the prize ribbons, the sod farm successes, the nursery, the Ford dealership, the implement dealership and the four apartment buildings, including the one regularly demolished by the fraternity boys "and their concubines." Frank's father was a self-taught, almost bookish individual, and he wore his education on his sleeve.

Among the fraternity boys was Frank, the son of the landlord, who had graduated a year earlier but who was now "managing the building" for his family, hoping to make it another of the family's successes. The occasion of his banishment was a theme party, the theme being Farm Life, a kind of witticism on Frank's part involving hauling three tons of straw into the building and piling it higher than not only the furniture but the heads of the occupants. Barnyard animals, chiefly pigs, were turned loose in

5

this lightless wilderness and the party began. It lasted two days. Tunnels quickly formed that led to the beer kegs and to small clearings where people could gather. There was a proscribed area for bodily functions, a circular clearing in the hay with dove gray shag carpet for a floor, and another for the operations of the stereo and its seemingly endless loop of the beloved Neil Young's "Are you ready for the country, 'cause it's time to go!"

The world of straw became damp and odorous with beer, marijuana, sperm, perfume and pig droppings. Frank would remember ever afterward the terror of crawling stoned, in his underwear, down a small side tunnel to meet headlong in the semidarkness a bristling, frightened three-hundred-pound pig. Right after that, clutching a beer and a joint and hearing the approach of another pig, he withdrew into the straw alongside the tunnel to let the pig pass, watched it go by ridden by the most beautiful naked sorority girl he had ever seen, Janet Otergaard from Wolf Point, now vice president of the First National Bank. Frank crawled after her but fell behind a bit, and when he caught up she was already going off into the straw with Barry Danzig, who was home from Northwestern Law School. This disappointment had the effect of making Frank long for fresh air. He made his way toward the entrance, and crawling out of the straw in his underwear, a bleak and tarry roach hanging from one of his slack lips, he met his father.

Mr. Copenhaver continued to wear suspenders long after they had gone out of fashion. He wore wide ones with conspicuous brass hardware to remind people of his agricultural origins. Most people hadn't gotten the news that farmers were as liable to be envy-driven crooks as anybody else, the stream of information having been interrupted by the Civil War; so, wearing wide suspenders was like wearing an "I Am Sincere" sign. Today, curving over the powerful chest of his father, they stood for all the nonsense he was not brooking. A bleary girl in a straw-flecked blue sweater emerged pulling the sweater down at the sides over her bare hips. She peered unwelcomingly at Frank's father and said, "Who's this one?"

"The owner of the building!" boomed Mr. Copenhaver. She dove back into the straw. Frank was now overpowered by fear of his father. He felt his drugged and drunken vagueness in muzzy contrast to his father's forceful clarity next to him, a presence formed by a lifetime of unstinting forward movement, of farming, warfare and free-market capitalism as found in a small Montana city. Next to his father, Frank felt like a pudding. As against making a world, he was prepared to offer the quest for pussy and altered states — an edgeless generation, dedicated to escaping the self and inconsequential fornicating, dedicated to the idea of the Relationship and all-terrain shoes that didn't lie to your feet. Frank's fear was that his father would strike him. Worse, he said to get the people out, clean up the building and appear at his office in the morning.

That didn't start out well either. He was exhausted from cleaning up the mess himself. His companions were unwilling to help until they had had a night's sleep. He found himself shouting, on the verge of tears: "Is this friendship? You know my back is against the wall? I'm about to get my ass handed to me. I need you to help me!" We need sleep, they said. So, he cleaned the mess up himself, hauling twenty-seven loads in the back of his car out to the landfill and simply, hopelessly, releasing the pigs into the neighborhood. They belonged to the family of one of the fellows who hadn't stayed to help. Frank found the most awful things on the floor: false teeth taped to the end of a stick, hot dogs and half-finished bags of miniature doughnuts dusted with powdered sugar, rotten panties, a Bible, a catcher's chest protector. He showered, changed into a clean shirt, clean jeans and a corduroy sport jacket. Then, having been up all night, he headed for his father's office. He drove up Assiniboine Avenue and then turned at College Street. His nerves were shattered by the sight of three of the pigs jogging up the center of Third Street, loosely glancing over their shoulders. Here and there, people stopped to watch these out-of-place animals.

He parked his car, an old blue Mercury with sarcastic tail fins and speckled bumpers, in front of his father's office, a handsomely remodeled farmhouse on West Deadrock, and went in. He presented himself shakily to the secretary, the very Eileen who now worked for him, who waved him on with a gesture that suggested she knew all about people like Frank and his friends. And perhaps she did, he thought. It's easy to detect motion when you're frozen in position, an old hunter's trick.

"Come in, Frank," said his father evenly.

"Hi, Dad."

His father stayed at his desk while Frank sank subdued into an upholstered chair placed in front of the desk, a chair so ill sprung that Frank, at six-one, was barely able to see over the front of his father's desk. The view of his father's head and neck rising from the horizontal line in front was reminiscent of a poorly lit documentary shot of a sea serpent and added to the state begun by Frank's shattered condition.

Mr. Copenhaver made a steeple with his fingertips. The high color in his cheeks, the silver-and-sand hair combed straight across his forehead and the blue suit gave him an ecclesiastical look, and Frank felt a fleeting hope that this was no accident and Christian forgiveness lay just around the corner.

"Frank, you're interested in so many things." His father glanced down; Frank could see he had the desk drawer slightly open so that he could make out some notes he had made for this conversation.

"Yes, sir."

"You like to hunt and fish."

"Yes, sir."

"You like the ladies. You like a high old time. You like to meet your buddies for a drink in the evening and you read our daily newspaper, indicating, I might have hoped, an interest in current events but probably only the ball scores. I rarely see you with anything uplifting in your hand bookwise and the few you've left around the place are the absolute utmost in prurience, illustrated with photographs for those who are unable to follow the very descriptive text. So far so good: at least it was confined between the covers of a book. There was a day in time when I had my own Tillie the Toiler comics and I am not here setting myself up to moralize about your condition. I have for a long time now, heaving a great sigh, accepted that I was the father of a drunken sports lecher and let it go at that. But when I gave you the opportunity to find some footing in the day-to-day world that would have implications for your livelihood many years down the road, you gave it the kind of disrespect I have to assume was directed at me. Last night, I felt personally smothered in straw and pig manure. That was your valentine to your father, Frank, thank you. And Frank, see how this flies: I'm not going to put up with it anymore. You're not going to run that building anymore and my hope that you would one day manage the old home place is dead. I think your brother Mike is the man for that job."

Mr. Copenhaver tipped back in his chair and began to talk about growing up on the old home place, the long walk to school, the cold, some parenthetical remarks about rural electrification and rural values. Frank tried to stare out the window but his eyes were too weak to get past the glass. He was cottonmouthed with exhaustion and prepared to endorse any negative view of his character. At the same time, he'd had enough. He got to his feet on his leaden legs and raised his hand, palm outward, to his father.

"Goodbye," Frank said. He went out the door and rarely saw his father again. Mike saw him frequently, even driving down from the school of dentistry. They had a nice, even relationship that Frank envied. Mike never made an attempt to be a businessman like his father. That, much later, would be Frank's job, seeking approval from someone who had departed this world for the refrigerated shadows of death.

2

First he went to Seattle, where he worked for a short time tying up seaplanes at Lake Union. Coming from a land of little rain, he felt his clothes would never dry. He lived with a Quinault Indian his own age who was studying marine biology at the University of Washington and who wanted to go home and manage the salmon fisheries on his reservation. Frank kept tying up the planes and admiring the pilots and waiting for the weather to clear. It never did. So, he went to Los Angeles and worked as a framer on what was to be the biggest semi-enclosed air-conditioned seaside synagogue west of the Mississippi, but the funding went tits up and Frank was again unemployed, living in a pleasant rented room one block off Westwood and going to lavish previews of off-the-wall motion pictures made by other hippies.

He had various girlfriends, ones who cooked, ones who didn't, ones who got on top and watched traffic at the same time, ones who passed a joint and held their breath while humping like a wild dog, flat-chested ones and ones whose breasts surged halfway to their belly buttons before trying to jump over their shoulders, ones who dealt, ones who typed screenplays for fake hippies from New York, ones who delivered singing telegrams and ones who sold airline tickets or served in-flight snacks and ones who like Frank himself were willing to support his weight but really just wanted to go back where they came from. It was sex en masse. It got monotonous and lasted one year, one month and nineteen days. He was out of there like a kerosened cat. He wanted to go back where he came from but he still couldn't quite bring it off. Everyone in California seemed surrounded by quotation marks.

He answered an ad promising travel and went to work for a crew that drifted around the country wrecking old homes and hauling the doors, chandeliers, windows and hardware back to Los Angeles for use in houses that duplicated other periods. They even demolished a few mansions in Montana. Frank thought of getting home but the brute work of making sure the booty made it to the West Coast was all-consuming. He would have liked a shot at the old home place but it was too much to ask. The old home places of others would have to do. The billiard table of a Butte mining baron ended up as a striking salad bar in Van Nuys, and numerous farm wagons and buckboards met a similar fate in steak joints, shrimp joints, king crab joints. Frank had felt a subtle change of character as he took on the world of atmosphere, as a thing unto itself. It was like the covering of straw and pig manure of the Farm Life party that had put him on the road in the first place. It was interesting to try to produce atmosphere directly, without tediously waiting for human life to create it.

Frank rose up in this work and became an independent contractor. His work had a look. If a chili chain wanted ambience, Frank went to the border and returned with wetback cafés loaded on tractor-trailer rigs. By the time the Cajun mania hit, Frank already was deep into Louisiana and in fact had inventoried the lower Mississippi, all the way to Plaquemines Parish, for an earlier gumbo empire that had stretched from Ventura to Redding before falling of its own weight and turning back into gas stations. It was in the minute town of Chalou, Louisiana, on the crumbling riverbend steps of a fallen-down indigo plantation house, that he met Gracie. She looked a little bit like an Indian. She was brown-eyed, black-haired, five-four and carried a two-barreled shotgun with big mule-ear hammers and a white ivory bead for a sight and had some connection with the building. He knew right then he had totaled his last heirloom. Ever afterward he would marvel at his own solitary experience with love at first sight. He stood there under her gun, as he would later be under the gun of her departure and then absence. His diagnosis, after she'd gone, was that he had spent their time together building something to please his parents when he should have been building something to please Gracie.

Once Frank was directed off the property, Gracie put the mule-eared gun in the back seat of the convertible she had driven out to the river and explained that the house had been in her family. Frank took her to lunch at a place on the road out to Thibodaux and they shared a huge platter of boiled crawfish. The waitress was a great big Cajun woman wearing a T-shirt with a red portrait of a crawfish on the front. The woman's T-shirt said, "You want me to suck what?" Gracie told him that real Cajuns suck the crawfish shells when they're done eating them. Then she told him her family story in compressed form so that he wouldn't think she was some trigger-happy hillbilly. Somehow they had been planters a century and a half earlier, been ruined, been "kinda like" rednecks for three or four generations and were now on their way back up. "Up" being a wholesale furniture outlet so successful they had acquired control of the headquarters in New Orleans. Gracie said that someday she hoped they would live back out on the river, in sight of the ruined plantation house. "Maybe you will," said Frank. At this point, he didn't realize that it mattered much. He guessed she had a romantic streak.

After lunch, Gracie took him to the furniture outlet. It was just outside the town of Houma, a vast cinderblock building that faced a parking lot that would have suited a small stadium. Something had been added to the gravel in the parking lot, causing it to sparkle, and the building itself was faced with a sparkling material. There must have been a hundred cars parked there. The great show windows rose almost a story and a half, and the name of the store, Bouget's Lagniappe Furniture, was written in neon script across the top of the building, where it flashed at an emergency level. Beneath the sign was an enormous portrait of Gracie's father wearing a shining crown to indicate that he was the king. There were low pines in the distance and the smell of a refinery in the air.

Inside, families and individuals wandered aisles of furniture, chattering in French and trying out merchandise. One olive-skinned paterfamilias was testing the mechanism of a TV lounger in front of his large and admiring family. He sat in the chair and pushed the footrest; the chair swept back so that Papa was gazing at the ceiling. The children sighed. Then Papa got up abruptly with a superior little smile on his face indicating that things were not so easily put over on him.

A little farther on, another family was seated at a dinette set pretending to have dinner. And beyond, an old man sat at a desk and imagined himself to be doing business while his wife pretended to be his secretary, scratching away at an imaginary writing tablet while he chattered at her in French.

Gracie led him to the back of the store and into an office, which was simply partitioned off from the vast warehouse–display area. Inside this office, Frank was introduced to Antoine "Fatso" Bouget, Gracie's father. He was not quite round enough, Frank thought, to be called Fatso; but with his oval, smooth, olive face and unmoving arched black eyebrows, he was very distinctly one of the locals. He deftly questioned Frank about his work and background, then turned to Gracie and said, "Him we have out to the house."

The house, on Bayou Teche, was a modern ranch house except that it had a big front porch on it filled with comfortable furniture for lounging and looking out on the bayou. Mr. Bouget gave Frank a tour of his property, which included numerous pens for pigs and ducks and a great variety of noisy fowl in general but especially the cautious-looking guinea hens that Mr. Bouget liked to toss into his gumbo. Gracie stayed in the house to talk to her mother, who was small and dark like she was and seemed to be continuously thinking of a very private joke. He showed Frank a loudly painted and powerful water-ski boat under a corrugated metal shed. A warm wind sighed in the trees and made an even ripple on the water.

"Dat's my pirogue, Frank. I use dat to find the crawfish in his home. I find his little chimney and dere I place my trap!"

With his left hand he gestured toward his big Oldsmobile until Frank acknowledged it and, as though they shared the same tissue of good fortune, he smoothly swept his hand to the boat. Frank nodded in vigorous complicity and said, "Uh-*huh,*" and now they were damn sure buddies. Mr. Bouget leaned toward Frank from the waist. His little smile was a V.

"By the way, Frank, my name ain't really Fatso. Dat ain't even my nickname. My name Antoine but my real nickname is Fais Dodo. Buncha ignorant Américains called it Fatso."

"Faye Dodo?"

"Yessuh."

"Why do they call you Faye Dodo?"

"Did. Don't no more, call me Fatso."

"But why did they call you Faye Dodo?"

"Why! 'Cause I always liked to party!"

This time, when Frank was unable to keep the complete confusion from his face, Antoine Fais Dodo Fatso Bouget pounded him on the back and shouted, "You better get some food into yo' ass. You peakit!"

"What do you call this body of water, Mr. Bouget?"

"This here's Bayou Teche."

"You always live here?"

"Aw hell, no. Maman and me come from Bayou Terrebonne. But you must go where your life take you."

As they walked back toward the house, Mr. Bouget jostled along in a comradely way, bumping into Frank and making amusing remarks, ending with, "You ain't by any chance Catholic, are you, Frank?"

"Yes, I am."

"Uh-*huh*. Frank, if you excuse me half a sec, I must have a word with Maman."

Gracie leaned out the door as her father went in. She was lightly dusted with corn meal from cooking. "You making out all right?"

"Just fine," said Frank, "just fine."

She went back inside and Frank wandered around the back, looked out at the dark water of the bayou, at the other houses and docks on its shore. Here and there boats were drawn up and there were piles of crawfish traps, net floats, defunct outboard motors, galvanized tubs and caved-in Styrofoam boxes.

Mr. Bouget held up two bottles of beer to call Frank in and Frank joined him. Inside, loud rhythmic accordion music played on the stereo. "Is that what they call zydeco?" Frank asked.

"Zydeco!" said Mr. Bouget. "Spare me, cher! Zydeco num' but nigga music."

"You're listening to the sweet sounds of Ambrose Thibodeux," said Gracie helpfully. Her mother returned to the kitchen and her father went into the living room to turn the music down. Gracie leaned over and said, "You should have never told them you were Catholic." Frank didn't mind. Though he rarely went to Mass, he took what he thought was the Bougets' view, that Catholics were different people.

Frank ate without having any idea what he was eating, except for the rice it was ladled onto. It was filled with beans and thick, furiously spicy sauce. Frank ate an enormous amount of it because it was better than anything he'd eaten in a long time. He ate so much that the family was fascinated by it. He drank a bit too much, and in his inebriation he knew how they approved of his overeating, both as a sign of admiration for Mrs. Bouget's cooking and as a sign to Mr. Bouget that he was comfortable with their family. He stuffed himself more than he really wanted to and elevated his voice. The Bougets asked Gracie vaguely set-up questions that would allow her to talk about her education and prospects. She had just finished at the University of Southwestern Louisiana. "Up in Lafayette!" shouted Mr. Bouget. That seemed to be the important part to him.

After dinner, Mrs. Bouget took Frank back to a huge closet where she was storing Gracie's trousseau — endless handmade quilts, sheets and pillowcases. Never have to leave the bedroom, thought Frank. While they were looking at the trousseau, Gracie and her father set up the slide projector. Gracie was filled with comic glee and Frank was uncertain what was causing it. They went back to the living room, turned out the lights and projected a photograph of the family standing in front of Bouget's Lagniappe Furniture headquarters in the Algiers section of New Orleans. Mr. Bouget was wearing the crown that he wore for his portrait on the front of the local outlet. Gracie looked proud in her white cotton dress.

"Sonofagun, look at Fais Dodo smilin'!" called Mr. Bouget to these images of himself. "He the king of the outlet!"

"He smilin' good now!" called Gracie.

"Show respect, Gracie," said her mother. "College smarty."

By ten o'clock, Frank and Mr. Bouget were both drunk and standing next to the bayou in the dark. There was a roar of nocturnal insects. Frank's high spirits had declined to a polite stupor.

"Want to run my pirogue, Frank?"

"No, sir. I can't see, hardly."

"Call me Fatso, Frank."

"Okay," said Frank, but he couldn't do it. Fatso wasn't a nice thing to call someone where Frank came from. But anyway, here came Fatso under his own steam.

"Frank, once Gracie come home from college, it was like she was lookin' for somethin', somethin' she couldn't find here in La Teche, somethin' she used to have but she lost up there at the college, and now she's back hangin' out at the old plan'ation thinkin' she can call back all them dead Creoles. I tell her, Cher, they gone, they gone. And guess what? They are gone but we are not. No sir, we are not. Anyway, all I'm tellin' you, Frank, is I know this girl 'bout as good as a father can, and you need to be paying extra close attention 'cause they ain't gonna make but one like Gracie." The day would come, years later, when Frank would recall this speech with anguish. "They ain't gonna make but one like Gracie."

Mrs. Bouget was winding down her household, pulling her

kitchen together efficiently and turning off lights from room to room. There was an inside staircase to the guest room, almost an attic room. Frank said good night to Gracie and her mother and followed Mr. Bouget upstairs. Mr. Bouget showed Frank his bed and turned back the covers for him. He told Frank he needed a little air and slid up the one window, letting the rich dampness of the bayou come inside. Frank was drunk enough to be able to abandon himself to this smell, filling his lungs with the fine air as though trying to store it for the year. Mr. Bouget watched him and then he began to do the same. Then they laughed and stuck their heads out the window. "Here's where it's comin' from," cried Fatso Bouget. They both took deep breaths.

"Antoine," came the voice of Mrs. Bouget.

"Yes, Maman," said Mr. Bouget, facing down the stairs with his thumbs in his ears and his fingers wiggling madly. "Here I come."

All the lights were out and the house was silent. It was a still night outside and Frank could hear fish jumping in the bayou. Many songs have fish jumping in the bayou, he thought. Frank loved to fish so much that even their sounds in the dark made his heart pound. By rolling onto his stomach, Frank could gaze out his window to the dim yellow light at the end of the pier and see the whirling moths that attracted the fish, the moist air, the light and water running together.

He awoke from a deep sleep. Something was happening inside his stomach. He rested his right hand on his swollen middle and looked at his watch on his left wrist: almost three in the morning. Years later, when Gracie left, he still had the watch but could no longer read the dial. He'd been asleep for over four hours and his stomach was getting ready to explode. He was thoroughly sober now and had a mild headache. He was going to have to relieve himself fairly quickly. The house was dark and for the life of him he couldn't remember where the bathroom was. He had great misgivings about going downstairs into the darkened house any- way. This family didn't know him well enough for him to go prowling at three A.M. One of these goofy Cajuns is liable to blow my ass off, he thought in his new hangover.

Then it was upon him. He jumped from the bed with only moments to spare. Unable to come to a decision, he threw off the shorts he had been sleeping in. He looked frantically around the room. He had but one choice. He thrust himself backward through the window, hanging on to the frame with both hands, and let loose. There was a prolonged stormy moment, and then it was over. He wiped himself with his shorts and then threw them as far as he could from the window.

He found he could sleep again. When he awoke in the morning, he immediately remembered what had happened and felt anxious and miserable. He got dressed and went downstairs for breakfast. The family was already eating, more or less in silence, and they scarcely greeted him. Remembering the high spirits of the previous night, the heavy eating, their enthusiasm over the slide show, he just took it to be a spell of recovery. Still, he tried to remember if he had said something awkward. His feeling of unease was exaggerated by his hangover.

When breakfast was finished, Gracie announced she was taking him back to Thibodaux so that he could be on his way. He escaped into his plan for work. He was supposed to meet a colleague in Nacogdoches, Texas, in another day anyway; and it was easier to think about that than this lack of friendliness and silence, especially from Fatso, who had been so voluble.

Nevertheless, Mr. and Mrs. Bouget got to their feet to see Frank off. Gracie walked out with him to the front yard. She bade her parents goodbye and got in to drive. Frank opened the door on the passenger's side, and turning to get in and to thank the Bougets, or even amusingly say "*au revoir,*" he chanced to see the streak down the front of the house under the upstairs window, the shorts dangling from a tree branch. A mop and pail rested next to the wall. But Frank thought that he would say goodbye as simply and quickly as possible and use his limited French on another occasion.

3

Frank sat in the bleachers at the sale yard reading the *Wall Street Journal* and ignoring a bunch of black baldie heifers being steered under the auctioneer's gavel. Bush's heartbeat was back to normal, Croats attacked soldiers at Split and high winds diverted the space shuttle *Discovery* from California to Kennedy Space Center. It's a bitch. Desperate new immigrants. Seventy-two percent of 3,500 police officers polled at John Jay College of Criminal Justice said they wear bulletproof vests. Image of Dan Quayle remains "bumbling." Worker stress was climbing toward widespread burnout and Japanese auto towers were under construction in Detroit. Out at the ranch the sage buttercups were blooming, supplying the blue grouse with spring forage; and the great horned owl had a nestful of gold-eyed downy young. And this just in — a point of pride for all Americans — the first AIDS patient, it would seem, was a Frenchman identified by the initials LAI, placing the American HTLV-IIIB in the situation of being little more than a "contaminant" of LAI. In landing the Sony account, the Burnett advertising firm announced it wanted to "communicate not only our products, but the lifestyles and emotions that surround us as a company." What sincerity there is out there in the business community, thought Frank, what personnel and marketing resources. Burnett claimed that its paternalistic and excellence-oriented approach to business helped land the thirty-five-million-dollar deal, that and changing the slogan "It's a Sony" to "Be Sony." Jesus fucking Christ.

Frank looked up. They were bidding on a group of steers. He raised his hand at seventy-eight dollars a hundredweight and went back out at eighty-six. Then immediately he thought, I should have bought them; it was scarcely a highly leveraged transaction for the dumb shit in the overalls who got them at eighty-eight. Bush's heartbeat back to normal and the dollar up. How could you sleep knowing that? Home oxygen tanks all the rage among the elite of polluted Mexico City. Fuck. I can't look at this.

This had been the year for Deadrock to lose its accustomed obscurity. It broke several winter weather records and got on national weather reports between the T-shirts, the giant cookies, the fire hall restorations and the jokes. Then in March, the weirdest of all months in the Rocky Mountains, a hijacker brought his shiny 747 to rest at the airport north of town. He didn't trivialize his visit with negotiations or threats but simply refueled, resumed his voyage into the West, then over the Pacific where he jumped from the airplane without a comment or statement or, more to the point, a parachute: a Caucasian male around forty. The stewardesses liked him so much, and said so on TV, that the mayor of Deadrock told the press it was a shame to lose a fellow who was "more sensitive than a five-dollar rubber." The plane went back to Seattle, but the big silver outlaw bird had brushed this small city with the wings of immortality.

There was plenty to be interested in but, living alone, Frank had found it hard to be interested in anything. He had set so many things in motion in his business that he could tap into that as he wished. He had several income properties scattered around the town, including the very remunerative clinic. He dabbled in yearling cattle and even owned a set of royally bred show pigs, though he never found time to go see them. The farmer who managed them, Jerry Drivjnicki, had sent him several postcards asking when he was coming to see the pigs.

He had a daughter, Holly, in college at Missoula and they went on liking each other tremendously; but the oddness of his house without Gracie made it a strangely formal place for them to spend time together. They did go fishing, but the season for that was closed eight months of the year, which left restaurants. He knew that Holly and Gracie often spoke, but Holly found it best not to discuss those conversations, a numbing artifice.

He'd had the Millmans over for drinks and it was a waste of time for everybody. Sandy Millman came in her hair all droopy with mousse, far too young for her. Frank could remember when Sandy was the young professionals' town pump, famed for love noises few had ever heard. Darryl Millman had come to town clearly on a large private income and opened a ski shop; and Sandy clamped on to him. Between the all-nighters and the recreational drugs, Sandy was able to slide Darryl straight to the altar, where his wealthy, lewd face was seen to say all the things that conveyed not only hopes of a happy life but fifty percent of his fortune to Sandy.

But Darryl was on a back-to-the-earth mission and put everything he had into a huge grain farm. He spent most of his time in his Beechcraft, meeting farm managers and going to agricultural seminars. It seemed a long way from the sap who supplied all the cocaine in the waning days of the seventies.

Frank had seen more of them since Gracie's departure because Gracie had barred them from Amazing Grease for attracting narco types, and then from the house itself for "character flaws." This was after several bitter remarks exchanged between Gracie and Sandy, Gracie getting the worst of a series of inquiries about what "she had ever done." Finally, the argument appeared to drift away when Gracie said, "All right, Sandy, let's hear these famous noises that have taken you so far."

A moment passed and Sandy spoke in a bell-like contralto: "Thanks for having us over. We see so little of each other. Next time, let's not let it be so long. Good night!" There was not a trace of irony in her voice. It was wonderfully disconcerting and its effect lingered for a long time. They never saw the Millmans socially after that.

Once Gracie was gone, Sandy seemed determined that she never come back. She introduced Frank to out-of-town women — wanton lawyers, nervous potters, divorcées of unrelenting ferocity. Frank made no effort to get around. He didn't have to.

But Frank's loneliness had begun to take some peculiar forms.

4

Frank stretched out on the broad-branched old apple tree with his back to the smooth, cool trunk. Within the canopy of leaves and remaining blossoms of spring he was engulfed in an even deeper darkness than that provided by this still, moonless night. Better yet, he was able to dreamily observe his travel agent, Lucy Dyer, whose office was just down the hall from his and who was one of Gracie's oldest friends, remove the last of her clothes and stand transfixed in front of the shuddering blue-gray light of the television. She dug her fingers into her scalp and pushed them up through her hair, loosening and letting it fall in a wonderful declaration of day's end. Frank sighed in his tree and rested his head against the trunk. This was serene.

Many times Lucy and her current beau had dined with Frank and Gracie, and sometimes Lucy came by herself. One wonderful Halloween, Frank, Gracie and Lucy had gone trick-or-treating together. Now her figure swam with the reflected light of world events on the ten o'clock news. When her window finally went dark, Frank slid slowly to the ground in an excited yet peaceful mood and walked through the sounds of the warm night across the subdivision to the railroad tracks, which he followed until the tall mountains behind the town could be made out against the starlight. To the west a faint flickering of lights arose from the interstate, and to the east the distant sound of trucks beginning the pull into the canyon had a kind of cheerfulness.

When he walked into the house, his phone was ringing. He ran to answer. It was Holly. Whenever he heard her voice, he felt something change inside himself: an indifference to time, for one thing, a floaty focus.

"Dad? I'm joining a sorority." Holly was a sophomore.

"You are?"

"Aren't you glad?"

"Well, yes, I guess I am. I just thought you were down on sororities."

"That was before. This is now."

"Well, yes, I am glad, especially if this means you won't be living in an apartment." She knew that was what he felt. He was nervous about her unguarded life at college. Something had gone amiss with men, and the weak ones were dangerous.

"That's not what it means."

"Oh, I was hoping it did. Well, did you join one in particular?"

She told him which one it was. He didn't know one from another. He vaguely used to comprehend all that Greek stuff, with its comic rituals as a precursor to the characters on little motor scooters wearing fezzes. He wished she would be living in a solid building filled with women.

"Actually, Hol, you know what? This is great." He was determined to be enthusiastic. "How can I celebrate this appropriately?" He was into this one and it showed.

"Why don't you come up when I get settled in?"

"I'd love to. Just give me the nod and I'm on my way."

"Yes, that's what we'll do. And now I'm headed for the library. Love you, bye."

Maybe he had become too dependent on Holly, but she didn't mind, or didn't let him know she minded. He didn't think so, but there may well have been an element of kindness.

For a while he couldn't quite think of his work in an orderly way. If he couldn't see how to get insanely rich or change the world in one or two days, he hardly wanted to go to work at all.

Finally, he began to take it seriously again. His work had a fairly large value to him viewed purely as routine. At forty-four (his friends had made him a cake, a corona of birthday candles and a chocolate pistol with the red number 44), he couldn't make out whether he was young or old, and for many reasons he didn't want to find out through the women in his life. After Gracie left, Frank detected that most people found him a little eerie. He could make them laugh, yet they always felt scrutinized. Some people could stand that and some couldn't. Examination was his disease. He often saw it in the faces of the people he cared for the most. Some of his adversaries in business saw him as a person of subdued and calculating malice. Frank was kind of proud of that. It was too bad when people he cared about felt eroded by his attention. But Holly wasn't one of them.

5

On Tuesday afternoon he drove to Harlowton for lunch with Bob
Cheney, who managed the JA ranch. The JA was a pioneer cattle
ranch that once belonged to the Melwood family; Mrs. Melwood,
the widow of the last rancher in the family, left it to the Salvation
Army and Bob Cheney managed it for them. Frank met Cheney at
the Graves Hotel, waiting for him a short time on its veranda and
staring out at the clouds over the prairie. They were as white as
shaving cream. Cheney arrived in a truck filled with fencing
materials and salt blocks, and parked right in front of the hotel.
They went inside and ordered lunch.

"How long has it been since you had yearlings on us, Frank?"

"Long time ago. 'Eighty-one, anyway. Are you going to have
any room for me this year?"

"I don't quite know yet. How many head?"

"I'll have to see where the market is, where the bank is."

"I don't think I'll be able to tend them. I'm short a man this
season. I could find you a fellow, if you want to pay him."

"That could work. Do you think you'll have room for three
hundred head of steers?"

"I might," said Bob. Their lunch arrived and he smiled up at the
waitress. Bob had a thin mouth, sharp nose and chin. He looked
like an English pirate. "Did you bring your clubs, Frank?"

"You know, I didn't. I have to go straight from you back to town."

"What a shame. Can't even make nine holes?"

"I can't," Frank said. "And you know what else? I haven't played since the year I last had cattle on you. I just kind of pulled my business life over my head and that was that."

Some war was on the radio and the café was quieter than usual. Conversations murmured on about the eroding price supports for grain, the cattle feeder monopolies, baseball.

"Your boy still at the college?" Frank asked.

"Getting ready to graduate."

"Is he going to come back to the ranch?"

"I don't think so." Bob smiled, shrugged.

You didn't work your way up in ranching. You might get the job but the owner was always someone else. Frank saw a man appear in the doorway with his dog. The continuity was going out of ranching, and Frank felt sorry for the people who had seen so much in it and couldn't go on with that, in their families or in any other way.

The waitress announced, "No dogs."

"No dogs?" the man in the doorway said.

"No dogs." She bent behind the counter and emerged with a large beef bone. "Take him outside and give him that."

The man took the bone and went out. He was back in a moment without the dog. "I gave him the bone," he said. He had a pushed-in upper lip and gray-black crinkled hair that grew well down on his forehead.

"Yeah, good. You going to have lunch?" the waitress asked.

"I might just have a cup of coffee while she's working on that bone."

"Yeah, that'd be fine," she said.

"Where'd that great bone come from?"

"Today's soup."

"Oh, sure. Well, she'll appreciate it."

Frank's father used to eat here regularly when he had an interest in the hardware store and then an insurance agency that later moved to Grass Range, where it was absorbed by an office in Lewistown.

Then he had a ranch at Straw, west of Eddie's Corner, and it was easy to use the Lewistown office for the ranch business. The ranch, as far as he was concerned, was just another file at the Lewistown office. Payroll, government programs, expenses, everything was just that one file, ran almost a thousand mother cows. Bob Cheney started at the Straw place when he was a young cowboy, later went to work on the JA for Mrs. Melwood and then the Salvation Army. All the same job except the Salvation Army didn't speculate but ran it as a conservative cow-calf place and in good years leased some grass. And it was good grass: buffalo grass and some bluestem.

Bob and Frank had always gotten along, once even worked together, so Frank got the first call on the grass. It wasn't insider trading; he paid the going rate, but it was an awfully good grass deal. Frank thought he could make some money on it, a little anyway. He did these yearling deals only when he thought he was having a good year. You took out a big loan and bet it on one throw of the dice. He liked being in business with people like Bob Cheney, liked talking to them.

"When's your girl finish school?" Bob asked.

"Two more years."

"She's at Missoula?"

"At Missoula."

"She got a boyfriend?"

"She did. I hesitate to tell you this, but he had a gold ring in his nose."

"Aw, come on."

"I ain't a-shitting you," said Frank rakishly. He wallowed in the fellow feeling produced by sharing this impression of weirdness in his child's generation. The nose ring was part of the bohemian stance of the young man, a stylish underpinning for his scheme to get into "pizza graphics." Frank hadn't asked about that. He'd just said, "Right." He was baffled by young people these days and knew full well that that was a cyclical thing. He just couldn't fathom how they could be so indifferent to their own future and security when it looked like the country had much to fear in years to come. Even the entrepreneurial adventure that Frank had more or less backed into was without appeal to them. Frank thought he himself must be a transitional figure, unlike his father, who had never wanted anything but a business life; Frank had waffled into it, then grown to like it. The young people he ran into seemed only to have a sense of entitlement to clean air and money.

"I don't know why I'm laughing," said Bob. "My boy brings his friends out to the ranch. They think it's a kind of zoo. He brought this big old football player out, boy about yay big, and he wanted to know which one of the animals he could pet. I told him, 'Size you are, you can pet 'em all.' He didn't want no part of that. Says he wasn't petting nothing he didn't know all about."

"What'd you tell him?"

"I told him to pet the goddamn lambs. He kind of flutters out in the pen and goes to petting. I tells him, 'You'll be okay.' "

They thought about this.

"Frank," said Bob, "I believe a man could put five hundred head out there."

Bingo. That was what Frank was waiting to hear. He kept talking but he was already running the numbers in his mind, already picturing the strategy with the bank, perhaps deferring some interest. He wanted a reason to have to come out here. Something about the other stuff was starting to go.

"Here's where we left off," Frank was saying. He was back in town. The banker George Carnahan was standing between Frank and the Dolan Building, which housed a shoe store and a row of second-floor apartments. There was a man in the window of the shoe store hunkered down in his stocking feet, arranging shoe samples. "You were going to go halves with me on the cattle. We were going to fix the rate at nine and there wasn't going to be any points or other charges."

"That's where we left off?"

"Yeah."

Carnahan had a young face and white hair. His mouth was small and level and it was right under his nose. It was like a face by someone who couldn't draw too well.

"Where did we have to go from there?" The banker smiled.

"Size," said Frank.

"Size?" asked Carnahan.

"Size," said Frank. "This is going to be what you guys call a jumbo product. I'd like a quarter of a million dollars. More or less. It's five hundred yearlings, basically. You'll have to get back to me, right?"

"Right."

"And remember this, it's only money."

"I'll let you know, Frank."

"And I hope we won't be talking about other collateral than the yearlings."

"Right, Frank. Frank, we walk it through. Don't always be so adversarial. I think it makes you feel you haven't sold out if you act like you're always in a fight with the banks." Carnahan laughed; it was really a sharp remark and he was quite proud of it. Frank had to smile. "I think you know it's kind of a joke about confining the collateral to the yearlings alone. We like you, Frank, but if you fuck up we're going to get you. We're a traditional small-town lender, just like it says in our ad."

Frank had come to rely on this fiscal narcosis in the last few years. He suspected it had to do with insufficient spiritual values, but those seemed to have gone out the window with his wife. Press forward, he thought. Buy things, then sell them. Try to make a profit. Embed yourself in the robust flux, the brushfire of commerce. Sometimes, when he ate at Julio's deli with his friends, he saw the university people here and there. They looked positively lost among the florid car dealers and subdividers. They winced at the loud townspeople or gazed fondly at the farmers and ranchers, who they thought were purified by their proximity to Mother Earth. Maybe they would like to have the farmers and ranchers up to try their special spaghetti sauce. And what a shame it was that some of the weavers and potters up at the college didn't take more time to get to know the snowmobilers. It wasn't just that fellow feeling was plummeting around the land but that the animosity was getting to be so detailed. Frank wondered if maybe he was getting morbidly sensitive to all this floating ill will. It was a terrible thing when a neighborhood deli felt like the Gaza Strip.

He got the loan, and in the wild fluctuations of the cattle market it was a dangerous loan. They were happy to walk it through when they thought it might blow up in your face. Despite his bold speech to the banker, it cost Frank a lien on the clinic.

The yearlings arrived in nine bunches, from Choteau, Camas Prairie, Sumatra, Sedan, Wise River, White Sulphur Springs, Ekalaka, Cat Creek and Geraldine. Frank stayed at the Graves, in Harlowton, and met each load with his summer cowboy, a very competent twenty-eight-year-old nephew of Bob named John Jones. When Frank sat down in the café of the Graves with Jones to do his W-4 form, he found that this bright young man could neither read nor write. For some reason, as he helped Jones, whose face blazed with shame, he felt like a transubstantiated version of his father, a patient and unambiguous man who would see Jones's illiteracy as just a small impediment in getting the yearlings onto the grass in an orderly way, where they could begin to gain weight and be worth more money. To Frank's father, every animal had a dollar meter on its back and the needle was always in motion. Sometimes it was going down. If you ran a thousand head, you had a thousand meters and you had to keep those needles going up.

Frank wondered what his father would have thought at a time when big calves were going for five hundred dollars a round and that quarter-million-dollar note was dragging its ass at nine and a half percent, compound interest all summer long, rain or shine, secured by a note on a medical clinic! He would have made money, Frank concluded, for the simple reason that his father never saw any romance in cattle. There's a little money in cattle, he used to say, not much, and no romance. A hundred years ago there was big romance in cattle because there was big money in it. There is no big romance combined with small money. Period. Frank's uncle Rusty once said: The lady doesn't marry the carpenter unless he's got a second home in Santa Monica or a two-foot dick.

6

Frank Copenhaver tapped a hard-boiled egg on the counter, slightly crushing the shell to keep it from rolling. Two old men next to him were lamenting conditions in the range livestock industry.

"Why does the Lord want me to serve him in this way?" inquired a leathery sixty-year-old with a short cigarette screwed into the corner of his mouth. Frank spread the *Wall Street Journal* out onto his part of the counter and ordered a pork chop sandwich from the waitress, who took orders and refilled coffee in one efficient trip down the counter. The old man slowly stirred a cream substitute into his coffee and Frank listened attentively. "Why, it's not as if we had nice childhoods, home alone sewing up prolapsed cows with hog rings and shoelaces — I'm sure you done that. Or digging a dead calf out of a cow by yourself when it's twelve below and you're twelve years old."

Frank looked up from the *Journal* into midair. It's quite unimaginable that they would secretly look into someone's bedroom window, he thought, and I have done it without remorse and, really, without having been driven to do it. Unless Lucy's being Gracie's oldest friend in Montana drove me to do it.

The old man's companion, a bit younger and with a distinctive furze of reddish silver hair around his scalp and the genial, unspecific face of an apprentice barber, said, "I was born broke and I'm broke now."

The waitress caught Frank's eye on this one and smiled at him. She wouldn't have smiled if she really knew about me, he thought.

"If steamboats was selling for a nickel," said the older man, "all I could do is run up and down the dock and yell, 'Ain't that cheap!'"

On the way in for lunch, Frank had been held up behind a crew of house movers who were taking a drive-in movie screen right down the interstate. He had stopped to talk to the sharecropper on his grain farm, then got behind the movers, and now he was cornered at the counter during the luncheon rush, something he usually avoided. He sat in the drifting cigarette smoke and waited to eat. This eavesdropping was irresistible and very much like looking in Lucy's window.

"I spent two years' days on an irrigated Indian lease," declared the older man next to Frank. "If I survived that, I can survive eighty-cent calves."

"We'll survive it," said the other, "and then they put us in the home." Frank was listening closely. He and his brother Mike had put their mother in a rest home and felt guilty about it. He always perked up for talk about "home," as the word was so charged with meaning, dread and guilt.

"I ain't goin' to no home."

"We're all going to a home."

"Kiss my ass, I ain't goin' to no home."

"Have it your way."

"By the way," the older man said, relighting the cigarette stub, "I believe my dog is superstitious. This morning he wouldn't go up to that green stock truck belonging to Vanderhooven. Do you recall Joker ever being run over by anything green or anything which was owned by Vanderhooven?"

"Joker's been around a long time. He's had plenty of time to think."

"Let's go. They need these places for lunch." The two left a dollar for their coffee and, pushing off the counter to get to their feet, went out. The waitress placed the pork chop sandwich right on top of the *Wall Street Journal*. Frank was still thinking about having put his mother in a rest home, thinking about the anticipatory dread of the two old ranchers. They were right, of course, but what could you do without these old folks' homes? You were not in a position to change the diapers yourself. Still, it was a wonder the roofs of those places were not adorned with vultures.

He had taken his mother to Fort Myers as a last try some years before, got her a little house; then a bar opened across the street with a nightly wet panty contest and a sign in front that said, "Guys, come as you are! If you worked in it, you can party in it!" So, he took her back to Montana, got her one more house which did for a year, then into the home. In Fort Myers, all the white-haired people with brick red faces, plus the tones of mayhem at night from the workingmen at the wet panty contest, had frightened her more, late in life, than anything up to then. Yardboy drug dealers stalked the sidewalks in pump-up basketball shoes as wailing police cruisers shot through the humidity. As if his poor old mother were to be allowed to miss no modern nightmare, a man in the airport had a condom full of smuggled cocaine burst inside him, producing a howling seizure in front of a booth that shipped oranges and coconuts to the folks up north. She huddled by the ticket counter and stared at the departure screen and the word "Denver," which was where she changed planes to come home.

The waitress was talking to the cook: "Dad, he wants to go to Searchlight. Mom, she wants to go to Elko. So, they stay home. I was going to get some peace."

The pork chop sandwich was delicious, juice sopping deep into thick homemade bread. A cowgirl grandmother took the seat next to Frank, big owl-frame blue glasses, hair teased up in a bottle blond pile, buck-stitched cowgirl boots, little radiating lines around her mouth, looked mean as a snake. She too ordered the pork chop sandwich, a house specialty, then gazed at Frank appraisingly while she slowly lit a cigarette. Frank said nothing.

Before his wife left, he had been a classic never-met-a-stranger type, but now he spoke mainly when spoken to. He kind of wanted to talk to this mean cowgirl grandma but he had lost his fluency in these matters, and had become an eavesdropper.

Frank went out onto Main Street where a crew was making repairs. It was still spring and the smell of hot tar was its classic smell on Main Street.

"Wake up!" said a voice, and Frank focused suddenly. A man stood in front of him in a seersucker suit, the tie pulled down and askew. He was hawk-eyed and intense. It was Dick Hoiness, his insurance man.

"Dick! God, I was elsewhere. You're right." Cars had started to pile up at the light on Grand. Spring sunshine boomed from all the car colors. Frank thought, Where am I?

"Well, how are you?"

"I'm all right," said Frank. "At least that." Someone tapped a car horn and Frank flicked a wave without looking into the glitter of windshields.

"Frank, when you get a minute, we need to go over the farm buildings I've got covered with you."

"You've got the houses, right?" Frank felt himself concentrate, somewhat unwillingly, on an inventory of buildings.

"I've got the houses and the main shops and of course the clinic. I just need to double-check before we renew. I think we're insuring more buildings than you really care about. You still got the grain farm and the ranch I know of?"

"Yes, but that could change. Mike splits the ranch bills. We own that together. What about the old hotel?"

"Untouchable firetrap, Frank," said Dick, backing off into the flow of pedestrians before continuing on his way. An exchange of waves and they parted into the sunny day. Frank thought about his insurance man; he'd known him for a long time. Dick had been a bassist in a local band, got his long hair cut off in 1980, then got in trouble for drugs, cleared that up, and when the Mission Mountain Band was wiped out, he took it as a sign that an era had ended and went looking for what was then known as a straight job. He had done well and now lived with his small family in Chokecherry Canyon. It was getting harder and harder to remember one's old hippie friends as they disappeared into local society; but like them, Frank Copenhaver went on with the vaguely disreputable feeling acquired during those years, a feeling that later gave him a coolness, a detachment toward his adversaries. A refrain went through his mind from an old song: "It ain't me, it ain't me . . ."

Frank glanced at an architectural magazine on his desk — "Bogus Colonials Invade Boston" — and a sporting magazine with a story about a man who pitches camp on the drifting carcass of a dead whale, hoping to ambush a great white shark. Definitely have to have his outfit dry cleaned after that venture. Frank couldn't bring himself to make his calls. I'm guilty, he was thinking. He dug into the morning news. Baby boomers were buying vintage guitars: bits of splintered lumber formerly owned by Pete Townshend, various "workhorse" Stratocasters, nostalgic early-middle-agers battling the Japanese for Buddy Holly's Gibson, flame-patterned Les Paul models sailing across the Pacific to museums.

He went to the window. An old couple in the yard of the small house next door, now surrounded by offices like Frank's, took in the midday sun. He had seen them before. They were very old, and she quite senile. The old man always wore a suit and his little wife a kind of sack dress, probably so that the weak old man could manage to pull it over her head when helping her dress. Frank observed while the old man slowly unwrapped a piece of candy for his wife. She watched patiently.

Frank went back to his desk. It was becoming hard for him not to think of work as something completely made up, no matter how remunerative. It seemed an excuse for not loafing. He was sometimes surprised everyone didn't see through it. This was Gracie's old pitch and he had never bought it. He had taken it that she was attacking his achievement. But it was time to go ahead and do something. The pork chop sandwich was starting to churn. He remembered that first trip down to Louisiana when he had taken a shit out his future in-laws' upstairs window. He rested his hand on his stomach and thought about how Bunker Hunt used to bring his lunch in a brown bag, creating a reputation for penury, when in fact the bag was filled with the kind of gourmet items you couldn't buy just anywhere. He picked up the phone and dialed Grant Weller, a cattle order buyer, and after a few formulaic remarks and parryings over price, bought another 500 six-hundred-pound steers, which he appended, with one more call, to the loan secured by his best property, his real trophy, the Alpenglow Clinic. He had a place to run them at ten bucks a head per month, about two bucks worse than he was doing with the Salvation Army. He needed to park them only a short while, until he could get them on feed.

"Good heavens. Where are these going?" asked his banker, George Carnahan, with a gasp.

"I'm going to background them at Mission Feeders. Call me for the deposits. Gotta go, bye." He hung up, sat back and thought. He returned to the window. The old couple were gone. He could see the candy wrapper on the ground and walked out of his office into the hallway. He went down two doors and into the travel agency, waved to the secretary and went past to a smaller office.

7

Lucy Dyer was at her desk, didn't really notice him in her doorway. The wall was covered with posters, tropical getaways for
people in the extreme north. He always looked at the brown girl
wearing little more than a dive watch under the waterfall in
Kauai. Lucy had a long brown braid wound up behind her head
and wore a navy blue jacket over a white open-throated silk shirt.
Once when Frank worked on a road crew in Yellowstone, when
he was young, a girl who looked like Lucy stopped in her convertible while a bulldozer crossed the road. They spoke briefly, Frank
put down his shovel and got in the convertible. When he returned
two weeks later, the job was gone. He could remember still the
smell of the evergreens and dusty tar, hear the mountain stream
that roared along that road, remember every instant of the two
weeks. She was a lovely rich girl in her own Mustang convertible,
but she did give him gonorrhea. He drove all the way to Laramie,
Wyoming, to feel anonymous enough to see a doctor.

He sat down opposite Lucy and tilted slightly in his chair. He
sighed and drifted forward in his imagination to winter, a scene in
which one shoulders from the front door to the car through
volumes of north wind. He rested on an image of jumper cable
attachment, his imaginary self disappearing in the rooster tails of
blowing snow that follow passing cars. Lucy was watching.

"How about a converted slave quarters on Nevis?"

"What month?"

"January." She pushed a brochure at him.

"I don't think so. I want something, I don't know, something that would take me back to the glory days —"

"The early seventies."

"But exactly."

"How about a hammock on Cay Caulker, Belize?"

"That's it?"

"That's it. It's a straight shot across the gulf."

"Meaning what?"

"Meaning you could pick up an oldies station out of Houston."

"Oh, Lucy." He thought for a moment. "Is there a brochure?"

"I think that would be very much out of keeping with the spirit of my suggestion."

"Quite right. How about the local weed?"

"I'm sure they can find you some . . . 'good shit.' And if you like the hammock, you can always grow your own."

"I see."

The room fell quiet. A car antenna moved into view in the window, backed up and rotated to a stop. Something was coming up inside Frank. Voices outside, laughter, more voices, deals, assignations. I hope it goes on for a million years, thought Frank gratefully, defying gravity and cold. Now he was nervous. He thought about his mother on her last day in her own house. She had a purse that weighed about fifteen pounds that had a lock on it; she had lost the key to the lock long ago and carried this massive purse whose contents no one could any longer remember. She even took it with her when she sat down at the disc-driven grand piano, shouting, "It's magic!" while the robot piano played Mozart like a barrel organ in a nightmare. It was a flat earth and they were all going off the edge.

"You're never going to buy a trip from me," said Lucy.

"I could," he said and thought, Here it comes. We have these jokey meetings almost daily and they go nowhere. Because she was Gracie's friend, I'm paralyzed to so much as ask her to dinner.

We leave the lightest moments red-faced and sweating, out of fear one of us will ask, "What do you hear from Gracie?" You move toward something that could mean something and all it does is produce fear.

"You're not like the others," Lucy said. "You won't go on a cruise. You don't like other people well enough."

"I deplore their eating habits."

"You won't go to the Bible lands."

Frank reached across and covered Lucy's hands with his own. "Not even Jesus had to worry about hijacking," he said.

"What's that have to do with it?"

"Didn't he, more or less, put the Bible lands on the map?"

"That's certainly a very strange way to say it, Frank."

"My problem in planning a trip is getting time and place in the proper relationship. For example, I would love to go to New York, but certainly not after 1925."

"That's a problem, and by the way, my hands are beginning to perspire. Don't keep coming on to me if you're just going back to your cubicle."

Astonished, Frank stood up. "You're a hundred percent correct." Her beauty was sudden phosphorus, ignited by her remark. He had a spell of immolating madness, wanting to offer himself in some way.

"How's it going over there?" She nodded in the direction of his office.

"I had one good transaction."

"Grain?"

"Cattle. How about you?" His mind was diving around like a hooked fish. If they could only get off this dead center.

"Pretty good. Mostly getting kids back from college. Nothing substantial in the way of trips. One screamer, didn't get his diabetic dinner on a Seattle flight."

Now Frank felt a wave of insubstantiality. The whole thing was getting away from them. The normal, pleasant prevarications of daily life were becoming unbearable. It would just zoom in like this and be awful. The terror had to be replaced by blind courage.

"Last night," he said, "I was sitting in your apple tree." This was it. This was it!

"You were?"

"Yes."

"What were you doing in my apple tree?"

"I was watching you . . . uh, get undressed and, uh, watch the news." What an exciting new world this was. He was perspiring. But no matter what the consequences were, he was going to accept them.

She withdrew her hands from beneath his. There seemed to be no motion anywhere in the building. His eyes felt dry. She got up and went to the window, but moved away from it. He waited for her to talk.

"You're quite a guy," she said in an extraordinarily flat voice. Everything seemed in jeopardy. He couldn't imagine what he had been doing there. He was walking home from the golf course in the dark. Two drinks. Not enough to explain anything. And suddenly he was there. It was too bad he told her. If he didn't tell Lucy, he knew there could be another time and then it would become routine; then he would be headed off the end of the world. It was time to put himself in her hands. He could tell when she turned around to look at him that he was not going to get off lightly, but it had been his only chance to stop and now he was going to have to take it like a man.

"I think the best thing would be if you went back to your office," she said. "I think you need a little vacation, Frank. Let me work on it. I'll give you a ring when I get this trip put together."

"When you get this trip together . . ."

"Yes. I'll call you when I put this little trip together. I can't do it in five minutes. But not to worry: this has been a long time coming and you're leaving town. You *need* to leave town. You haven't been anywhere since Gracie left. You've got to break the pattern."

"Fine," he said dully. "Call me."

In a couple of hours, she dropped off his plane tickets and itinerary without a word. He read it with amazement. He swallowed several times but the feeling his trip gave him wouldn't go away.

8

Frank pulled the parka up around his face and looked out at the river. Pack ice from the slow breakup of winter had crowded the river from bank to bank. The Eskimo shacks along the shore seemed to reveal no signs of life except for the old caribou hides nailed to their walls and flapping bleakly in the north wind.

Frank wandered back to the hotel to play video games with the Eskimos. The town had the appearance of a military supply dump: windowless storehouses, pyramids of fuel barrels, vehicles abandoned where they would never run again and where they would endure for centuries of refrigeration.

The hotel, like the other buildings, rested on top of the ground on blocks, out of reach of permafrost. It was a carelessly constructed building, mostly prefabricated, and was not expected to last many more winters. From its windows could be seen the endless granite landscape, streaked with snow and running water, more of a plan for country than country itself. Through this unchanging vista, hundreds of Eskimos appeared each night on hot-rod four-wheelers, heading for the hotel bar. Frank went down the first night to have a drink with them, but they took him outside and tossed him in a blanket until he passed out. He definitely avoided drinking with them thereafter, because after three or four they became sharply conscious of the injustices Frank's

43

race had committed against them and began to get psyched up for another blanket toss.

The desk clerk and manager was an Englishman who had come during the sixties to do good work among the Eskimos. Funding for that had disappeared and, not wanting to leave the North, he took on the hotel job. He was a stolid Yorkshireman, settled here now with his family. He said that his children were veteran smokers and drinkers by the age of ten. "Bloody little Inuit, they are," he told Frank.

An Eskimo woman who had gone to Toronto, a three-hundred-pound crack addict who listened to rap music on her Walkman all day, wandered into the dining room to order breakfast.

"Have I had any calls?" Frank asked. "Anything on the radio?"

"Nothing at all," said the manager. "Your vacation winding down, is it?"

"You really never know," said Frank. He was reduced to reading the last newspaper he had bought in the airport and speculating about the life he had left behind, if only for one of the longest weeks of his life. He learned that California community planner Richard Reese hoped to produce a more "nurturing" lifestyle in his new planned communities. Reese intended to use psychologist Abraham Maslow's hierarchy of needs to build a town that functioned as a kind of golden stairway to wellness. On the count of three, thought Frank, all will cut off their dicks on the road to wellness. Reference made to Seaside, Florida, the assemblage of playhouses on the Gulf of Mexico. Says here that business is flat in the world of bronzed baby shoes, an admittedly "schmaltz-oriented" enterprise. Frank sighed. The faster he became an Eskimo, the better off he'd be. Then he could go home, having repaid his debt to Lucy. He could chew blubber in his office like a gentleman.

Now he mostly played the video games with those Eskimos who preferred not to drink. There was a two-seated Grand Prix game with a screen revealing a pair of racing cars ready to race if you had fifty cents and a partner. Frank played this regularly and came to know many extended Eskimo families. The steering wheels of the racing game, once black, were worn silver. Passing the winter, young Eskimos pondered the images of the red and blue Ferraris as they surged down a simulated narrow lane in pleasant southern France. Frank Copenhaver wheeled his racer among the palm trees and blue glimpses of the sea even if, as today, there was no one to race but himself. He got up and joined the crack addict for breakfast. She seemed glad of the company. She was shaky from her vice and seemed to bear an infinity of sorrows. And just when he wished to think of average things for discussion, like weather, her interests were entirely millennial: world war, the antichrist, the hole in the ozone layer.

Tuesday he went home. It had taken him half his trip to look at the return reservations on his ticket inside the Sunseeker Travel Service folder. He went through customs in New York and didn't declare the snowshoe keychain that was his only purchase. Lucy picked him up at the airport, where he took great breaths of the smell of new grain fields in the advancing summer in the Gallatin Valley. This alone gave him the feeling that his trip had been a success. Lucy had a twinkle in her eye. "I know I have a good figure," she said, "but was it worth it?"

"I hate it when all and sundry are so literal."

"May I take you to dinner?" she asked.

"The hotel, if you can call it that, was out of hot water the last two days. I haven't had a shower."

"Will that prevent you from eating?"

"I guess not. All I've had is smoked almonds all day."

Frank shoved his duffel into the back of Lucy's gray Volvo and got in. The radio was still playing, a disc jockey crying, "Oh, no, not again!" They started toward Seventh. Frank could see the odd spook shapes of the cottonwoods toward the Bridger Range. The radio announced the coming appearance of a "gospel magician" at a gathering for teenagers. No wonder they stuffed themselves with drugs. Then the folks from Coca-Cola came on and said Coke has always been there for you, always at the heart of the things you do. They said that with Coke and days off, you'll never be able to beat the feeling. Frank's spirits sank slightly. The Civic Center, said the radio, was going to have professional wrestling, including a ten-man battle royal in a steel cage; afterward, Sir Lathrop versus The Animal.

"Well, how did you like the Arctic?"

"It was real different."

She handed him her sunglasses. "Look at the clouds through these, they're so vivid." Frank put them on and in fact the clouds thickened up brightly, wet and full of color. With these enriching glasses clamped to his head, he felt a lewd stirring.

"And how have you been?" Frank asked, handing back the glasses. He really didn't want to get into this.

"I get up in the morning. That's half the battle."

Traffic slowed down as an old lady in white headgear and black wraparound sunglasses crossed the road carrying a bag of clothes. She walked straight across through the cars without looking right or left. She reminded him of his mother, at her worst a decrepit scheming shadow who lived to interfere.

An old sedan passed, pulling a cage on wheels filled with white Muscovy ducks. The Volvo crossed Main and entered the parking lot of the Thai restaurant. Lucy got out. "Let's play the hands we were dealt," she said. "We will begin by eating."

Frank looked around the dirty parking spaces under the trees and felt a wonderful lightness. "Remember Gram Parsons's 'Grievous Angel'?" he asked.

"Sort of."

He sang: " 'Twenty thousand roads I went down, down, down, and they all led me straight back home to you.' "

"How extremely sweet!"

"This is a perfect time and place," said Frank sincerely. They walked into the restaurant. It had that wonderful feeling of restaurants that had recently been houses: walls in the wrong places, the waitress emerging from what seemed to be a parlor, carrying a tray. The room was nearly full, with couples, families and even two cowboys who, Frank noticed with irritation, had not removed their hats.

"Hello, Frank," said one of the cowboys.

"Hello," said Frank, staring fixedly at the unremoved hat.

Behind them came a great big man in overalls, freckled arms as big around as most people's legs. Frank looked at him. "Hello, Paul."

"Hello, Frank."

"Lucy Dyer, this is Paul Smith."

"How do, ma'am."

"How do you do, Paul."

"Frank," said the immense man, his face creasing in two with a pained smile, his head settling down and driving out one more row of wrinkles around his sunburned neck. "I burned the feed bunks and farmed right up to the walls of the barn."

"You're better off," said Frank. "You're much better off, Paul." It was nice to tell someone they were on the right track. It was nice to notice that people sought his approval in their business decisions. He decided not to tell Paul that he was even deeper into feeder cattle. With his current low spirits, he wondered why he had ever let that happen.

The waitress seated Lucy and Frank at a small table slap against the wall and handed them their menus. Ordinarily, Frank ordered Mongolian beef extra hot and kept washing it down with beer until he felt somewhat crazy.

"I nearly froze up there."

Lucy stared at him. She said, "It was supposed to be *a joke*."

"It wasn't a joke to me."

"I mean the travel arrangements."

"I don't have much of a sense of humor."

"Here she is, let's order," Lucy said. "He doesn't have much of a sense of humor," she said to the waitress.

"You don't need one for Mongolian beef," Frank said.

The waitress was looking on to her next table. The two cowboys were staring past each other in silence, waiting for their litchi nut. Paul Smith, the farmer, was now at a table by himself, looking like a freckled mountain. Frank turned around: every time the kitchen door opened, the music of Neil Young poured out. Frank loved these sentimental tunes. "I'd cross a mountain for a heart of gold . . ."

He looked back and it wasn't Gracie. It was Lucy. His face broke out with sweat. He was starting to go loose with panic.

"I gotta go."

He stood up and abruptly went out the door.

"Do you have any idea where he was going?" Lucy asked Paul Smith. Smith looked embarrassed. He got redder. "I mean, what was that all about?"

In the parking lot Frank thought, I'm not gaining, I'm not getting anywhere. Lucy came out of the restaurant a minute later. She stopped in its lighted doorway and stared around at the cars parked under the trees. "There you are," she said. She came over and gazed at him. Frank could just make out her face; she came up to about the middle of his chest and she was not looking at him. She took the edge of his shirt in her fingers. He smelled violets.

They crossed in front of the car and got in. As soon as she began to drive, he felt a tension in his legs from wishing to work the pedals himself. They drove out of the parking lot to Deadrock Street. Homebound traffic from the mall kept them tied up at the stop sign in silence.

Lucy pulled into the takeout line at McDonald's and, seeing that it would be a wait, turned on the radio low, too low to really make out the music or the excited patter betweentimes.

"We're down among them now," said Frank, listlessly contemplating the menu painted on the side of the building. But when the food was handed to them in a bag, the car filled with the appealing trash aroma of fast food. He reached into the bag and felt the hot, salt-grainy ends of the french fries as they wheeled back onto Deadrock. It was wonderful to stare openmouthed into traffic with the radio muttering and the lousy food steaming on the seat between them. Splendid to take what you are given. He smiled, felt the happiness go over the top of him. A long-ago day came back.

"It's 1964 and news of Dad's hole in one has just shot through town."

"What are you saying?"

"I was just thinking back . . . It must be hell being a travel agent."

"It's not so bad. You get so you don't want to go on a trip."

"I got some slides from the Far North. Would you like to see them?"

Frank ran the projector. The air was warm and stale in his house. Lucy sat next to him in the dark while he listlessly clicked one snapshot after another of Eskimos passing the time on the banks of an arctic river, working on their Japanese ATVs and smoking cigarettes. They had a way of smoking that looked like they were eating the cigarettes. He had bought these souvenir slides hoping they would trigger reminiscences when he got home. The trouble was, they didn't. They scarcely mitigated the effect of the humid old couch.

"I wonder if we're missing something, giving up cigarettes," said Lucy. She saw the deep satisfaction of the smoking Eskimos.

"I think we are."

The last slide clicked through. The wall lit up with a white square. A car passed on Assiniboine Avenue and light wheeled on the ceiling and again it was so dark.

"It's something how lonely life is," said Lucy.

Man, thought Frank, she just chirped that out. He thought of her at work, helping people plan their trips. It had been outlandish of her to suggest his going to the Arctic, outlandish of him to accept. It had been a way of saying something they couldn't say in any other way. He didn't know if it had gotten through. It probably hadn't. He hated travel. When he was away, he just thought about being the child of deeply unhappy people, something he forgot about when he was at work, never having such a thought. But that first airport and, wham, there he was alone with his people. Besides, he thought, it's not true; they're not deeply unhappy, they're dead. The Eskimos were up there watching the river melt, go by, freeze, melt and go by, and it was simply very familiar. And Lucy went on sending people on vacations, drew herself up each morning to design a holiday, people of the world staring at each other, all somehow more real in brochure form, just as the solitude of the Eskimos came to him on his living room wall in the mustiness of his semi-absent housekeeping.

Lucy stood up in the square of light on the wall.

"Is this better?" she said.

He froze. "Are you going to do something?"

"Yes, I am."

9

Frank watched the small television set atop the dresser while he shaved. A new "young country" singer was performing, his long curls falling out from beneath his ten-gallon hat. "Put a futon on your wish list," he hog-called into the microphone while his hair fell over his harmonica rack, "I'm kicking you tonight!" Perhaps it was very good music. He simply didn't know anymore. It could be great.

He turned off the television set. Then he sat down and thought about the previous night, the previous brief evening and its love-making, which might well have been less an episode of spontaneity than an unfolding of earlier matters, something fearful, a sort of cowering behind one's loins for want of a better idea. Not like the old days of rear back and let it rip. In these times, there was a surfacing of themes, the collision of culture, a pilfering of one's own existence to direct dial three abdominal nerves. Life itself, thought Frank wearily, and at these prices!

From his shower, Frank could see lights on in a few houses, but most of the roofs from his angle huddled in the dark of their trees, scarcely outlined by moonlight. He felt he was up alone with the news crews of New York.

He dressed and went outside. It had been a warm night and the air was filled with the smell of juniper and damp garden beds. The sidewalk shone slightly, and as the road mounted the hill toward the south, the houses were raised in increasing angularity until they stood silhouetted at the crown against the stars and foothills.

He walked into the dining room of the Holiday Inn and waited for a seat. There was one gentleman reading *USA Today,* a Northwest Airlines crew of pilots and stewardesses, and June Cooper. Frank hoped the waitress would take him to an empty table before June spotted him, but no such luck. She seemed to realize that that might have been his hope and flagged him to her table grimly. Frank went over and sat down.

"Join me," she rasped. "You don't have that many friends, at least not at this hour." June was a striking forty-year-old with almost black hair and blue eyes, an amazing combination. She had blown in from Oklahoma twenty years before as a veterinarian's assistant, gone through three marriages to three previously married men and ended up with a successful Buick agency of her own, a gleaming single-story showroom and office that scattered its inventory of sparkling Buicks across one of the most valuable commercial lots in town. Her last husband hadn't made much of it, and it seemed, after a decade and a half as a barracuda, June's real gift was in running a business. She once told Frank, "The way I was raised, the only business open to women was marriage. I opened a chain. Right?"

"If you don't want to sit with me," she drawled, "don't have breakfast at the Holiday Inn. I eat here every day."

"Got you." He liked June very much but she was so shrewd that he feared her seeing how dilapidated his spirit had become since Gracie left.

The waitress arrived and filled Frank's coffee cup.

"He'll have bacon and eggs and hash browns," June said. "Eggs over lightly."

He nodded. "I ought to eat a bowl of cereal."

"You can have cereal at home. This is where we turn our backs on the things we do at home."

Frank looked around the room, gathered in the footloose merriment of the Northwest crew, the bleak movements of the waitress, noted the silver cast of the windows as sunrise commenced. He lifted his coffee cup.

"How's your love life, June?"

"I'm sublimating. And you?"

Frank thought, actually thought, about his current situation. He could hardly tell her that after learning he had peered at her from an apple tree, Lucy had virtually shipped him to the Arctic Circle. Nevertheless, he told her the truth: "My love life is nonexistent too."

"I don't love anyone," said June, pulling the little square of foil off the marmalade container. "Life is a highway and love is the potholes. I don't say it's good, but that's how it is."

"How about the Buick Family? I see on television there's this nationwide thing called the Buick Family."

"I don't love them piss-ants neither."

"So what do you do?"

"Occasionally, I get some sleepy type to go to bed with me. There is a burst of excitement but then they sense my needs are fairly much physical, and that's all she wrote. We get a good bit of turnover. I do try to keep several of these donkeys on line, however."

Frank's breakfast arrived. "What about surrogate children?"

"I still have that dog, what's his name, Jake. I still have Jake. I'd hardly call Jake a surrogate child. He's supposed to be a trained retriever. But what is there to retrieve in my life except possibly self-esteem, and I can hardly expect Jake to do that. I have a niece at Oklahoma State, a real bum. She tried to work me for a car, but it didn't take and I no longer hear from her."

"Everyone used to have one of those overtrained water dogs. They were socially required."

"Exactly, Frank. I noticed that when I came up from Oklahoma, but to no avail. I married three duck hunters in a row. Quack, bang, quack, bang. Such a life."

"Now I'm too excited to eat," said Frank.

"Is it the thighs?"

"Not really. It's more like seeing things as they are. Kind of like the old acid days."

"Well, it gets you rolling in the morning." She stood up abruptly with her purse under her elbow. "Call me," she said, and went out.

Frank felt a little gust and thought, I will. He paid for breakfast and went outside where a parking lot full of cars rested, seemed to await their mission. Wonderful when day had not begun, when only the breakfast waitresses and airline crews were conspicuously there and ready for the rest of the world if it ever woke up. Frank looked off to the silhouettes of the city and the mountains beyond. Odd hours always took him back to the days of weirdness, to the exhilaration of being out of step. He went on contemplating the way the world was reabsorbing him and his friends, terrified people coming to resemble their parents, their dogs, their country, their seatmates, after a pretty good spell of resembling only themselves. This, thought Frank, lacks tragic dimension almost as certainly as podiatry does. But it holds me in a certain ache to imagine I'm actually as much a businessman as my father.

But Frank was apprehensive about going to work. He was, after all, across the hall from Lucy. That hadn't changed. And he was disquieted about seeing her this morning. Despite twenty years of trying to reduce sex to the same status as the handshake, its reduction was unreliable and it frequently had an unwelcome larger significance. Lovemaking still seemed to test the emotional assumptions that led up to it, and in Frank's case he somehow found out that he was never going to be in love with Lucy. It was important to act on this perception before her nose seemed to grow or her mouth to hang open vacantly, her vocabulary to shrink or her feet to slap awkwardly on the linoleum. He was going to have to drum up some drippy conversation about friendship, a deadening policy statement that would reduce everything to awkwardness.

He needn't have worried. She was in the hallway when he arrived. She wrinkled her face at the sight of him, shook her head and disappeared into her office. He went into his own without greeting Eileen, his secretary. He tore down the Eskimo poster with disgust and, briefly, hated himself. A new set of tickets and itinerary lay on his desk. He opened the itinerary. It said, "Hell." Nothing else.

He picked up his phone.

"Eileen."

"Yes, Mr. Copenhaver."

"Good morning."

"Good morning."

"My mind was elsewhere."

"Don't worry about it."

"Thank you. Now, can you get me Lucy across the hall."

The phone rang only once.

"Lucy, Frank."

"Yes."

"Is there something wrong?"

"Is there something wrong . . ." she said. He knew now, of course, that there was.

"I thought we'd had a nice evening."

"We had, to a point."

"And at what point did you think it went downhill?"

"At the point you called me Gracie."

"I did that, did I?"

"About seven times."

"Sorry."

"I suppose it's not your fault, Frank. But I'm not your old wife."

"Of course not."

He hung the phone up and leaned on his hands. He could have said, "No, you're not my old wife. You're my wife's old friend. Some friend!"

For some reason, he called June up at the dealership. They had to page her on the lot. By the time she came to the phone, he had forgotten why it had seemed so necessary to call her. Nevertheless, he told her what had happened. She listened quietly. He explained as discreetly as he could that he had said one or two inappropriate things during a spell of delightful lovemaking and it had ruined everything. June said, "I can't get into it. When they're doing their job, they can call me John Brown for all I care." Frank thanked her anyway and hung up, then thanked her to himself for this burst of redneck health.

He went down to Lucy's office and sat under the waterfall while Lucy watched him and waited for him to say something.

"Are you still angry?" he said finally.

"No. I never was angry."

"I don't want to lay this on you, but if you weren't angry, you were hurt."

"Then I was angry, but I'm not angry now."

Some hours ago, he thought, she was chewing sheets and going "Oof, oof, oof!" while, evidently, I was going, "Oh, Gracie, oh, Gracie!" Quite a picture. Oh, dear.

Then she smiled and said, "This time, I'm not sending you anywhere." The air had apparently cleared. Frank left her office, thinking, What a nice person.

Frank straightened up his desk and went back out through the reception area. "I'm going to the ranch," he said.

"Can you be reached there?" asked Eileen.

"No, but I'll be back."

Frank drove north out of town, cutting through the subdivisions that lay around the old town center. Frank had a reluctant affection for these suburbs, with their repetitious shapes and lawns and basketball hoops and garages. He appreciated their regularity.

The road wound up through dryland farms of oats and malting barley, golden blankets in the middle of sagebrush country, toward the tall brown of snowy mountains. The city had almost disappeared behind him, yet from the front gate of the home place he could still make it out. A bright serration against the hills.

Frank stopped right in front of the house where his family once lived, a substantial farmhouse with a low, deep porch across the entire front, white with blue shutters and a blue shingled roof.

The house sat on a fieldstone cellar with deep-set airyway windows at regular intervals beneath the porch. The house was locked up. In front, the tall hollyhocks his grandmother had taken such care of stood up boldly through the quack grass and competed along the border of the porch with the ocher shafts of henbane. The junipers hadn't been trimmed and streaks of brown penetrated their dark green masses. It was a fine old house that gave Frank the creeps.

He drove slowly past it toward the barn and outbuildings, looking for Boyd Jarrell, his hired man. He had already seen Jarrell's truck from the house, and when he crossed the cattle guard into the equipment compound, he watched Jarrell walk past the granary without looking up at Frank's car. He saw that Jarrell would be in a foul mood, and felt a slight sinking in his stomach. Boyd liked Mike but didn't like Frank. Mike came out here and played rancher with Boyd, building fence on the weekends or irrigating, and in general dignifying Boyd's job by doing an incompetent imitation of it. Frank could never understand why this would ingratiate Mike to Boyd, but he guessed it was a form of tribute.

Frank parked the car and walked toward the granary. Jarrell now crossed the compound going the other way, carrying an irrigating shovel and a length of tow chain over his shoulder.

"Boyd," Frank called, and Jarrell stopped, paused and looked over at Frank. "Have you got a minute?"

"I might."

Frank walked over to him.

"I spoke to Lowry Equipment on Friday," said Frank, "and the loader's fixed on the tractor. So, that's ready to go whenever you need it."

"If that's all it was."

"That's right. But I assume it's okay."

Jarrell looked away and smiled. Frank let it fall silent for a minute.

"I've got a buyer to look at our calves on Monday."

"I hope he can find them."

Frank looked at Jarrell. Jarrell had him by fifty pounds and ten years. But he had put down his mark.

"He'll find them," Frank said. "You'll take him to them. Or you'll get out."

Frank turned to go to his car.

"Fuck you, Copenhaver," he heard Jarrrell say, like a concussion or a huge sneeze, and Frank kept walking. He heard Jarrell walk up behind him, and in a moment Frank's hat was slapped off his head. He bent to pick it up, then kept going to his car. Jarrell laughed and went to his truck, parked alongside the barn.

Frank stopped, then turned. He went back to where Jarrell stood. "Why did you do that, Boyd?"

"Because I don't like people telling me what to do."

"Well, Boyd, you should have thought of that."

"Thought of that when, you goddamn sonofabitch? When I let you tell me what to do?"

"When you came to work for us, Boyd. You knew what the deal was. I told you what the deal was. And I might have been the guy to give you your last chance." Jarrell crossed his arms and smiled at a faraway place. "I wouldn't hesitate to fire you right now except for the thought you might go back and beat up your wife like you did last time." Jarrell swung his gaze from the cloudy faraway and stared hard and flat into Frank's face. If it happens it happens, Frank thought. I couldn't live with myself if I shut up now. "Don't look at me, it was in the papers. And you know what? I had the same thought everybody else did: what kind of guy puts a hundred-ten-pound woman in the Deaconess Hospital? What kind of man is that? Good luck on your next job, Boyd."

Frank turned and began to walk toward his car. He hadn't gone many steps before he heard Jarrell behind him again. He kept walking and the steps ceased. He got in his car and drove out of the drive, past the unlucky house, and tried to picture the exact spot where Jarrell stood when he left.

When he got back to the office, he called Mrs. Jarrell and explained that he had had to let Boyd go, that Boyd was a fine man and a fine worker but that the time had come for each of them to get on with their lives in a different way. He had had to tell people before that it was time to get on with their lives. He said this in a conciliatory voice that sounded, after a bit, like that of a radio announcer or an advertisement for a commercial halfway house for disturbed youths. Mrs. Jarrell at least let him finish, then called him every foul name he had ever heard, including a few he was unsure of, like "spastic morphodite." Frank squinted in pain through this barrage and said that, nevertheless, he wished them all the luck in the world. His voice was a croak.

"Eat shit," said Mrs. Jarrell. "I hope you have a stroke."

Pause for thought. Some direct suggestions from Mrs. Jarrell. The same day Hell was suggested as a travel destination — and by a lover of the previous night! He went to see his brother Mike.

Mike was an orthodontist, and Frank had to wait until almost noon in his office, with bucktoothed preteens, reading kids' magazines before Mike had him in. They sat in the dental lab and talked, fat Mike still in his pale green smock, his round red face revealing the constant optimism that came of doing some one small thing in the world, namely pushing young teeth back and keeping them there. Frank looked around at the instruments, at the remarkable order.

"Mike," said Frank, "the ranch is making me crazy."

"You always tell me this when irrigation starts."

"I fired that cocksucker Jarrell."

"I wish you hadn't done that. He's a hard worker."

"I went out there today and he was in one of his cowboy snits."

"You shouldn't have gone out there. You know this happens when irrigation water runs. Everybody becomes an animal."

"I have to go out there. I had the tractor fixed for the filthy shit. He busted it, bent the bucket and blew the hydraulics. But he can't talk to anyone so I got it fixed. I tell him this and it just seems to make him madder. I told him we had to have the buyer look at the calves. This makes him mad. He knocks my hat off, salutes me with a 'fuck you.' It's unbearable, the cowboy mentality. I don't want to hire any more cowboys. They're all like Jarrell — drunken, wife-beating, snoose-chewing geeks with big belt buckles and catfish mustaches. They spend all their time reading magazines about themselves. College professors drive out and tell them they're a dying breed. I hate them. I tried to make things right with his wife so he doesn't put her in Deaconess again. What'd ya think she said to me?"

"Another 'fuck you'?"

"No, you're close. She said, 'Eat shit.' And she called me a 'spastic morphodite.' Ever hear that one before?"

"I have to admit, that's a new one on me."

"This would be a half-man, half-woman and very uncoordinated."

"Huh, real circus stuff."

"Yeah. And I don't want anymore. I'm a businessman, an ordinary businessman, and I want to keep it that way."

"Why don't you sell it? I really don't care, Frank. Marny would like a place we could take the kids picnicking when they get older, but there'll always be somewhere we can go."

"I'm going to get it out of my life whether we sell it or not. I would sell it, but I'm a sentimental asshole and it's ruining my life. I can't put anything behind me. I'm an asshole. I'm an asshole."

"I agree with your evaluation," Mike said.

"We never lived there, for God sakes."

"Yeah, but Dad grew up there."

"He hated it, Mom hated it."

"It doesn't matter. That was long ago. Now it's the 'old home place,' Frank. I don't know why you keep applying these truth tests. It doesn't matter what really happened. It only matters what people think is true, and Mom and Dad thought they spent the happiest years of their life there. It's true they argued for thirty years, but I'll tell you this much, it wasn't an old folks' home. It had that much going for it."

Frank didn't want this to be the last word, but nothing came to him and he had to let it stand.

10

The Fourth of July. Few people knew the country had not always been an independent nation. Most citizens took it as a day in honor of the invention of the firecracker, and towns like Deadrock bloomed with smoke and noise and pastel streamers of light on the evening sky. This year, what no one expected was that the hundreds of Indians who lived away from their reservations, on small plots or in tenements or in streets and alleys, would march on this quiet city with its sturdy buildings, broad central avenue and flowery neighborhoods, and ask for their land back. It ruined the Fourth of July. Indian ragamuffins, crones, wolfish men, pregnant women, fancy dancers and boys dressed as prairie chickens carried hand-lettered signs or simply chanted, "You know it's not yours, give it back!" Finally, the police frightened them off with flashing lights and uniformed appearances. The Indians dispersed. Some were seen at their jobs in town the next day. Like a dream without an obvious explanation, the event went unmentioned. It was pushed out of the newspapers by perestroika.

As soon as the bank opened after the holiday, Frank went to the drive-through window for some cash. Whenever he felt bleak, and for whatever reason, he always made sure he had cash. The teller looked at him from a high window and talked to him over a loudspeaker next to the vacuum delivery box. He sent his check

up to her in a tube, and when she looked at it, she asked him if he
had a dog. He'd had, in fact, a beautiful border collie named
Scott, but Boyd Jarrell's predecessor, a little Oklahoma cowboy
with a huge ring of keys on his belt, ran over Scott trying to drive
and light a cigarette at the same time. When Frank asked him how
he had run over his dog, the Oklahoman said, "Dog ain't got no
business under a tire." Frank brought Scott's body into town and
buried him next to the raspberry canes behind the house, and felt
very sad for a long time. He still felt sad. So he said to the teller,
"Yes, I have a dog, a beautiful border collie named Scott, black,
brown and white." When the teller sent Frank's money, she also
sent a package of dog biscuits down through the vacuum tube.

"What's your name?" Frank said with moistening eyes. He
couldn't see her, far off in her high window.

"Joanie."

"Thank you, Joanie."

He now felt closer to Joanie than to any other woman in his
life. When he got to the office, clutching his dog biscuits, he retreated into his room and rang out to Eileen. "Eileen, get Joanie at
Security Merchant on the line."

"Joanie," he said breezily, "this is Frank Copenhaver. Uh, to
refresh your memory, I cashed a check for a hundred bucks and
you were kind enough to send down some little sort of cookies for
my dog Scott, a tricolored border collie."

"Yes, I remember."

"Well, I wonder if you would like to uh" — blank, his mind
went blank, then filled back in vaguely — "to meet Scott."

"If I would like to meet Scott?"

"Yes, meet Scott."

"The dog?"

"Yes."

"If I would like to meet your dog?"

"Yes, that is what I am saying."

"I don't know, Mr. Copenhaver, if I would or not."

"Think of the dog as a device. I'm saying I'd like to meet you.
I'm quite safe, quite reliable, an old customer of the bank, endless

paper trail and so on. Well, what do you say?" He was conscious of yammering.

"Okay, where?" she said in a lusterless voice that suggested she was on to his game but would meet him partway. The absurdity of having gotten into this with dog biscuits must have struck her by now, or it would soon.

He gave her his address and set the time at seven o'clock, a nice hour close to the crossroads between dining and tomfoolery. He hung up the phone and could have gasped with relief but for the helpless smile that spread across his face.

Joanie was on time. By some rude standards, she was not presentable. She was a hearty, open-faced country girl, big enough to play for the Steelers. Frank told her right off that Scott was dead, but she came straight in and looked around his house as though she were the most unimpeachable ticket holder in a public place of amusement. Frank then decided he would cook for her, an impulse he had but seldom. After dinner, he promised, they would walk around the neighborhood and distribute the dog biscuits. She beamed at these suggestions, pulled things from the shelves for examination.

Frank established Joanie on the comfortable sofa in front of the television. She made it even more comfortable by propping herself all around with pillows, removing her shoes and putting her legs up. She seemed to be in for the long haul. He gave her the channel changer and she made immediately for the baseball game. While Frank chopped and prepared, she called out key events in the game, the Indians and the Tigers, and at one point burst into such raucous laughter that Frank went in for a look: a Detroit player was shoving an umpire backward across the infield. Frank returned to his cooking, stir-frying chicken and raw peanuts, thinking about how welcome these coarse shouts from the living room were, when the doorbell rang. He took the wok off the flame and answered it. It was Lucy.

Frank said, "Um."

"Is this a bad time?" she asked, peering into the hallway.

"Not at all," said Frank, backing inward and gesturing toward the living room with his spatula. "Please come in and introduce yourself to my guest —" Frank didn't know Joanie's last name. "And be so kind as to join us for dinner."

"Oh, I —"

"Of course you can. I know your habits."

"What the heck." Lucy came into the house in a cloud of jasmine perfume and by the time Frank heard her speaking to Joanie in the living room, he was back in the kitchen. Frank wondered what Lucy's reflections were as to her spot on the totem pole of desire when she found this cheerful elephant on the sofa. He could hear the game and the conversation from the living room and was reminded how pleasant plain human noise could be.

This time when the doorbell rang it was June, straight from the car lot in the sensible suit she'd worn at breakfast. "You're just in time for dinner," said Frank without an invitation or explanation. He shooed June into the living room and went back to the kitchen to chop every fryable thing in the refrigerator. June knew where the bar was, and wanton cackling soon poured from the living room. It's a shame I had to show up, Frank thought. He now had so much food in the wok it was hard to turn it over with the spatula and keep the bottom from burning.

"Anybody gonna help?" he called.

"No!" June said.

He ground up Szechuan peppers with the butt of the cleaver handle and sprinkled them into the cooking food. He tried it and added garlic, then rice wine vinegar. It was getting there. He opened the refrigerator with the toe of his shoe and looked for beer: there was plenty, and the food was going to be hot.

"Come and get it or I'll throw it out!" While the women came from the next room, he piled bowls and utensils, placed the six-packs of beer on the table in their holders, shoved the soy sauce and other condiments to the center and set the wok on a pot holder. They swept into the room with an audible rush and sat down. Frank rubbed his hands and said, "New blood."

"You wish," said June. "They're bad," she said to the other women.

"It's never new enough for these butterflies as they float from flower to flower," Lucy said.

Frank was always surprised by the capacity of women for a kind of clubbiness with one another. These three already seemed to be old friends. Men would still have been eyeing each other's shoes and watches, listening for accents.

"What do you think of this, Joanie?" Frank asked her.

Joanie looked rural and lost for just a moment, then focused on the food. "What is it?"

"Gallatin County Thousand Sighs Resfriados."

"Oh."

Frank dished out the food. It was like summer camp. The women were artificially elated, and the energy of unexpressed wit seemed to fill the room.

Joanie took one last doubtful look at her food and said, "Over the lips, past the gums, look out stomach, here it comes!"

Frank quaffed a beer to catch up. June told about a customer who constantly complained about his Buick, coming to the agency to gripe about mysterious noises. Today, she finally gathered a group of mechanics and sales people and placed the complaining customer, a circuit court judge, in the middle and asked him to imitate the sound his Buick was making in the hopes one of them would know what it was. The judge made a series of whining chugs — which June tried to render — followed by a low whistle, repeated them five times for his appreciative audience, only to have June tell him, "We'll have to get back to you on this." Wild laughter filled the dining room. The immense Joanie rose to a semi-crouch and popped four beers. "More beer for my lieutenants," she said, astonishing every sweating face around the table as she passed them out. June filled her mouth with stir-fry, widened her eyes and said, "Shit fire!" Lucy quietly slid her hand up the inside of Frank's thigh and Joanie shouted, "Drop his dick, lady, you're busted." The gaping faces stared around giddily.

"What a dinner party!" Frank yelled, surprised at the volume of his own voice. He looked across at Joanie's beef red slab of a face and wondered what would come out of it next.

"Guess who stood outside my window watching me undress last month?"

"Who?"

Lucy jabbed her thumb sideways in Frank's direction. He raised and lowered his eyebrows, kept chewing. This wasn't real insouciance.

"Oh, Frank," crooned June. It was hard to tell whether or not she was disapproving.

"So what did you do," Joanie asked, "call 911?"

"I sent him to the Arctic Circle," Lucy said. She looked around at the bewildered faces and added, "I'm a travel agent." It didn't seem to clear up much, but she didn't enlarge on it and "Arctic Circle" was absorbed as some sort of expression, descriptive of a deplorable state reached in many modern relationships.

It was here that Frank thought he would try to explain. He would tell them about the sense of freedom he had prowling around in the middle of the night, the sense of surprise, but Joanie jumped in to call, "Curiosity killed the cat," and raised her arms like a choirmaster as the others cheered, "Satisfaction brought him back!"

"I was trying to get to the bottom of things," he said, and got booed. He opened another beer and pushed his bowl away from himself. The others did the same. It was like a women's locker room and he was the towel boy. Lucy belched without self-consciousness and looked off in thought.

"We should count our blessings," she said with faint gloom, "that we haven't arrived at the moon of the cruise and package tours."

"What's this all about?" June asked, rifling her purse until she found a lipstick. She screwed it up into her view, squinted and began applying it to her lips. Frank knew June as someone who deplored all avoidable melancholy.

"I mean, my company should be called Last Fling Tours. I don't know if I want to work there anymore. It's sort of depressing."

"That people get old?" June asked. "I can't wait to get old. I thank God I'm not a day under forty-one."

"No, that they should do all this catching up at the end. Do you have any idea the quantity of adult diapers a cruise ship carries?"

"Oh, Lucy, come on."

"I'm serious."

"I think it's touching," said Joanie, "and if the ship goes down, it makes a kind of romantic ending." Frank missed Joanie's point, seeing only diapers bobbing on an empty sea.

June said, "I suppose we could take this view of everything. Every silver lining has a cloud. You guys think everything is a tearjerker. I sell convertibles to some very desperate people. I'm just sorry there's not more of them. I'd have me a big rolling ranch outside of town like the cook here. Walking horses. Hounds. Yeah, that's right. Y'all come. Sayonara ragtops."

"You don't want a ranch, June," Frank said. "Or if you do, I'll sell you mine."

"You can't sell it," said June. "It's the old family place."

"Watch me."

"Ever since I first met you, you've been wanting to get rid of it. Why's this?"

"None of us live out there and it's hard to keep it going, keep the weeds down, keep it irrigated, keep it fenced. You can't find ranch hands. If they're easy to get along with, they don't work, and vice versa. I just fired one today. I hated it. Hard worker. I shouldn't hire people because I can't stand to fire anybody. This was a little different. He got me off the hook by insulting me. So, at first I was comfortable about letting him go. Now I'm unhappy again. I called his wife. She was literally savage to me, but it didn't cure anything. I wish I knew how they were getting through this evening. He's going to be job hunting tomorrow. But he and his wife are a pair of mean Joses."

The women sat patiently through this maundering, then Joanie said, "Let's go out there and look in their window and see how they're getting along!" Frank shook his head, but June and Lucy shouted their support for the idea. Frank raised his hands to bring this to a stop but it had the opposite effect. He went into the kitchen to start coffee. Things were spinning along too fast. When he got back to the table they were deep into their plan of spying on the Jarrells. "What's to become of this cowboy couple?" asked June. "Enquiring minds want to know."

"You got any fucking brandy?" asked Joanie. "Schnapps?"

Frank doggedly hauled out the brandy, a pretty good cognac. They tossed it back without ceremony. They drank coffee too, which ought to have helped. He held out for a while but they got Jarrell's name and conferred over the telephone book. "Here it is, and it's a perfect address," said Joanie with her finger on a page. "All cottonwoods along a creek. We can sneak around in there like real Indians." Frank had a shot of brandy. This was going to be both exhilarating and mildly dangerous: the disconsolate Jarrells could come out blazing.

First, the dog biscuits had to be distributed.

"Let's go down Tracy," said Frank. "There's a mutt every ten feet on Tracy. Let's go down Tracy."

Frank carried the dog biscuits as they walked along the array of lawns. Lights shone from the painted porches. Schoolchildren studied in lighted upper windows, and where they passed dark houses, the cool stars glowed close overhead. At each stretch of chain-link fence, a dog bounded out and received a dog biscuit. The starlight glowed on the roofs of automobiles along the curb and there was a faint murmur of radio and television, music and typing, the hollow tap of Ping-Pong. In a basement workshop a bandsaw sang. The air was full of the breath of cooling silver maples and effulgent spruces. The four walked in peculiar contentment and a feeling of rightness, afloat. On every side, life went on.

"I hate to break the spell," said Joanie, "but I'd like to see how the couple is getting along."

The idea teetered here on the edge of collapse. There was a quiet moment when the right words seemed out of reach, time enough for Joanie to say, "On your mark, get set —" and start the hysteria up again and a stampede for the cars. A relay of barking dogs marked their progress down the street.

11

By walking the creek bottom through the sparsely settled neighborhood, single file, they approached the small, run-down house of Boyd Jarrell. The muddy banks of the creek made a coarse sucking sound around their shoes as they walked. By the time they got close, hunkered down in the red willows and startling clouds of red-winged blackbirds, only Frank still had shoes on, and that was because his laced up. The others had lost theirs in the mud. Their legs were black almost to their knees, and those who had tried to retrieve their shoes, Lucy and June, had black arms. Frank tried over and over again to get them to be quiet, but they chattered away and laughed through their noses when he signaled at them with downward cuts of his right arm and mimed the words "Keep it down!" When they were close, he stopped and said in a low anchorman voice, "If he hears us, he might start shooting." He got perfect silence.

A bank of untended lilacs enclosed a small back yard with a picnic table that had built-in bench seats on either side, a burn barrel, a clothesline, a swing set (Does he have kids? Frank wondered. How can I not know if he has kids?), a barbecue with a red enamel lid and a crooked little crabapple tree still in blossom. An open lighted window faced into this yard and there was a table just inside the window at which sat Boyd Jarrell, apparently asleep with his head on his arms.

They managed to slip through the lilacs quietly and Frank whispered his plan for them to sit at the picnic table and observe. They didn't quite understand, so he went forward and sat on one end of the bench seat facing the house. He gestured for the others to follow. June came and sat next to him, then Joanie. Finally, Lucy came and sat. It was her relatively light extra weight that caused the picnic table to flip over on top of them. Frank felt the wood press his face and heard June's hissing Okie curses. Joanie was on all fours, bucking, trying to get it off all of them in one powerful gesture but then complained she had gotten splinters in her rump. Frank grasped the table and raised the whole thing back into place with a red face. Lucy remained sitting on the ground, cross-legged, muttering, "I just hate it." Frank's first concern was Jarrell, but he saw his position hadn't moved. They sat again at the table, two on each side.

Then they watched.

"Is he asleep?"

"I don't know."

"Is he passed out?"

"That looks the same as asleep."

"Where's the little woman?"

"Nowhere to be seen. But you know what? He's moving."

He was. More than that, a continuous murmuring could be heard. Riveted, Frank tried hard to make it out.

"What's he saying?" Lucy asked.

"I don't know. If you promise to be quiet — Joanie, this goes for you — I'll go up and listen." Joanie covered her mouth with both hands. The others nodded compliance and Frank crept to the window. He listened until he could understand what Jarrell was repeating.

He was saying, "I have nothing, I have nothing." It was a choking voice and Frank felt an immense weight fall upon him. He stood looking in the window until Jarrell became silent again, his head rested in his arms. And it wasn't for a long moment before Frank was conscious of the burning eye that gazed out at him.

"Ladies," he said in a clear voice. "I'm afraid he has seen me. Why don't you get home as best you can. I'm going to have a word with Boyd."

Boyd Jarrell rose slowly to his feet and his shadow shot across the yard. The women screamed and ran headlong into the willow bushes.

Frank wanted to slip away too, but this was his responsibility. He walked around to the door, which was unlighted. He tapped on it and got no response. He tapped again. Nothing. He opened the door. It seemed to open into the abyss.

"Boyd?"

He walked in.

"Boyd? It's Frank."

Frank walked around the house calling Boyd's name. It was a plain house with a beer company print of Charlie Russell's *Last of the Ten Thousand* for decoration. In the bedroom were a pair of dirty jeans over the back of a chair. The empty drawers of the dresser were pulled out. There were coat hangers on the floor and the closet was open, with a handful of worn snap-button shirts hanging inside and a battered pair of rough-out cowboy boots with curled-up toes.

He went back to the kitchen and looked in the pantry. There was a bottle of whiskey in there and he poured himself a shot at the sink and sat down. It was quiet. He sat and listened. He made out a train a long way off, then perfect quiet once again. He sensed that he was being watched from the side but didn't turn that way for a moment, instead sipping the whiskey before deciding to look. He turned slowly and discovered a deer staring at him through the kitchen window. Beyond her, two others stood high on their back legs and ate the crabapples out of the tree in the yard. The deer faded from the window and Frank sighed. He made a note and weighted it with the whiskey bottle. The note said, "Stopped by — Frank."

"Who's the note for?"

Frank looked up. Boyd was in the room with him.

"Why, it's for you, Boyd. I couldn't find you."

"I told the old lady to get lost. She didn't want to get lost. So I helped her get lost." His face looked dazed with backed-up rage. "Now I'm back." Frank looked at the face. Boyd was almost beyond anger, his rage was so abstract. Frank felt himself turn helpless. This was just the moment when blood should have been flowing to his limbs, but it seemed to be going the other way. He felt like a flounder. He thought he might try defusing this situation by telling Boyd that he felt like a flounder, but there was not a lot of humor in the air.

"While I've got you," he began.

"While you've got me?"

"Yes, while I've got you."

"You're not funny."

"I didn't think so, no," Frank said. "What about the can. I use the can?"

"You gonna wet your pants?"

"Actually, possibly."

"Go ahead, and then I want you right here." Boyd gestured toward the hall with a jerk of his lips. He slowly wiped his mouth with the back of his hand as he watched Frank.

Frank went into the bathroom and closed the door. Then he turned around to look at the door. Good, a bolt lock. He locked it. Then he took in his surroundings. A toilet, a bathtub with a pipe ring around the top and a telephone-shaped shower head on a flexible metal pipe, and a big open window with the breeze pushing its plastic curtains.

"You better open up," came Boyd's voice. "I heard you lock it."

Frank could see the door flexing against the restraint. He didn't answer but looked at the window. He knew Boyd was thinking about the window too.

"I hope you're not gonna watch me take a leak," Frank said in a loud voice. He turned on the tap and hot water came out at a hard volume. When the steam billowed from the spray, he detached the shower head and stood next to the window. A few moments passed and Boyd lunged into the window space. Frank let him have it full in the face with the shower head. Boyd howled and went over backward. Frank ran through the bathroom door, up the hall, through the kitchen and out the front door.

Seeing Boyd come around the corner with one hand clapped to his face, Frank jumped into Boyd's black Chevy half ton and got the doors locked before Boyd could arrive. Boyd picked up a rock from the driveway and brandished it alongside the driver's window. Frank looked out, expressionless as a manikin, as he lifted his right hand slowly from his knee and felt the keys rattle against the back of his hand. He started the truck. Boyd went a short distance away and began beating a cottonwood tree with the rock. Frank felt he had no choice. He turned around and went out the driveway.

It wasn't until he got out to the highway that he looked into the rearview mirror and saw Boyd crouched in the bed of the truck. So he went up Sand Hill Road to Blind Creek Road, the most potholed road in the county. He drove up Blind Creek Road as fast as he could and still successfully wrestle the wheel. Sometimes Boyd was four or five feet in the air. He could now see that Boyd was ready to beat the window in if he could, but there was nothing in back but a spare tire that bounded around, seeming to chase Boyd from place to place in the bed.

Blind Creek Road rejoined Sand Hill and took him into Belwood, still at a high rate of speed. As he entered Belwood, he could see the cloudy security light in front of a single-bay car wash and a green Chrysler Coronado starting to nose into the huge, whirling, soapy brushes. He drove in behind it, blowing his horn frantically. The Chrysler stopped and he bumped it from behind, still blowing his horn. The Chrysler pulled forward and Frank eased the Chevy into the car wash, looking up into the rearview mirror just in time to see Boyd vanish under the brushes. He pulled forward just a bit more and slid across the seat, letting himself out the far door. By crouching next to the wheel well, he was able to slip out without getting soap-brushed.

The big rack overhead rolled forward, transporting the huge

spinning brushes and their load of hot water and soap. By the time Frank stood up enough to see, the owner of the Chrysler, a heavyset man in a nylon windbreaker, was standing next to the left fender of the truck, presumably waiting for the driver to get out. Frank slipped around the side of the building, and by the time he got across the street where there was a bar, he could hear oaths and the exchange of blows.

12

Saturday morning, first light, a silvery gleam along the ridge of the Lutheran church. The few cars reflected the sleepiness of their drivers as they eased up Assiniboine Avenue. Frank cleaned up the mess he had made, got the drink glasses out of their crevices in the living room, scraped the solidified mass out of the bottom of the wok with his cooking shovel under a stream of hot water and opened all the windows to let in the day.

He gathered up his rod, his fishing vest and waders, and drove over past Connolly Park where some children were already kicking a soccer ball back and forth between them. He stopped a few blocks beyond, where a street ended in a view of the stockyards, got out and knocked on the door. It opened and Phil Page came out carrying his tackle. Page was tall and thin with a long black beard that came down to his chest. Almost all that revealed expression were his eyes, which were detached and suspicious. Frank and Phil had played on the same baseball team in high school. Phil was a first baseman, and Frank always thought he had the right sort of detachment for that position, a driftiness in responding to the facts, a kind of lag timing peculiar to first basemen.

"Hi, Frank."

"Phil. We'll go in my car."

Phil put his tackle in the back seat of Frank's car and got in.

Phil Page was a brakeman on the railroad. Their friendship, which went back a quarter of a century, had been revitalized by troubles with their marriages. It was just like being back on the baseball team together. Phil usually fished with him on the weekends, but only if they made what he called a reasonable start.

"How's the railroad life?"

"Rolling."

"Making any money?"

"A little."

"Where are we going?"

"Let's go way the shit up the Sixteen," said Phil. "I'm in a brook trout state of mind."

They stopped at a twenty-four-hour convenience store to get some lunch supplies. The woman at the cash register was watching television so intently that Frank was able to slit the plastic wrap on a porn magazine and get a glimpse of the photographs, one after the other; it was like a seafood catalogue. Hard to maintain fascination in the face of that. The vagina was a splendid thing, but viewed as a monument it was entirely terrifying. The tiny, out-of-focus heads in the shadows behind those colossal, multicolor Mount Rushmore–sized cunts made Frank sorry he had looked. He wondered if these young women were discovered at soda fountains the way they used to discover Hollywood movie stars.

Phil came around the corner. "Man cannot live by bread alone," he said, then held up a jar. "He must have peanut butter." Phil displayed the two described items. "What else?"

"Two six-packs."

The country opened up quickly as they came down out of the Bridger Range going east toward the route of the old electric railroad. Blue skies, white flatiron clouds, sagebrush and grass, rhythmic hills betraying sea-floor origins, a sinewy black road that lifted on occasion to afford a glimpse of sparkling watercourses in the willows, cows of different colors but the same expression, doe-eyed calves, hawks contouring an air cushion on the surface of the land, the golden skeletons of tumbleweed blown into the fence corners, pictures of politicians on the telephone poles grinning insincerely into the vast space, and gophers running, heads down for speed or heads up to alertly observe themselves being run over.

A truck went by with a pair of scowling ranchers in front.

"I wonder if their mothers tie weights in the corners of their mouths," Phil said. "You know, kinda like the Watusis do to their ears and lips. I bet that's the case, the mama rancher hangs weights in the corner of baby's mouth. Then the little boy baby gets a little cowboy hat and little boots with little spurs and weights for his mouth. Next they give the little shit a little lariat and stick a pair of steer horns on a hay bale. Most generally, the little shit is called Boyd, and in ten or twenty years' time Boyd's getting drunk and beating cows with his stock whip, abusing his old lady and stubbing out cigarettes in front of the TV."

"During this entire time," said Frank, "your railroader is mostly in church or tending his kitchen garden or cuddling a litter of rabbits to help them through a blue norther. He's a man of few words but they are always the same words: 'The Railroad Built Montana.' "

"Turn left," said Phil. "Asshole."

The road took them off into a prairie with brilliant pale stands of bear grass and, below, a spring surrounded by aspens. A quarter mile beyond the spring a long slough solidified into a shining expanse of canary grass, deep green and dense. The Sixteen River meandered between parallel bands of willows, a true sagebrush trout stream heading west to rattlesnake canyons and the wide Missouri.

They stood beside the car, rigging up their rods and tying on flies. "Attractor patterns today," said Phil. "And death to all streamside entomologists."

"D'accord, sport. I'm putting on a royal Wulff tied with me own pinkies."

"I long to feel that creek push in on my waders."

"I long to hear the Pflueger opera as I drag the first hog to the gravel."

"I doubt there's any hogs up here. Not enough water."

Frank suddenly thought about Boyd Jarrell. Boyd hated people who fished, although he spent plenty of time watching television or sitting in bars. Sometimes after he'd been in a bar for two days and spent every cent he'd made that week, Boyd would tell people, "I've lived next to these cricks all my life, but I've never had time to fish."

"Walk down about half a mile and I'll fish behind you," Phil said. "We can hopscotch." He was pulling on his beard and looking through the willows into a small pool. "I can see about nineteen of the fuckers from here," he said in an enraptured voice. "Time to rip some lips."

Frank started along the stream bank at a brisk walk. A covey of partridges took to the air in an ivory rush, brown terrestrial birds against the blue of outer space. After a bit he looked back and watched the heron-like figure of Phil Page forming a bow of line in midair over the stream, a slight breeze lifting his black beard from his chest. A meadowlark stood atop a Canadian thistle and poured out its song, barely pausing as Frank passed by. The prairie grass rolled away to the north. About halfway to the horizon, a sandstone seam made a long wavering line in the silvery grass. The sun dilated toward noon and Frank felt breathless to be in this very spot.

The line straightened and fell, and the bright speck of fly soared on the current. It lifted into the air again, then returned to teeter along the quick water on its hackles until it disappeared down a small suction hole, and the trout was tight, vaulting high over the water again and again. The rod made a live arc in Frank's hand, and in a minute the fish splashed in the shallows at his feet. He grasped the fly and the trout wriggled free. Frank let out a deep sigh and looked down the meander of wild water; it spiraled away forever.

He could see Phil fishing behind him, hovering on the stream bank and probing with his fly line like an insect. Every so often his rod tightened in a bow and Phil scrambled down the bank to grab a trout. Frank caught three in a row from a flowing pool. Miles and hours went by and it was time for lunch. Frank stretched out on the stream bank, his fly rod crossed on his chest, the sun warm on his face, and waited for Phil to catch up. Ants were crawling on his forehead. He was drifting off, thinking how easy friendship could be.

"Good grief," Frank said and sat up. "I'm suddenly starving."

"I'm afraid we're talking PB and J here, sport."

"That'll do just fine."

"Doesn't really go with beer, but who really gives two shits what goes with beer when you got beer?"

"Not me," said Frank, pulling the top and smelling the spray of hops on his face. "Oh, boy."

"The little creek's hotter than a two-dollar pistol today."

"I lost count."

"So did I."

They ate and watched the stream as though something very important could happen there at any moment. Some jelly leaked into the palm of Frank's hand and he licked it out. A band of antelope drifted over the top of the sandstone seam and began to graze toward the west. The clouds climbed like a low ladder toward the west and a darker blue.

"You been going out?"

"Some," said Frank. "No one special." He thought about it: was that true?

"Anyone I know?"

"You know Lucy Dyer?"

"Wasn't Jerry Caldwell fucking her?"

"I really don't know."

"I'm pretty sure she was fucking Jerry. This'd be a year or so ago. But what's the difference? The only thing that'll stop them from fucking the mailman is AIDS. My old lady's probably fucking somebody right now. Who gives a shit." He pulled his beard straight down while he thought. "It's inflation. The consumer is king."

Frank thought of saying something but he didn't. He just tried to watch the country. Phil soon went on to something else: out-of-staters. Seems every time Phil tried to go downtown, he had to plow through out-of-staters to get anywhere he was going. Things, no matter how you looked at them and as more time went by, were a bitch. Phil had set his face.

"How can you tell they're out-of-staters?" Frank asked.

"Shit, you just look at them. For one thing, the motherfuckers take little tiny steps."

"Oh."

"And they're dressed for an Everest assault. I don't have to tell you that there's a world of difference between Deadrock and Mount Everest. The cocksuckers will come into the Dexter, read the menu and leave, go down the street to O'Nolan's, read the menu, leave, then drive out to Wendy's, tie up everyone in the drive-up line, customizing their goddamn burger order, hold this, hold that. I hate to see it, man. I wish they'd go back to where they came from."

"I can remember when you were an easygoing first baseman."

"Yeah, well, I wised up. I've got plenty of anger in me now and it gets my ass out of bed in the morning. That's the only way you get anything done. This country was built by pissed-off people."

"Maybe that's what I need," Frank mused. "I don't know, I just get sad. When you get comfortable you tend to brood on your losses. Hunger produces optimism. You're on the move and that big Dagwood sandwich is just around the bend."

"Well, I hope I catch up with it. Them boys at Rail Link busted my union and cut me to the bone."

Frank felt the quiet that ensued, two men on a riverbank, didn't used to be here and someday would be gone. Just now their lives seemed so important. Frank had made a killing in real estate; Phil would never be out of debt. Both of them loners, by choice or not. Brief stories of local life. Frank felt it made sense to think of it this way.

Through the afternoon, Phil fished on ahead. A breeze came up, and casting the pale fly line was not quite the pleasure it had been earlier in the day. The small clouds that rode the westerly cast racing shadows on the ground. Trout kept coming to the fly. The riverbank curved like the rim of a bowl. It was taller than Frank was on its outside edge and its face was speckled with the borings of swallows who came and went incessantly. There were small groups of ducks occasionally floating toward him, and when they struck an invisible boundary, they took flight and wheeled to the east. A small island divided the river and balanced the two halves of water in an even flow across a pure white bar of gravel.

Frank noticed the great length of Phil's shadow on the ground as he walked toward him. Moths arose in clouds from the prairie and nighthawks began to soar in the violet light. The day of fishing was over. They broke down their tackle, got in the car and started along the empty road toward home.

"That was all right," said Frank.

"I guess it was."

"I really stop thinking about everything else when I fish. I think about how to catch a fish, period."

On state and local news, Mr. Medicine Horse, a prominent chief in the sun dance ceremony, was running for sheriff of Hardin, promising to join his opponent, Mr. Rogers, in avoiding undue mudslinging.

"Good luck, Mr. Medicine Horse," said Phil to the road ahead.

"If he didn't learn mudslinging at Crow Agency, he better study it now before it's too late."

"So, what's happening with your ranch?" Phil asked as they bent around toward the south.

"It's ruining my life. I fired Boyd Jarrell."

"It's about time."

"Well, he had his merits. Hard worker, good cowboy. This was the usual deal, he was hunting for a quit and he found one."

Phil looked out the window rigidly. "I thought he needed to be elsewhere a long time ago."

Frank drove and thought for a moment. "I'm surprised you feel one way or another about him."

"I have to be honest, Frank. He spent all his free time running you down. I told him I didn't appreciate it. He said it was a free country. I thought he was no good."

It was absolutely silent in the car except for the hiss of wind around the doors. Frank felt something in his stomach. "I didn't know that was the case, Phil." Frank realized he had been naïve in thinking his problems with Boyd had been between them.

"That was the case."

Frank kept driving. He was no longer thinking about Boyd; he was thinking about Gracie. The last time the ranch had meant anything to him was when Gracie kept Archie, her little paint gelding, out there. One spring he just disappeared. Frank was later told on pretty good authority that a rancher up the road had shot him to make a bear bait. After that, Gracie didn't want to go out there anymore. Frank couldn't help his silence. He wanted to say something to make Phil feel better, but he couldn't speak.

"I shouldn't have said anything, Frank," said Phil.

"Actually, I started thinking back . . . about Gracie."

"That's good. I didn't think you were that worried about what anybody said."

Frank waved the whole thing away. The silence resumed and it was oppressive. "Yup, old Gracie." Phil writhed around in his seat, trying to watch out the window. He fooled with the radio, then turned it off again and took a great sigh. He dropped his fist to his knee.

"Okay, me and Kathy, we're married like twenty years. It's not perfect but it's okay. The day we get the news Denny Washington's gonna bust the union, I take off a half day and head for the house. I walk in. I hear it in the back room. I have to see with my own eyes: Kathy's fuckin' our family doctor. You know him, an asshole backpacker in your clinic, Dr. Jensen. And I can see he's trained her in a couple deals I'd never found out about. I go out and sit in the hall. I sit there and think: *A,* do I shoot them? *B,* do I divorce her? *C,* do I shoot myself? I'm going round and round. The doctor walks by. Kathy walks by. And that's it. Life goes on. End of story." Phil went back to gazing out the window and they rode the car together as if it were a time machine.

"I appreciate that, Phil."

"I guess that if we didn't have trout fishing, there'd be nothing you could really call pure in our lives at all."

Frank stared at the road ahead, filling with joy at this inane but life-restoring thought. "I do like to feel one pull," he said.

"Yes!" Phil shouted and pounded the dashboard.

"Yes!" shouted Frank, and they both pounded happily on the dashboard. "Trout!" The volume knob fell off the radio. Phil dove down to look for it, muttering "Fuckin' douche bag" as he searched.

A few miles down the road, Frank drove past a hitchhiker sitting atop a backpack with a thumb out.

"That was a girl," said Phil. Frank hit the brakes and backed up a quarter of a mile. The girl stood up and looked in the car. She had a sweater tied around her waist and sunglasses held by a bright pink strip around the back of her head. She evaluated Frank and Phil and got in.

Frank said, "You want to get up here in front?"

"No, back seat's fine."

Phil caught Frank's eye. "Let me get that pack for you," he said, and wrestled it into the car. As she clambered in behind the tilted front seat, Phil mouthed the words "Not bad" so that Frank could see. She had a strong fresh smell of woodsmoke.

"How far you going?" Frank asked.

"Deadrock."

"Where you coming from?"

"The Highwood Mountains."

"The Highwoods!" said Phil.

"What were you doing in the Highwoods?" Frank asked. She was watching the roadside go past.

"I was trying to see a wolf."

"A wolf!" said Phil. "There's no wolves in the Highwoods."

"Maybe there is and maybe there isn't," said the girl.

"Are you an out-of-stater?" asked Phil.

"What's that got to do with it?"

"Just wondering."

"I'm from Minnesota originally. There's wolves there too."

"I'm Frank and this is Phil. What's your name?"

"Smokie. Watch out for that truck —"

"Sonofagun was halfway into my lane."

"You were halfway into *his* lane," said Phil. "That's why he was blowing his horn."

"Was I really? I'll be darned."

"Have you guys had a few?"

"We been fishing. It has the same effect on us."

"So, where's the fish?"

"We let them go," said Frank, glancing into the back seat. Smokie had a rope of ash hair in a braid that hung over her shoulder. She was young.

"You let them go?"

"Yeah," said Phil. "We train them so out-of-staters can't catch them."

"You're a riot," said Smokie.

Phil looked like he'd been slapped, if lightly. He stared straight through the windshield. The elevators appeared, then the stockyards, then the fast food and car lots, agricultural supplies and used furniture, pawn shop, video rental.

"God, this is getting built up," said Phil. "I mean, where the hell's the town? Used to be right over in here."

The last thing Phil said that day was "Shit." Frank had pulled up in front of his house and Phil thanked him for a great day, another great day on the stream; then Phil snagged his shirt getting out of the car and said his last word for the day. Smokie moved to the front seat. Frank glanced over at the front door of Phil's house. Kathy was not there welcoming him home, glad to see him. Frank thought of the day she and the family doctor strode out of that modest doorway. It sharpened a pain inside him.

"Where can I drop you?" Frank asked.

"Anywhere around here is fine."

"No, I'm happy to take you where you're going."

"I haven't picked a spot, I guess."

They drove on past the hospital and a light-truck repair place. The trees curved right overhead in the old neighborhood as they approached Main.

"Do you have a place to stay?"

"No."

Frank turned his head to look. "You don't?"

"Uh-uh."

Frank thought for a long moment about his afternoon and looked at this fresh-faced, vital creature. "I know a spot you can stay," he said and drove her back to Phil's.

"Phil," he said with a look, "I hate to impose, but Smokie needs a place to stay." Frank thought Phil would be grateful, but he stood there and complained about what a mess the place was. Finally, he agreed that if Smokie walked around the block for half an hour first, she could stay on the couch. He was quite grouchy about that. Frank thought as he drove off, I'm so cynical I thought he'd take it as a favor.

13

Frank went straight to his breakfast meeting with Doctors Jensen, Popelko, Dumars and Frame in the dining room of the Dexter Hotel. They were his renters. He got there a few minutes late and the doctors were telling stories over their first cup of coffee. Dr. Popelko, an obstetrician who had taught his specialty, explained how he had tried to get his university to hire prostitutes. He chuckled, his little round face completely wrinkled, his bow tie bobbing and the shoulders of his loud plaid sport jacket shuddering. "How do you teach students to do a vaginal?" he bayed across the dining room. "It's no different than learning to ride a horse. *You need vaginas!* Where are you going to get them? In the old days, we used poor people's vaginas in exchange for medical treatment. Now everyone has insurance. The chancellor's wife isn't going to let you use her vagina, is she? The chairman of the English department is not liable to suggest that the medical students train on his daughter's vagina. The only answer seemed to be prostitutes. But when I suggested this as a budget item to the university, I damn near lost my job. It made the papers and the born-agains were marching. I went into private practice. I had to!"

"Morning, Frank," said Dr. Dumars. Frank carried his own coffee and roll and set it among the more complete breakfasts of the doctors. Dumars was an older doctor, close to retirement, and bore himself with the gravity old doctors sometimes had as a result of all they had seen. Jensen and Frame were young and ambitious, with huge split-level homes. Jensen, the seducer of Phil's wife Kathy, had blond hair which he had arranged in pixieish bangs, a modern and alert young man with staring eyes. Frame was somber; the skin under his eyes was dark and his lower lip hung in a permanent pout. He was staring at Frank.

"Been fishing, Frank?" Jensen asked.

"Yeah, I went Saturday over on the Sixteen. It was pretty darn good," Frank said. Jensen knew he fished with Phil. This was a way of taking Phil's temperature at long range.

"Huh," said Jensen, "we went to the Big Horn over the weekend. Sixteen-foot leaders. Antron emergers. Size twenty-two."

"A little tough for me, sounds like." Frame was still staring at Frank.

Jensen shrugged. "I wanted to get a couple of days in. There's a marathon in Billings next weekend, then a prostate seminar in Sun Valley the following weekend, and so on, and there goes your life."

Dr. Frame spoke abruptly. "Do you uhm know what?" He was trying to look right through Frank.

"I shudder to think."

"The rent at the uhm clinic is too high."

"No, it's not," said Frank.

"Too high, too low, it's more than we're uhm willing to pay." Frame was teaching Frank the ABCs of running his building.

Frank sipped his coffee, peered over the top of the cup at the other doctors, who were not tipping their hands, letting Frame run point. Popelko had a purely inquiring look on his face; he wanted a factual outcome. Jensen was just being serious about whatever it was. No one was going to mediate on Frank's behalf, that was clear. Frank said, "Why don't you move out?"

"We haven't paid last month's rent."

"I hadn't noticed."

"We just wanted to uhm send a signal."

"I don't understand signals. I understand English."

"I tried English," said Dr. Frame. "You didn't seem to uhm understand."

"I understood. I was short on information. I didn't realize you hadn't paid the rent last month. You're evicted."

At this the other doctors clamored. Dumars immediately pulled Jensen toward him by the coat and spoke into his ear. Frank stood up. The doctors were all trying to look like one unit, a little tribal dance group or something. Frank knew they didn't want to move out; they just wanted to improve their deal. Frank read once that ninety percent of doctors went to medical school for business reasons. That made it easier for him to keep the rent where it ought to be than to imagine they were sheltering sick orphans.

"Get your stuff out. Or hand deliver last month's rent. I'll be able to give you the new figures for next month, if you decide to stay. I don't see last month's check in my office today, you're going to have to work out of your upstairs bedrooms."

Frank walked out into the street. The sunshine hit him. He could never think about property, or its problems, if the sun was in his face. A ranch couple walked by in matching denim; she had a dramatically tooled purse and he wore a bandanna. They were gazing around at the buildings and gesturing to each other with show-business savvy, projecting their feelings. What a big town this is! they seemed to say.

Frank turned and went back into the hotel, feeling his thoughts roll forward like a barrel going down a hill. The doctors were still at their table. Frank stood at its edge.

"That building is killing me," he said. "Six percent of its capitalization before expenses. Why don't you buy it? No, hold it, I know why. Because the return is so low. We'll let Frank Copenhaver go on owning the sonofabitch. Let me tell you something: nobody's getting such gentle rent treatment in this whole town. But don't be greedy, don't be greedy."

Outside, the sun was still shining. He saw crisp newspapers in their stand and smelled the bakery on Reno Avenue. There was a white vapor trail angling upward in the blue sky. He returned to his office in bounding spirits and gave Eileen Joanie's, June's and Lucy's names and asked her to get them on the phone for him. He went to his desk and waited. His desk phone rang and Eileen told him none of the three was in. He suddenly wanted company. It was painful.

14

It was beyond stillness; for a moment he didn't know where he was. He felt the heat of her body against his right side and her open-mouthed breathing on his neck, the uneven breathing of a pounding heart.

"Who is it?"

"It's not Gracie."

"Oh, hi, Lucy."

She eased upright and drew the covers back. "A little birdie told you," she whispered. "A little birdie told you a woman devoid of self-respect had stolen into your bed. Man, you've been out like a light." He could see her breasts, pushed somewhat together by her upper arms. She was looking straight into his eyes as she reached up between his legs and took him in her hand, her hair hanging straight down alongside her face, a faintly superior smile. "Ooh," she said, "it's harder than Chinese arithmetic."

"Uh-hm."

"You pretty swift with this little deal?"

"If everything goes according to Hoyle."

"We'll see."

She was gradually drifting away as she held him, moving her hand up and down, her form almost rigid, head hanging down. Then she stretched her face toward the ceiling, murmured something and came slowly down on him with her mouth — a white arc of scalp visible where her thick hair was parted — all the way to the back of her throat, and she tried to say "We'll see" again. The *W* was the only thing she could pronounce.

"Ooh, hold it, hold it, hold it," he said, grasping the sides of her face.

She lifted her glistening mouth. "Too much?"

"Yeah, too much."

"Can I put it in?"

"Yeah, put it in — no! Just hold it a sec."

She made her finger slick on the end of his cock and swirled it around one nipple. "Let me put it in."

"You've got to hold it a sec. Don't even say it again."

"In."

"Sh."

Her hips were still moving. He had to look off at the wall, the blank window, the drapes, the dresser. "Okay," he said.

She lifted up to kneel over him on one knee, one foot flat on the bed, and reached down to barely put him inside her, then slowly let herself down. All grace went out of her and she began to fuck out of control, a look as if of horrified surprise on her face, going "unh unh unh unh." Then she added, "This could get habit-forming."

"Thanks."

"This *is* habit-forming!"

He hoped she wouldn't say it could get habit-forming again. It was the sort of remark that could bring him to a screeching halt. But she went on until he felt the hotness loosen then shoot up out of him. He felt a long fall, thought how men didn't want to shoot *into* anything, but simply, in the vulgarism, *off;* so much more abstract. *Off,* as in off into space or off we go into the wild blue yonder. Women would be insulted if they ever pictured this solitary deed. Actually, maybe they'd gotten wind of it already. "Shooting off" — it was outlandish.

In a moment, she closely curved beside him and said, "It's easy. Two syllables. Lu-cy."

Frank thought, This isn't working. This isn't making me feel good. She is having to act extremely silly and it can't be very good for her. Except for about a minute, this is worse than work.

When Frank woke up again and realized she was still there, he was suddenly annoyed. He had been through this before, but to find his morning solitude erased was too much. A young woman smelling of cocktails and bar smoke from her last stop before this one was asleep in a key location of his home. What next? He went downstairs to the kitchen and put three shredded wheat biscuits into a bowl. To his aggrieved eye, they looked like sanitary napkins. He mashed them down so they'd stay within the rim of the bowl. He poured milk carefully into the center and it just disappeared until finally its white sheen rose around the cereal.

A bird hit the window hard and he jumped up, threw the window open and looked out. A black and white magpie was staggering on the ground. It sat down and fluffed out its feathers and looked around groggily. Frank whistled and the magpie looked up. It didn't feel well enough to fly away, just walked off in a hunched, disconsolate manner.

He returned to his breakfast. He was wearing a bathrobe that had an old box of goldfish food in the pocket. The goldfish had long since moved to the office. Probably ought to throw the robe in the wash. The low, white, nearly silent German coffee machine quit drizzling and the half-black pot was filled with steam. Frank poured himself a cup of coffee, a cup of Mexican Pluma to be precise. He was continually changing brands in the hope of tasting something. He drank so much coffee, he might as well have put caffeine pills in boiling water.

Frank was thinking about all the good times he had had with Gracie and Lucy. He recalled the time he went trick-or-treating with them on Halloween, drunk and out there with the kids. They cut holes in a sheet and stuck their heads through; they went as a *ménage à trois*. By the time they got home with shopping bags loaded with M & M's, Good & Plenties, Milky Ways, Snickers, Hershey Kisses, candy apples, caramel popcorn on strings, they were filled with a crazed and diffuse lust; but it went away and they didn't go through with anything because at the last minute Lucy went on a crying jag, something about proving her mother wrong and what was left, what happened to meaning, and so on. Lucy had knelt on the floor, face on the rug, sobbing, while Gracie and Frank continued to sit on the sofa, their heads through the sheet, trying to think what in the world to do. And Frank was burdened with what seemed to be an outlaw and omnidirectional lust.

He had a bad feeling about his night with Lucy. His skin was clammy. He felt guilty of everything, no matter what it was. He felt as if he had shot poison into the blameless uterus of a travel agent and old friend of his wife, the kind of thing he had tried to avoid, at least in his mind, if not on the actual mattress. He could hear her now, of all times, singing in the bathtub, a buckaroo tune to the meter of " 'Twas the Night Before Christmas" which might have been composed for the musical saw.

Frank went upstairs to look in on Lucy. She was sitting in the tub, bubbles up to its gunwales, and when he entered she grabbed her breasts with soapy hands and said, "Come in and make the ficky-fick, Frankie!" Frank wondered if most property investors were addressed in this manner. He was startled by this new Lucy. She had evidently had some conversion since he last was with her, one that seemed entirely foreign to her personality.

"I don't think so."

Nothing about Lucy moved. Her big eyes searched Frank. She looked like a deer caught in the headlights. Steam lifted from the tub and went out through the tilted window. She had invented this character for herself and now she didn't know what to do with it. Real empty-headed wantonness didn't quite work for Lucy.

"I knew if I lived long enough, someday I'd get turned down," she said. "They say it builds character."

15

Frank stopped by Dick Hoiness's insurance office and asked him to join him for a drink. It seemed to be a wonderfully burgeoning insurance world in there, with all sorts of things pressed into service to hold down papers, even rocks. There were two secretaries on suave gray rolling chairs faced in opposite directions, operating computers. Dick got the jacket of his seersucker suit off the coatrack in the corner of his office. He was watching Frank quizzically. Frank had known for some time that he was going slightly downhill since Gracie's departure, but this odd gaze from Hoiness confirmed it.

"Man, it's ten A.M.," said Dick. "Can I join you for something other than a drink?"

"No, this is more of a drink situation. You're going to have to roll with me on this one."

They drove back to the Dexter Hotel and went into the Meadowlark Bar with the Art Deco aluminum cocktail silhouette in front.

"Is this important?" he asked.

"Important."

"Do I have to drink?"

"Yes."

They had the bar to themselves. At such an hour, even the bartender viewed one with suspicion, barely accepting that in hard times problem drinkers help make ends meet. The light was dim, designed really for chatting up the opposite sex; but at this hour it seemed just gloomy.

"Let's sit in a booth," Frank said.

The bartender rolled his eyes. They each ordered a beer. Dick gathered his toward himself on the tabletop without actually taking a drink from it. He still had a kind of nocturnal demeanor from his rock-and-roll days. Frank looked at this well-adjusted insurance man and remembered him calling out over the top of reaching hands and transported faces, "I didn't know God made honky-tonk angels!" with a death grip on the bucking neck of his guitar. Long time ago.

"I don't know why I had to tell you this," Frank said, "but I've accumulated a good many things and you've got them insured and I just had to tell someone that I am not enjoying any of this, including the accumulations, and it's probably because I haven't gotten over Gracie." Hoiness looked at him in astonishment; it confirmed Frank's sense that he was coming adrift.

"You're telling me this? I'm flattered you would think of me to tell this."

"You're in insurance. You deal in the values the world accepts or you'd be out of business. I pay you to insure things that are starting to have no value to me."

"You're not canceling . . ."

"No, I just need to have things spruced up so I can keep playing. I want to be a player. I don't want to get benched just at the point I'm getting a few things done. I want to play my ass off. But does this ever happen? Do you get clients that say they don't want things insured until they rediscover their meaning?"

"No."

"You don't? It's worse than I think."

"I'm not saying that . . ." Hoiness lifted his hands in confusion. "I guess we all get the feeling we're doing something wrong. It's like walking alone through a store at an off hour, trying to act like you're not shoplifting. In other words, your only choice is to go on about your business. How is your business?"

"My business is good," Frank said. He didn't mention any doubts he might have had.

"Now we're businessmen," Hoiness said.

"Yes."

"How did it happen?"

"I don't know," said Frank. "The Theys have taken us in."

"We're pretty cozy. We're one of them. I married a They — nice tits, mother of my kids, never seen me on drugs, never seen me with my dick through the back of a park bench waving to the nuns. It's outa sight. It's PTA."

"We're pretty cozy in here," Frank mused, "right in the golden hearth of American life. We should thank our lucky stars." Frank stared at the picture of the elk and the waterfall behind the bar. "I don't want to get booted out of the hearth, Dick. I think it's possible to appreciate it. I think you ought to be able to sit in front of your hearth even if you are all by yourself."

Dick looked at him and said, "This is from the point of view of the committed life insurance salesman: I've noticed that people who lose the point of everything don't seem to be around too much longer."

"Said like a true They."

Karl Hammersgard came in the door out of the blinding light, the sleeves of his blue oxford shirt rolled up, the pleated khakis straining around his midriff and rising slightly above the tops of his oxblood loafers. You could see the comb lines in his blond hair going straight back from his ruddy forehead. He was short and tough.

"Holy cow," shouted Hoiness, "a real drunk!"

Hammersgard went to the bar and got a shot and glass of water without seeming to notice there was anyone in the place but him. He knocked back the shot, sipped the water, got the shot refilled and came to the table. He looked at Frank and Dick. "Ain't that a pair to draw to," he said.

"Join us, Karl," said Frank.

"I thought I was the only day drinker in our group," said Karl, sitting down.

"Normally you are," Dick said, "but Frank's not feeling too good."

Karl raised his glass to Frank. "What's the trouble?" he asked.

"The escalating boredom of life in the monoculture."

"Good, Frank. Is that what this is?"

"Yeah," said Frank, "like something you grew in a petri dish." Then Frank didn't feel particularly well. But it was hard to be solemn.

"So, what's with you?" Hoiness asked him.

"Well, the usual. We're four and oh." Karl was the high school baseball coach. "So, I'm happy. We play Red Lodge tomorrow and they're tough, or supposed to be tough. I've saved this one kid — pitches, unbelievable slider — for tomorrow. This kid is pure baseball. Being scouted already. It's an away. I want to see him at that altitude. I think his stuff will absolutely shine. When you see this kid walk out there, it's like seeing baseball itself, with a kind of glow. I'd like to put him in a glass case and suck out all the air. He's that good. So, like I say, I'm happy, things is good."

Frank looked at Karl. Karl was normal. Have a couple of shooters in the middle of the morning because they taste so good. No other reason. Big, life-loving Scandinavian brute. That's what Frank hated about having a crooked personality — the weirdness, the glancing impulses, jokes going wrong, worldly mania one day and pining for a monastery by sunup the following. It was good to have companions like these, large mammals. In fact, overwhelmed by his love of them, Frank lustily ordered another drink.

The smoked glass of the barroom windows darkened rhythmically with the passing of pedestrians. The bartender went to his radio and turned on the livestock reports, which became the country music station, Hank Williams Jr. love marches and boasting.

"Turn that shit off," yelled Karl, "or change it."

"There ain't a Norwegian station," said the bartender.

"Jesus Christ," said Karl, but the bartender changed it to something like background or elevator music.

"That we like," said Karl in a firm voice. "And another round

all the way around. These boys'll take shots with their beer."
Frank and Dick tried to object but the drinks came and even
seemed good, and they ordered the same thing again.

Frank was now at the end of the bar whirling with his right
hand a rack of snack foods — ruffled potato chips, beef jerky,
cheese popcorn. His left hand was deep in a three-gallon wide-
mouth jar of pickled eggs. The pickling solution soaked into the
sleeve of his jacket and he paused to feel the slippery eggs bumping into the back of his hand, never the front where he could grab
them. "Hey, can't catch these bastards," he cried. He tried putting
both hands in, but it made the juice slop out onto the bar. By the
time he got an egg out, he had about ten of them in his hands and
the bartender was watching him sharply. He went over to the
booth, where Karl and Dick were forehead to forehead in a heated
conversation about the Middle East.

"Who wants a pickled egg?" he called out. Hoiness waved him
away without taking his eyes off the passionate explanations of
Karl Hammersgard. This hurt Frank's feelings and he thought of
slugging Hoiness. He stood cradling the rubbery, strong-smelling
eggs against his chest. "Well, then," he said, "I don't want them
either." He went back to the end of the bar and tossed them one
after another with a splash into the jar.

The bartender was right in his face. "No egg?" he said.

"My eyes were bigger than my stomach."

"You think it's a good idea to handle them a lot, then toss them
back in for the next customer?"

"Only a sucker would buy one of those eggs," said Frank.

"You're buying them all or you're out."

"Put them on the tab, Hal," called Karl from the table. "Frank,
get your ass back here and stop wandering around stirring things
up." Frank seemed to respond to this suggestion and trudged back
to the table and sat down.

"What's the subject? Still Middle East?"

"No," said Hoiness, "the spotted owl."

"Another round!" bayed Hammersgard. "Get in here and don't

act like you want to go out and face the world. Be a gentleman, even if it kills you."

"The world is just an illusion anyway," said Hoiness. Most of Frank's friends were able to revert to hippies in a heartbeat. He knew plenty of middle-aged people ready and willing to discuss karma at any time.

"Not in Red Lodge it ain't," said Hammersgard. "They got one of the best defensive ball clubs in the state of Montana. They got a third baseman who's like the Crest invisible shield. Nothing gets by this monkey. That's why I'm fielding my man. When he turns his shit loose, the Red Lodge nine will make appointments with their optometrists."

Frank leaned across the table and said, "My face is numb."

"I'm close to hysteria," said Hoiness. "I've got an appointment to sell a group plan to the cement plant in Belgrade. Before I sell them even one leetle premium, I'm gonna show them how the big boys puke."

"Euphoric," said Frank.

"How's that?"

"Euphoric."

"Oh, good, Frank," said Dick, "that's good."

Four cowboys burst in the door. They were in high spirits, laughing even before they came in. The bartender checked the shortest one's identification and the others ridiculed him and pointed out that Shorty didn't need to shave because the cat could lick his beard off. In a moment, tall draft beers were arrayed before them.

"Kids," said Hammersgard cheerfully.

"But loud," said Frank.

"It's part of their deal," said Hoiness. "Frank, it's normal."

"Loud is?"

"Mm-hm."

"How are you?" called one of the cowboys, a tall man with a rag tied around his neck.

"We're fine," said Karl.

"Why, that's all right," said the cowboy, turning back to drink with his fellows.

"What did he mean by that?" Frank said. "What'd you mean by that?" he called across to the cowboy. The cowboy put his beer down on the bar and came over to the booth. He wore a green flannel shirt and a belt buckle with some sort of animal head on it, a sheep or a goat.

"I guess I meant, how are you," he said.

"Do we know you?"

"Frank, Frank," said Dick.

"I'm not acquainted with Tex," said Frank. "What difference is it to Tex how I am?"

"You need us over there?" called one of the cowboys at the bar.

"Not yet," said the one at the table. "Just doin' an attitude check here."

"Let me save you some time," said Frank. "The attitude is bad. I may cancel my insurance." His head was full of clouds, the day, the misunderstanding, the drinks. "I may cancel your insurance," he added in a ridiculously ominous tone.

"Let me help you to your feet," the cowboy said, and reached across Karl to take Frank by the shirt. Karl roundhoused him onto the floor with such concussion, the three other cowboys had to more or less jump over their companion to reach Karl, Frank and Dick at the mouth of their booth. "Not again," said Hoiness in a voice of despair; yet in pretending to rise to his feet, he was able to surprise one cowboy with a stomach butt and knock the wind out of him. Frank bent over the airless man sitting like Raggedy Andy and pressed him for his social security number. Frank was slugged solidly in the right ear, which removed his sense of humor instantly.

The bartender moved quietly to the phone, and the cowboy who had come to the table first, seeing this, slipped over to the farthest bar stool to feign quiet drinking. Karl charged the entire row of bar stools and the cowboy went down in a wilderness of chrome legs and red naugahyde. The front door parted just enough to flash in some sunlight and the prospective customer failed to enter. Gripping each other's ears, Karl and the tall cow-boy began a grim waltz down the center of the bar. Frank and his new acquaintance were silently trying to lift each other off the floor by the ears. Hoiness had succeeded in recognizing the smallest of the cowboys, who looked like a penguin in a big hat, and knowing his ID was false ("I know how old you are, I sold your father crop insurance this summer"), urged him to go out the back door before the police got there. It must have been Hoiness's years of barroom rock and roll that sharpened his instincts, because he slipped out the back with the youngster.

When the police arrived, the ear-grip dancing was still in stately progress, and the hair lifting too, though handfuls of it were scattered here and there around the booth. The arrival of the police was like the sound system quitting at a disco. Everything just wound down and stopped. The bartender was fooling with the dial on his radio. One policeman, a handsome young man with curly black hair and a jawline like Superman's, leaned close to the entrance and kept an eye on things while his companion, a much older man with a bright gold tooth, helped the fellows with their handcuffs. "You can make nice or not," he said in a jolly way that made everyone feel better, "but it's down to the hoose-gow we go."

In one way or another, they all agreed to go; they were eager for someone else to plan for them. It was only human. Frank and Karl slipped quickly into the back of one of the two squad cars, embarrassingly surrounded by pedestrians in a town where everyone knew everyone else. Karl said to Frank, "It would have been nice if you hadn't called that feller over to our table."

"Hindsight is twenty-twenty," said Frank as a joke. But it didn't go over.

"I thought hindsight was when you had your head up your ass," said Hammersgard coolly.

"Want me to knock the piss out of you?" Frank inquired, adjusting his suit jacket. He was still trying to look his best.

"No, and besides, you couldn't. In fact, pull yourself together, Frank."

The police officer with the gold tooth got in and twisted around like a cab driver to look in back. "Looks like we're all set," he said. "Next stop, jail."

Sheriff Hykema was there to help process the five. The cowboys trooped down to their cell quietly. "Karl, what's all this about? Don't you have a game tomorrow?"

"Red Lodge."

"Go on, get out of here."

Karl ducked his head slightly and went out the door before the sheriff could change his mind. Then Hykema eased up to Frank. "My lucky day," he said with a big smile.

"Eat shit," said Frank, not mincing words.

"Right," said the sheriff, and turned him over to a deputy with a short crew cut and the kind of clear-rimmed glasses they issue in the armed forces.

Frank went through a very long checking-in period, including fingerprinting and some interviewing against questions on a computer, the answers to which were logged and sent out via modem. "I'm so sleepy," Frank said to the officer.

"Shut up," said the officer.

"Right you are. Turn other cheek."

"It'll have to be one of your cowboy friends."

"Oh, those guys. They don't like me."

When they put Frank in the cell with his three adversaries, he told them to eat shit just so they would stay away. But they were sick of Frank. He was able to curl up near the drain and pass out with the sense that he was sinking into disarray and hellishness. At the exact moment of sleep, he seemed to plummet.

16

He awoke alone in the cell, filled with dread. He very slowly allowed a few details to seep in, wincing at each one. He sat up and gazed at the drain in the floor. A few apologies in order, he thought, one or two at least. A glance at the high window and he could see it was dark. He thought back: drinking started in the morning, must've been hauled in around midday. He went to the door of the cell and called out. An officer he didn't recognize came to the door. Just then, he remembered his remarks to Sheriff Hykema. The present policeman looked like an old pensioner with remarkable bags under his eyes.

"You ready to go?"

"It'd be nice."

"Sheriff said to send you home when you woke up."

"What time is it?"

"Few minutes after eight."

That seemed like an especially odd time to Frank. He must have slept all afternoon.

"When did the other guys leave?"

"A long time ago. You slept right through it."

He felt he was rising from the dead. That was about as much loss of control as he could stand. The officer opened the cell door and Frank followed him out. He had a few things returned, watch, wallet, car keys. "Where's Sheriff Hykema?"

"Gone home."

"Where's he live?"

"Quartz Canyon."

At Frank's request, the officer wrote the sheriff's address down on a scrap of paper. "Your stay will cost you a few bucks, one way or another. You mind stopping back and taking care of it?"

"Not at all. You have any idea how much?"

"Maybe a hundred bucks," said the old policeman.

Frank knocked on the front door of the sheriff's small lilac-surrounded house in Quartz Canyon. He could hear a great horned owl in the woods nearby and there was a stirring canopy of stars that seemed just higher than the house itself. Frank craned his head back and stared at them when the door opened. A sixteen-year-old boy with a blue and orange Mohawk haircut answered the door. Under this warlike hairdo was the face of a child.

"I'm Frank Copenhaver. Is Sheriff Hykema in?"

"Yes, you want to come in?" Frank followed the boy into the hall, where he saw the sheriff's gray uniform jacket and three or four Stetson hats. "Dad!" the boy called. In a moment, the sheriff appeared in his stocking feet and introduced Frank to his son Boyce. Frank and Boyce shook hands gravely.

"Come on in," said Sheriff Hykema, and Frank followed him into a nearly dark den where a baseball game was on television. Hykema picked up the channel changer and muted the game, then gestured for Frank to sit in one of the deep chairs that faced the television. Hykema sat in the other.

"How you feeling?"

"Better than I deserve. I'm afraid I remember a couple of things I said to you last night —"

"This morning."

"Right. And I sure apologize."

"Don't give it a thought," Hykema said. "Let me see if they're going to call that foul." He turned the sound back on for a moment, then off again.

"Well, I am sorry."

"I hear that sort of thing every day."

"Well, I wish it hadn't happened, but it did."

Hykema gave him a long look, disinterested, almost scientific in its detachment. "You must have had a lot on your mind."

Frank was able to meet his gaze. They both seemed to drift off on very different tracks, lit by the pale green image of the baseball diamond on television. It was very quiet. Suddenly, the sheriff seemed to come back into focus. He clapped his big hands down onto the thick fabric of the arms of his chair. "Copenhaver," he said, "that's the first time we've had you down at the jailhouse. I don't know what your problem is, but when folks start appearing there, it usually ain't an accident. A big portion of them keep reappearing until something real bad happens and then it's too late to go back to where the problem started."

Frank felt a ticklish surge to be receiving sincere advice. He could tell that his gratitude seemed a little out of place to Hykema, or exaggerated, further proof he had lost track of the normal. "I like to think it was an isolated event," he said.

"I like to think it was an isolated event too. But a lot of times it isn't."

"That's good to know," said Frank. Everyone was so helpful.

17

Frank lay in his bed and listened to an educational radio program sponsored by the National Endowment for the Arts, some kind of marathon in progress about the relationships between men and women. Frank paid attention for a while. There seemed to be an invisible audience that gave the background a hint of poll tax riots. A woman with the tiniest voice imaginable read a paper, "Pocahontas, First Governor of Virginia," which was challenged by a man who sounded as if he were trying to talk around his pipe stem and who said that the myth of the coping female had led to nationalistic suicide in the South and to "the recycled panty hose of Robert E. Lee." Frank's feeling that he was already out of balance was exacerbated by this educational radio program and he turned it off with a diving twist of the knob. He lay in the dark wondering why he could be so disoriented by a program sent out to Americans by a happy government whose work resembled that of kindly parents who distributed colored eggs in the hedge and the garden the night before Easter. But maybe there was just too much spin on the eggs.

He managed to sleep through the night, off and on, breaking into the occasional moan and going to the bathroom three or four times just to have something to do. Day came in a gray opening of minor renewal. Frank got up and clung to his routines of breakfast and bathing. When he shaved, he examined his face over and over with his hand to check for missed spots. This day could be set back easily by a missed spot, a lone whisker in a weird place. He put on polished cotton slacks and blue socks, a pair of Church's English oxfords, a green-striped Egyptian cotton shirt and a green and red silk tie. He brushed his hair until not one hair was out of line and his scalp tingled sharply. He applied St. Johns bay rum. He put on a light gray seersucker jacket and stood in front of the floor-length mirror raising and lowering his chin until it was at just the exact level. He tried smiling mirthlessly, then let it go back to neutral. He smiled sincerely and decided that he still got a pretty big reading off a sincere-looking smile even though, as was usual in business, it was apropos of nothing. Then he headed for the Holiday Inn for the early bird breakfast and there was June.

"Oh, God," she said, "join me."

"Are you sure?"

"I'm sure. What've you been doing?"

"I was in jail yesterday."

"I thought they'd have you in."

"No, this was different. This was a bar scrape."

"Who started it?"

"I did."

"Shame on you. That's the old you."

Frank told her about the experiment in front of the dressing mirror, trying out different expressions, preparing for insincerity. He said most of it was about conquering women, no matter how deeply it was buried.

"What is it about you guys?" she said.

"I know," said Frank. "Something's not right."

"You know, we get horny too."

"Yes, I know."

"But we don't go around trying to lead platoons over it."

"Yes, yes, we couldn't be bigger pigs," he demurred.

"A couple of nights ago, I was feeling the strain," said June. "I rented an X-rated video."

"No."

"Called *Businessman's Lunch*."

"How was it?"

"Terrible. The main character was certainly not a businessman. You would have been irate. They put him in front of a row of boxes with a clipboard in his hand and had him pretend to go over the inventory." June's rather loud and raspy voice got her an audience once again, the usual airline personnel and early delivery people, not many, half a dozen or so sleepy eaters waiting for their coffee to work. Then the waitress interrupted things and they ordered. When the waitress left, June resumed. Frank thought that by looking around boldly he could keep people from listening, but it was hopeless.

"Naturally, our boy seduces everybody and that had its appeal, though anyone with a room-temperature IQ would quickly get bored with the oral business under the desk. It was one of the most ineffective ads for office furniture I've ever sat through." Frank shrank as though dashed with cold water. "But the scene that seems very important to these movies is the festive ejaculation. This scene is shot like a Disney nature film, in slow motion. We get the holiday droplets flying through the air with frequent cutaways to the 'businessman.' Our man is reared back, howling like a baboon and apparently trying to uproot his own member like a stoop worker on an Alabama row-crop farm. This does not look too bright." Frank sheepishly stole a glance around the room; the show was a big hit. "Meanwhile, the starlet seems to have forgotten she's in a movie. She scoots around on the queen-size, trying to avoid the barrage." An appliance repairman with the dead-giveaway blond bangs of a born-again Christian came to their table. The script on his shirt read "Rance."

"Ma'am," he said from a smoldering face.

"Don't tell me you're the director," cried June.

"Ma'am, I'm gonna tell Holiday Inn, nice folks can't eat in this place if you're here."

"They're crazy about me," said June. "They'll throw out the nice folks. Might try Days Inn."

The waitress arrived as Rance drifted back sullenly to his table, right after he suggested that if June hadn't been a woman, something very dire would have awaited her. June turned to her breakfast with delight. "I must be his first dirty old broad."

"Must be," said Frank.

June spread jam on her toast. She held it up admiringly. "Imagine living such a sheltered life," she mused. "I think Holiday Inns sustain those illusions. There's never any discord in the Holiday Inn."

They ate with reflective gazes for a time. They were both thinking. Rance got up after a bit, shoving back his chair noisily so as to suggest that he had never had waffles under such circumstances before. June blew him a pouty kiss and went back to contemplatively eating. In this eternal ambience, with its perfect standardization, exemplary and American, Frank felt he could age quietly or be part of a trend. The pressure was more on time itself than it was on him. This thought alone took some of the pressure off.

He tried to make it through an entire day at the office. Eileen had him stacked up with calls to return and letters to respond to. He had to sort out gas line easements across the ranch. The city was asking him to abandon an old head gate that was now on the grounds of a small park. There was a request from the doctors to confirm that they could always lease at their current rate, which Frank responded to with a number of built-in slides for inflation, cost of living, exhausted depreciation schedules and the offer to raise the rent at once. There was a call from Phil to say that he and Smokie were going to the movies, if he wanted to join them. No, he thought. The building that had housed Gracie's old lunch-counter restaurant, Amazing Grease, was being converted to a light-truck repair shop and the shop's proprietor was making an offer to purchase it. Again, Frank declined. He sent the animal shelter written permission to exercise animals on the ranch and he tried to return his brother Mike's five telephone calls but failed to find him in. He prorated Boyd Jarrell's last paycheck and asked Eileen to call him and find out what he wanted done with his tax and workmen's comp withholdings. Eileen returned to say that

Boyd was out of town but that the wife wanted the money forwarded to her. "Okay," Frank said, "do that." He felt quite absent. He was thinking about his house. He was thinking he could barely picture it and didn't want to live there anymore. Once a poetic edifice, it had become an annoying heap.

He recognized that he was going to have to move his mind more into the foreground and out of the world of regrets and ambiguities. The desk was piled high with reminders of neglect. He couldn't run a business this way. "You can't run a business this way," he said aloud. He thought he heard Eileen say "Amen," but he knew very well she didn't have that sort of wit. He must have imagined it. It did seem, though, that he had heard an "amen."

18

He met Mike at a quarter of twelve at McDonald's for a quick lunch to discuss something on Mike's mind. It was already crowded at this old fast food place, with its amusement park shapes and colors now well battered by Montana weather. Even the fiberglass animals and carousel horses looked like they'd come up the trail with the longhorns. Inside, the stainless steel handrail in front of the counter was bowed out toward the condiment and napkin counter by the pressure of tens of thousands of buttocks.

This was Mike's favorite restaurant. He prided himself on being a prosperous professional who had never developed an interest in the good life: "I live like a dog and I eat like a dog." This wasn't quite true, and in Mike's identification with ordinary people there was a kind of dandyism. They carried their trays to a small table in front of a window where they could see traffic and the pretty farmhouses across the road that had been overtaken by the strip; their deep and shady porches now faced a blazing modern highway. When they sat down, Frank unwrapped his cheeseburger and tipped the cardboard container of french fries on its side.

"My doctor friends say you're trying to gouge them on the office building." Mike made this statement with a crazy grin.

"Cheapskates."

"You got that right. But again, they're my friends."

"Why don't they leave?"

"I don't know."

Mike rarely asked Frank to come to McDonald's. Meeting there for lunch almost always meant something, since even by Mike's standards the dining was not the issue. When their mother had been in the nursing home, after the fiasco in Fort Myers, she had gone rapidly downhill. Frank tried having her at home and so did Mike, but she no longer knew where she was and would prowl about at all hours. Once she set fire to Mike's house trying to cook on the gas stove at three A.M. One of Mike's children found her, nightgown on fire, and Mike had to spray her with a fire extinguisher. "Go ahead, kill me!" she had cried.

Adding to their problems was the fact that she had never liked them as children. She had been a famous local beauty and children had never fit her plans. She had associated Mike and Frank with her decline throughout her life, so that by the time she was old and infirm she openly disliked them. But she got pneumonia from the fire extinguisher and nearly died. So they put her back in the home, which was pleasant but inhabited almost entirely by what looked to Frank like zombies, who sat and stared or held playing cards but didn't play them or who waited for the meal bells or simply watched television with perfect vacancy or took on small tasks that didn't need doing, like curtain arrangement or extra dusting.

Frank had loved his mother but got nothing much in return, and even Mike, who hadn't cared, understood that his mother's situation was not one to be desired. She reached the point that she no longer got out of bed, then no longer ate and was on life support equipment. This went on for a good while; they visited regularly even though most of the time she didn't know they were there, and when she did, she was unpleasantly reminded of how little she liked them. Finally, she failed to return to consciousness altogether. After a couple of months, Mike called Frank with his decision. He had spoken to the doctor. An absence could be arranged if Mike and Frank wished to remove her life support system.

"I couldn't do it," said Frank.

"You don't have to do it," said Mike. "All you have to do is agree it needs to be done and I'll do it."

"I just don't know, Mike."

"Maybe she's living in a bad dream, Frank. I'd want mine pulled."

They agreed that they would do it. Frank wondered, after she died, what the actual moment of death had been: when this decision was reached, or when her pulse stopped and her temperature started down? It was actually Mike who removed the . . . stuff, the equipment, the tubing. The last thing she said — and they had to go back a number of weeks for this — was something that had just bubbled up from a Johnny Carson show she had seen, and they would never have known that except that Mike had seen the same show. In a crooning, faraway voice, she repeated the words of a famous model who was a guest on the show telling about her photo safari to Tanzania. Their mother seemed to become the model, down to peculiar expressions of enthusiasm like "off the graph": "The lions were really off the graph!"

They waited a long time after the apparatus was removed and she lingered on. They decided to stay with her in shifts. Mike went home to eat with his family; Frank stayed and watched. She never moved. Frank thought about her for a while, then thought about himself. He considered the compartments they had gotten into over the years, starting with his father the farmer entrepreneur, his mother the town beauty of the famous Geranium Festival, Frank the investment manager and Mike the orthodontist. Gracie was about to join the former-wife class, and his mother had eased into the class of the soon dead. Frank's daughter was in the college class, to enter either the professional or the homemaker class and join them all in the grand march off the flat earth. He decided to stop thinking about himself and about all that this meant under his flat-earth view, and to listen. He heard nothing. He got up and stood next to his mother. Her small hand lay open on the bed. Her wrist was terribly thin. He rested his hand next to it and lay his finger across her wrist. Nothing. He remembered how superfluous she thought he was. She said he was the boy who held the lantern while his mother chopped the wood.

"There's one of my patients," said Mike. "See that pretty teenager there? Carrying the milk shake? Well, you oughta had a look at her when she arrived on my doorstep. Looked like a church key."

"She looks fine now."

"Nothing whatsoever to prevent her from falling into your basic local social pattern. When I got her, she was headed for a life either alone or with a wheat farmer."

Frank asked himself how two brothers could have turned out so differently. Everywhere Mike looked he saw certainty, definition and meaning. And yet, when they were growing up, Frank was always optimistic and Mike suspicious. Mike's suspicion had paid off. He knew absolutely where he was going and it didn't bother him that it was one mouth after another. The inevitable things about life didn't bother him either. Even death struck him as one more piece of local color, a nostalgic event.

"Frank, what in the hell are you thinking about?"

"I was just thinking how different we are."

"You just figured that out?"

"No, it still is hard for me to understand."

"Not me. You're a year older. You had to break trail. Plus, Dad made more sense to me than he did to you. That's why everything has seemed so much clearer to me. You always seemed to think Dad was crazy."

"I suppose."

"I may be missing a whole layer of life, you know," Mike said. "Its seriousness. But I don't strain my mechanism like you do. Sometimes I think you're like an airplane that keeps taxiing and never quite gets airborne. I'm dumb, I just fly."

"I was airborne for a while."

"Maybe you were. But I don't crave struggle. I enjoy my life. It goes by smooth as silk and I'd just as soon have it that way. I'm a big fat happy guy with a big fat happy wife and several extremely average children. I like it. I'm flying."

"I don't blame you," said Frank. He looked up and saw Dick Hoiness coming in, the old guitarist hidden in a summer suit, and signaled him to come over.

"Hi, Dick," Frank said coolly as Hoiness reached the table. "I wanted to thank you for slipping out of the bar the other day."

"It had to be done."

"Had to be done," Frank said. "I ought to cancel my insurance."

"Life will go on."

"You cancel yours and I'll cancel mine," said Mike, always loyal. This might have gotten serious.

"What a day," said Hoiness, starting for the counter. "Let me know what you want to do, fellas."

"We forgive you," said Frank. "We just wish you were more of a stand-up guy."

"Musicians aren't like that," called Hoiness from the counter. "We're gentle escapists — you know, four-F."

"What about your claims adjusters?" Mike asked.

"Different breed," said Hoiness. "Hard-boiled but compassionate, realistic but generous, universally loved. Montana natives one and all. Low rates and prompt attention. Our claims adjusters stand for family values and a decreased dependence on foreign oil." He turned to the smiling girl behind the counter and ordered. He pointed to each item he ordered on the wall menu behind her, as though she had never heard of these things before.

Frank watched and thought how much he wished things would change faster at McDonald's. Americans had overtaken their product line, if he was any judge, waiting for McThis and McThat. If there were only a few departures or insights — McShit on the toilets, anything — it would be so much easier to take one's seat in this American meeting place and not feel such despair that the world was going on without you.

"How's your deal going?" Mike asked.

"It's all right. Hasn't been much to it this last little while. Exchanged some cattle. Everybody's getting run off the national forest. There's a bunch of timid traders out there. I had the idea to do a warm-up lot somewhere, maybe Billings, but the way this yearling thing has been looking, the price of feed and everything else, I just didn't have the juice to do it, not and guarantee gains where they need to be."

"What about the water slide at Helena."

"Sold it."

"The Hertz franchise at Helena — I got to tell you, Frank, I'm hearing all the time now that you're overextended."

"It's true, but I'm getting by with it. The Hertz franchise is fine. I wish I had a bunch more."

"Frank!" Mike, at first incredulous, was soon off in thought.

Young people had started to fill up the place and were blowing the straw wrappers off their straws. They all looked so intense to Frank, so ready to burst into something. The ones who got crowded shoved back. The ones who were hot, coming in from outside, took off their coats and fanned their faces hard.

"I say we dump the ranch," said Mike.

"Count me in," said Frank, still looking at the youngsters clamoring for hamburgers. That should have been a signal to get back into the cattle business more seriously. He had bought and sold thousands of cattle the way other people played pinochle on Thursdays and he had done it with other people's money as well as his own. Now he was thinking that once he got out from under the present loans, he might not want the risk, responsibility, commitment, whatever. So, sure, sell the ranch. And thus would end an American family's place on earth.

"You want to list it?" Frank asked.

"Let's run an ad."

"Mike, why don't you write it."

"Sure, let me write it," said Mike. "You know, I'm not a reflective guy, but at a time like this it might be nice to sit down and compose a few words about the old place."

"You want to try it now?"

Mike got a ballpoint out of his shirt pocket, where it had made a dime-sized blue spot. "Fire. You start," Mike said, and turned over his paper placemat. "Give me a headline."

"Old home place," said Frank. "In capitals. OLD HOME PLACE."

"Okay, then underneath: 'In same family four generations.' Didn't our grandfather start the place?"

"It was *his* parents. Fattened oxen that came off the immigrant wagons."

"Gotcha: 'Local farm dynasty decides to relinquish ancestral headquarters.' This I like. Don't say anything against it. 'Long-awaited decision. Priced to move. Principals only.' Got it. Hoss, I'm putting it in the *Wall Street Journal*. I'm going to say that Hollywood types forced us out of the cattle business. That's one of the best ways to get a Hollywood type to buy it."

"Add: 'Moose, deer, bear, elk, grouse, trout.' "

"Why?"

"They all have that, all local ads. One keystroke on the IBM. You don't want this ad to look like it was done in L.A. They never mention the one kind of wildlife they all have, rattle-snakes."

"All right," Mike said, writing. "What else?"

"What's the view?"

"There isn't one."

"We better come up with one or we're going to have to go on owning it. Can we just say, 'Big sky'?"

"I think that's fair. That doesn't really misrepresent anything. I mean, what's big to one person may not be big to another. Anyway, people who are out there trying to scoop up old family places are in on this bullshit. It's kind of like date rape. You can't get fucked if you don't spread your legs."

"You're great, Mike. You always see things so clearly. I get bogged down thinking about the lives that have been lived out there, the crops gathered, the calves shipped."

"It just gets in the way, Frank."

Frank left it in Mike's hands and walked out to the parking lot while his brother visited with the many normal people he knew inside. Whenever they talked business, Mike liked to act tough. That's why his deals were all stiffs. Frank barely cared, but he did care, and an undetected slyness had worked for him long enough that he was dangerously overextended. He had to keep a mental buoyancy or go under.

The parking lot was now full of cars and the great white clouds were reflected on their colored roofs. Frank looked up and got the feeling he was looking clear into outer space. A truck piled high with yellow split firewood went through the drive-up line with two laughing cowboys in front, their hats on the back of their heads, the radio blaring the Neville Brothers' "Yellow Moon."

Frank stopped and tried to feel his detachment against this throbbing daily intensity that was all around for the asking. Whenever he jumped in, he overjumped; when he tried to stay reasonable, he was like a cat burglar in the homes of everyday people, or someone who had broken into the zoo on a day when it was closed. The street was busy; people were pouring in and out of the restaurant. People sat with their car doors open, their feet on the pavement, and ate ice cream. And yet the big vacant sky seemed to proclaim their isolation. Frank found it attractive in a way even he knew was ludicrous, like the impulse that sends shy people to nudist colonies. Or even the one that landed him among the Eskimos. This is why bland people buy sports cars, he thought; things get lively around them and they have to jump in there with their car. He remembered how he and his friends used to dance through the night to the rock bands, none more extreme than Dick Hoiness's Violet Twilight, or the Great Falls screamers Standing Start, or the psychedelic band from the Assiniboine reservation, Arthur and the Agnostics, with its stupendous lead singer Arthur Red Wolf, or the great all-girl hard-rock band, the Decibelles. And what fun those darn drugs were. Marvelous worlds aslant, a personal speed wobble in the middle of a civilization equally out of control. And it was wonderful, however short, to have such didactic views of everything, everyone coming down from the mountain with the tablets of stone. Hard to say what it all came to now. Skulls in the desert.

Frank set out for the ranch in somewhat higher spirits, the possibility of not owning something that had always been in their lives throwing the place into sudden and blazing relief. He was able to go over its every feature in his mind now, from springs to dragging gates to the smells of the cellar and the loose boards in the parlor, the paint on the cupboard doors with the previous contrasting paint job, the flour bins with the odorless mummified mice. Yes, he thought, a lost home and the gates of hell.

There was little traffic, and clouds distinct enough that one could navigate by them. A distant tractor plowing a summer-fallowed field trailed a plume of brilliant dust high in the air. The yellow-and-black-striped gates at the railroad crossings stood out vividly in the farm greenery along the tracks. "Slippin' and a-slidin'," sang Frank to himself, "peepin' and a-hidin'." What a day. What freedom, what breezes. What life ahead! "I been told, baby, you been bold!"

When he drove into the farmyard and looked at the fine old white house with its porches and chimneys, its slanted stone-sided cellar entry, its small chaste cedar shingles, the outbuildings, fenced and ditched small fields beyond, he could already feel it floating into abstraction like a diploma, into a rather glamorous distance.

Things seemed to be in apple-pie order, just as they were when Boyd left. That whole thing was entirely unfortunate. He thought with a bit of a thrill that he ought to go over to Boyd's house and express his regret that things had ever come to such a pass.

19

There was a car parked in front of the Jarrell house, not Boyd's black Chevy half-ton pickup. Frank walked briskly to the house. He shot his cuff to look at his watch, suggesting that there would be many stops today. When he knocked, it was to a jokey little rhythm. He whistled and cast an admiring glance at the scrubby vegetation. The door opened and there stood Mrs. Jarrell: middle height, close-cropped hair, blue tank top and a face that saw through everything. She held the screen door in her hand and kept it between them. Frank was surprised to see her.

"I don't want to talk to you," she said. He could see the little irritated red dots in her armpit where she had shaved. The shadows that fell on her face from the door made her seem even more grave and unreachable than the already frightening tone of her voice.

"I won't take any of your time. But I do need to reach Boyd. It's business, that's all. That's all it is."

"Maybe you'd like to come in."

She opened the screen door a little more, just enough for Frank to sidle through, which he didn't want to do. It seemed that if he declined he might set her off, and so, as obsequiously as he could, feeling the spaciousness behind him, he turned sideways to enter. She seized him by the shirt and pulled his face to hers, a knot of hatred and the pale ocher eyes of a weimaraner, her words full of spit. "Don't flatter yourself," she hissed. "You listening real good? Now get the fuck out." And then he was looking at the discolored white mass of the locked door. He went around to the side window, which was partly opened.

"I'll bet you're a good cook too," he called out. "Probably have a million friends, bunch of adoring nephews and nieces —" Glass exploded over the top of him as an electric flatiron came through the window. He picked a few shards from his hair. "I'll catch up with you later. *Ciao!*"

Now as he drove he took no pleasure in the car. The way out of town had had all the expectation. It almost always does, thought Frank; all the movies, all the old westerns, had their great flavor in the road out of town. Going back to town was always somehow with your tail between your legs, kind of falling-on-your-sword in effect, and was just generally a joyless direction, devoid of chance. But going back with glass shards in your hair and the spit of a stranger on your brow would test anyone's mettle. He liked to picture Mrs. Jarrell with her hand on her stomach, unable to find satisfaction, heading for the milk of magnesia. And there was no reason, short of the general rat-maze conditions of modern life, that they should not be kind to each other:

"Hello, Mrs. Jarrell. Just looking in. I know you've had some troubles lately. Anything you need? Anything I can do?"

"Oh, Mr. Copenhaver, leave it to you to worry about me. I'm adjusting quite well, thank you. In fact, I start today on a continuing education program up to the university. I don't know if I told you this, but next year I plan to run for the United States Senate. I guess it was time I got on with my own life. I suppose I should thank you for firing Boyd. He got a great job at the White House, greeting dignitaries. George Bush will go anywhere to find hidden talent."

"I just got lucky. Boyd playfully knocked my hat off my head. When I stooped to pick it up, I suddenly felt a new understanding to his working future."

"We all just need our own space," said Mrs. Jarrell. Evidently she felt it was time Frank knew more about her body because she . . .

The panel truck slid to a stop at Frank's door and its horn blew continuously. Frank could practically reach out and touch the driver. And Frank could tell by the way the red-faced man was beating his steering wheel with both fists that he had not been driving attentively. He ducked his head apologetically and drove through. Pay attention or die, he told himself.

20

Wonderful suburbs! Wonderful with their regular streets and amiable rivalry of lawns! They were as successful as that assemblage of animals that make up a coral reef. Frank strolled through the heartening rectangles of Antelope Heights, savoring the color schemes, the orderly parking habits, the individuality of the mailboxes — some mounted on wagon wheels, some of fiberglass with brightly colored pheasants molded into the sides (must be a hunter in there!), some that anticipated only letters and some that anticipated great big packages. One or two lawns had the outlines of snarling rottweilers with blazing red eyes on stakes driven into the sod to indicate the presence of a guard dog, but by now everyone knew you just bought the sign and saved on dog food. There was a sweet cacophony of sounds which included television, radio, stereo, practice on musical instruments and the muffled shop tools in the basements of hobbyists. Frank wanted to be here among the families, to watch them in their ordinariness, that most elusive of all qualities. To simply carry on and ignore all that is unthinkable seemed to require a special gift; and, in the end, the world belonged to those who never thought about nuclear holocaust, the collapse of the biosphere or even their own perfectly predictable deaths. Carry on! Who made the playoffs? Let's eat! Let's eat something!

Frank walked softly past one of the rottweiler signs toward the well-lighted outline of a small mock Tudor painted in the cheerful colors of the Bahamas, pink and blue. There was a side yard that separated this house from its neighbor, a house with a For Sale sign in its yard, perfectly dark so that Frank could observe this family without thinking about the house behind him. Unfortunately, when he reached the beginning of the side yard, the guard dog exploded into his view, rigid against a short length of steel chain. Its rage and astonishment at finding Frank there reduced its snarl to something so internal as to be past a warning and simply the prelude to an attack.

"Ooh, datsa big fellow," Frank murmured, backing away. He made himself feel, through waves of terror, real affection for this dog on the theory that any insincerity on his part and the dog would uproot the chain and tear his face off, leaving not even lips to offer an explanation to the homeowners. Frank made like a love-sodden star of some Podunk gospel hour and backed away into the next yard where he fell over the For Sale sign. A floodlight went on and, even though he was seated on the lawn, he cast a long black shadow in its harsh light. There was somebody standing on the front porch of the house.

"Frank?"

"Yes?"

"Frank Copenhaver?"

"Yes?"

"It's Steve Jensen."

"Oh hey, Steve!"

Steve, one of the doctors who rented from Frank, was having a wonderful time atop Phil's wife Kathy, a remarkable lapse in his closely planned life. Frank was conscious of the acrimony over the clinic rent. He was even more sensitive to looking like an intruder.

"Frank, what are you doing?"

Frank decided to go into microfocus. "Tripped over this blasted sign," he called out. "Fell on my butt!" He had a hold of the stake of the sign and was looking closely at the lettering. He could see the brush strokes in the paint.

Jensen walked over to where Frank now stood dusting the seat of his trousers. He looked at Frank blankly and then very slowly a knowing smile came over his face. He laughed to himself. Frank just waited. Jensen looked off, smiling, then turned back to Frank. "You're checking out this house, Frank. I know you. You don't want the realtors knowing you're interested. Talk about your covert operations!"

"You gonna tell?"

"No, I'm not gonna tell."

Frank batted him playfully on the shoulder. "You promise you're not gonna tell?"

"I promise I'm not going to tell."

"Steve —"

"What?"

"I owe you one." Frank dropped his head submissively.

Frank declined Steve's offer of a drink. He didn't want to get into anything intimate about the clinic, much less discuss his hosing Phil's wife. Gesturing to the house next door, Frank said that he had seen enough, and indeed he had; but the desire for the ordinary was still in him and it was heightened the minute he contemplated returning to his empty house. Steve commented that it was amusing that Frank even left his car elsewhere, calling it "extreme realtor fear."

Frank could only go along with these spiraling witticisms. These days, everything took such a long explanation, it was turning smart people into mutes. Combining the knowing look with absentmindedness was the great modern social skill as far as Frank was concerned, and he thought he had it down pretty fair. It would never occur to the doctor that this was a new Frank, certainly not the one who acquired and managed the clinic so acceptably over the years. This was the night Frank. This was the solitaire who feared that happiness was past. This was the roaming dog.

But he had extraordinary luck just a few blocks away, a couple helping their daughter, who was maybe twelve years old, with her homework. They sat around the kitchen table, the mother right next to the struggling child, the father sipping coffee and pitching in when he had an answer. Frank tried to remember how much of this he had done with Gracie and Holly. He tried to be ironic about the golden light that flooded these three people from the opulent globe over the table. The schoolbook lay open in front of the pretty child next to a heap of marvelously rumpled papers. Steam rose from the coffee. The mother had pinned her hair up to keep it out of her way. The father sharpened a pencil. Frank thought these people had not always lived in town and were buoyed by the convenience of their suburb, the handy shopping, the populous grade school. Good grief, it was an American family! Frank rested his chin on the windowsill and gazed upon this rapturous scene, shriven by time, tears pouring down his face. We used to be one of those, he told himself. We had that in our hands.

21

Frank put his car in the short-term parking lot and walked into the airport, a low and rustic-looking modern terminal just past which could be seen the tall silver tail of an airplane. It was dusk and the airplane was tinted with the dusty pink of sunset. Frank was sure it wasn't Holly's plane, and when he got inside he found he had almost ten minutes to spare.

He stopped at the newsstand and bought the paper, skimmed the local news and left it on a plastic chair. The plane on the ground was being loaded and there was a short line at the security x-ray. A few of the older and more countrified travelers who perhaps had not flown much put their purses and other belongings on the conveyor belt with extreme suspicion. Frank hunted around for a tearful goodbye and found one, a plain girl in dowdy navy blue slacks and jumper, squeezing the hand of a vague-looking youth with long sideburns and a catfish mustache; she wept silently. She stared into his face almost imploringly while he gazed around in a rubbernecked way, as if to say, "Get a load of this."

Frank was eager to see which one was leaving. When the ticket agent announced the final boarding call, the girl released the young man's hand and boarded the plane. The young man looked around anxiously to see if anyone had been watching, and in case someone had, he wiped his brow with the back of his hand and flicked the imaginary drops of perspiration to the ground. In a matter of time, Frank thought, this loving relationship would be converted into a marriage.

Frank joined the mixed group at the big window in scanning the sky for the next inbound flight. For some reason, he remembered a winter trip to St. George, Utah, he had taken with Gracie and Holly. He and Gracie had had an argument at their motel and Holly pretended to be drowning in the swimming pool. It was a realistic imitation of a drowning person — face down, limbs slowly sinking — and it ended the argument. Frank and Gracie were startled that Holly would go to such lengths. The desert abruptly seemed pointless.

A glint appeared to the north, right at the level of the horizon, and began to enlarge. A moment later, the plane was taxiing at right angles to the terminal, a good way off, and then it turned and came straight in — pure, pretty silver, pink in the dusk with wriggling heat waves behind it and a big sound that suddenly penetrated the building.

Frank stared at every passenger emerging from the expanding tunnel that attached itself to the plane. Some passengers took their own sweet time getting off and held up people behind them. After the first press, only a few passengers remained and Frank was afraid Holly wasn't among them. But then she emerged, burdened by carry-on luggage, magazines and rolled-up newspapers, with the beaming smile that still filled Frank with complete happiness. She affected a rolling, impatient sailor's gait until the last passengers were out of her way.

He put his arms all the way around Holly and her luggage and squeezed. It was wonderful to feel plain love, even stupid love, just this sense of everything mattering all at once. He began hanging the luggage from one arm as he unloaded it from Holly's. "Do you have a suitcase?"

"Nope, this is it."

They walked toward the lobby. Frank gazed at her from the side while she walked, looking straight ahead, occasionally smiling at him. Holly had a serenely pretty olive face with brown, almost black, eyes that were as intense as the eyes of a sleek, quick animal. But when she grinned every bit of her face was affected in a crinkled way that swept Frank away with appreciation. She was wearing baggy cotton pants and a washed-out pink mountaineer's jersey. She had an old green bookbag with a drawstring of the kind that prevailed during Frank's college years. And she wore a big, cheap man's wristwatch without a strap safety-pinned to the jersey. She looked a little like her mother, but even more definitely she had inherited Gracie's careless prettiness and the unpretentious assumption that, somehow, she was being admired. Our only child, thought Frank. It's true!

They got in the car and started toward town. Along the road out to Seventh, clouds of grackles showered down from power lines and swept back up again. Holly picked up one of Frank's cassettes and smiled. "Can I play this?"

Neil Young filled the car, guitar feedback and all. Holly played it loud and looked out the window at the weedy ditches flying by, the crazy, day-in-and-day-out blue sky of Montana, and the mournful howl of Neil Young: "Your Cadillac got a wheel in the ditch and a wheel on the track." It was funny, Frank thought, how that tone of apocalypse just kind of went away.

When the song was finished, Holly turned it off and looked fondly at Frank. She said, "Dad."

"Weird Dad," Frank said.

"Weird Dad." She punched out the cassette and held it up. As she peered at it, it seemed to acquire the quality of an artifact. "Where do you find these things?"

"They find them when they demolish old mansions."

"Like you used to do?"

"Yeah. They tore down this copper baron's mansion in Butte. The walls were filled with Bob Dylan. When they got to the attic there was a mountain of Big Brother and the Holding Company posters and Jefferson Airplane albums nearly devoured by pack rats." Frank was getting into this. He saw the black hand of times gone by lying on this treasure trove.

For some reason, Holly liked to toy with the idea of her parents' great and irreversible ancientness. She loved anecdotes about the sixties, which she associated with her father; she viewed him as a romantic rebel of ambiguity. She knew that he not only wasn't fighting or protesting, he was demolishing the mansions and heirlooms of unguarded America. He was furnishing franchises with salad bars — and he never ate salad. He hated salad. He liked T-bones and potatoes. He even tried to tear down Mama's indigo plantation! This last was a shared family-origin tale, though Mama owned no such plantation. Daddy the opportunist appears on the levee with a wrecking bar in his hand and a Los Angeles restaurant-chain contract in his hip pocket like a four-shot derringer. Gracie allowed a barbaric rakishness to seep into her version of Frank's fomenting the spread of neon down the Mississippi. Holly always wanted to hear little stories of how they met and married.

"What would you like to eat?"

"Are you cooking for me?"

"Have I ever not?"

Holly puzzled through the tense, then said, "No, you've never not."

Frank had already started her favorite, a monster of calories and simplicity known as New England boiled dinner, featuring corned beef, rutabaga, new potatoes, hot mustard and coarse grain bread he got from the Blue Moon bakery, whose sweet-smelling baked goods were proscribed by every responsible doctor. And beer. He loved to guzzle yellow cans of Coors with his beautiful daughter and talk football, school work, America, money, romance, the evolving life of the Great American West.

She always asked about his fishing. Sometimes he showed her a new rod or an English reel or curious flies like sparkle duns and olive emergers and flashabou woolly buggers. They'd pull open his desk drawer at home and peer into the pewter-colored fly boxes with their exotic mysteries of silk and steel and feathers. He'd mention favorite river names: the Sixteen, the Ruby, the Madison, the Jefferson, the Bow, the Crow's Nest, the Skykomish, the Dean. When she was a little girl, he would make up stories that took place in the great drainages like the Columbia or the Skeena or the Missouri, and the place names would restore their years together. He could still thrill her with the story about the time the great brown trout towed his canoe past the city of Helena in the middle of the night, past the glow of its lights on the night sky of August, a fish he had to break off at the head of thundering rapids whose standing waves curved five feet high in the cold white moonlight.

They listened to the local news and weather as Frank finished cooking and Holly set the table. She laid out the utensils and napkins; she centered the hot pad and then Frank served the meal and poured the beer. They sat down and Holly sighed.

"This is it," said Frank.

"No food on the plane. I'm ready."

Frank gazed with pride at his own cooking. Most of the time, he ate Lean Cuisine microwave dinners, Campbell's tomato soup or leftovers dumped into half-limp taco shells while fixated on the livestock reports, the index of leading indicators, new home starts, west Texas intermediate crude or some other fool thing that seemed to connect him with the economics games there were to be played. In some ways, he loved money; he certainly loved the sedative effects of pursuing it, and if that was all money did for him at this point, it had much to be said for it. The year he tried to escape into bird-watching, into all the intricacies of spring warblers and the company of gentle people, he had been forced to conclude that nothing got him out of bed with quite the smooth surge of power — as the Chrysler ads used to say — like the pursuit of the almighty dollar. Also, he was good at it and always had been. His mother had said he had his father's nose: he could pick up the scent of a deal from a good ways off, as sharks are said to do with blood. He actually had the knack to a greater degree than his father.

"I regard this as a quality family atmosphere," Frank said to Holly.

The superb golden light of evening came down through the leaves of the Norwegian silver maple and through the windows of the dining room and lit up their faces and the things on the table.

"Who's your current boyfriend?"

"A fellow named Mark Plante."

"I don't like the sound of this. What's he like?"

"Kind of a comical little nitwit. He won't be around long."

"I like this guy more and more."

"There's plenty where he came from. They're like fleas on a dog. I've had several lunches with the leader of a citizens' group. I've also had a few attentions from a young history professor."

"They've begun preying on the students, have they?"

"I thought they always have."

"Well, with these bountiful federal grants, there's more time for dalliance than there was in my day."

"They had other problems in your time — keeping you people from breaking into the president's office and smoking the cigars, burning the flag, describing the pink spiders crawling out of your desks to the biology professor who can't seem to make them out."

"Don't ridicule, Holly. That stuff's coming back. What about this bird from the citizens' group? Haven't I heard of him?"

"He gets in the papers from time to time. He wants to keep Montana for Montanans." Holly smiled with a new potato rakishly poised on a fork. "Would you ever let your hair grow again?"

"No. I don't think any of us would. It's better to hide these secrets. To infiltrate. To duly note the action of the scavengers who have followed us down the great American highway."

"The secret drifter."

"The secret drifter."

"You *are* a drifter, aren't you, Daddy? In your heart?"

"A drifter."

"But you don't move much anymore."

"This is my home. Recently, though, I visited the Eskimos."

"And?"

"About what you would expect, sans igloos. They're in a place that's hard to live and it seems to get them down. They have TV. They know what's going on. They want to know why they got dealt the permafrost. There are anthropologists and sociologists up there teaching them to curse their fate and cast their blame in a wide circle."

"I don't understand what you were doing there."

"I wanted to get away. Remember Mama's friend Lucy? She's a travel agent. I told her to just put a little trip together for me that would really be a break. I told her I'd go anywhere she sent me."

"How is Lucy, anyway?"

"She's bored, a fine person. She sits under the posters of tropic isles and doesn't really care if anyone goes anywhere or not. You hear it in her voice. She doesn't have that big belief, that Kathie Lee Gifford sort of booming view of people getting out and about on a cruise ship. She doesn't really see why anyone bothers. And of course this pops up on the balance sheet as self-fulfilling prophecy —" He stopped abruptly. He could hear himself talking exactly as he would if he were talking to Gracie. When he looked at Holly, who was not eating but simply gazing both fondly and reflectively at him, he knew she was having the same thought, or something very much like the same thought.

"Do you know why I stopped talking?" he inquired.

"Yup."

"I thought so. Well, what can you do."

Holly said, "I'll wash, you dry."

He turned on the radio, the oldies station, and Van Morrison sang while they worked.

> You can take all the tea in China,
> Put it in a big brown bag for me,
> Sail right round all the seven oceans,
> Drop it straight into the deep blue sea.

"As we boogie to the suds," said Holly, arms deep in the soapy water, Frank with his towel and lost in his dreams. "I know you're thinking about Mama," she said.

That night Frank lay in bed and watched the full moon from his window, the great pure shape rising through the telephone lines, the treetops and over the roofs to race cool and smooth and alone in the sky. Its pale light barely illuminated the distant mountains. He couldn't sleep. He almost felt he'd gotten a hold of the moon and was being towed along in the chill.

He wondered what was to become of Holly. She was certainly the most reliable person he knew, filled with plans she was capable of achieving. He did not think she was liable to be swept away by someone she had failed to size up correctly. He liked life's randomness, its buckshot absurdity and disconnections, but he didn't like them for his daughter. The story possibilities for his life were getting narrower by the minute and randomness was perhaps what his life needed. Holly, he thought, needed narrowing story possibilities. Lying in his own panel of cold moonlight, Frank thought only of the madmen, the crazy drivers, the pretty boys, the flamboyant professors, the head of the citizens' group, the careerists. He was worried sick about Holly and that was that.

22

Frank and Holly carried their coffee outside into the cool morning. The early sun slanted across the street in bands between the rows of spruce and silver maples. The street climbed rapidly to the south, and on either side were the old pioneer houses with their eclectic and eccentric architecture. They walked along and looked up onto the old porches, the hidden off-center doorways and the neat clapboard walls, the tall chimneys with recessed sides and fancy crenellated tops.

Frank didn't want to eat at the Holiday Inn for fear of running into June, whom Holly liked but who seemed, when anybody else was around, entirely too raucous for Frank's taste. And invariably, she tried to get Frank to buy Holly another car, a Buick, when she already had a good one, a jaunty green Honda Civic. Frank thought he was bending over backward in the friendship anyway by driving a Buick he couldn't bear, a car as loose-jointed and ungainly as Rozinante. So they went to the Dexter; but it was such a beautiful day, they ordered the Travelers' Special in order to get back outside as soon as possible. He thought Holly might want to fish, but today she just wanted to visit the ranch. He didn't mention that he and Mike had decided to sell it.

On three different occasions, as they walked back up Main, people swerved toward them and waved gaily to Holly. "Who's that?" Frank asked each time, and it was always some old friend from high school. He said she had a lot of friends and she agreed unaffectedly. When he added that they could use some help with their driving, she gave him a look of comic exasperation. She had been more or less humoring her father since she was six or seven, or at least, when times got tough, tolerating him.

Holly sat in the car looking out at the pastures, her door open, one foot on the ground. He considered telling her that he and Mike were going to sell the place. He knew he wasn't paying as much attention to its management as he should. Frank's father had wanted Holly to own a piece of family land one day. Holly was the only person to whom his father had ever shown open affection, and when his mother had told him that this was the only way the old man knew how to show the emotion for Frank he had never been able to express, Frank didn't believe her. Anyway, he didn't think he ought to be asked to believe it. At thirty-eight years of age he had found himself tearfully telling his mother, "If he loved me, he should have said so."

When he remembered that moment, he writhed with discomfort. But that wasn't fair either. His mother assumed that it was her fault. He felt worse, and deserved to feel worse. He had spent half a lifetime directing his dissatisfaction with his father at her. Does anyone really mind? he wondered today. Or does the world just go on by, like one of June's Buicks, with some fool's foot through the firewall. Maybe it was just more of that outlandish concept of his youth, "lonely teardrops," romantic solitude at its most heightened, made into a way of life for a middle-aged man.

They began walking, and followed the little creek that came down through the corral, a muddy-banked trickle that grew as they followed it up into the timothy pasture where it forked. Above the fork it was bigger still and had more speed, deep and undercut, and finally when they were both winded, it was a real mountain stream bouncing through the junipers. The new movement of morning air up the slope carried the wild grass smells on the blue light. They could see across the valley into a tall, absolute sky. Frank looked over and thought, I have the sweetest little girl in the world. Why not have a thought like that? he asked himself.

"Let's sit here."

"I'd love to," said Frank, and did a split-knee lowering of himself to the ground and put his knuckles together, fingers turned up in imitation of a meditative pose.

"No, no, no," said Holly, and sat in a correct lotus position, face elevated perfectly into the breaking day. "Like this."

"I could do it if I had a beer," said Frank.

"Boy, you look apprehensive."

"I am apprehensive."

Holly gazed vaguely across the valley. They could hear the train heading for Bozeman but couldn't see it. The whole valley was a green and gold grid of farmland and country roads and silver threads of irrigation. One big sprinkler gun to the west drew a pale drifting feather of water across a dark green stand of alfalfa. From this perspective, the valley seemed quite unsettled. The warmth of the new day was making the air hazy over the irrigated ground.

"What we're going to do is we're going to talk about Mama," she said.

"Uh *huh*." Frank stretched his legs out in front of himself and leaned forward to try to touch his toes.

"Okay?" Holly tried to prod him.

"Let me think."

"I honestly believe you owe it to me."

" 'Owe.' I see." Frank's first instinct was that she looked far too much like her mother for this conversation to be anything but squeamish. "I don't know where to start," he said. She wasn't looking at him and she wasn't looking at anything in front of her. A little dust devil picked up a twist of yellow cottonwood leaves and flung them.

"Let me start, then. First of all, I think the wake or the funeral, or whatever it was, was unnecessary."

"It was necessary to me."

"In what sense?"

"I had to close that chapter of my life, darling. I was in terrific pain."

She reached over and held his hand but did not quite soften the expression of determination on her face. He felt his heart racing. She said, "And I consider that group of pallbearers to be a no-good bunch of traitors."

"Sweetheart, they were simply my friends. They wanted what was best for me. They wanted me to be happy. They knew that my heart was broken. I'll always be grateful for the way they carried some of that pain away." Frank was conscious of a stuffy, artificial tone creeping into his voice, obviously meant to hold Holly at a certain distance. His mind kept trying to escape into the idea of buying a sports car, another thousand yearlings. Time had taken something away from the funeral.

"Did any of you wonder what that outrageous wake must have made me feel like?"

Frank thought for a moment. "Maybe we didn't think about that as much as we should have."

"Going down Main Street with a *coffin*? A loudspeaker truck playing 'Paint It Black' by the Rolling Stones? The pallbearers were all . . . bombed. Very few people in that huge crowd had ever even met Mama. Some of them believed she really died! It was a disgrace and now it has become a famous disgrace, the big event of the last ten years."

"Well, it was a lot of fun for some people. Folks remember the good times."

"Oh, boy."

Frank scratched around in the dirt with the point of a stick. He was in trouble with Holly.

"Want to play tic-tac-toe?"

"No."

"So, what is this?"

"I'm going to graduate one of these days. I'm going to come back here to live. Mama's having a pretty tough time. Maybe she'd want to come back. But how could she, after that stupid funeral? Or was that the whole point?"

Frank lay back on the deep wild grass and all he could see was sky, a few white clouds, nothing but blue sky.

"I don't know what to say." He sounded like a little kid. He felt kind of funny.

Holly was peering at him. "You really don't, do you."

"It just doesn't seem like the conversation I should be having with you."

"Are you uncomfortable?"

"*Yes, I'm uncomfortable.*"

They drove back to town when they got hungry, and Holly made him eat in the health food store, with its otherworldly waitresses and bland food. Then they went to the used bookstore, where he found *The Conspiracy of Pontiac* by Francis Parkman and Holly found *Thus Spake Zarathustra,* which had unfortunately been recommended to her by the head of the citizens' group, Lane Lawlor. They went to the hardware store and bought a Rainbird sprinkler and a hummingbird feeder. Later in the afternoon Holly went to see her friends and Frank went home to try to catch up on some work.

23

He was dreaming:

"I would like to have sex with you," Gracie said.

"That would be nice."

"It's more or less free, you know."

"More or less?"

"Free. Plus options, taxes and dealer prep. Hope that eases the sticker shock."

"It does."

Where exactly were they? Frank woke up and stared toward the ceiling, not quite making it out in the faint light from the street. They were in Texas, that was it. Victoria? Corpus Christi? He couldn't quite remember. It was outside of town in an old motel, so the sign said "Motor Court," with mesquite and cat's-claw growing right up to its dirt parking area. There was a little store across the road that said "Smith Gro." The town was just beyond. Someone had painted on a viaduct, "El North Side."

Frank leaned over on his stomach and adjusted the clock's face toward himself. It was after three. It was awful lately, seeing all these crazy hours, which had remained undisclosed for years in a zone of sleep safety. There was a gasp of air brakes and Frank held himself, face sweating into the pillow, until his cock jolted in his fist. He thought lightly, This is no way to live. The phone rang and was quickly picked up in the bedroom across the hall. Holly talking to a boyfriend in the dark. Three in the morning. Hot wires to Missoula.

Frank left before Holly awakened. He wrote her a note as he ate his breakfast, listening for movement in her room. She might have been on the phone for a long time. He walked to the office, taking in the songbirds' cascade of music from the garden beds along his way. Birds are very important, he told himself, trying to peg in one value to start the day. An old man pulled handfuls of wet green grass clippings from beneath his lawn mower. Across the street, the yellow cherry-picker arm of a phone company truck rose slowly through the branches of a maple tree.

Eileen acknowledged him with the least movement of her chin she could manage. He had left her sequestered by paper mountains, offering no leadership whatsoever for weeks now. She could take anything — murder, mayhem — but not lack of management, and he could see her sullenness growing by the second. It was just like Boyd Jarrell. Frank was now what the Mexicans called a *perro enfermo,* a sick dog, something in his center not quite as it was supposed to be.

He was perfectly well aware of how he was letting things slip. Nevertheless, he went straight past to his own quarters, sat down and tried to reignite the importance of title reports, brand receipts, sharecropping contracts, rent receipts, tax assessments and reassessments, the basic paper trail of doom as he currently saw it; hostile letters from the Forestry Department, Bureau of Land Management, Fish and Wildlife; partnership offers and get-rich-quick schemes as they were understood by a limited business environment such as his. He longed to prowl once more in the subdivisions where the tough insurance men and car dealers and rising doctors lived. He longed for the sight of a booze-disheveled bank vice president vaguely picking his nose over a Book-of-the-Month Club notice in his veneered den. He loved those rare moments of capturing people without their game faces on. By the time he got to work in the morning, the world was already in a three-point stance, resting its weight on its knuckles. He wanted to reacquire that stance, learn what he had once known but what had seemed to slip away with his wife.

He had spent his life with his guard down and wanted to return the favor. He remembered when they first moved to town and the Episcopalians came out during the evenings before Christmas to carol. Frank and his family felt blurred and unfocused behind their window while the Episcopalians, with long scarves and song books, with real singing voices, tenors, basses, sopranos, baritones, round singing lips and red cheeks like people on Christmas cards, sang to the goofy Catholics in their house. "Look at them," said his father, watching the snow sift down on their quality faces. "If I don't bankrupt a few before it's over, I won't have lived."

The first spell in town had been a strain. His parents fought continually in their small house, culminating in his father's stringing a taut strand of barbed wire down the middle of the marital bed to make sure there would be no mingling. His mother complained that she couldn't get the bedding on the mattress without great difficulty and that she didn't want to be on his side anyway. "This way we're sure," said the old man, still trying to learn how to run his apartment building and live in town. He had a bunch of Indians in there too, loud reservation Cheyennes who were always cooking in the middle of the night and playing the radio.

Frank picked up his phone and asked Eileen to come in. He had made a list of minute things she could not possibly have remembered and put them in his top drawer, which was open just enough for him to read them, an old trick of his father's. Eileen entered seeming to wonder what on earth he could want with her. Her discontent was taking new forms every day.

"Everything all right, Eileen?"

"Just fine," she sang.

"That's good. I'm afraid I have been a little absentminded lately, which can't have been pleasant for you." Silence. "But I'm sure you got along without me just fine." Silence. Eileen smiled slightly and Frank's eyes dropped to his list in the drawer. "Eileen. Couple of things. The Willow Creek place. I asked you to get the water rights adjudication info from the county. May I have it now?"

"When was this?"

"I asked you to get it two months ago."

Eileen barely moved. "I'll have to get it now."

"I see, Eileen. Okay. And the double billing from the surveyors. Is that in hand?"

"I'll have to check."

"Where is the video cattle auction literature I asked for?"

"I don't know."

"You don't know."

Frank slipped the drawer shut and tilted his chair back. He let the last trace of sound leave the room. Eileen was back on the job now and not wallowing in the managerial vacuum Frank had created. But he didn't want to release her. There was something else. He didn't know what it was yet, but he could feel it rising toward the surface with a slight dread. Then it was here.

"Tell me, Eileen, does my wife ever call you?"

Eileen looked down.

"I see. And what does she want?"

A helpless shrug.

"Does she want money?"

"____"

"She wants money, then."

"No."

"She doesn't want money. Then what does she want?"

"I don't know."

"She wants information. Where is she, Eileen? And this time I want an answer."

Eileen said, "You find out yourself, playboy."

This was too astonishing. He had to imagine he had misheard. He tried to think of other words that sounded like "playboy." Frank wandered to the window, his temples pounding. He had pushed Eileen too far. Instinctively he looked for the old couple, remembered the old man unwrapping his wife's piece of candy. The sun slanted like an examining light into the corners of the yard. A bright and slumbrous column of dust marked a recently departed automobile. A magpie sat on the single telephone wire that soared in and attached to the wall. He realized that Eileen had pretty much said what he thought she had said. He would come in from another direction.

"Quite right, Eileen," said Frank. "I haven't been what I should have been of late. We'll see what we can do."

Eileen listened and Frank imagined that she was comparing him perniciously to his own father. It left him with the feeling that in speaking to Eileen, he was never quite speaking for himself, with her mustiness of another era.

24

Frank adjusted the gooseneck lamp over the oak desk in his den and pulled up chairs for himself and Holly. Holly had been studying most of the day and had tied her hair back with a bandanna. "Let's have a look," she said. Frank opened the drawer and pulled out two aluminum fly boxes. Holly drew them toward herself and tipped open their lids. Inside, they each had twelve compartments with glassine covers that could be opened by tripping a small wire latch. About half the compartments were filled with flies. Holly frowned.

"Where are the pale morning duns?"

"Must be out of them."

"Don't go anywhere without pale morning duns."

"I make the light Cahill do the work for me."

"Not on big fish," said Holly, "only on dumb fish. I see you have Adamses in about nineteen sizes."

"I believe in the Adams."

"The Adams is pretty vague."

"It's not vague. It's a strong generalization."

"Where's the vise and stuff?"

Frank dug out his fly-tying vise, an old Thompson A, and set it up on his desk. He pulled out the lower left-hand drawer, revealing a collection of feathers and pieces of moose and deer hide, small blue and white boxes of hooks, spools of different-colored threads and silk flosses. A nice smell of camphor arose and Holly took a deep breath.

"You and Uncle Mike are really going to sell the ranch?"

"If we can! All we need is a buyer! All he needs is American money! Who told you?"

"Uncle Mike."

"I didn't want to tell you."

"Could it be sold before I get home again?"

"That would be too good to be true, but it could happen."

"Then I'd like to go once more before I catch my plane."

"Who's picking you up in Missoula?"

"Mama."

"Mama!"

"Yessir, this is a clean sweep. She wanted to come up and check out my boyfriend. Maybe she'll give you a report. This boyfriend is special and I want you and Mama involved."

"Well, send her my best."

"I will. I'll give her your best. I don't know if I told you, I changed faculty advisers this term."

"You didn't tell me. You're still a history major?"

"Still a history major."

"Why did you change?"

"Oh, I don't know. Dr. Carson — that was his name, huge redheaded guy — Dr. Carson had been reading all these statistics about increasing American ignorance ever since I got there. How many Americans had never heard of the Civil War, never heard of Roosevelt, couldn't guess the dates of the First World War within fifty years, on and on. He collected these things as a joke and" — she put a size 16 hook in the vise and began winding cream-colored thread on it, almost too quickly to watch — "saved them for me as a kind of gesture of friendship. It got more and more obsessive with him until it became an icky form of intimacy. I tried to agree with him. But he just never seemed to feel I was quite negative enough about proclaiming the awfulness of everything."

Holly rubbed beeswax onto the thread, then spun pale yellow

fur onto it; she wound the thread on the hook until it looked like the eggy, delicate body of a bug. "I had to meet with him every week, but we couldn't really talk about my work because the stupidity of the American people was becoming so ominous to him that he was paralyzed, and it was starting to paralyze me. Finally, about two weeks ago, I went into his office determined to take a course on the French Revolution even though I hadn't had the prerequisite, and he said, 'Do you know how many books the average American reads between graduation from high school and death?' And I said no and that I really didn't care because it was not in my plans to become an average American. But I could see he was in this vortex. He said, 'Guess!' I mean, he sort of croaked it out. I refused to guess. He stuck his arms straight out from his body and made little fists. His face was red. 'Guess!' When I backed out of his office for the last time, he was shouting, 'Statistically less than one! Statistically less than one!' So I got a new adviser."

Holly set two minute white feathers on top of the hook and figure-eighted the thread around them until they stood up.

"Who is the new one?"

"A very quiet, very pleasant dwarf with a Ph.D. from Harvard."

"Are you calling him a dwarf because he went to Harvard?"

"I'm calling him a dwarf because he's four feet high."

"Oh. Did you get the course?"

"Yep, Dad, yep I did." Holly wound the hackle around the hook shank and the hackle points spun like a bright little cloud around the base of the wings. She wound the thread to the front of the hook and tied it off in a precise whip finish to make the head of the fly. She opened the bottle of lacquer and, when its good smell came out, looked over at Frank and smiled. She dipped the end of her bodkin in it and touched a clear drop of lacquer to the head of the fly. It gleamed for a second and soaked in. She took the fly out of the vise and put in another hook and started again on an identical fly.

"I was kind of surprised when you told me you were going to come back after graduation."

"It's home."

"I know, but it's not a place of much opportunity for people your age."

"Think of the places that are."

"That's true."

"I might even reopen Amazing Grease."

"Please."

"Well, I might."

Frank watched while Holly finished another fly. She used to tie flies for the anglers' shop, for spending money in high school. She had always fished with Frank. When she was in practice, she could outfish him. She couldn't cast as far but she was a great water reader and better at stealing up on trout and making her casts count. She'd had a boyfriend down in New Mexico who fished; she even brought him up one time. Frank didn't like him — Miles something or other. He seemed to think his being a fisherman covered everything. He was an avid, excited young man who took the position that he and Frank had known each other for years. It was part of the angling camaraderie. Frank despised him. Later, Miles gave up fishing to work at the Chicago Board of Trade, where he became a drug addict and dropped from sight. Holly put in another hook and wound the thread onto it.

"Where've you been fishing lately?" Frank asked.

"I haven't been. I made a couple of trips to the Tobacco River, mostly to get away from school for a bit. It's nice, small stream, a lot of small fish. Come up and I'll take you."

Frank was glad she was coming home, though he thought it a bad idea. Holly was a bit high-powered for her old society and her sharp tongue would make it no secret. She was a good-looking girl who did almost nothing on purpose to be attractive. It was hard for Frank to see her falling for one of the up-and-coming young men in town. He didn't like any of them, found them stylishly callow and opinionated.

"What kind of fisherman was Grandpa?"

"Honestly?"

"Yes."

"Not very good," said Frank.

"That surprises me," said Holly.

"He wasn't very good, but nobody loved it more."

"Because I remember him fishing constantly."

"He did, when he had the time. But his approach was too direct. He tried to overpower trout, go straight at them. It was one of the many areas where fishing and life are not at all alike — or at least fishing and business. Your grandfather's problem was that he didn't trust anything or anyone but himself. He had to have a hold of things. A good trout fisherman has to understand a slack line. A slack line is everything. That was too much for Grandpa. If that line wasn't tight, he believed it was out of control. I never knew him to catch a big fish. Big fish are caught on a slack line."

"Well, what kind of a person was he?"

Frank thought for a moment. He'd never looked at it that way. "He was a pretty good fellow. The way he grew up, he got pretty trained to look straight ahead. I got the impression that people who grew up with him who hadn't learned this hard, straight-ahead look were ground up, gone, blown away. He didn't really understand or respect people who hadn't come out of a Depression background."

"You must have had trouble with this straight-ahead business?"

"I sure did. I can't believe that's a serious question."

"Is that why you became a hippie?"

"Here we go."

"No, seriously."

"I don't know why I became a hippie. And maybe I wasn't really one anyway. I never thought I was a hippie at the time. I liked the music. I'm still a child of rock and roll. Lots of us will never escape that. And when we're old, we'll probably let our hair grow out again, if there is any. Right now we're in the swim of things. It's not perfect but it is highly tangible, you know what I mean? We're kind of running the store. Know what I mean?"

"I'm not sure."

"Well, you're in your youth. You're washed around from possibility to possibility. God is telling you nothing matters but meeting the perfect partner, nothing. The world seems to be out ahead but nothing is real. It's all ideas. You're racing toward these balloons that the air currents move steady in another direction. But you get older and you catch up to some of those balloons. You get even with things and they're not drifting away ahead of you. I know that I've settled into the limited possibilities of feeder cattle and rental property and grain sharecropping and the ridiculous limited characters of my friends and my own rather fascinating inadequacies. And all these things are so real! I can feel my limitations like the surface of marble a sculptor touches. And there's only so much grass to be leased in the summer, and even subirrigated ground can only produce so many bushels of grain, and Budweiser and Coors are only going to accept so much malt barley, even if we do get it combined and delivered and past the tests for moisture content. The only things that undermine my happiness are things I can't lay hands on."

"Like what?" said Holly.

"Oh, I don't know."

"Just give me an example."

"I can't."

"Is regret one of them?"

"Sure."

"Do you ever get lonely?"

"Of course. That's a bad one. It's not like other things that strengthen you. Loneliness makes you weaker, makes you worse. I'm guessing that enough of it makes you cruel."

"Two more pale morning duns and we can call it quits," said Holly. She turned and looked at her father in thought. She smiled. He shrugged. She laughed, reached over and squeezed his nose. "Poor little friend," she said.

25

The sun was just coming up. They could make out the light in the tops of cottonwoods. And dropping smoothly out of sight was the pale disc of the moon with its wonderful discolorations. It was like being in a big church in the middle of the week and the only light was in the high windows. They put their rods together and leaned them against the hood of the Buick. Frank opened the bag of doughnuts and set them out and Holly poured coffee from the steel thermos.

"It's already warm," she said. She screwed the lid back on the thermos and set it down decisively. The steam curled up from their cups. There was a dusting of powdered sugar from the doughnuts on the black paint of the hood.

"It was good we started early."

Holly turned her head and listened. Then Frank heard it, a coyote insinuating a thin pure note that seemed to fade into the sky. He could almost feel himself carried with it into a pure blue place. "Are you going to take a net?" Holly asked. She still cocked her head in the direction of the coyote. She smiled to indicate that she had heard it. The little wolves had been here for thousands of years.

"I don't think so. The lanyard always stretches in the brush and fires the damn thing into my kidneys. You know what, though?

Maybe I better. Think if we hooked a big one somewhere we couldn't beach it."

"Gosh this coffee is good. Didn't that 'yote sound pretty?"

"Beautiful."

"Beautiful . . . That's right, beautiful."

Frank went ahead and found a cow trail through the wild roses with their modest pink blossoms. The cottonwoods left off quickly and they were on a broad level place. Here and there were stands of cattails, water just out of sight. And while they threaded their way on a game trail through the brush, they could hear waterfowl chatting among themselves about their passage. When they were almost to the stream, they walked under a huge dead cottonwood, a splendid outreaching candelabra shape festooned with ravens who nervously strode their perches and croaked at the humans beneath them. One bird pirouetted from his branch and, falling like a black leaf, settled on the trail ahead of them. They stopped and Frank tossed his last piece of doughnut. The raven hopped up to it, picked it up in his beak, flew back with it to his roost. "This isn't his first day on the job," said Frank.

Before they reached the edge of the stream the sun was upon them. There was no bank as such, just the end of the wild roses and an uplifted ridge of thorn trees where magpies squawked at the intrusion. But they could hear the stream, which emanated not far away from a series of blue spring holes at a water temperature that stayed constant, winter and summer. Frank loved to arrive at a stream he knew as well as this one. You could strike it at any point and know where you were, like opening a favorite book at a random page.

They stopped at the edge and gazed upon the deep silky current. A pair of kingbirds fought noisily across the stream, and on its banks were intermittent pale purple stands of wild iris. Holly said, "Ah." For some reason she looked as small as a child in her chest waders; whenever she stopped, she stood her fly rod next to her as a soldier would, while Frank flicked at the irises with the tip of his. He stared at the steady flow of water.

"Nothing moving," Frank said. "Needs to warm up."

"Where is the otter pool from here?"

"Well, right above us is the long riffle —"

"With the foam buildup in the corner?"

"Yup, and then the long ledge with the plunge in the middle of it."

"Okay, I know where I am now. Otter pool right above that."

"Holly! We're a little foggy on details."

"I'm a history major. The foreground erodes for history majors. We like an alpine perspective."

They worked their way along the bank, blind casting to the undercut far side, hopscotching upstream until they could hear the shallow music of the riffle. Frank tried to watch Holly without making her self-conscious. She was an accurate close-range caster, her line a clean tight loop, and she had the ability to slow the line down, almost to the point of its falling when she was presenting the fly. She soon hooked a fish.

"What have you got on?" Frank asked as she fought the fish, her rod in a bow. The fish jumped high above the pool as they talked.

"Elk hair caddis. Just something that floats." She hunkered next to the bank and slipped her hand under the fish, a nice trout of about a pound. She let it go, stood up and smiled at Frank while she cast the line back and forth to dry her fly.

At the broad ledge they were each able to take a side of the stream and fish at the same time, casting up into the bubbled seam beneath the rocks. Holly pointed to the plunge at the center and said to Frank, "After you, my boy." Frank cast straight into the center of the plunge. The fly barely had time to land before he hooked a rainbow that blew end over end out into the shallows and held for a long time against the curve of his rod, a band of silver-pink ignited by the morning light. Soon Frank had it in hand, a hard cold shape, gazing down at the water while he freed the hook. Frank let it go and rinsed his hand. He looked upstream and said, "The otter pool."

"You forgot to thank me for that fish."

"Thank you, Holly."

The sun was still too low, and so they waited quietly before they started upstream. The tall sedges grew down so close to the bank that it was necessary for them to stay in the stream to get up to the otter pool. They waded in the center where the current had scrubbed the bottom down to firm sand. Frank was in over his hips and Holly was almost to the top of her waders. She held her rod up in the air and pressed the top of her waders to her chest with her free hand so that water couldn't splash in. They made two great V's in the current. "This is the moon," said Holly, "and I'm on tiptoes."

"Smell the cold air on the surface of the river."

"Stop," said Holly, peering closely at the water. They were on either side of the thread of current and mayflies were starting to appear, unfurling their tiny wings and struggling to float upright. Every few seconds one would come by, some still in their nymphal stage, the case just beginning to split and release the furled wing; others were sailing upright like pale yellow sloops.

"*Ephemerella infrequens,*" said Holly.

"Little sulphurs," said Frank.

"Pale morning duns," said Holly, "like I told you last night."

Frank hung on to his old names for flies, had never learned the Latin of Holly's generation of anglers. "Pale morning dun" was the compromise, reasonably objective compared to the sulphurs and yellow sallies and hellgrammites and blue-winged olives of Frank's upbringing.

At the bend, the wild irises looked as if they would topple into the stream. The narrow band of mud at the base of the sedges revealed a well-used muskrat trail, and on this band stood a perfectly motionless blue heron, head back like the hammer of a gun. It flexed its legs slightly, croaked, sprang into wonderfully slow flight, a faint whistle of pinions, then disappeared over the top of the wall of grasses as though drawn down into its mass.

Around this bend was the otter pool, so called because, when Holly was twelve, she and Frank had watched a family of river otters, three of them, pursuing trout in its depths. Holly took the position that the otters were just like their family: one otter was Frank, one Holly, one Gracie. When the three seized the same trout and rent it, Holly cried, "Oh, poor trout!" and sent the otters into panicked flight upstream.

They stopped quietly at the lower end of the pool, which was wide and deep and surrounded by aspens and cottonwoods. At the top of the pool was a rocky run that looked like a watery stairway. It enlivened a silvery chute of bubbles that didn't disperse until a third of the way down the pool. The movement of water folded into a precise seam of current only at the end of the pool. All along the seam, trout were rising and sipping down the mayflies under a tapestry of reflected cottonwood leaves.

They stopped to watch. "Hm," said Holly.

"An embarrassment of riches."

As they watched, a fish rose about halfway up the pool, a quiet rise that displaced more water than the others, sending a tremor out toward the sides of the pool. Holly grabbed his arm.

"See that?" she asked.

"Mm-hm."

The fish rose again and, in a minute, again.

"Has it got a feeding rhythm," Holly asked, "or is it just taking them when they come?" The fish rose again, its dorsal making a slight thread against the surface.

"I think it's on a rhythm. There're just too many bugs coming off now. What kind of leader have you got on?"

"Twelve-footer, five-X," Holly said. "You're not going to make me cast to that thing, are you?"

"Didn't I thank you for that last rainbow?"

"Can I get by with this tippet?"

"You'll have to. I hate to take the time to change it now. I don't know if you could hold this fish with anything lighter, assuming you make the cast."

"Assuming I make the cast . . ."

A light breeze moved across the water and turned it from black to silver, a faint corrugation that obscured everything that was happening. "Right-hand wind," Holly said gloomily. Then it went back to slick black. "Am I going to line those little fish, trying to reach him?"

"I think you've got to take that chance," said Frank, easing over to the bank in a slight retreat to the ledge where the heron had stood. "If you think about them too much, it'll throw you off." The fish fed again. Even Frank had a nervous stomach. Holly stood and stared. Frank said, "I'm going to try to get up the bank where I can see this fish better. Why don't you try to get in position?"

Frank left his rod at the side of the stream and pushed his way through grass as tall as his face until he got up onto the top of the bank. He worked his way back through the brush until he could look back and see the pool glinting through the branches. Then he got on all fours and crawled to the slight elevation alongside the pool. By the time he reached it, he was on his belly and perfectly concealed. He could see right into the middle of the pool. "Ready to call in the artillery," he said.

"I can't even see you," said Holly.

"Nothing going on."

"Do you think he's gone?"

"No."

Small fish continued making their splashy rises. Frank could see well enough to make out the insects. He rested his chin on the backs of his hands and didn't have to wait long. He tracked a dun mayfly out of the bubbles at the head of the pool, then another, then another. When this one reached mid-pool, a shape arose, clarified into a male brown trout with a distinct hook to its lower jaw and sipped the fly off the surface. It was a startlingly big fish, leopard-spotted, with its prominent dorsal fin piercing the surface. The low pale curve of its belly appeared to grow out of the depths of the pool itself. It sank almost from sight, but even after it had fed, Frank could make out its observing presence deep in the pool, a kind of intelligence.

"See that?"

Instead of answering, Holly began to strip line from her reel. She had the fly in her hand and blew on it. "I'm just going to cast," she said. "I'm thinking too hard. How big?"

"Big."

"Oh, I wish I hadn't asked."

"You have the fish marked pretty well?"

"Yeah, here goes."

Frank could see her false casting, but the fly tailed the loop, turned over too soon and hooked on the line. "Shit!" Holly brought her line back in and cleared the fly.

"You're rushing, Holly. You're turning it over too soon. Cast like you always do. Don't press." She started again. "Slow, slow." And she did, resuming her elegant cadence. The curve of line opened. The fly floated down and the fish arose steadily from the depths. "Whoa whoa whoa," said Frank. "Don't strike, he's taking one in front of yours. Let the current take your fly away." The fish eased up, made a seam as he broke the surface, then sank. Frank heard a pent-up breath escape from Holly while he watched the heavy fish suck an insect down. The fish held just beneath the surface, both the dorsal and tip of his tail out of the water; his gills flared crimson and a faint turbulence spread to the surface from either side of his head.

"Try again while he's still up," Frank said, and an instant later Holly's fly fluttered down from above, right in the feeding lane of the trout. He could see the fly rock around on the bright hackles Holly had wound on the hook last night, slowly closing on the fish. The trout elevated slowly and the fly disappeared down a tiny whirlpool in the water. "There," said Frank, not too loud, and the thin leader tightened into the air, a pale cool spray the length of it. "You've got him!"

Frank stood straight up out of the brush as the trout surged across the pool. Holly held her rod high with both hands and said, "Oh, God God God God God."

"Let him go."

"I *am* letting him go."

"Don't touch that reel."

"I'm not touching the reel!"

Frank got back below the pool and waded out to Holly. The reel was screeching. She was looking straight ahead where the line pointed. There was a deep bow in the rod. She moved her face slightly in Frank's direction. "I'm dying," she said. The fish started to run and the click of the reel set up a steady howl. "I am going to die."

Frank wanted to take some of the pressure off Holly. He moved his ear next to the screeching reel and looked up at her. "Darling," he said, "they're playing our song."

"Daddy, stop it. This is killing me!"

"I thought this was supposed to be fun."

"It's torture. Oh, God."

The fish stayed in the pool. It might have sensed that Frank and Holly were at the lower end, and the rapids above were probably too shallow for a fish this big to negotiate. If it went that way, the light leader would have quickly broken on rocks. All Holly could do was keep steady pressure and hope the fish was well hooked and that none of its teeth were close to the tippet. She was doing her part perfectly. The fish began to work its way deliberately around the pool, staying deep. "I guess this is where we get to see if there are any snags," she said gloomily. This fish swam entirely around the pool once, an extraordinarily smart thing to do; but it couldn't find something to wind Holly's leader around. And it was having increasing difficulty staying deep in the pool. Holly continued to keep the same arc in her rod and watched vigilantly where the line sliced the surface. Finally, the fish stopped and held, then slowly let itself be lifted toward the surface. For the first time, Holly cautiously reeled.

Frank undid his net from the back of his vest and held it in the water to wet the mesh. The fish was coming toward them. "Let me be in front of you, Hol," he said quietly. When the fish was closer, he held the net underwater toward the fish. He could hear the unhurried turns of the reel handle. He looked straight at the fish from above. It turned quietly around and went back to the center of the pool, accompanied by the steady whine of Holly's reel. "Oh, how much of this can I stand!" said Holly. But when the fish stopped, she resumed her steady work.

"We'll catch this fish, Hol."

"Do you think so?"

"I think so."

"You're just saying that, aren't you?"

"No, I foresee the fish in my net."

When the fish reappeared, Frank stared hard and moved the net toward it. The fish seemed pressed away by the net. Holly brought it closer and the net pushed it away but it didn't move off quite the same way. "I'm going for it," Holly said, and pulled hard enough to move the fish toward Frank; the fish turned and chugged toward the other bank but was unable to dive. Holly brought it back once more, and this time the fish glided toward the pressure of her rod and Frank swept the net in the air, streaming silver and slung deeply with the bright spotted weight of the fish.

"I'm so happy, I'm so happy!" Holly cried as Frank submerged the net to keep the trout underwater. "I never caught such a big fish!" He slipped his hand inside the net and around the slick underside of the trout, unveiling him delicately as the net was lifted clear. With his left hand under the fish and his right hand around its tail, he was able to hold it. The little pale yellow fly was stuck just in the edge of his upper jaw. Holly reached down to free it and the fly fell out at her touch. Frank held the fish head up into the current until the kicks of the tail became strong. "You want to do the honors?" he asked.

"You."

"Grab," he said. Holly took the wrist of the fish's tail just above Frank's hand.

Holly let go, then Frank let go, feeling the weight of the fish with his left hand and the curve of the fish's belly with his right. Underwater, the trout seemed to take its bearings and balance itself. Then it kicked free, gliding to disappear into the middle of the pool. They began hollering like wild hog hunters, gesturing at the sky, Frank with his fists, Holly with her rod.

"I'm the champion of the world!" Holly yelled.

There seemed little point in doing anything but contemplate the bewildering size of a trout that must have rarely let down its guard in a long life. They were confident it would never make that mistake again. It was strange to feel affection for a creature finning secretively, almost below the light, disturbing the gravel bottom with an outrush of water from its broad gills. They were silent in the glitter of cottonwood leaves.

Later, as they drove home, they sang. Frank pushed off the steering wheel to belt out his small part and Holly twisted in her seat operatically.

"Hey!"

"Hey!"

"You!"

"You!"

"Get offa my cloud!"

And Holly's visit home was over. When her plane went off in a shrinking silver spot that disappeared, he felt his chest go all fluid with emotion that rose up through his face before he controlled it. With so many of his family, people he had known, gone, to have someone he loved as much as he loved Holly poised early in her life, facing out onto the flat earth, was overwhelming. Today he had had her attention fully and he knew that wouldn't always be true. It was hard to take that in.

26

Eileen was in the doorway of Frank's office, brow furrowed and seemingly reluctant to disclose what was on her mind. She did a lot of this sort of telegraphing with her face and Frank got the sense she would love to go through life with these meaningful dumb shows, like an Indian in a cowboy movie, pointing at things, listening to the night wind, smoke signals from a nearby hill, message tapped out on the plumbing. It was very hard for Eileen to make a direct statement. This never annoyed Frank when Gracie was around, but now poor Eileen stood for business, and anything about business was slipping in Frank's esteem.

"Yes, Eileen."

"Someone to see you, Mr. Copenhaver."

"I believe this has happened before, Eileen. Any reason you can't show him in?"

"It's Mr. Jarrell, Mr. Copenhaver."

This was the ranch, the unimproved heritage. "Have him come in," he bayed. He looked at his papers without seeing them. For once, Eileen's mugging amounted to something. Frank rested his hand on the phone. Boyd came through the door and closed it behind him on a glimpse of Eileen craning inward. Frank noticed that he was empty-handed. Boyd nodded. Frank nodded. For some reason he found himself saying, "Haven't seen you since the night of the suds."

"Yeah."

"Skip a couple of showers after that, ay?"

"Yeah."

"Well, today is another day, and what is it I can do for you?"

"I went out to the ranch yesterday and had a look around. It don't look very good at all."

"We haven't found a new man. You kind of left us in midstream."

"Alfalfa all burning up, deer gone through the fence —"

"I believe Mike has taken out an ad in the *Agri-News*."

"— place where the RV boys shot off the lock on the east pasture, just riding around in there and flattening the grass."

"Like I say, I'd have to check with Mike and see if we've had any responses."

"But when I got to the troughs and the salt was completely gone, I realized —"

"What did you realize?" Frank asked because Boyd had paused.

"I realized we'd got our deal backwards. It don't matter about you and me. Cows have got to have their salt."

"So, what are you telling me?"

"I'm starting back in today."

"And what about — what about our conflict, Boyd? Be honest."

"We're going to have to set that aside, Mr. Copenhaver. Like I been trying to tell you, the cows are out of salt."

"One thing you should know. Mike and I have decided to sell the place."

"You ain't gonna do no such of a thing."

Frank thought for a minute. Boyd was a perfect cowboy. All he cared about was cows, but he did care about cows. He could see a sore-footed one from almost two miles off, as Frank had one day found out. He was as kind to cows as he was unreasonable to people. Frank might well have been more assiduous in staying out of his way. Boyd once clobbered Mike with a frying pan, but Mike thought everyone was crazy anyway and didn't take it personally, though his nurse complained that he staggered around the office for two and a half days and may well have suffered a concussion. Frank thought about the cows being by themselves, without Boyd tending to them. Big, easygoing, helpless creatures dragged onto this prairie by white folks, always pregnant and always out of something they needed. There had to be someone who tried to close that gap between cows and an environment not always friendly to them. He had to admit to himself that there was real satisfaction in seeing Boyd ride through a herd of cattle, knowing that when he got out the other side he'd have learned as much about them as the graduating class of the average veterinary school. If I knew that much about anything, Frank thought, I wouldn't be nice to anyone. But I'm so ignorant I have to go on treating people decently.

"We took you off the rolls. You'll have to stop and let Eileen know. You deal with it."

"Yeah."

"And I'm not kidding. Mike and I are thinking about selling the place." Why? thought Frank. Boyd could hold it together as an heirloom.

"Check with me first," said Boyd. "You don't need to be selling good land like that. You'll piss it away."

"You think so?"

"Hell, I know so."

27

He phoned Saturday to see if Holly had arrived safely in Missoula. A man answered. "Just say her father called." Frank had a feeling he'd encountered this bird once, a transfer from Colgate, shoulder-length curls and a nose ring. He had made a sardonic remark at the time, something about Missoula, something about the West Slope. It fell on its face.

Frank went outside and looked around at the street, with its operatic ascent to the south through shafts of light crisscrossing the maples. Cars seemed to coast around town, their motors ticking placidly. Their shapes and array of colors jumped and disappeared in the front windows of the houses. Students appeared at the crown of the hill on bicycles and plummeted heedlessly past, then on into town. The sidewalk climbed the hill in an erratic line, its track interrupted here and there by lilacs and caragana bushes.

He enumerated his obligations with the feeling that they kept him from soaring into this vista as one of its colors. Holly, easy. And Gracie — what obligation? He did not know. He had let slide Holly's notation that Gracie was doing less than well. Bad luck or stewing in her own juices, he didn't know. But Holly was going to see Gracie and that was exciting. Maybe she could help finalize the divorce and they could start to get past the pain.

He walked on down the street. Something useless about Saturday, a day of loathing to the self-employed. Eileen would be home taking care of her older sister, a woman afflicted with multiple sclerosis and a lack of funds. He passed St. Anne's, his family church at the corner of Shoshone, and saw its door ajar, a dark band at the lintel with the glimmer of yellow interior lights. He stopped and went in, the old pull; he paused and was swept in as by a current. And then the smell of stone and old burnt incense, of the varnished pine pews, was comforting. He walked halfway up the middle aisle, genuflected and took a seat, gazing at the empty altar. He wondered if it was any different than the tumuli of Druids, fairie rings, sun dance circles, or if that in fact suggested a reduction. Maybe it expressed a zone of the subconscious that produced the murdering popes and ayatollahs. What if there was nothing there but the belief of many that there was something there? That certainly added to the importance of matters. He walked up and lit candles to his mother and father. He returned to his pew. Anybody here? Release the white bird now, please. Let a beam of light pass overhead. The faint voice of a bell. You see, we are desperate. We are here to say *stone* and *water* and *sacrifice; house, crops, fish*. And to say them plainly. To say *Gracie*.

He was sorry he included "fish" because it started him thinking on a lower plateau. He left the church and went to his house and began gathering his tackle. Inside an hour's time, he was standing waist deep in the Gallatin River. Swallows dove just above his head, catching mayflies. Trout moved among the current seams like phantoms. Darkness would overtake him only a few yards from here, deep in a mystery.

Frank stopped at Valley News and bought the paper. There was a young man in front with long dirty dreadlocks. The well-bred golden retriever he held beside him on a length of clothesline looked hopelessly out into traffic.

Lucy passed in front of Valley News just as Frank came out with his paper. He nodded slightly. She nodded slightly, passed, stopped and came back. She looked handsome in a blue cotton skirt and oversize gray sweater. She said, "Frank."

Frank said, "Lucy." He wanted to be decent and let no smile cross his face. But he suddenly remembered going to a whorehouse in Livingston with Mike and hearing Mike's voice boom out from behind a closed door, "Great Caesar's ghost, it's a cunt!" And now he began to laugh. He really ought not to remember any of Mike's views on women, including the one that the only people who understood women were the Africans who practiced female circumcision, nipping off the clitoris with a clamshell. Mike would pantomime the action of the clamshell, like Señor Wences and Johnny.

"What are you laughing at?" she demanded.

"I had a completely inappropriate and unwelcome memory. I'm sorry. Lucy, have dinner with me." He felt a little ashamed.

"This early?"

"I could eat."

"I could too, I guess. Well, sure."

"That's good. Thank you, Lucy."

"You're welcome, Frank." They went down the street to O'Nolan's, a quiet, unpretentious place filled with well-educated nouveau Rockies people whose bland love of recreation fascinated Frank. They sat opposite each other, silently looking into their menus as though they were secret documents. They knew each other well enough to read their menus without nervous chatter or commentary on the offerings. Frank was feeling a weird flutter.

"It's amazing this place is so busy at this hour," said Lucy.

"They probably want to turn in early. Wild-mushroom seminar at daybreak."

"What?"

"I'm surprised too."

"Well, Frank, we left off on a sour note. But we're mature people. I think we're moving right along to a new tone and I find that very welcome."

"Hear, hear. Nutone."

"This is your treat, right?"

"Right."

"May I say that I had no right to impose my romantic schemes without more input from you — please don't make a rude joke about input."

"I wasn't going to."

The waitress came and recited the specials. Frank had no interest in food. He wanted to say, Who gives a shit? He was always interested, though, in the way the waitresses could rattle off the specials along with a little description of the sauces and methods of preparation. And phrases like "*fines herbes*" and "*crème fraîche*" had a certain dorky melodiousness that seemed to work on the other diners and that Frank, therefore, wished would work on him. They did have a rib eye steak of splendid dimensions and he ordered that. He ate so fast that when he was in restaurants he had to order large-volume meals to avoid having a lot of time to kill. Lucy asked for a couple of the oddities. They also ordered drinks.

Frank made a mental note to watch the drinks closely so that some immensely complicated stirring of the old trouser worm didn't get started. Lucy was very real to Frank. Sometimes women got so real you couldn't have sex with them anymore: you and the real person had to get involved with some third entity to have the atmosphere of wished-for intensity. It could be a child or a business or pornography or the desire to do away with your people's enemies. Prowling suburban couples ambushed unsuspecting individuals in off-color lash-ups. Car, rooftop or diving-board sex. Love that referred to something. "Love." Frank sauntered through these notions in what he thought was a pleasant atmosphere.

"Frank?"

"Yes?"

"I don't seem to have your attention, Frank."

So, okay, how do you field this one. "I'm sorry," he said.

"Don't be sorry."

"Right, then. Say, what did I order?"

"A steak."

"And you, dear?"

"Veal Bolognese."

He knew very well this was not veal baloney. But a thought of a lone slice of flat meat, something isolated-looking even in a school lunch, went through his mind. "I'm looking forward to my steak," said Frank. He thought of his cattle deal. He thought about the yearlings slowed to a stop by the depth of his Salvation Army lease grass. He saw those melting pounds forming along the calves' ribs.

Their drinks came. The bourbon went straight into his thoughts as he gazed across the room. He was quite conscious of their hands resting on the table. Lucy excused herself. He nodded slightly and watched with vague attention until he realized that she was not going to the rest room, she was going out the door of the restaurant, and if his eyes didn't deceive him, she had succeeded in snagging her coat en route.

He snapped to attention and quite properly chased after her out the door. He caught her at the curb. Her eyes were brimming.

"I'm perfectly capable of buying my own dinner," she said.

"What did I do? What did I do, Lucy?" He knew that without their rueful camaraderie he could never ask this seriously.

"You drifted off. You simply drifted off, Frank."

"Oh Lucy, it's true. I'm guilty. Come on, let's go back in. I did a big cattle deal and sort of scared myself. I started worrying about it. Come on. Our steak and baloney will be there in a jiff. One more chance."

"So of course she buys this," said Lucy. "She plods back into the mediocre restaurant. Life is just going by a step at a time. He has his deals and their eyes never quite meet, much less their thoughts. She begins to ask herself, What sort of discount can I offer the Methodists for Machu Picchu? Does Royal Holland Lines have any interesting guest hosts this year? Was it Viking that had the bad comedians?" Frank's eyes sparkled.

They were back at their table in time for the entrées. Lucy looked abashed, as though she had forced him to pay closer attention to her. Frank thought he could see in Lucy a sort of formal decision to take her own destiny in hand. She had had an unsuccessful marriage; and Frank's biggest reservation about her was that she was heading back into another unsuccessful marriage by hook or by crook. She never seemed to know which cards to play, and Frank was not attracted to women who wanted a lot of help with their cards. Everything else he liked about her. He was so much the sleepwalker lately that it may have been the peculiar floundering way she fucked that brought him back to the bright lights of the reality he craved. He was always interested in people's businesses and Lucy had a business with some reality in the community. People wanted to get away from time to time and she helped them efficiently. She had a good feeling for the different ways they wanted out, and was a successful sales person. She had led a few tours, even did a Lindblad bird thing in the South Pacific with a group from the university, cramming bird lore and successfully staying ahead of a group that prided itself on being at an information advantage. Before the celebrated busts of the television evangelists, Lucy had a reliable Holy Land trade but that had fallen off, and the region's reputation for violence took care of what was left.

"Frank?"

"?"

"What's it all for?" She made this seem a radiant question.

"I knew you were going to ask that."

"But it makes sense I should ask you. We have our business interests. We're beyond survival. What are we trying to achieve?"

"Hm."

"Well, I think it's important to find out."

Frank stopped eating for a moment. He often liked just being a businessman, much of the time, enough of the time. He was very absorbed in Holly's emerging story. Maybe he had transferred too much of himself to that. He realized that his compulsion to watch people going about their lives, watching them through their windows as though they were in a laboratory, came from some sense that not enough of the right things were going on in his. If life seemed anything, it seemed thin. It had an "as if" quality. He sensed that everyone was living in an atmosphere of postponement.

He wondered why people didn't acknowledge this. If President Bush had said he felt "as if" he were waging war on Iraq, Frank would have seen it as a breakthrough in candor. "It's as if bombs were falling on people." It was for others, real people, to actually receive the bombs, to have nationalist struggles, to lose the crop, to suffer the red tide, to feel an inner joy at the way the new Audi handles the winding road, to be cheerfully fooled by the instant coffee served secretly to them at Antoine's in New Orleans, to be disappointed by all the cotton wadding in their little bottles of aspirin. Yet there was a real bravery as Lucy decoded the birds of Micronesia for the know-it-alls who hadn't taken the time, on those snowy days in Montana, to prepare for the intricacies of a cruise ship's pecking order. This also put her cheek by jowl with the ship's biologist and it was only a matter of time before they pretended to make a baby in his stateroom. She told this to Frank once before, when she had wondered if you could always detect a lust scenario if you were diligent.

"The Beatles used to call their girlfriends 'birds,' " Frank said. "I remember John Lennon introducing his girlfriend as 'me bird.' "

"Me bird . . ."

"Yes."

"Frank, what in the fuck are you talking about?"

"You said you studied birds for your trip and ended up kind of a bird yourself."

"Oh, I get it. I don't really remember the sixties."

It was warm and dark when they left the restaurant. It seemed easy, not needing a decision, to walk into the neighborhoods that spread to the north behind Main Street. Between streets there would be an unpaved road that divided the backs of two rows of houses, an alley where people had their garbage cans, rowboats, woodpiles, and where their windows looked out unguarded onto this cheerful lack of arrangement. Frank heard the sound of a stringed instrument and was drawn toward it as they walked. He saw the window and crept to its light, gesturing to Lucy to follow. From a few feet, he gripped Lucy's arm and felt safe looking in. A man in a white undershirt was playing a cello, drops of sweat on his forehead as he stared grimly at the music stand. Next to him, in a plastic bassinet, a baby watched its own waving fists. It was an empty room with a wooden floor, and for furniture only the chair the musician sat on. Frank couldn't make out the source of light and there wasn't a shadow anywhere.

When they got back to the alley, Lucy said, "That scared me."

Frank gave her a comradely squeeze to reassure her. "An original scene, wouldn't you say?"

They walked a short distance into a shadow and began to kiss. They kissed for a while and he slid her arm down until her hand was between his legs. He held her buttocks from behind and worked her dress up until he could get his hands into her panties. The globes of flesh felt cool. He stood back from her so that he could get his hand in front and his fingers inside. She stood in the alley and moaned, moving against his hand as it grew slippery.

He led her into a garage. There was an old Buick parked inside and he opened its back door. God, it was just like his own Buick. Lucy hesitated, then sat on the end of the back seat, then slid back. He took his pants down and his cock was straight out into the air as he reached inside to lift her foot over the front seat. She undid her blouse and pulled it apart so her breasts stood up white in the faint light. She bit the side of her hand and watched him as he entered. She lost caution and tried to come before he did. Big tendons on the inside of her thighs stuck into his hips and her feet were on the roof. He wanted to make sounds as he felt the spurts loosening into her but kept quiet. "I'll turn over if you stay hard," she said. He said "Okay" experimentally, and stood outside the car where he could make out the pale curve of her rear. He felt crazy bafflement as phrases went through his mind, like "travel agent" and "Old World charm." So, that part of it didn't work out.

Frank regretted that Lucy had such a time getting out of the car gracefully, the white awkwardness of her buttocks emerging from the door, her right foot pedaling toward the ground. Unable to pull up his pants because he was standing on his own cuffs, Frank did little better. A couple of creeps, he thought.

They went on down the alley to where it opened up into a small park. Lucy was silently weeping. He could reach up in the dark and feel the cold, drizzling tears. There was not one thing he could say or had any right to say. Tears began to pour from his own eyes. What was this? He took Lucy into his arms in such a way that she could feel these tears of his, until a kind of easy solitude let them laugh rueful snot bubbles from their noses. Pretty soon they were laughing. At first they tried to laugh quietly. Then Frank tried loud laughter. So did Lucy. They began to guffaw like two people in an opera. It was literally, "HA, HA, HA!" They were bellowing. They were having fun at last.

Frank walked Lucy to her car. It was parked a block behind Main Street and he could read the names of the old businesses: grocers, hardware merchants, even a blacksmith. The stores in front had long since become something else: florists, clothiers, boutiques, office supplies.

"What is this?" he asked her.

"A Toyota Corolla."

"Is it any good?"

"Yeah, it's fine. Well, Frank —"

"Lucy."

"I enjoyed it."

"So did I."

"Nice big laugh there at the end."

"You can say that again," said Frank.

"Nice big laugh there at the end."

"Good, Lucy."

"I'll see you at the office."

"See you at the office."

28

Frank liked to think he occupied some middle ground between his father and his grandfather. His father had been an Eagle Scout and a good scholar. He had also had a fanatical desire to better himself financially, a personal pride in the score, not unlike the athlete bent on achieving a four-minute mile, a thousand-yard season. Frank's grandfather was a dour farmer who rarely said much but seemed to take in everything with his great stern eyes. When Frank's father had first made money to any degree, he took Frank, then nine years old, and his father to the country club for dinner. He made everyone eat a lobster. He drank far too much and stuffed crumpled bills into the waitress's hand. Frank's grandfather watched this in silence, then finally boomed out over the lobster shells, "If you can't drink any better than that, Bill, you had better not drink at all."

The whole country club heard it. Frank saw his father's sudden, startling vulnerability, saw both his face and his pride fall at one time and understood the astonishing power of deflation fathers have over their sons. In a way, it made Frank happy not to have a son, on the slim chance he could ever accidentally use this terrible weapon, this atom bomb. He was having the opposite problem with his daughter: he daren't say a word against the one with the nose ring for fear of receiving a good lecture. Or the head of the citizens' group, who wished to save Montana for Montanans. He could only learn to feel something was missing from his life, not having a nose ring of his own, a butterfly tattooed on his butt.

On Monday he did not go to work at all. This had almost never happened before. And instead of asking Eileen to hold the fort, he called early in the morning and told her to take the day off too.

She was delighted and said she would go to Helena to watch minor league baseball. "Thank you, Mr. Copenhaver. I'll be there bright and early tomorrow morning."

"As you wish, Eileen."

"Can I ask where you're going?"

"I'm looking for a mental health professional within comfortable driving distance."

There was a long pause and then Eileen said in beefy, almost British tones, "I'm going to take a chance here, Mr. Copenhaver, and assume that you are serious. I'm going to tell you that I think that that is a very good idea. I hope you realize that it's nothing to be ashamed of."

"I do, Eileen," Frank said thinly. In fact, he had already made an appointment with a therapist. He was looking at the picture of a movie star in *People* magazine who was attending a Crow Indian sun dance ceremony, hanging by thongs through his chest from the lodge poles of a prodigious tepee.

A short time later, it seemed to make sense for Frank to stand inconspicuously in the parking lot behind Mullhaven Hardware, watching people park their cars. His eyes were covert slits. An old rancher came in, parked his big Toronado, with its pink and white paint job, and climbed out pocketing his keys. A heavy red-haired woman in jogging pants arrived in a green Wagoneer, thrust the keys under the seat and got out. A man who looked slightly costumed in his gardening clothes drove up in a white Ford station wagon and went inside without making any special movements toward the ashtray, the visor or beneath the seat. When he was out of sight, Frank went to the car and got in.

The keys were in it. There was a crisp, unopened *Wall Street Journal* on the seat and Frank took a moment to glance at the headlines. The Fed had cut the interest rates again but it was not expected to impact the recession. He started the car and backed out of the angled slot into the alley. He swung around to Main and turned east, enjoying the commodious volume of space behind, thinking of it filled with kids' bicycles or fitted with a dog barricade or redolent of a well-used rotary mower, green polished off at the corners to a pewter gleam under its veil of 30-weight oil. Unfortunately, it was a brand-new shell of a station wagon and had the familiar, disconcerting, prop-like quality of the unearthly exercise equipment that freighted the yard sales of America.

That feeling went right away as he tooled over the pass, eyeing the various gougings of the nearby mountainsides and looking forward to the prospect of pouring his guts out to a stranger. Then quite suddenly he lost all sense of what he was doing in this car and began checking in the rearview mirror for the police, staring between the retreating twin columns of mountainside reflected down toward his eyes, then scanning the silver-gray bands of pavement and the spheres of white clouds on a dome of blue sky: no cops. The fear passed and he resumed his confident occupancy of the station wagon, custodian of the deeply throbbing wheel and air-light accelerator as the pass opened to the shallow plains of cattle pastures.

It was then that he spotted the cellular phone. It seemed comforting, as if a car thief would scarcely drive the speed limit and make a few telephone calls. First he called Lucy at her office. "I've been looking for you," she said, "and you didn't come in today." She didn't sound hurt, nor did she seem reticent about looking for him.

"I'm trying to make some adjustments, Lu."

"Who isn't, Frank? Are you coming in today?"

"I don't think so."

"Well, let me get something off my chest then."

Frank thought about her chest, the receptive undercurve of her resting bosom. A wonderful homey thing that helped pass the time. "Fire away, Lu."

"Frank, I don't think these 'episodes' are good for me."

"No?" He pictured the Buick's interior, the upended Lucy with a whelk curve of open pink flesh.

"No. Sure, there's pleasure. But just now they make my, uhm, plight seem more extreme, and it lasts longer than the pleasure. I've been noticing that."

"Aw, Lu." That sounded unhelpful, but he couldn't touch the white whale of a subject that buried everyone just now, the deep distaste men and women had for each other of late, the unstable truces of the new marriages, the warlike affairs. Frank hoped they had bypassed that with an avalanche of sheer lewdness, but it was just wishful thinking. Indelicacy was not a cure for everything.

"Anyway," said Lucy, "I had already come to that conclusion before the other night, and suddenly there I was with my feet on the roof of those people's car —"

Frank felt a fever go through his face at the very thought and as billboards emerged from pastures, with skiers and swan divers and stylized silhouettes of the Big Sky on them.

"— and I realized that I simply have to ask you, as a friend, to make sure that that never happens again. People like us have a special need to look out for each other, and what we've been doing hasn't been good for me."

She's asking me as a friend to quit fucking her!? With all that energy spent on venery, the intricate, often baffling pursuit would turn to poison. Poison! Plus, Frank thought, it's guilt because of Gracie. We've descended from Heartbreak Hotel to Heartbreak Bed-and-Breakfast.

"Okay, Lucy."

"You make it sound so flat," said Lucy.

"Well, I don't want it to. But I guess it makes me feel sort of flat to promise you that." A candy-apple green Mazda went by at about a hundred. It seemed to have a sidling shudder induced by its pure speed as it mounted the long hill, then disappeared from sight.

"Why?"

"Why? Because I enjoyed it, Lu. I enjoyed *you*."

"I enjoyed you too, Frank."

Right at the interchange where two peninsulas of trailers gathered on the high banks along the highway, a girl was hitchhiking with an aluminum-frame backpack, holding up a sign that said "Madison." Heading east — that must mean Madison, Wisconsin, not the Madison River. This was Frank's turnoff but he was going to forget that and give this young woman a ride, this fresh-faced stranger. Frank wheeled over and gestured for her to get in, smiling, indicating that he was on the phone and therefore not able to help much. She put the pack in back and got in. He grinned, tried with shifting and grimacing to indicate he'd be off the phone in a sec.

"But if you want it that way, Lu, we can sure leave it at that."

"I ask myself if I really want to leave it like that."

He made out the inner curve of her thighs with sheer peripheral vision. The girl smelled like sagebrush. Brunette, long hair held together low in back with a piece of knotted blue cloth. He started to sweat. He had the tip of one finger on the rim of the abyss, but Lucy's voice was sucking him back in.

"I guess I can't answer that one for you, Lucy."

"Even as I hear myself speaking, I know I'm lying."

"You do?" How's that for stupid.

"Yes, I do."

"How do you mean, exactly?"

"I want you. Frank, I want you."

"Uh-*huh*," said Frank, as if, lifting the hood to add a quart of oil, he spotted smoke coming out from under the valve covers.

"Shall I tell you how?" she asked in a numb, involuntary voice.

"Sure," he said, absolutely confounded in his effort to bring this to a stop. She began to roll on as in a trance, overcome by the erotic power of her telephone. Frank looked over at the girl, who had raised her eyebrows in a coolish look of inquiry. To underscore his helplessness, he removed the phone from his ear and held it out. Lucy's voice, reduced to a tiny scratchiness like a little witch doll's, projected into the car's interior: ". . . when you're all the way in my mouth and I feel your big balls . . ."

"Stop the car," shouted the brunette. She had thrust her legs out and seized the door handle as if to suggest that she would jump if he didn't stop.

"Frank!" shouted Lucy through the phone. "Are you with someone this very minute?"

"Call you back, gotta go." He hung up and pulled off to the side of the road, where the girl jumped out, turned and flung open the back door, hauling out her backpack.

"I'm really very sorry," said Frank.

But she was walking already, eating up the miles with her long legs, her house on her back, free of filth. His shirt was stuck to his skin. He was furious with himself for not going to the office. Plus, why steal cars? He started backing up along the side of the road, to reach the interchange where he was supposed to have turned. He had backed up nearly a half mile when a police car came over the crown of the hill, then pulled off the road in front of him. In a moment the cop was at Frank's window, a world-weary veteran with small features and a collection of loose wattles falling from beneath his chin.

"Miss your turn?"

"Yes," Frank breathed, "I'm afraid I did."

"You know you aren't supposed to back up along the interstate like that."

"I'm sorry," said Frank, with such feeling the officer gave him a long look. "I know I'm guilty and I'm sorry."

"Let me see your driver's license."

Frank leaned forward to free his wallet and the cop backed around the car with his clipboard to get the number on the license plate. He looked up just as he started writing, and said with considerable annoyance, "There's one of them college hitchhikers again. That's been illegal for ten years." Batting the clipboard against his hip, he strided toward Frank's window. "I'm going to let you back up and turn off. But you aren't supposed to and I am not supposed to let you. So don't do it again."

Frank left and let the cop drive up and bust Miss Clean.

At Gracie's request, he had once seen a therapist, a meeting that went very badly from the beginning. There was all sorts of persiflage about his holding or not holding the door as they entered her office, and Frank could feel a kind of electricity coming from between her shoulder blades as she moved around her desk to sit down facing him.

There was a large photograph of a crowd scene over her desk which said underneath it, "How many forms of abuse can you find?" As he looked at her, he thought of the word "pig." Not, strangely enough, that he thought she was a pig, but he could sense that she had already decided *he* was one. He knew that that was the totem animal not only of ugly women but of overeaters and men of exaggerated masculinity. He had tried to work up a wussy shuffle for his arrival, but then they had the little showdown about what he was "trying to say" in holding the door for her. Everything about being here was awkward. In a conciliatory way, he told her he couldn't help acting like a pig because he was the owner of some of the best show pigs in the state. She didn't react. The gender thing was dialed up to where he couldn't even figure out how to sit down. They ended up seated across the desk from each other. The window was behind her and he had to squint as he answered her questions.

"Do you drink?"

"Yes."

"Have you ever been drunk?"

"Yes."

"More than once?"

"I'm afraid so."

"Has it occurred to you that you may be an alcoholic?"

"No."

"Has it occurred to you that you are in denial?"

"What's denial?"

"Denying that you are an alcoholic?"

"No. Sometimes I forget to drink for half a year at a time."

"Are you familiar with the term 'dry drunk'?"

"Well, just sort of."

"Often, if we don't drink and at the same time fail to seek counseling, we become what are called dry drunks."

"I'm not following. Are you a dry drunk?"

The therapist's face flared red. "Hardly! Is it the position you are trying to take with me that any little help I may try to be of to you is simply mud you are going to sling back into my face?"

"I'm sorry."

"I am a mental health therapist and must accept, in the line of duty, a certain amount of punishment. But just so you know, if you were outside the walls of this office, what you just tried to dish out to me is a little verbal abuse. It is virtually diagnostic of denial."

Frank nodded gamely but he really didn't get it. "How much this thing gonna come to?"

This gave Mirabelle time for thought. That was her name and she asked to be called Dr. Mirabelle, an odd mixture of formal and informal. In his confusion, he still viewed her as a dry drunk, though he wasn't sure what it was.

"You're changing the script, Frank. We're talking sideways anger, here. Attempts to control me through undermining questions about my financial arrangements with you or any other patient will go, you'll find, nowhere."

"You don't have to stare me down. It was an innocent question."

"Sixty dollars! I'm not ashamed of being recompensed for my hard work. You can take your control questions elsewhere. That issue fails to appear on my agenda."

"Everything I say seems to upset you so much," he said nervously, fishing his checkbook from his shirt pocket.

"It's not 'about' being upset," she shouted. "I'm not buying into that!"

He wrote frantically. It was like spending sixty dollars to get out of jail. He slid the check across the desk. She made as if she didn't even see it. Her lips were so pursed, it looked like someone had just stolen her cigar.

"In all honesty," Frank said, "this sort of thing doesn't really seem right for me. Crazy as it may seem to you, I feel sort of abused myself, kinda gypped."

"Welcome to the human race," she said. "It's about welcome.

It's about accepting your ordinariness. It's about finding meaning in the everyday." Frank sensed she was trying to jam in some advice to make this sixty-dollar bum deal seem more palatable. "It's about letting go, Frank, and sensing a sharing that takes place for those who know what it is to be human." Frank left her seated at her desk, knowing that when he was out of sight he would pick up his check and that, painful as it might be, it was somehow "about" cashing the check.

And at the same time, he felt poorly. Most everyone he knew was in a program for recovery. He had felt quite isolated by not joining something, had never really felt anything applied to him, but he got the very strong message that he had not tried hard enough. Gracie really wanted him in a program and he would have been willing to meet her halfway, but somehow they got lost in all the choices, all the initials. Now, in his first skirmish and probably his last, he had failed. It was better to have never tried at all than to have failed a program so abruptly. It was as bad as feeling all right, when it seemed to be plain to everyone that this was a sign of his detachment from his true inner feelings. It was like flunking life. The dialogue dropped away and even his considerate and hopeful fibs about "the child within" sagged pitifully. He felt like some bogus stoop who didn't actually have a child within. Certainly, Edward Ballantine had one, even as big and hairy as he was. That might have accelerated Gracie's departure.

Instead of going to his appointment with the therapist, a new one named Bob, Frank drove back toward town, went into the Long Haul Saloon and had a glass of draft beer. He used the pay phone to call the receptionist and cancel his appointment. He told her that he had "this thing that's been going around." When he went back outside, squinting into the sunshine, he found the police preparing to tow the station wagon and was impressed by their efficiency in locating the vehicle. He walked over to Powell Street, bought the paper and caught a westbound bus with but three people aboard. Two were girls who seemed to be sisters in their early teens, with similar bangs and anachronistic pageboy haircuts that looked homemade — country girls who averted their eyes, looked at each other and smothered grins by burying their chins on their chests. The other passenger was a trucker with a four-day beard, leather vest and chrome chain leading to his back pocket.

Riding back toward home, with no obligation for guiding the vehicle, sitting with strangers, he savored the anonymity and wondered if the mild euphoria was based on simple movement or avoided responsibility. On the other hand, what was his responsibility? He was eating, he was clothed, he was out of the rain. He was making his way to the edge of the flat earth. He wasn't as driven as the people who, to protect their own product, circulated the rumor that Corona beer contained dog urine, nor the New York soft-drink interests who claimed Tropical Fantasy soda pop was manufactured by the Ku Klux Klan and contained ingredients for sterilizing black males. Air Sununu was grounded. And the art market was in a recession. "Unlike stocks and bonds, many works of art are unique," said the *Wall Street Journal*. And in the wake of a Royal Dutch/Shell Group refinery fire, the price of crude was up while pork bellies settled sharply. Constant busyness out there, no time to think, but the four of us on this bus are lost in our thoughts, our fortunes turned over to the man in gray up front there at the wheel who drives us but never indicates his intentions. Frank allowed his gaze to settle on the driver, feeling despair at the smooth movement of his hands on the wheel.

29

Summer was beginning and Crest would be available in a new dispenser that sucked unused toothpaste back into the container when the customer stopped squeezing. It really looked like it would be a beautiful summer. Queen Elizabeth II planned to attend her first baseball game and might try a hot dog, though it was made clear that she could distance herself from the hot dog, since in British tradition the queen cannot express private views.

Even though his doctors abandoned his building without warning and with a month's rent unpaid, Frank at first avoided thinking about it at all. But when he drove past and found the lights off and a youngster practicing wheel stands on his bicycle in the sprinkler-softened ground, he felt that the clinic needed to be taken care of and carefully rerented and managed. He pined for video games with the blubber-thick crack addicts of the Far North. Those knife-wielding Eskimos would have made short work of these rent-dodging white boys. He was slow to face the implications of the emptying of his clinic. It was, as they say, a highly leveraged transaction in the first place.

If the prospects of failure had crept toward him from the day Gracie left, they were now at a full gallop. He quickly reckoned whether he could slow this down. He was conscious of a kind of force bearing against him. He drove toward home but then stopped in front of his office. He got out and looked around as though checking the address. The wind up the street frightened him. It seemed like the movie wind that blows away footprints.

Two cattle buyers from Nebraska were in his office, smelling of the lots and the diesel fuel of the outbound loads, with snap-button cotton shirts, Copenhagen lumps under their lower lips and Stetson Open Road hats pulled just over the tops of their eyes. The older of the two wore eyeglasses with colorless frames. He had buck teeth and looked like he never smiled in his life, not once. His counterpart had a round chipmunky face and eager brown eyes.

Frank started out by denying everything. He spoke with a booming voice he used only around cattle buyers. His mind quietly ran on in several directions, one of which was that the bank, noticing poor crop-growing conditions and consequent low feeder replacements, was desperately trying to keep themselves, and Frank, from taking a bad blow. The bank must have alerted these boys. Force him to take the loss now and suck it out of his other collateral. The wind was blowing away his footprints.

"What do you mean, I stole those cattle?" Frank boomed.

"I don't mean literally stole," said the older man.

"I paid about what their owners wanted for them," shouted Frank in a voice that would have been unfamiliar to his own mother. "But I sure picked my time and I bought them right. If you want yearlings, that's one thing. But I don't allow folks to discuss valuation with me at that level. Now I know where these are going and I know what feed is. I can background them till hell freezes over, you know that. But I have told you like a white man what I've got to have and the two of you look at me like a pair of Chinamen. You tell me that not only have I stolen these cattle in the first place but that I am not entitled to fair market value for them. Which is: eighty-four cents a hundredweight with a nickel slide at, what, six hundred pounds?"

"Five seventy-five slide," said the younger man.

Frank shrugged. He minced over to another spot in the room in a golden fatigue. Even he could feel a sort of doom. At least these fellows weren't rubbing his nose in it. A pleasant, protective code was in the air.

"Five seventy-five," Frank repeated.

Part of the formula, which comforted everyone in a cattle deal, was to lose deal points without losing face. This price slide really knocked the wind out of Frank, but he didn't let it show. His mind was moving fast. He knew he wanted to be out from under these cattle, but this thing on the slide was a fucking double hernia. He was in too good a mood when he bought them, and lately he had quit tracking them in the marketplace, a loss of interest that could get costly if it went much beyond this. With the doctors out of his building, the bank was surely wondering about him. It was time for the parachute before the USDA issued one of its devastating inventory reports or some bullshit about lighter cattle going on feed, various ruinous allegations about seasonal erosion of fed cattle marketings. He used to track this sort of thing like radar, but with Gracie gone he had begun to notice that often he just didn't know. He didn't really know now, but he had the urge to take flight, to bolt.

"I guess we could write you a deposit," said the man in the glasses.

"No, I don't expect you could," Frank said, trying not to get in a rush, trying not to spill, trying not to let on that this was something he wanted out of now. He wanted to get this thing down to the bone. They had to know he was hurting.

"Mister, we're a good ways from home."

"Yeah," said Frank, "this one I've also heard. You don't dare show your face without ten pots of yearlings. You can't even go up to the house without a thousand head because of what people expect of you in the Sand Hills." He thought this would warm things up toward a closure, and he was right.

The older man said, "They expect quite a little, don't deny that."

"If you're shipping as quick as you say, I need to show this stock paid in full. Get out your checkbook and start writing." Frank was really saying, Don't tell me you can't write me a great big check for these cattle, I know you're plenty stout.

The older man slid his eyes to his companion, moved his chin very slightly. They were going to leave Frank his shred of dignity. It wasn't costing them anything. The round-faced younger man reached under his coat without looking and elevated his checkbook from his shirt pocket.

"I used to know a man who wrote checks for a million dollars," Frank said, "then lit his cigar with them. Can you tell me who I can call to verify the funds?"

Frank was back out of the cattle business again. If the check didn't bounce, he could go to the bank and tell them that although they just lost fifty thousand dollars, it could have been way worse, blah blah blah. No surprise to them. Changing times, like an ice water enema. They sent these guys. They knew there was a loss. It was just a question of how bad a one a man could take. That evening, as he walked home from the office, he made his way over to Endrin Street, to the small storefront building he owned there, the former locale of Gracie's restaurant Amazing Grease, a modest institution she referred to as a "bio-feedbag mechanism." The very recollection of this phrase reminded Frank bitterly of the witless companionship he had enjoyed since. No, that was ungrateful; but it didn't give him anything like the same feeling, to say the least.

He let himself in and sat at one of the six tables. He looked around, taking things in by the light that came through the front window, past the small counter and the doorway to the kitchen. Next to the kitchen doorway, the blackboard still hung and he was able to make out a few words. He got up and went closer, peering at it. It said "Crawfish Etouffée" and it was written in Gracie's hand in that powdery, fragile chalk script. He sat down at the table again and looked out through the window into the declining light of day.

He had a sharp feeling that he had lost his touch, a feeling that once the slide reached a certain speed, it couldn't be stopped until it reached the bottom. He felt a chill. "Gracie," he said aloud, perfectly aware that it was not a great thing to begin talking to yourself. "I think I'm going broke."

30

This feeling stayed with him so long that it was not exactly a surprise when his accountant asked to see him. John Coleman was one of the most reputable accountants in the city and Frank enjoyed going to his office for a sense of the pulse, a cool office with muted traffic sounds below and an undisturbed air. He showed Frank a chair, then swung sideways in his own after asking his secretary to hold his calls. He always gave Frank the feeling that he had set aside more time than they would ever need. "Are you all right?" he asked. John still wore wide, soft ties restrained in the middle by a tie clasp with a little chain.

"I'm fine."

"You haven't been by."

"Not much happening. It takes almost a year to absorb the blow of last year's taxes."

"You're a success, Frank. It's expensive to be a success." Coleman wrapped his hand around his forehead.

"In more ways than one."

"Quite right. It's either too much or too little, isn't it? I mostly see too little. But Frank, you've always had a nice light touch, a nice feel for the situation."

"John, I appreciate the valentines. What's up?"

"I don't know."

"What do you think it is?"

"I think I see problems."

"Are you talking about my cattle deal?"

"Partly."

"I'll tell you what that was. That was a bum deal and we all have them."

"The clinic?"

"That was a case of drawing the line. Where'd those assholes go, anyway?"

John said in the tone of an elementary schoolteacher, "They went elsewhere. They went to the new clinic." He pursed his lips, raised and lowered his eyebrows.

"There's a new clinic?"

"Out near Nineteenth."

"Oh. I thought that was a day care."

"See, Frank? You would have known that before."

"Anyway, we'll fill the building."

"You will."

"I believe so."

John laced his fingers over the top of his head and looked straight at Frank. Frank thought it was a rather artificial gesture. He asked, "What about Gracie?"

"What about her?"

"Hear anything?"

"Nope."

"She divorce you yet?"

"Not yet. I don't really care. I guess she'll get around to it. I couldn't give a shit less."

"I'm just trying to imagine its impact on your finances."

"I guess she'll take me to the cleaners." Frank yawned. "Little coaching from the boyfriend, they'll see a big future. Takes money. Might want to make a hit in Sedona. Oak Creek Canyon. Strong showing in Scottsdale. I'm having trouble with the future. It's my least favorite tense."

"Frank, I'm your accountant. Are you saying you don't care?"

"No, I'm saying my focus is elsewhere." He wanted to get up.

"Do what you can, John. I'm not much help just now."

"Do you have a plan?"

"Yeah, yeah I do."

"What is it?"

"I'm gonna drive around. Take in the sights."

Frank felt very heavy in his chair. John's healthy interest was unbearable. His comfortable office had become a cell. Frank resolved to make a smooth, unjerky exit so that he didn't seem disturbed or alarmed to John, who always had his best interests at heart. It was astonishing how the smoothness could go and leave an alarming jerkiness in its wake; it was astonishing how lightness could become heaviness. He was reduced to longing to be elsewhere. He thought he was within an inch of jumping out the window or breaking into a crippled trot.

Frank feigned a smooth tone. "John, you know about thick and thin. This is thin. We'll be fine." He lifted his hands and dropped them to the desk with a dead-fish sound. It was not really smooth, a geekish gesture actually. It was as if he had emptied a couple of detached hands from a basket.

"I know we will," John said in a warmly formulaic tone that indicated the numbness was catching.

"Well, I gotta go," said Frank, not knowing where to put his gaze.

"It was good of you to come," said John with an averted look of his own. This was torture for both of them.

"So long, John," said Frank. He was sweating bullets.

"So long, Frank. Hope everything goes okay."

"It will, John."

"Good, Frank."

"This is me, then," Frank bleated, "heading on out."

He made it through the door with a sense of rebirth, went down to his car and was suddenly fatigued again and wanted to curl up and sleep in the back seat.

He drove back to his office. Eileen did a cute little number about not knowing who he was. Wanting to fire or kill her, he laughed amiably. He closed his door and gazed at the surface of his desk with its notices and mail. The short-term interest rates that were presumed to stir a recovery weren't doing that, and of course they couldn't save as bad a calculator as Frank was on his cattle. Shell Oil and Chrysler posted losses so huge Frank felt his didn't matter. A human rights group was disturbed by its tour of China, and Canada's ban on tobacco advertising was overturned. Israel declared itself unpersuaded of the need for peace talks. Makes my failed marriage seem like a small thing, Frank thought. We never indulged in penny stock fraud, and unlike the Ceausescus, we never built underground mazes or had group sex with Nazi soldiers. But while I was buzzing around in a stolen car, Cadbury Schweppes enjoyed some modest gains on the strength of North American operations. Charles Keating's exciting new show, a securities fraud trial, would be opening to standing room only in beautiful, easygoing Los Angeles, California. Indeed, Frank's follies notwithstanding, Deadrock, Montana, seemed fairly quiet, with street scenes innocent of arbitrageurs.

The bank agreed to treat the loss as a simple debt, to be repaid over the year at simple interest, one point above prime. At first they wanted to exploit their position on the clinic, and Frank told them where they could put their position. He felt so blue, he looked at the stream of receipts for the mini-storage. It didn't matter that it was chicken feed; it was steady. He began to think about an entirely new life, fueled by mini-storage facilities scattered around in midsize towns in Montana. He thought this new life could be in the Tongass wilderness in Alaska, a de Havilland Otter to get him around the half-drowned climax forest. This perked him right up.

Holly called while Frank, with forensic calm, was trying to clean out the refrigerator — a single olive floating in a quart jar of brine, cheese slipping into decay, a plastic dispenser with old ketchup running down the side, a carton of whipping cream with a vicious odor, a huge wedge of angel food cake folding in on itself in desiccation. He had the willies.

"Will you buy me a little computer? I'll pay you back."

"Sure," he said, and closed the refrigerator door.

"I took some lessons to see if I like it, and I like it."

"Sure, if you think you need it. I guess everyone is using them."

"Thanks, Daddy. Also, I'm in love."

"Oh no, not again. This one got a ring in his nose?"

"Nope. I'm not going to describe this one. You never get the picture from my descriptions. You'll have to see for yourself."

"No hints?"

"I'll give you just one: he's older than you are."

"Older than I am!"

"Mama's meeting him tonight. She's not too happy."

Frank walked around the block, then down toward town, where he thought he glimpsed Smokie coming out of Sage Records. When the wolf was extinct, you could go to Sage records and get a wolf tape. Frank even felt that he would feel less dolorous about his situation if there was a good tape of himself.

It was early Friday evening and Frank walked along the sidewalk in front of his building, formerly the clinic. It was a cool, low, sanitary shape with an even hedge of potentillas along the front and specimens of paper birch and seedless cottonwoods in bark-filled beds. An old man was running a Weed Eater along the base of the building with a fanatical small-engine raving, a monofilament hiss as the weeds tumbled neatly. The building was pale ocher brick and overhead the sky was deepest cobalt, the clouds white, white, white. The street seemed to climb into a magnificent cloudland.

The Weed Eater man watched Frank let himself in with a key. The doors were self-closing and made a soft cushioning sound as they shut off the outside and exposed the silence of the interior. Frank hiked himself up on the receptionists' desk and looked out into the waiting room. Magazines, fireproof curtains, green naugahyde ("unborn naugahyde," Gracie called it) chairs, shin-high tables; no anxiety, nobody waiting to hear what was wrong with them, no news of a baby they weren't supposed to have, no maintenance reports on wearing-out bodies, no heartbroken fat girls waddling back to the doctors' offices carrying their own records. It was a true dead zone, with decorations by Cézanne, Matisse and Charlie Russell. He picked up the phone, also dead. The Rolodex was opened to Bungalow Pharmacy and some wag had written on the desk blotter, "Eat Shit and Die, Motherfucker."

As he walked back through the hall past the receptionists', looking into the denuded lab and trying out the scales, peering at an anatomy poster and, finally, stretching out on an examining table, he asked himself what else you could do with a clinic, for Christ's sake; acoustic tile ceiling, nonglare lights: time for self-examination. Oh, no, wait a minute, not just now. Let's rent the building first.

It was such a nice little cash cow, when you matched up its receipts with its credits and depreciations. In low moments, he had waved the records in Gracie's face while she struggled with Amazing Grease — its moody pothead cook, its recalcitrant swampers and dishwashers, the steam heating system, the hot sauce whiners and check bolters, the food and wine experts, the academics who weren't sure if they were out on the town or ironically observing those who were. Quietly, throughout this mayhem, the cash cow clinic went on. Now? Dead in the water. The boats gathered 'round the carcass; flensing knives drawn . . . Helplessly, Frank had started rotating his equities through his head, noting the pattern of erosion. He was in need of an introspective convalescence. Too much was going wrong and he hadn't taken the time for lamentation or simple worry. Worry took time, and it must have taken energy because it often produced a terrific appetite. Heartbroken chow hounds were familiar figures. But he would have to take that time before things turned to powder.

It was interesting to ponder the meat color of the arm-spread man in the anatomy poster. He looked at all the little parts doctors have to memorize or they don't graduate. This poster was supplied by the makers of Valium and this big muscular fellow with the cutaway face that seemed like a fierce smile didn't look like he was the tranquilizer sort. Yet no one was above tranquility, however it was achieved. Frank imagined that this was Holly's boyfriend, flayed for science, howling at the very movement of air, cradle robbing the baldest crime.

Frank sensed that he was not alone. He listened and heard someone walking in a neighboring office, more than one person. He opened his door an inch or two and watched. In a moment, he made out the forms of men carrying out the scales — the doctors, in jogging spandex. He couldn't quite remember who actually owned the scales and so he hesitated before stepping into the corridor, but finally he did emerge and the doctors hesitated for a second, played it as if they knew he was there all along. Then when they steadied the scales on their shoulders, the weights ran across the bars and clattered to a stop, and Dr. Frame said, "Frank."

"Get 'er all, boys," said Frank. "She'll never be a clinic again."

Dr. Jensen said from beneath his bangs, "We'll only get what belongs to us."

"My lucky day," said Frank. He waved them on in their work and seemed to mean it.

31

He drove five hard hours to Whitefish, where he took a room on the lake. For most of the next day he watched the cat's-paws move across the blue water and listened to a train travel through the woods above the dark, stony beach. He lay out on the dock and watched the cutthroats fin around the pilings. There were numerous smoke-blackened fireworks fragments and Frank, lying face down with his nose between the boards, smelled gunpowder. He loved that smell. He occasionally thought it would be pleasing to shoot several people in particular, accompanied as that would be by this fine smell. A plane went by overhead; no reason he couldn't be in that plane. A boat glided past and there was no reason he couldn't be on that boat.

Just at sundown he paddled a floating cushion out to the middle of the lake, legs dangling in the cool green water, where he met a radiologist, a woman in her forties, also on a cushion, hers with parti-colored seahorses and an inflated pillow. She worked in Kalispell and came here, she said, anytime she found a cancer, to float between earth and sky and to sustain, on her seahorse floatie, a sense of deep time that could accommodate life and death. Frank looked at her long, melancholy face with its thick, seemingly puffy lips, stringy hair and short square brow and said, "You have a hard job."

She took a moment to consider. "Yes I do. My job is to search for something I hope I don't find. That *is* a hard job, mister."

Darkness seemed to be forming, a circle of contracting shadows from the shoreline and faint stars overhead. There wasn't a breath of wind, and when Frank reached out to take the tip of the radiologist's finger, he was able to draw her raft to him with an ounce of pressure. Her face was now an inch away and they both moved imperceptibly toward each other to kiss. Her mouth was open and he tasted a mentholated cough drop. He slipped his hand a small distance inside the top of her bathing suit and felt a hard nipple. He opened his eyes and thought he could make out trembling water around her raft. The bottom of her bathing suit was drawn across the points of her hips and a flat stomach.

Very quietly, Frank moved to board the radiologist's raft, a delicate matter that worked, right up to the point that it didn't work; and with a sudden rotary motion the radiologist shot out of sight. "Hey!" Frank shouted impulsively, and trod water between the plunging shapes of the floaties. He felt the radiologist's head under the arch of his foot and struggled to get a hold of her. She came up spraying water from her mouth and with a minimum of floundering she got onto her raft again, on her stomach, and began to paddle toward shore. Frank followed her.

"What's your *prob*lem?" she said when he overtook her.

"Same problem as everybody else."

"Oh, this'll be good," she said. "What is it?"

"I'm just trying to get some meaning in my life." Frank felt he was leaping from line to line.

"Ha, ha."

They walked together along the railroad track in the last light. There was enough curve in the lakeside route that the rails were always disappearing on the geometry of creosote sleepers just ahead in the woods. Honeysuckle grew wild down the steep banks where lake water glimmered through the trunks of tall old pines. Elise, that was her name, chatted along amiably and was very good at naming the birds they saw — the chipping sparrows, the yellowthroats, the kinglets. There was something about the way she touched her fingertip to the droplets of resin on the pine bark that made Frank think, I may be headed for a world of poontang.

In Frank's room, she peered examiningly at his cock. "The baleful instrument of procreation. Ooh," she said, squeezing hard, "I can tell I shouldn't have said that."

"Don't worry about it."

"Are you having a nice time?" she asked.

"Like my grandpa used to say, 'If this ain't it, you can mail mine.' "

They kissed and she slipped a cough drop from her mouth into his; it was like a cool breeze. He slid down the length of her and, spanning the backs of her knees with his hands, licked deep into her. She moaned, then jumped out of bed and ran around the furniture. "That cough drop has set me on fire!" she hollered, and went into the bathroom. He heard her running the water and tried to decide what to do with the cough drop. Finally, he spit it down the wall behind the bed. He tried to blot his tongue on the wallpaper. She came back in with a washcloth clamped to her crotch, got into bed and sent the cloth back toward the bathroom with a kind of hook shot.

"Just quit pussyfooting around," she said, "and stick it in."

She had a long, firm body that she must have worked hard to keep in such shape, and she flung it around with great confidence in its appearance. Frank hadn't made such buoyant love in memory. He got happier and happier until he wondered briefly if her energy was connected by some means to having found a cancer that day. He felt exultant and did not consider asking about it.

Then, when they were through, he did think about that. Lying there, he must have been looking off and she caught it, scrutinizing him. The room was silent. She leaned across him, picked up the phone and dialed. After a moment, she spoke. She just said, "Hi." Then the other person spoke. Then she said, "Sorry, I couldn't make it," and hung up. It was out of the question to ask who was on the other end; something in the flat way she spoke made Frank know that she was supposed to have been fucking this other person and not over here at the lake fucking him.

It was late and the only thing they could get was the weather channel. Elise was smart and it was fun to talk to her about the possibilities of weather. There was a stalled-out high where they were and they could see it on the national weather map. Elise knew where it was going to go when it began to move; it was headed for the Dakotas. She stood naked beside the television set and pointed to where it was going. Their drought was over but it looked like others' had just begun. She came back to bed. Frank could see where the heat spread west from Bullhead City, Arizona, then hit a kind of Pacific wall and stalled, rising slowly up the coast of California . . . She had her mouth on him now and the antics of the weatherman with his pointer didn't make any sense at all.

When they'd finished, Frank turned the weather off and got back into bed. They talked awhile about property. Frank said housing starts were way up in his part of the state. "The contractors who hung in during the eighties are really booked. Everybody's working. We're all trying to woo these new businesses, but our unemployment rates are so low and our warehouses so full, we know we're askew on their shopping lists. I've got a little building I rent as a clinic-slash-boutique to four doctors."

"Oh, that's great."

"Yeah."

"I'm just there at the Valley Hospital. It's okay. I don't pack anything home with me. I'm still in my hippie mode, down deep."

"Were you a hippie?" he asked.

"Yup."

"Huh, so was I."

"I mean, I was pretty motivated compared to some of them, but I consider myself an old hippie. What do you think I'm doing here?"

"People were doing this before the hippies."

"Not with the same spirit," said Elise. "I was hitchhiking around Europe, and in Italy they called us *I amici di Liverpool*, because they thought all the hippies came from Liverpool, kind of a hangover from the Beatles era."

"I guess Italians get the news a little late."

"They just get it when they want it . . ." She seemed to drift off and then spoke again. "What's the policy on your toothbrush?"

"You can use it."

"Mm." He could feel her drift off, her back to him. He put his arms around her and thought about considering the weather with someone else . . . thundershowers in Indiana . . . lake effect . . . Then he thought, To be living.

He woke up in the dark. He was alone. That was probably why he woke up. The bathroom light was on. He made out a knee beyond the lighted doorway with the corner of a newspaper over it. He heard a deep, solid fart. He remembered a map-reading scene in a movie about the Civil War, when the noise of cannon fire was muted so you could hear the dialogue of strategy.

She sensed something. "Are you awake?"

"Just."

"Is this your *Journal*?"

"Yup."

"Have you read it?"

"No, I haven't."

"It says, 'Natural gas is the fuel of the future.' "

"I see."

"It's a joke," Elise said. "I know you were awake when I made that little noise."

"I'm afraid I was."

" 'The 1990s were supposed to bring a golden era for the gas industry. Repeated threats of oil shortages, ever-toughening pollution laws and federal tax credits refunding up to seventy percent of exploration costs seemed to guarantee that gas would become the dominant fossil fuel.' What do you think?"

"I don't have a strong feeling about this one way or the other."

"Yet you lay there like a secretive little mouse because I cut one lousy fart in the privacy of a motel bathroom."

"I wasn't being secretive. I was asleep."

Elise came back to bed in a flood of warmth and immediately cuddled. "You married?"

"Separated."

"Since when, since breakfast?"

"Long time. How about you?"

"Yup, nice husband, two nice kids, boys."

"So, what's this all about?"

"I belong to a dick-of-the-month club."

"Seriously."

"How should I know? You paddle out to the middle of a northern Montana lake to be alone and a decent-looking guy paddles out and rolls your raft. There's nobody else out there. It's determinism, it's fate. Fate says: Put out, Elise. So, Elise puts out. You seemed to welcome the fate of Elise and its atmosphere of festivity. You seemed to salute the cheating heart of Elise."

"This is an unusual thing for you?"

"Not particularly."

"Was that your husband on the phone?"

"Nope."

"What about the cancer?"

"That was pretty much true. I confess that it's also sort of an unimpeachable excuse. But don't you think that most personal freedom is built on other people's misfortune?"

"Good grief."

"I never look at a set of x-rays without being reminded how short life is. Lust follows. It's like living in a city under siege. And here's another weird thought: I'd hate to ever have to x-ray someone I've had sex with."

A few minutes later, Frank let his eyes close. What an adorable woman, he thought, a little crush forming; so full of life and now asleep with an untroubled conscience. Her peace was catching and he was soon falling asleep with a feeling that was a lot like love.

In the morning, they got doughnuts and coffee from a gas station–convenience store. The sky was clear except for a huge white thunderhead to the west that caught a pink-orange effulgence from the morning sun. Elise slid into her yellow Jeep Cherokee. Traffic headed toward Flathead streamed past behind her.

She nodded, smiled as if to say "yes" or "yep" or "uh-huh" and pulled into traffic. He knew she loved him too.

He finished his coffee and went back to the motel to check out. He felt a goofy pride to see the thrashed and discomposed bed. "Good job, Frank," he said aloud, and climbed into the shower, letting the needles of hot water drive into his revitalized flesh. Then he shaved. Frank loved to shave. It was a daily challenge to get the little groove in his upper lip and to make the sideburns come out even. He had to stretch the skin of his neck to shave it smoothly, as it no longer stayed taut on its own. What difference does it make if my flesh is firm, he thought smugly, if they're going to put out like that anyway? That simple fiesta of venery has restored me. I'm like the happy duck that spots the decoys.

32

He checked out and drove south toward Missoula, where he fancied the prospect of running into Gracie while he was detumescent, indifferent, superficially inquiring, amiable. The only thing new he had to talk about was whether or not he had lost his touch, and he didn't expect to admit or say that.

There was a fair amount of traffic on 93. Summertime seemed to reveal the ranches along that route in all their nakedness: junk-filled yards, small corrals with a couple of steers or sheep in them, modest flower boxes, yards that seemed meant only for their occupants and not the careering tourists of 93. Huckleberry stands appeared between Whitefish and Kalispell, then, as he started down the fjord-like shores of Flathead Lake, stands selling the incomparable Flathead cherries, cars nosing out of steep lakeside driveways to peek onto the highway. A condominium rose next to its white reflection on the black, clean surface of the lake.

Frank pulled over and bought a couple of pounds of cherries and placed them on the seat next to him. He rolled the window down and spit the pits out as he drove until the hot buffeting wind made him feel deaf on that side. He rolled the window up and began spitting the pits onto the dashboard. He turned on the radio and listened to an old song called "Big John": everybody falls down a mine shaft; nobody can get them out because of something too big to pry; Big John comes along and pries everybody loose but ends up getting stuck himself; end of Big John. Frank guessed it was a story of what can happen to those on the top of the food chain.

On to an oldies station and the joy of finding Bob Dylan: "You've got a lot of nerve to say you are my friend." No one compares with this guy, thought Frank. I feel sorry for the young people of today with their stupid fucking tuneless horseshit; that may be a generational judgment but I seriously doubt it. Frank paused in his thinking, then realized he was suiting up for his arrival at Missoula. In a hurricane of logging trucks, he heard, out of a hole in the sky, the voice of Sam Cooke: "But I do know that I love you." Frank began to sweat. "And I know that if you love me too, what a wonderful world this would be." He turned off the radio, looked into the oncoming chrome grille of a White Freightliner and shouted, "My empire is falling!" Then he twisted the rearview mirror down so that he could study his own expressions. He now permitted himself to think about Gracie. He knew that she might be in Missoula and he wanted to be ready but he didn't know how. He was nervous.

All the little questions. Will they lose interest when you go broke? Sam Cooke: "Give me water, my work is so hard." What work? Tough to believe both Sam Cooke and Otis Redding are dead. Heading for a white world: polo shirts, imported beer. The back nine. Lawn care. Etiquette. Epstein-Barr. Then he thought with disturbance about trout fishing. Blacks didn't seem to care about that. They liked fishing off bridges, though. It was hard to picture Otis Redding and Sam Cooke fishing off a bridge. Maybe they did before they were famous.

Holly's apartment was on a small side street behind the university, about three blocks from the Clark Fork River. Frank first stopped at the river and watched it rush through town. There were some small trout dimpling along a speeding current seam about ten feet below traffic. Because of the previous night, Frank felt it was going to be out of the question to develop a truly huffy tone. But he meant to do his best. There were several cars parked in front: Holly's green Civic, a well-kept old tan Mercedes 190SL and a National rental car with Utah plates. Next door, a pretty college girl was hanging out wet towels while a Louis Armstrong solo played its scratchy uproar from the windowsill. In the space between houses a steep hillside angled away, green and dotted with small white stones. Frank could smell the nearby paper mill and just make out the iron red top of a crane moving beyond the roofs of buildings. He felt faintly sick to his stomach.

The door to Holly's apartment opened and instead of Holly, there was Gracie. That's what he was afraid would happen. Frank was partway out of his car, still cushioned by the sounds of the radio as well as by the accidental moods of a neighborhood of temporary college housing; but it nearly stopped his heart, a feeling so intense it resembled fear more than anything else. He felt as if his brain were photographing everything in an exhausting superrealism that he couldn't absorb. He was experiencing flu-like symptoms.

"Would it be better if I left?"

"As you wish, Gracie." He could scarcely believe the bland tone of his voice.

"As I wish?"

"As you wish."

"Okay, I'll stay."

For the second time in a weekend, Frank thought he had found himself in hailing distance of dramatic poontang. If nothing else, such a puerile thought was heartening in the face of his shakiness. He was swept under by self-contempt. He didn't even have time to imagine who was the wronged party or, still worse, account for the water over the dam. He feared old rooted love more than anything else, blunt and tragic, like horrible news from the doctor.

"Gracie, how are you?" he asked, now at the door.

"I'm fine, Frank, and yourself?"

Bad English, thought Frank, but said, "I'm fine. Holly here?" Gracie sort of smelled his little thought and squinted before speaking. Her squint was perfect, eternal.

"Yes she is, Frank. And she's with . . . Lane."

"Who is Lane?" Frank asked, titrating just a bit of conspiratorial intimacy into his conversation. She stayed rigid. It didn't appear she wanted much to do with him. He was a jerk.

"Lane is Holly's gentleman friend. Shall we?" She backed away from the narrow screen door to let Frank into the hallway. Frank stepped in and then Gracie followed, a panicky situation in a small spot. There was a brass holder for umbrellas, to remind Frank that he was in a rainy area. Beyond a pair of divided-pane glass doors was the old parlor of the house, which Holly had furnished with junk shop furniture, including a folding card table, a cream-colored La-Z-Boy recliner, a television set with its futuristic insides exposed, cinderblock-and-board bookcases and a large public drinking fountain. On one wall was a poster so out of keeping that it startled Frank. It showed the bomber *Enola Gay* with the mushroom cloud over Hiroshima behind it, and underneath the legend "It's Miller Time." There was a miscellany of small, uncomfortable metal chairs in one of which, gesticulating feverishly, sat Holly, and in another a gaunt figure with a shock of gray curls, wearing a three-piece suit and lace-up cowboy packer boots, Lane Lawlor. He dressed the same way Frank's grandfather had, only that was sixty years ago and the old fart had had a Maxwell touring car. Who was this costumed geezer courting his daughter? Frank wondered.

As he held out his paw, Lane Lawlor actually said to Frank, "Put 'er there."

"Daddy," said Holly, "this is Lane Lawlor." She smoothed the front of her dress and shrugged up one shoulder. She shifted her look to Frank and said, "And Mama, she's met."

Gracie came in from behind and almost secretively found herself a chair. Everybody looked over at her and she reexplained, "We've met."

Frank gazed at Gracie. Love had turned to rage. It came out in some rather sharp questioning of Lane.

"Where you from, Lane?"

"I'm from Fort Benton," he said, "right where she all began."

"Right where what all began?"

"The history of Montana, the fur trade and so on."

"Oh, the *white* history of Montana." This wasn't quite fair, as it suggested subtextually that Frank spent a good bit of his time fighting for the rights of Indians. He really meant Otis Redding. "What's your line of work?"

"Water."

"A swimmer?"

"I'm an attorney. My practice is confined to water issues — apportionment, adjudication, priority and so on."

"You've been at it several summers, I take it," said Frank, allowing his eyes to drift to the gray curls.

"Sure," said Lane, ready to take him on, which seemed to be looming.

Holly made a presentational gesture with both hands toward her mother. Her interest in Lane had made her into a bit of a simpleton. She had an expression of appalling devotion, a Nancy Reagan gaze directed at the side of his head. "Well, what do you think?" Holly asked.

"She looks well," said Frank. He wasn't controlling his projected tone very well. He was usually better at this. Either more was at stake or the background of his slipping business was seeping in. He tried it again. "She looks well." This time it sounded as if he were saying she didn't look well at all or was actually ugly.

"You look well too," said Gracie.

"Thank you. Anytime."

"Oooh," said Gracie, and this almost got away from them. Holly was frozen. Frank noticed that Gracie was angry.

"You want to hear how we met?" Holly asked.

"Yuh," said Frank. "How?"

"At a rally for We, Montana."

"I'm terribly sorry, darling," said Gracie, "but your father and I don't know what that is."

Despite his pleasure at Gracie's figure of speech, Frank said grimly, "I know what it is." We, Montana was an organization of citizens who hoped to keep any water from leaving the state, through the erection of dams and diversions. They had some reputed connection with the Posse Comitatus as well as the radical tax protesters of the Dakotas. They spoke to the press sardonically about their interest in "white water issues," by which they meant water for white people. Frank especially remembered their Western Family archetypes: the John Wayne male and his bellicose, gun-toting woman, their cold-eyed, towheaded children.

"Then we started going to the pistol range together," Holly said.

"Why were you going to the pistol range, darling?" asked Gracie.

"To be able to defend myself," said Holly flatly. "I shoot two hundred rounds a week."

"I never thought of you as being in danger," said Frank.

"You're not in danger," said Holly, "until you develop a few convictions. I found that out. There are some very peculiar out-of-staters on campus that give you the feeling that happiness is a warm gun."

"I guess that's why we've been so safe," said Gracie to Frank. She seemed lost by this new Holly. Frank was numb.

"I hope you'll realize with what love I say this," Holly said. "Your generation, especially with your own out-of-state experiences, has been pretty much bent on self-discovery. Something very different happens when standards enter into it."

Frank missed something here. "What are out-of-state experiences, darling?"

Holly laughed. "Experiences outside of Montana!"

"Uh-*huh*. Just what it sounds like."

Gracie turned slowly toward Lane. "Lane, do we have you to thank for this?"

"I'm not sure what 'this' is, but probably you have Holly to thank."

"Mom, you're not even *from* here!"

"Where are you from, Mrs. Copenhaver?" Lane asked quietly.

"Louisiana."

"Louisiana," mused Lane. "I've often heard how colorful it is."

"Don't be a wise guy," said Gracie. "It's a great place." Lane bobbed his head agreeably. "You can get a soft-shell po' boy there which sets it apart in my eyes."

"I've heard a good deal about your organization, Lane," said Frank. "What do you hope to accomplish? Elect some people?"

"First of all, it's not *my* organization. We see ourselves equally vested in Montana. We don't want to elect anybody. We simply wish to provide an atmosphere of accountability throughout the state."

"Who's trying to hide the water . . ."

"Exactly. That's the magnetic issue which collects all the other iron filings. We take the position that no water leaves the state, period. That tells you all you need to know. It tells you who the tree huggers are, the wolf recovery sleazos, the grizzly kissers, the trout pinkos —" Frank glanced over to Holly to see if he had become a trout pinko. She looked straight back at him, through him.

"Uh, Lane. Some of the state is twelve thousand feet high and, uh, water goes downhill, as I remember. Seems like some of it's going to leave the state."

"Not if you impound it."

"Not if you impound it . . ."

"Exactly."

"But then all the streams and rivers would, would be impoundments, all the beautiful streams and rivers."

Holly and Lane chanted at him, trying to help him see the light: "There's no such thing as a free lunch!" This phrase must have held some philosophical importance to them.

"I met one of the wolf enthusiasts," Frank said noncommittally.

"Those people — the birds, bees, wolf and buffalo people — need to know that Montana is not a zoo," said Lane. He got up, went to the kitchen and came back with a plate of little reddish brown discs. It was elk jerky that he had made himself. He passed the plate around.

"I start every session of the legislature passing out jerky to my fellow Republicans."

"We're Democrats," said Gracie. "What do you give Democrats?"

"A piece of my mind — no, just kidding. I try to give them a sense of our ideology. Liberals think a victimology is an ideology — just line up victims and the policy will dictate itself. T'ain't so, McGee. There's a way of looking at this world and this country and, more importantly, this state that begins with saddle leather and distance, unsolved distance. And water. American government is run on the squeaking wheel getting the grease. In Montana, we not only don't need grease, we don't need the wheel. We need water, *and we're going to keep every drop that's ours.*"

Frank was looking down at his disc of jerky, held between thumb and forefinger. He was trying to sink his nail into it while wondering what sort of family or town could produce a dipshit like this. Lane had the gleaming true-believer tone of a James Watt, but with his own beetling menace. It was the knowledge that people like this existed that made Frank really fear that he was losing some advantage in business. Given that Lane was dating Holly, Frank felt that if this were an Arab nation and he, Frank, were a middling sort of emir, he would go on ahead and have Lane beheaded. Maybe arrange to have the head fall into a bag so that Holly wouldn't be traumatized. Have the headless corpse float out to sea after dark; try to do it in a thoughtful way. Maybe have an orchestra. So long, head.

Frank excused himself to use the bathroom, which was at the end of a corridor behind the steep stairwell. Lane followed him back there. Frank was surprised.

"I'm going to the bathroom," he said.

"Just a quick word with you," said Lane.

Frank stopped. "What is it?"

"Well?"

"Well what?"

"What do you think?"

"About what, Lane?"

"About me and Holly?"

"As a couple?"

"As a couple."

"How old are you?"

"Fifty-three."

"You're several decades older than Holly, Lane. I think that's a bit extreme."

"Don't get yourself off the hook with that, Frank. What do you *actually* think?"

Frank appraised him for a moment, feeling challenged. "It's not so much a matter of thinking, Lane. It's more a feeling."

"A feeling of what?"

"Of being sick to my stomach."

Lane smiled evenly and said, "Fair enough."

Frank went into the bathroom and closed the door, bouncing a douche bag that hung from a hook there. It looked like some tired thing from a yard sale. There were small porcelain fragments of an angel fastened to the wall, children's towels with cowboy and Indian scenes on them, a sunburst on the toilet seat and a claw-foot tub. He realized that he didn't need to use the bathroom and that the reflexive trip down the hallway to its door was out of hope that Gracie would follow for a heart-to-heart talk, bandied remarks or whispers of assignation. He was eager to tell her that he thought he had a real chance of going broke, but he didn't want Lane or Holly to hear. He desperately wanted her to know that he might fail. Nevertheless, his short absence produced a change. When he got back to the living room, Gracie, Holly and Lane were standing. Holly had a class and Lane had to get back to the office. Frank heard each of these two before letting his eyes drift to Gracie. She was looking at him.

"I'm available for lunch," she said, "if you are."

Frank just smiled and offered a poor joke at departure. "I look forward to seeing you again," he said to Lane, adding, "Don't forget your annual physical."

The women looked over at him in barely concealed astonishment. This was beyond the pale, even for Gracie.

"And you," said Lane levelly.

"My family's up and grown," said Frank.

"Yippee," said Lane. "By the way, I'll be down in your town lecturing. You ought to come and see me, see my constituents, before your mind closes completely."

"Boys, boys, boys," said Gracie.

Lane stood without motion, made even taller by the lace-up boots that stuck out incongruously from the cuffless bottoms of his suit pants. Don't want to get fooled by this arch-bumpkin livery, Frank thought; guy like that'd run a Dun and Bradstreet on you in a minute. Instead, he looked at his daughter, who had become a bit corn-fed, one of the few predictable effects of zealotry. As soon as he could get to a phone, he meant to offer her a trip around the world. Any horizon-broadening at all would reduce this Lane to a dot. Furthermore, he suspected it would be Gracie's view that Lane was the sort of thing to be expected when Frank was functioning as a solo parent. If he could get her to a restaurant, he would disabuse her of that, big time.

They saw Lane to his pickup truck. Holly kissed her fingertips and reached through the window to touch Lane's liver lips. Frank watched him bat his eyes in mock collusion; it was unbearable. Lane wound a gray curl around his forefinger and said to her, "So long, pard," then nodded curtly to Frank and Gracie.

"Get us a table at the Red Lion and I'll be along in just a minute," Gracie said.

"Okay," Frank said. He turned to Holly and squeezed her. "Bye, pet." The embrace had become awkward. Holly was unresponsive.

33

He drove several blocks to the restaurant and went into the air-conditioned semi-darkness. He bought the newspaper from a stand next to the cigarette machine and got a table overlooking the Clark Fork River. The staff far outnumbered the customers. He ordered a Löwenbrau and leaned up against the plate glass window with his paper, trying not to think about family matters at all. He turned to soybeans in the Chicago Board of Trade report, then remembered you couldn't really tell where things stood, as it would be another month until their moisture requirements peaked. And here was real live news of the drought elsewhere: corn stockpiles were the lowest they'd been in eight years, with estimates lowered by a hundred million bushels. He danced through his favorites: barley, flax seed, feeder cattle, orange juice, cotton, heating oil — no surprises, no atmosphere of opportunity. Maybe because he wouldn't know an opportunity if he saw one.

Throughout the business world, there was a desire for clout. Clout was what Frank would want if Lane tried to investigate his financial health. Clout would prevent his bank from cooperating with Lane or any other lawyer. Cloutlessness sent politicians to pollsters. Frank wanted clout. Clout enabled you to fly your daughter around the world. Without clout, you grabbed your ankles and waited for the big boys to shred your undies. Frank's curiosity about clout had sent him staring into the windows of neighbors to see what they were doing with what clout they had on the off hours. It seemed quite proper to seek information in a covert way — what the police called a fishing expedition.

A negligible domestic instant like meeting Lane made Frank want to start a riot, a civil disturbance that would ventilate his own malaise and sense of peril. Frank had felt for years that the new man in him was prepared for a debut, but it was locked in a lingering postponement. A galoot was after his baby.

"I'm devastated by this clunker," Gracie said, as if reading his mind. She had pulled her coat off her shoulders and was standing next to the table.

He stared at her and attempted to think. "As who is not?"

This was not conciliatory. Frank had made the least of the opening. He just wanted to be in motion, not caught flat-footed, and he came up with something not so nice. But he jumped up to hold Gracie's chair. She made a wry smile and sat down. He glanced at the top of her dear little head, then took his seat in despair. He could just make out the soup of the day on a chalkboard: cream of broccoli. His life reeled past, continuously taxiing, rarely airborne. When the waitress arrived, they vied to order drinks, Absolut vodka and grapefruit juice for both, pharmaceutically powerful choices.

"For some reason," Gracie drawled, as though they'd been talking all along, "I don't think we're the quality of people who can finish some long-term thing like raising a child. I should have known that what we thought we'd done with Holly would turn out to be an illusion. That cluck is far from what I had in mind for her."

"Your great anthem was, Never give up your illusions."

"There's illusions and there's illusions."

"Well, Holly's illusion is that this water-hoarding bozo is a romantic figure."

It was hard to be indignant about this. He didn't really know where Gracie had been and the look of defiance he had expected wasn't there. Gracie was mostly a practical person and she looked as sad as it was practical to be. The biggest thing that they had once had together had been themselves — not some third thing, not a business or a child or even a view of the future, but just this enveloping situation that had lasted a long time — had lasted, in fact, right up to the very second that it didn't. And then it was truly gone.

"How did you get here?"

"I drove. Frank, do you know what? I don't think I can sit in this depressing place long enough to get something to eat. Would you mind terribly if we went someplace else?"

"No, not at all. I — not at all."

"Maybe we can get the girl to put our drinks in to-go glasses. Or I'll tell you what, we'll just gulp them and split."

"I'm not hungry anyway."

"Neither am I."

They drove to a small park with modest houses around its sides, a concrete tennis court without a net, a swing set and a steel flagpole. There was a light overcast sky and it was pleasantly cool. The only people in the park were those crossing it to go elsewhere, including an old woman making agonizing progress on a cane. Sitting on one of the wooden benches, Frank looked around and thought how easy it was to feel sunk into one of these spots where the world goes by. He thought of the doctors decamping from his clinic, now a pathetic shell, and the bath he took on the yearlings, the sort of *faux pas* he once never made. You could sit in this park and in a couple of months get a warm sweater and sit in it some more and feel yourself either immersed in the small human routines of a town or perched on a cooling planet hurtling through time and space. It was dealer's choice.

He couldn't understand sitting next to Gracie. Either this was an illusion or she had never gone, never really gone; or if she had gone, she would be right back; or, how was this, she had gone but she'd *had* to go and then would be back. It was satisfying to think in little crazy units like this, kind of absorbing to avoid sweeping concepts. Gracie was there, then went forth, then returned. She was following her star! He was stuck in the mud. She was on a high wire. He was sucking wind. Other times, it was his star and her mud. Other times, for each of them, it must have been like leaving the house to go to work while the old dog watched from the lawn and wondered why he didn't get to go along. When he had been young he barked; when he was old he just watched; and then he was dead and gone.

And Frank remembered how poorly he had dealt with solitude — well to remember that, because he was going back to it — how he had slunk around like a coyote, encountering other lonely prowlers, joyless, glancing occasions, losing ground with every event in a steady regression. What was the name of that girl he met at Hour Photo? Picking up her nephew's school pictures? Gone. He covered Gracie's hand with his. She removed her hand and laughed. Out the window went his dream of mystery poontang.

"What are you laughing at?" Frank asked, wondering if she could read his mind.

"Remember when Holly was little, she used to drink out of the hummingbird feeders?"

"Yeah."

"I was just remembering."

"Well, it takes a big dog to weigh a ton."

"Sure enough?"

"It seems funny, though."

"What's that?"

"The way things have flown by."

"Flown by," said Gracie. "They've flown by, all right."

"I think once I get over being bitter, I'll feel we had a pretty good run at it."

"I'm already at that point. I never was bitter."

"What did you have to be bitter about?"

"Oh, Frank, let's not start."

"Okay." He was inches from an unproductive fugue state, the very trees in the park darkening as though in an eclipse. He looked around at the beaten paths in the grass, a lot of anonymous human use. He wished they were living together now in a raw Sunbelt subdivision with no history whatever.

"I feel kind of guilty about this," Gracie said. "I promised that this trip would be highly focused on Holly's situation."

"I don't follow."

"I wasn't anxious for any renewal of intimacy."

"Is that what you think I have in mind?" No sense in trying to fool her, he thought. "I imagine you're pretty loyal to Ed . . ."

"It's not that. He's been no solution to my problems. But his problems may be more serious than mine and I can't push him off the brink, which is where I think he is currently living."

"In what way?" Frank asked, his heart leaping. What did he hope for, cancer? bankruptcy? AIDS?

"I don't want to get into it. He's still married too."

"Leave him — ?"

"God, just look at you!"

"I can't conceal everything, Gracie."

"What's the difference, Frank? You couldn't get rid of me quick enough, a regular hanging judge. Anyway, I'm going to need to get a few things out of the house," she said.

How was this to be understood? "To be continued"? She was certainly a bit agitated. "Okay," said Frank boldly, "so you're out of this relationship at some level and it's, what, reconnaissance time?"

"Fuck you, Frank."

"Uh-*huh*."

"I hate it when you look so triumphant. What a disgusting man you are, Frank. Yes, disgusting."

"You act like you lost match point and that's not at all the way I'm viewing this, Gracie, honestly it's not."

"You'd just like to find some alpha male one-liner for the coarseness and lust that drove me from my home. I know your every thought, you rotten shit."

Alpha male, that was a good one. Is that why he stared down from his bedroom window at the college couple as they waited for a summer shower to pass, jerking off into his curtain? Is that what an alpha male does? Frank knew perfectly well he was sinking into a pure shadow state as several of his dreams turned to dust.

One was showing a faint glow of light, but mostly it was a broad flowering of shadow.

"Anyway," Gracie said, "I thought this was about Holly."

"It is."

"I've been thinking."

"And?"

"It's none of our business."

"Gracie, I think that's an abdication. *No más abdicación.*"

"Yes, I suppose it is. But I think that's what you do. Abdicate. In fact, I'm going to get into it, on several fronts. I'm going to set an abdication track record."

"I tried that. They're stripping me of my belongings."

"This must be a ball buster for you, champ."

"Not as much as you might think. As discussed, your comprehension of me was never as deep as you thought."

"Give me a call the day you learn to accept failure," she said. "I'm in the book."

She looked down into the wilderness of her purse, found some Carmex and slicked it onto her lips. She reflexively glanced at him to see if he saw her finger touch her lips, and then averted her eyes sternly. "There's a tone, Frank, almost like dictating a letter. It's unbearable."

"They're stripping me of my belongings. Tone's the first to go. Plus, finding Holly infatuated with the Lord Haw-Haw of the northern Rockies —"

"Let's not make it worse than it is."

"Let's not make it worse than it is!"

A youth with a punk haircut, riding a mountain bike one-handed and drinking an orange soda with the other, shot past them a few inches from their toes and Frank told him to slow down. The youth wheeled around in a big circle, came back at higher speed, shaking the soda can, and hosed Frank in the face with it as he surged past. Frank jumped up in pursuit but it was hopeless. When he turned back to the park bench, his face and hair sticky and wet, Gracie was doubled over with laughter.

Frank wiped his face on his sleeve and sat down. He decided

not to discuss it. He indulged a little reverie wherein he ran down the boy on the bike, shoved his head through the spokes of his front wheel, then kicked him in the ass at his leisure. Frank smiled to think that he was making less of a distinction these days between what he imagined happening and what actually happened. His carefree jerking off had come to seem advantageous compared to the time-consuming alternatives. But it was laziness, really, or weariness, a collapse of the casual utopianism of his earlier days in which ecstasy was but a hop, skip and jump away.

He watched a young woman in bombacha pants teaching her dog to chase a Frisbee, several robins stretching worms under a sprinkler. An extremely small Asian woman in her sixties set up an easel that faced the dun-colored hills behind the neighborhoods. He felt Gracie next to him. A robust and amiable erection tortured his chinos into an asymmetrical tent.

"My God, what a problem I've got," he said, accepting that it was inconcealable. Gracie gazed around, pretending to search for the object of his enthusiasm.

"You're all boy, Frank."

"Thanks, Grace. Now why don't you come on home. The coffee pot's on. I've hobbled the old goat —"

"And what? We could make some feta cheese? I'm not following. The other thing is, an indecent-exposure rap would go a long way in weakening your case against Lord Haw-Haw."

Frank thought for a moment. "I have a lot of faith in Holly. She'll go through this thing and right out the other side."

"I hope so. I also suspect it as something we're using for our own purposes."

"Exactly."

Here was another ruse, the candid discussion, elevating essentials to a cooler altitude, often accompanied by bad acting and owlish solemnity. It was an ungainly moment. Frank wanted to fall upon his wife like a Saracen.

Just then, Gracie began to sob. Frank said, "Oh, dear, what's this," and had no idea what to do. With any slip of control he was going to join in, but he held on and stared off into nowhere to contain himself, and felt sunk. His tear ducts ached under his eyes and a film dropped suddenly over the park as though the credits were about to run on the last scene. At that moment, the boy on the mountain bike shot past once more. Frank elevated his over-wrought face in the boy's direction in time to receive another blast of orange soda, and the can, which bounced off his head.

Frank jumped up and began to race after the boy, who was riding on the rear wheel only and pulling away. He followed him out of the park and into traffic. The boy darted between oncoming cars to an intermittent song of horns, his green shirt shrinking, then wheeled to the right down a side street. Frank himself went to the right and walked a block and a half to an alley, then up it a short distance, where he climbed into a garbage pail and waited, surrounded by a deep vegetable stink, trying to reconcile his desire to kill the boy with his desire to be close to Gracie. He was close to retching but confident the boy would circle back this way for one more look. He meant to explode from the can into the boy's face and do what he had to do. While he waited, he tried to remember what it was costing to hedge yearling cattle. No one else was doing that, but it was probably a good and original idea for this part of the world. You could certainly do it and the bank would help. Well, maybe not his chickenshit bank.

Gracie wasn't going to wait around indefinitely. He was beginning to cool down. He thought of Gracie's tears and he wanted to see her now. He stood up in the garbage pail and found himself facing a screaming old woman in her bathrobe. The woman dropped the black plastic bag she was carrying and scurried into a door that opened onto the alley, yelling "Police!" in what Frank took to be an uneducated accent because she paused too emphatically between the syllables. He looked up to see the boy do a sliding U-turn on his bicycle and head out the opposite way.

Frank made a rapid trudge to the street, where he tried to blend in yet knock the loose garbage from his clothes. He crossed the park from another angle, but their bench — he could tell it was theirs because he could line up the swings and the flagpole — was empty. Now, from a distance, he could see the boy leading two foot policemen his way. There was no time to think; he just had to run forward until he was out of the open space of the park, into an intimate blue-collar neighborhood, through back yards and under clotheslines, knocking a bird feeder out of his way in a spray of seeds, frantically navigating his way to Holly's house, bursting through her front door and virtually into the arms of Lane Lawlor. Frank was acutely conscious of smelling like sweat and garbage. "Hello again," he gasped, tilting his head and smiling, a gruesome shot at charm, ungainly in the extreme.

Lane watched him for a moment before speaking. "Let me build you a drink," he said, making a point of forcing a smile, like pressing his own weight. "I came back to use Holly's phone." He paused, as though there was no telling what to expect from someone standing in a slight crouch with an unmistakable tincture of back yard garbage.

"Just catch my breath," Frank said, moving to the living room and falling into a chair. He remembered seeing a redheaded man who had just had a heart attack at the airport, seated on the floor in a busy Salt Lake concourse, rushing travelers eddying around him, a look of perspiring embarrassment on his face, a morning newspaper at his side. Probably no one but his mother could have comforted him. His pupils were the size of dimes and he definitely seemed to be watching something coming his way.

Lane brought him a drink, the kind of strong drink you made when you meant to let your hair down. Frank was going to be careful of it. And it was a relief to be here with a highly objectified creature like Lane. It had been too much with Gracie. Every attempt to modify his emotions recently had gone upside down. He had just felt wild, and that was too much. He didn't want that wild feeling taking him off. He wanted the type of steadiness that is always praised, in sports, in life, everywhere. With Lane it could be strenuous yet polite, like an old-fashioned sea battle: gentlemen captains getting their guns into position and altogether out of the question to act or feel wild.

Lane sat down. "Kind of a turbulent time for you," he said.

"Afraid so."

"Sometimes it helps having something to set all these tribulations against."

"Yeah," said Frank, "like, we sleep for eternity or something."

"Not quite that dire. Maybe a few values."

"What kind of values, Lane?"

"The kind you come in from the desert with, the kind that stand you in good stead. The kind that make you one with your own people."

Lane probably had him here. The people who wanted to stop every river, kill every inconvenient animal and reduce every forest to usable fiber had a remarkable solidarity. They believed that every thing in the natural world was part of a conspiracy against the well-filled lunch bucket, the snowmobile with its topped-off fuel tank and the proper utilization of a deep clip of cartridges. Frank looked at him and tried to imagine him as a child, concluding that Lane had never been a child. He was born a full-sized spokesperson.

"You know," Frank said, "I have a feeling if we share our philosophies we're going to end by tearing this apartment up and it doesn't belong to us."

"Ha ha ha," said Lane.

"I'm not kidding."

"Okay, so another tack. Frank. You're a businessman. You share my climate."

"I've become a worse and worse businessman."

"I'll lay you three to one it's because of the negative climate that we operate in — workmen's comp, et cetera."

"No, it's not. It's something else. It's closer to chronic fatigue syndrome." He didn't tell Lane about his flat-earth theory or the exhilaration he sometimes felt when he thought of the big, brusque, variegated planet going on without him, like a Spanish galleon leaving a swimmer who had just walked the plank. This vision always ended like an old comedy going into reverse, with him rising from a big splash to run through the air back up to the end of the plank, run back down it into the crowd of sailors on deck. He wouldn't leave earth voluntarily, given the paltry stats on the other shit-planets with their faded canals, daffy moon rings.

"I'm very motivated toward having a pleasant relationship with you," said Lane. "I'm very drawn to your daughter." Frank got the awful feeling again. "I'm not getting much encouragement from her." He laughed. "It's a credit to you and your wife that she has grown into such an intricately developed personality. I wish she would give me stronger indications of our future together."

"That's good," said Frank. "It's an inappropriate relationship."

"I think the principals, and the principals only, are entitled to that view."

"Couldn't you find a conservative American your own age?"

"I could."

"You could?"

"But I don't want to."

"Ah."

"And Frank, your daughter is getting more conservative by the minute. And that's not bad. We're the ones who look around our nation and want the same thing: swift, retributive justice."

Frank thought about this alarming and obviously premeditated phrase, without picturing where it could lead. "Anyway, do you know when they'll be back?" he asked.

"They won't. Mrs. Copenhaver has gone down to Deadrock, I think, and Holly's at class."

34

The streetlamps streamed slowly past as he headed to a downtown Deadrock bar on foot, the lovely curves of automobiles with intricate paint jobs and personalized license plates displaying the state's pride in the Big Sky. An elderly cripple made his way along the sidewalk with gritty determination and shouted at Frank, "Watch where you're going, you crazy jerk!" This filled Frank with a reassurance of the indomitability of man. He stopped to look up and down a cross street, noting a conspicuous whistle from his nose and shadowy rings around his vision. He gave a loud laugh and a car slowed down to look at him. Wave to those people! They didn't wave back. We don't care! Another big laugh. Ha, ha! More waving . . .

Frank found himself in the bar. He didn't know how long he'd been in here, or how many drinks he'd had, but he decided to make a request by tracking the bar to the dance floor, pushing through all those dancers to the bandstand and asking the singer, who was usually the leader of the band, to play something special. There was Lucy Dyer! Hey, talk about special!

Lucy sat at the bar turned around on her stool so that she could watch people dancing. There were men on either side of her when Frank approached to take her request. No matter how he pressed her, he couldn't get her to name that tune. Finally, the man on her left, a tall and unsmiling cowboy in a black shirt, said, "She doesn't have a song to request. Hadn't you been listening?"

"Frank," said Lucy, "I'd like you to meet my honey, Darryl Pullman."

Frank was right in his face with a warm greeting and a handshake. "What do you do, Darryl?"

"I'm a spray pilot."

"That's all right."

"And a big-game guide."

"Well, what about you, Darryl, anything you'd like to hear?"

"If they knowed any Dwight Yoakam, be okay."

"Dwight Yoakam it is."

Frank hated the way he seemed so sprightly in the presence of these salt-of-the-earth types, but he succeeded in getting in the request and the band played "Guitars and Cadillacs." Up till then, he thought Darryl was kidding him, requesting some relation of Mammy Yoakam. He went back to Lucy and Darryl and said, "Would I be pushing my luck if I asked Lucy to dance?"

"Whatever blows your dress up," said Darryl.

"Thank you, Darryl. Thank you very much."

It was crowded on the dance floor and seemed to be no more than a large disorganized group of people. Frank couldn't detect any relationship between the music and the movements of the dancers. The large number of cowboy hats seemed to cut down on the available space. But Frank was enjoying the familiar weight and heat of Lucy in his arms. He knew it as common lust, a profound simplicity. The prominent bulge in his trousers spoke reams.

"You've got your nerve shoving that thing at me," said Lucy.

"The worst hanging judge in the world doesn't penalize folks for that which is involuntary."

Frank danced her around the room, feeling loose enough to fall on her. It was swell. When the song finished, Lucy pushed off and Frank went back to the bandstand. The singer leaned over his guitar and moved the microphone away from his face to listen to Frank.

"Do you do 'Happy Birthday'?"

"Sure do. Who's it for?"

"Darryl Pullman. He is one hundred years old tonight and he came just to hear y'all play." He had filched Gracie's accent.

"Be tickled to death," said the singer, reverberating the familiar six notes that punctuate the annual walk off the flat earth: "Happy bir-thday tew yew!" He leaned toward the microphone to talk out of the side of his mouth as Frank made his way back to Lucy. "Don't often in our business get to celebrate somebody's turning *one hundred years old* like we're fixing to do right now. This one's for Darryl Pullman, who's with us tonight. Darryl, here's to a hundred more!"

Frank looked Darryl right in the eye and said, "I didn't think they'd even invented the name Darryl a hundred years ago."

"They hadn't," said Darryl, who began to sing along with his own birthday song. "But this is a great opportunity for me to look forward to what it'll be like, you sorry little shit."

When the song came to an end and the applause died down, along with the back-pounding that forced Darryl to act happy about it all, Frank said, "Darryl, let me lay it on the table. This may be too much for you, and if it is, I don't blame you. Can you reach me my drink?" He gulped it down. "But I have absolutely got to have a word with Lucy and it will not take but a minute. I've absolutely got to." Darryl didn't say anything. "Darryl, I gotta. I've absolutely got to. We're right down the hall from each other. It's not that whatever. Please."

"Is this an emergency?"

"Yes! That's exactly the word I was looking for. Emergency."

"How long?"

"Six minutes, twenty-one seconds. There will be no time-outs or delays for commercials."

"I ain't too worried about it," said Darryl, "if you want to know the truth."

As soon as they stepped outside, Frank began to struggle with himself. He looked up at the theater marquee across the street and saw its perennial sign, "Closed for the Season." He discovered the unsteadiness of his limbs. "Is there anywhere we can sit down for a moment?"

"Yes," said Lucy in a firm and businesslike voice, "we can sit in Darryl's truck. I know he wouldn't mind because he is not petty. He is not petty and he is not inconsiderate."

She directed Frank to the Dexter Hotel's parking lot, where they found the three-quarter-ton Ford with a stock rack. Frank got in behind the wheel and Lucy went around to the other side. Frank smiled at her and pretended to steer down the road, mashing the brake at the same time. Lucy said, "What's on your mind?" Frank saw the keys and started the truck. Lucy gave him a look, but he just turned on the heater to cut the chill.

"I just hadn't seen you. I haven't been to the office."

"So we've noticed." "We" was Lucy and Eileen. He knew the subtext here was that Gracie was back in town.

"Oh, Lucy."

"And don't 'oh, Lucy' me, either."

"At least don't treat me mean. I've built an empire."

"And you're letting it fall apart."

"That's what they do. Read your history. None escape."

"And what about Gracie? A wonderful girl. How did you spoil that, Frank? She was a big reason I was attracted to you. I had to find out. Ever since that Halloween we dressed up as a *ménage à trois*. But Gracie was my friend. There's something about you but it may not be such a nice thing and no wonder she hit the road. No wonder! Yes, Frank, no wonder. And I want to tell you this: in your case, absence doesn't make the heart grow fonder. Once a person gets away from you, for however short a time, that person asks themself, How, how did I do that?"

"Soiled yourself with my love wand?"

"Frank, please."

"I was only trying to make things lighter. Besides, I've bent over backwards. You sent me to the Arctic Circle, I went. Wasn't that a living testimonial?"

"You were just trying, you . . . it was awful. What an utterly artificial attempt to cast a romantic glow over things. All you ever

225

did with any sincerity was fuck me, take me to the show and fuck me, take me to dinner, fuck me — in other words, *fuck me fuck me fuck me!*"

Looking into the truck window in time to hear the end of this speech was Darryl Pullman. Lucy saw Frank's glance, looked back at the window and moaned in loud despair. Frank slipped the truck in gear and moved out onto the street. "You can't talk like that around a cowboy," Frank said. "Not if you want to stay in one piece." Darryl called to another cowboy standing in the doorway of the bar. The cowboy pointed to his own truck, a big green Dodge, and he and Darryl ran toward it. Frank turned sharply into an alley, came out its far end, went through a closed bank's drive-up lane the wrong way, down another alley — all alleys he had played in as a child — and emerged in the middle of a Chevrolet used car lot. "Let me out here, Frank."

"You don't want to get out. You want to see this thing through, Luce."

Frank watched the darkened street over the tops of the cars. It felt dangerous. Feeling the heat and smelling the perfume, he sensed that the feeling of danger was very close to the feeling of lewdness. Overpowering presences, riveted attention, a kind of desire. And no purpose, a wonderful freedom from purpose. He threaded his way among the vehicles of the car lot.

There was Darryl and his friend in the Dodge, coming around the front of the railroad station. Frank cut his lights out and slumped in his seat. Lucy did the same, thrilling him with her complicity. He watched closely as the Dodge rolled by just beyond a row of used cars, its headlights splintering around their shapes. The two cowboys never looked his way, and when they had gone a block and a half east, Frank eased out and headed west. He reached down for the headlights as he was moving through the dark. He pulled the switch and heard a screech behind him. Looking into the rearview mirror, he saw the Dodge wheel in a semicircle, its lights jutting upward as the truck squatted with acceleration.

"Oh shit, oh dear," said Frank while Lucy covered her face.

Out on the highway, they were able to maintain an even lead over the other vehicle, but they were going a hundred and Frank didn't want to do that for long. "I don't know if you remember Sterling Moss," he said over the noise. "Great driver, but tore up every car he drove. Juan Fangio was even faster, but his cars never seemed to have even been driven. Something simpatico between Juan and machinery . . ."

"Frank, please."

"I can't stop now. Can you imagine what kind of mood those cowboys are in? I have no choice but to put it on them before they put it on me." Suddenly, he didn't seem to be moving at all. He watched the stars through the windshield and thought he simply liked Lucy. But the piercing beams behind him brought him back. Bold is best, he thought, then hit the brakes and managed to turn onto a gravel fork in the road. He turned off the lights again. "Frank!" Lucy cried. He could make out the road well enough, and he was sure that he was nearly impossible to see.

He slid onto another fork that went into dense trees but he could still see lights behind him. In another mile, the road wound around to the north while climbing a washboard hill. They were now in a forest but had to go much slower. There was a logging road going deeper into the woods but he knew that Darryl would just assume he went up it, so he went on, passing another logging road, then another. He turned up this last one. It was muddy and he had to get out and lock the hubs so he could travel in four-wheel drive. When he got out of the truck, he could hear the Dodge laboring on the grade without being able to tell if they had found them. It sounded like they were about a half mile behind.

Frank and Lucy's truck was all over the road. The mud was getting deeper and the engine was over-revving as the wheels lost traction. The road was sufficiently crowned that it was all important that Frank keep from sliding off the top of it. The truck was swimming upward from side to side like a tired old salmon going up a river. Then it just wallowed off the crown and buried the hood in muck. Frank and Lucy found all their weight on their legs, as though they were standing under the dashboard. Frank tried the accelerator and the rear wheels became whirligigs of spraying mud. When he turned the engine off, he realized the radio was still on faintly and Merle Haggard was singing: "Not so long ago you held our baby's bottle. Now the one you hold is of another kind." He turned it off and sighed.

Lucy said, "I can't live like this."

"I know how you feel."

"No you don't, you aimless bastard."

"You're just trying to hurt me, Lucy."

The windshield was steamed over. She slapped at him while crying out in despair. Then she quit.

"We can't just wait here like sitting ducks," he said. "The moon is shining. Let's walk out of here." He pushed open his door against the weight of gravity and looked down. "It's a bit of a jump," he said.

"Don't start talking like an Englishman!" Lucy cried. She seemed completely out of control. Frank took her arm and guided her to his side of the truck. When he jumped out and turned to help her, the seat was at the level of his chest. He held her hand. She looked all over for a place to land and then just made a wild jump that took Frank off his feet. He sank in the mud under her weight. He tried to make as little of it as possible because he sensed she was about to go mad. But his nostrils were plugged and the necessity of breathing made it impossible to put a completely good face on things.

Instead of just wading out of the mud, Lucy kept trying to jump feet first like an immobilized kangaroo. Frank crawled toward her, determined to help. Lucy opened her mouth and began to howl like a forlorn dog. Frank kept saying, "I don't blame you, I don't blame you. How could I have done this to you?" She was flinging something at him, probably just more mud. Mud didn't matter now. No matter how much of it, it was just theoretical. He well knew that he was stinking drunk, but he lacked any desire to resist its worst effects. He wished to be free of all conflict.

Dry ground was only a couple of yards off and soon they were standing on it, kicking out first one foot, then the other, like old-timers recalling their days in the chorus line. Frank smiled broadly and pointed to the west. "Town is that way. And what a lovely night for a walk!" With a look of despair, Lucy trudged in the direction he was pointing, on the small marginal road that went off into the woods. There was a ribbon of stars overhead and Frank was hoping that his head would begin to clear. He took Lucy's hand in his own and she sort of threw it off. He let it flop on his hip as though he weren't doing anything with it anyway.

It wasn't long before they came to a clearing where several pieces of heavy equipment were parked, including a big articulated log skidder. Frank stopped and looked at it for a long moment. He knew the answer to his troubles lay in technology.

"Lucy, if I can get that thing started, I can get our truck out of the mud in a heartbeat."

"Forget it."

"And accept defeat? Not this boy."

With the skills of his youth, Frank lay upside down under the dashboard of the skidder and cut the ignition wires with his pocketknife. Touching them together, he felt the diesel lurch. He sat up, pushed in the fuel cut-off, set the throttle, crawled underneath again and hot-wired it. The diesel chugged steady, caught and ran. The hinged cap on the exhaust stack fluttered with pressure and neat puffs of smoke arose and disappeared against the starlight. He twisted the wires apart and let them hang.

"Climb aboard," Frank called. Lucy considered it, then struggled up beside him. They were far from the ground. The skidder seemed as big as a locomotive, with a powerful hydraulic forklift in front of it. When Frank put it in gear, steering by hitting first one wheel brake and then the other, the great machine crawled forward on a serpentine course, flattening everything in its way. Lucy seemed almost fascinated, though she must have known things were out of control. And Frank had fixed upon the bogged-down pickup truck as an emblem of everything preventing him going on with his life.

He got the skidder turning off one way and couldn't quite get it back on line until a blizzard of saplings went down before them, leaving the air filled with the rupture of small trunks and descending clouds of leaves. This grand machine made its own road, and with their seats high above the destruction, they could feel some of the detached power that intoxicates those at war with the earth. They were back on their road and could make out the strip of sky overhead, which was a better navigation tool than the dark road ahead of them.

"Where do you suppose those fellows are?" Lucy asked over the engine noise.

"Long gone."

"Are you sure?"

"They're back in town by now."

"To do what? Get the sheriff?"

Frank felt a shiver go through himself. He didn't want to think about implications. He still had a wonderful feeling of living in his own dream. Everything seemed loose and guileless and free. He thought about the rumble of the big diesel going up through Lucy's butt, making her a real part of his assault on reason.

"Sunup can't be that far away," said Lucy.

"Oh, don't say it," he said, looking back to see if the long yellow shape of the skidder was following him, under control. I'm unbelievably good at this, he thought. He felt he made a handsome picture atop this ten-ton machine, throwing shadows of its combustion through his companion's interior.

He had a plan beyond simply keeping up appearances. He would ease the skidder up to the truck, place the forks underneath it, hydraulically lift the truck back onto the road and drive quietly back to town. He thought about explaining it to Lucy but realized she might not care. She was watching to see how this would turn out. To Frank, she had the detached clarity of real despair. She was a goner. Her head bobbed with the movement of the lurching machine. Her mouth hung open.

He found the truck again without any trouble. He had to turn off the road to get sideways to it. The skidder crawled down off the crown like a big weasel. By flattening a wide swath of brush, Frank was able to get perpendicular to the pickup. He stopped a moment to experiment with the forklift. It was simple: a hydraulic valve lever raised and lowered it smoothly and powerfully. Now he eased forward to the truck. The forks were almost on a correct line to go underneath it, but the muddy bank stopped him several feet short. He backed up and tried it again. This time he might have been even shorter. Once more, and the same result: there was a slick berm that wouldn't let him crawl up next to the truck.

He was going to have to use some power. He backed up and revved the diesel. "What are you going to do?" asked Lucy sharply over the roar of the engine. Frank engaged the gearbox and they leapt forward, up over the berm, and speared the truck with the steel forks. "Oh, no," Frank said. He took it out of gear. The forks were buried clear to the hilt in the lower part of the door. He was sure some lever would get him out of this. He yanked back on the hydraulics and the truck began to rise, streaming mud and water from its undercarriage. Lucy let out a noise of despair as it lifted over them. By the time the skidder stopped lifting the truck, it was possible to see the chassis, the muffler and exhaust pipe. Lucy was still letting out an awful noise.

"This baby could end up in our laps," Frank explained. He had to change the emphasis fast. He knelt on the floorboards and thrust his head up under Lucy's dress. This usually gets them, he thought, and buried his face in her crotch. It was pure magic. Her dress seemed to light up around him. He could make out its flower pattern in a thrilling illumination. He could hear her voice, "Frank! Frank! Frank!" and felt her fingernails dig into his scalp. She wasn't enjoying this. The thrashing got worse. Better have a look. He sat back on his haunches and threw the dress back over his head.

They had him in their high beams, Sheriff Hykema, Darryl and Darryl's friend from the bar. Frank looked around like a blind possum, trying to process all this information. Lucy was pushing her dress between her knees as she sat on the tractor seat of the skidder. High overhead, Darryl's pickup dropped clods of watery mud onto the engine-heated hood of the skidder. Frank stood slowly, held his hands up and surrendered.

It wasn't until they reached town at sunrise, in all its harrowing colors, that Frank realized that Lucy too would be booked and jailed. Darryl followed them to town in his truck, which they had carried to dry ground with the skidder. When they reached the courthouse, Frank immediately began to bargain with Darryl. He would like to have kept this secret from the bland and somehow alarming sheriff, but it wasn't possible. Darryl didn't want to speak to him at all. Frank knew he'd have to go quickly to a viable offer. They wouldn't even have had this moment if the sheriff had realized that a bargain was in the offing.

They were sitting in a room where Frank remembered taking a written test for his driver's license. There was still an eye chart on the wall.

"Darryl, there's no sense in my apologizing. Things just got away from us there, a man-versus-machine deal fueled by alcohol. I see this doesn't strike you as funny. But . . . how many miles your outfit got on it?"

"Sixty-one thou."

"You do take good care of it."

"I *did*."

Frank saw that he was touching a deep issue here. "Well, look here. Can't I just take your truck and buy you a new one?"

Darryl looked over, right into his eyes. Welcome to the twilight world of prostitution yawning before you, thought Frank.

"New?"

"New."

"And what do I have to do?"

"Drop the charges, hoss." Frank could see the clenched motion in the sheriff's shoulders from his seat in back. Lucy just watched things going by. There was a long silence from Darryl, not a sound. The sheriff looked at Frank. Frank would think about that gaze for a long time. He seemed to be taking in the long way Frank had fallen.

Lucy, Frank and Darryl got into Darryl's truck. First, they went to Lucy's house. She got out and in shame, rage or both, walked straight to her door without a word to either Frank or Darryl.

"I think she's sore," said Frank. He was getting depressed.

"Yeah." Darryl looked depressed too. They sat for a moment in front of Lucy's house, the truly ghastly colors of a new day rising behind the tall ash trees along the street, jerky bird movements among the branches.

Darryl said, "I wonder if there's anything we could have said."

"Like what?"

"I don't know. The whole thing is a bad deal."

"It wasn't your fault," said Frank.

"Well, it wasn't *her* fault."

"Let's get you your new truck. Maybe if I take a good hammering on that I'll feel a little better. I'm almost suicidal."

"You're just sobering up."

"There are a couple of other things."

"They call it self-pity."

"Okay, Darryl, I've got it coming."

Darryl put it in gear and headed up the street to Frank's house to get his checkbook. "I'll just be a sec," Frank said, and went in the house. He pulled out half the drawers in the kitchen before he found what he was looking for. He could have waited a bit and stopped at the office, but he knew Eileen was so demoralized that his appearance would have put her away. He also knew he couldn't bring himself to break in a new secretary. But now he had the checkbook and went back outside.

Darryl was gone and a note fluttered on the sidewalk gate: "Forget it."

35

He sat with his fishing tackle at the great corrugated base of a black cottonwood tree whose broad and leafy branches shaded an undercut run. He rolled over on his back and watched the big white clouds, barely moving toward the east, drifting on in a unit against the insistent deep blue of the sky. This seemed to him to be a grand and wholly acceptable arcade where his various sins were simply booths to be revisited with amusement. He wondered how Dante had failed to perfect one of his circles for the philandering sportsman: ravaged by his own hounds, flogged with his own fishing poles, dancing over his own buckshot. He joyously felt himself idling, an unreflective mood in which water was water, sky was sky, breeze was breeze. He knew it couldn't last.

He got up and strung his rod together and in a minute he was in the river with a box of flies in his shirt pocket. He could barely sense his business behind him, spinning toward failure. He didn't even have waders but was comfortable in the summer flow. The river was low and the gravel bars were prominent. He moved along until he could find some fish feeding. There was nothing going on where he had slept, in the deep run, though surely there were fish there. Nothing in the sparkling tail-out below the next big pool. But in a slender side channel he saw a string of fish feeding on flying ants.

Did he have a flying ant imitation in his fly box? He looked and yes, he did. He tied it on and made a very cautious presentation to the most downstream fish. The fish took in a silver swirl that faintly betrayed the colors of its flanks. Frank gave it some slack; the fish dropped back where it couldn't scare its fellows and in a minute was in hand, an East Slope cutthroat, a rare bird on this river. He let that one go and eased up on the next and caught it, a little butterball brown trout that jumped four times. He hooked the next one; he could see it was a brown trout by the yellow flash as it took his fly down. A smart fish, it moved up through the others, scared them off, bolted and broke the fine leader.

Two hours had gone by. Frank crawled up on the bank, pushing his rod ahead of himself, and when on dry land, rolled over to face the sun and dry off. A slight shadow went through his mind as he reflected that this was Wednesday, conventionally viewed as a workday. But this soon passed. Work? The question chilled him. He'd better figure that out fast. He'd better work for something or quit taking up room. Though what was wrong with taking up room? He hadn't asked to be put in this position. He was a byproduct of his parents' sex life unless, given those austere times, he was the entire product. Hard to picture from the current carnival.

The worst was that he had been "meant" for someone and now he was not "meant" for anyone. His fear was that if he was not meant for any*one*, then it might follow that he wasn't meant for any*thing*. He wasn't a scientist or an artist. He was just a businessman, really. Still, he believed that he asked the big questions. He knew that scientists and artists believed that only they asked the big questions. They believed it was their job to ask the questions the answers to which the general population required for their well-being, but never asked themselves. Why? Because, it would seem to follow, the general population was too fucking stupid. This belief was behind the impression that artists and scientists often made among ordinary people, of being blow-hards, or assholes. He admitted loving his bouts of brainlessness: the fish tight against the rod, the strange woman smiling across the corridor as the light from the Coke machine shone on her lipstick, the dog barking beyond the railroad tracks. When you analyzed something, it owned you. You ought, as the Bible suggested, to watch, and wait. Frank smiled at his own thoughts, rolled onto his stomach and watched the river.

By the time he got to the office, several things had changed. First, he had certainly come to realize that he was going to have to take hold of practical matters while he could. He pretended that his emotional hegira had been a kind of renewal, but his body and the vague feeling of being stunned denied that. He had evidently recovered his old abstracted yet purposeful self because his secretary had lost her sardonic aura and fell right in behind the renewal of his routines. There was a mausoleum tidiness about his desk that implied absence and neglect of business.

Second, he was coming down with something. Eileen told him it was going around. He felt shaky, and there was the sense that sweats were not far away. Aspirin was wearing off about every two hours but work had to be done. He began to look at his activities: his antagonizing the renters at the clinic, his gross failure to track the cattle market, his open boredom when talking about the fate of the family ranch. He felt he was awakening from hypnosis. What in God's name could I have had in mind? he wondered.

And finally, he had learned in a phone call from his daughter, marked by a coolness he had never experienced from her before and which was so baffling to him that it had the effect of overshadowing the information it conveyed, that Gracie had returned to town and would be living on Third Street with her friend Edward. She, Holly, would be down for a visit, and to accompany Lane at one of his Brandings.

This made things neither better nor worse. Gracie had left him and the finality of that blow could not, he was sure, be increased by her being in town. At least he didn't think so. There would be the pain of running into her. But how often did he run into anyone by accident? There would be a powerful temptation to slip over to her place at night and see what was going on. But he was going to stop all that, or if he didn't stop, he would resume his observation of conventional families pursuing a long-shared idea in our country, one he had lost.

"Eileen, have you been following the fortunes of this Centennial Wolf Pack?"

"I think they killed them all except one."

"*Who* killed them all except one?"

"Whoever. They don't know."

"How many were there?" Frank asked.

"There were six, weren't there? There was the black female, the mother — the one they called Alberta because that's where she was supposed to come from. They shot her —"

"Who?"

"They don't know," Eileen said. "The senator said that environmentalists were shooting them to make ranchers look bad."

"Then they poisoned the male, I believe. Two pups were shot off the highway. How many does that leave?"

"Oh, yes, Mr. Copenhaver, they poisoned that other pup at the campground over in the Gallatin. I believe the senator explained that the Bozeman Girl Scout troop might've done that to help protect fawns. Although I heard the Girl Scouts denied it and their troop leader wasn't real happy about the senator. So, there's just one, and he's this real silvery male they had on TV going across the Cayuse Hills. He's almost grown. They've got a radio collar on him. Fish and Wildlife says he's doing great."

"He might be a little lonely, wouldn't you think?"

"A wolf?"

"Anyway, I have a friend who's been following the wolves. It's a passion with her. I haven't seen her in a while . . ."

Eileen looked on with vague incomprehension. She wasn't big on these lateral, associative kinds of things. He'd been through this before. Anything beyond the declarative sentence aroused a suspicion in her that a plot was afoot. And in his case there was, a plot to locate Smokie.

"You don't look very well, Mr. Copenhaver."

"I'm afraid I'm just hanging on. But I can't give in to it. I've neglected so much."

"You have indeed," said Eileen. "I'm very worried for my job."

Frank took this in, looking at her to gauge the depth of her worry. But Eileen stranded him. She didn't exactly wear her heart on her sleeve. Frank had a split second of admiring the consistency of her out-of-fashion clothing, eyeglasses that made her as unattractive as possible, pale plastic-rimmed things that were a pure optometric solution to seeing poorly.

"You won't lose yours unless I lose mine," said Frank heartily.

"That's what I mean," she said.

"I see," said Frank. Once he saw this all from a great altitude. His benevolence in directing his widespread world was immediately accepted for the simple fact that he was in motion and provided a kind of leadership. He had learned that people will follow damn near any moving object, but that if it falters, they will quickly move to another moving object and follow that one. He once read an essay by Robert Benchley describing a newt falling head over heels in love with a pencil eraser because it resembled something in the mind of all newts. Frank once thought of this as a very complete description of human love.

Next Frank talked to John Coleman, his accountant, the man who once crowed, "You're a success!" at the crossing of some threshold of net worth or another. He could tell that John was even more worried. Well, Frank was worried too. In fact, he knew so much more than John that he was inclined to overreact to John's worry. John had a deep, measured voice that he cultivated purely for phone use. He rarely used that phone voice on Frank, but now he was, candidly nattering on about a few accounting strategies — he knew Frank was not interested. Evidently, he had bumped into Edward Ballantine on the street and gotten some very aggressive questioning as to whether Frank was deliberately devaluing his estate by way of anticipating his divorce. All that was meant to say was that this was now street knowledge and, accurate or inaccurate, it was hardly a salubrious business climate.

"Frank," he said, "I think you are perilously close to failure." This would have had greater effect if John hadn't used the phone voice, but it had some effect. "If a divorce is impending, then what I say is certainly true."

Frank didn't want to let any of these people get to him. "I think I'm coming down with something," he said.

"That's one way of putting it."

"I mean a bug. I got a flu shot but this one flies below radar."

"Failure," said John. "It's almost like getting killed."

When he got off the phone, Frank tried to think about having nothing and couldn't respond to the idea. He'd had prosperity for a good little while now and obviously it hadn't done enough for him to form a background for terror when he contemplated its absence. He tried it on himself: "I am a failure." Nothing.

He made himself have a productive day, getting the most important mail out and returning the calls of those who were angriest or most offended. He did not talk to the bank. He was not prepared for any more of a bottom-line view than he had acquired from John Coleman. Then he went home and went to bed. He was sick.

He woke up at about eight P.M. and was still sick, but he was hungry. He had wound up the bedclothes in a twisted confusion and he was sweating. The phone rang and it was a wrong number, some old man. He found himself trying to prolong the conversation but it was, he concluded, the result of fever confusing him about how long things took. He thought he was simply not rushing when the old man said, "Look, mister, this is a wrong number. You follow me? I can't talk to you all night."

"You've got to go," Frank said. It was attempted wit. He hung up the phone and rolled over. There was still some light coming in through the curtain on the high window. The curtain made it gray and Frank lay looking at the gray light on his hands. He tried to pretend they were someone else's hands. What sort of person were they the hands of? He couldn't tell. They were just hands. He was sinking into despair.

Maybe a shower. He let the hot water run straight into his face, trying to get some feeling back. This is like twenty gallons of tears a minute, he reflected as the water surged down off his chin. He tried shampoo, half a handful of golden gel. It swelled his hair into a foaming white crown. He took a piss this way, white-headed, hot water in the face, pissing against the wall. There was this movie scene, she was blowing him in the shower, suds, hot water, some crosscutting between orgasm and the water going down the drain, various arty annoyances. Then the movie went on to something completely different.

When he got back into bed he thought, My mother and father didn't love me. What would a psychologist say? Probably, Oh, Frank, they loved you; they just didn't love you in the right way. I don't buy this about love, Frank would say to the psychologist. You're worse than an asshole blowhard artist, you psychologist. Love *is* the right way. If it isn't "the right way," it isn't love.

He was at an abyss of self-pity and he knew it but couldn't seem to get around it. Sick and alone. If this was a preview, it was altogether frightening. It didn't help to be so much cleaner. And in a moment, he was back in the bathroom to throw up. Afterward, he brushed his teeth but he couldn't get the taste of vomit out of his mouth. He tried turning on the television. He was lonely and his accountant had said he was failing. His mother and father didn't love him. That last fish broke his fly off. Darryl showed that he was a bigger man than Frank was. Lucy would have liked him if he could have just figured out who Lucy was so that he could do something in return. "Travel agent" wasn't much of a beginning.

He got a thermometer and lay in silence, the covers pulled up under his chin, the glass rod sticking out only an inch from his lips. He had a fever of about 103. That was a pretty good fever. He got up and put on a bathrobe and a sweater over it. He went downstairs and drank a quart of milk with a marmalade sandwich and went back to bed. His hands were sticky. He lay there trying to remember the details about the marmalade. He had read the label. There was something about Seville oranges. It was foreign marmalade, but there was something about the family who made it that he had read and this was now completely gone from his mind. Maybe he was getting Alzheimer's disease.

On the other hand, he remembered his first joke and there was a connection. He'd heard it from his Brooklyn-born barber when he was a kid. Somebody put an orange in a robin's nest and when the young birds came back, one said to the other, "Look at the orange Mama laid." In the barber's accent, it sounded the same as "orange marmalade." There was a time when he thought that was a really fine joke.

Many people he had talked to on the phone, before he came home, used the phrase "What are you going to do about . . ." Frank thought about this locution as though it were a specimen phrase from a foreign language. It seemed to imply that the person addressed was a kind of lever or something. He wished to state that he was no lever; he was a bystander, and on days he felt a little better, a pedestrian. He thought of himself and Holly singing "Hey, you, get offa my cloud," and he began to weep in silent bitterness. *People* magazine was always talking about the glitterati. Well, he belonged to the bitterati. This thought caused him to burst out in a laugh, but snot flew from his nose onto the bed covers. He wasn't about to be overpowered by snot, and so, covering first one nostril, then the other, he recklessly blew snot all over everything, then lay back in thought. This was meant to show he didn't care about anything. He turned on the radio next to the bed, at low volume, and fell asleep.

36

When he awoke the next morning, he had the sense that complete chaos was occurring outside his window. Horns were blowing and some piece of roadworking equipment was backing up with its fierce signal going. People were trying to go to work and, with admirable simplicity, were flying off the handle at any delay whatsoever. A new sun shone an all-creating light over the vehicular uproar wedged between two lines of sidewalk. A single construction worker strode between the cars giving the finger to men and women headed for work, to students and to families. "Can you see this?" he asked through windshields and side windows. Magpies flew through the trees. Frank watched the motorists staring straight ahead, not seeing the mad construction worker whose rage showed through every shambling stride he took. At all times, someone was blowing a horn and it was clear that the construction worker would have keenly murdered everyone.

Frank didn't think he could go out to get any food. He tried to watch the news but it seemed totally out of kilter. There was Gorbachev. He looked like a fucking mouse. A college football player showed the new convertible he got from his dean for improving his forty-yard-sprint time by a full second. Then an enormous weatherman, the beloved Willard, completely out of control. He turned it off and called June. She was already at work. She said he sounded terrible.

"For many perfectly good reasons," Frank said, "nobody loves me anymore."

"You're probably right," said June.

"June, is it true?"

"No, Jesus! What ails you, Frank?"

"I'm sick. And I'm starving to death. Junie, I can't quite get it together to take care of myself. I'm running a fever. Everything is so bad, it might be psychosomatic, though I doubt it. Eileen said it was going around."

"So, you've seen Eileen."

"June, please, I can't handle much."

"Okay, I'm coming over. It might take a bit. I'll stop by the grocery."

June brought him some sweet rolls and coffee and a carton of orange juice. She spread a towel on the side of the bed and set these things out. Then she pulled up a chair, sat down, crossed her legs and got a paper cup of coffee out of the white paper bag. Frank was propped up in bed and was conscious of the disarray of his room: drawers half pulled out, closet door ajar, one end of the rug rolled up, an overflowing wastebasket. The curtain was still pulled aside from watching the traffic jam.

June blew on her coffee and said nothing. Frank ate. She was wearing a navy blue dress with a string of pearls. She had her hair twisted up into a bun. She had a thin, off-center cheap Oklahoma face that was appealing and self-sufficient. June was his friend. She was a fighter. Unlike most women he knew, she wasn't astonished to find that life was a fight. So her feistiness lacked the indignation, the bruised quality, that gave relationships between men and women these days their peculiar smelliness. She had once said, quite evenly, "I can look after myself," when Frank had offered to intervene with a supplier trying to gouge her at the dealership.

"I have underestimated what a delicate thing life really is," Frank began. "I was rolling along there like a house afire for well over a decade. I knew this thing happened with Gracie. It wasn't what I wanted. But I certainly thought I would survive it and I guess I will. But I'm certainly not the same guy and it sort of pisses me off."

"I love it when you're lonely," said June.

"That's really not it."

"I thought this was some bug going around."

"It is. But you know Gracie better than anybody. You're both from the South. Is Oklahoma in the South?"

"Sorta. And yeah, that's half our trouble. You don't have the love of people that we have. When you go to falling out here, there's no bottom to it. They'll just watch you fall."

"Huh. Do you think Gracie agrees with that?" This hurt his feelings. He wanted everyone to love the West.

"She had you. She had Holly. She had friends. She was making a beginning. But these are the meanest white people in America. Your kids up and grown, your marriage fails, nothing holds you."

"What holds *you?*"

"The 'ninety-two Buicks. They're beautiful. Make your mouth water. Each one is a little world." She smiled. "The 'ninety-threes will be even better."

God, it was wonderful to hear someone looking forward to something that was actually going to happen. Next year's cars. He told June that.

"Well, it isn't going to last," she said. "You're gonna have to take aholt, son."

"I know this."

"And Gracie's in town. So, maybe you ought to spend the time to polish off those jagged edges. You've both got to go on. You don't want to leave off like you did. And this is the first time in your life since I've known you when you didn't seem to care about making money. You better take advantage of it."

"Okay. But Gracie's okay. That guy's probably got a lot of money. I know money isn't everything . . ."

"He's a sharp one, that Ed. He knows how to make it. Do you know what his big trick was?"

"I hadn't really heard. I suppose Gracie told you."

"She did and she wasn't happy. He used to be a dealer of Indian artifacts but he got crossways with the law. I guess he married one of his wealthy customers but she was in a bad car wreck. Now he buys life insurance policies from people who have been diagnosed with AIDS. He cashes them out at a discount. He says that gives them money for medicine, which he knows won't work, and it allows them to buy a little dignity, which it may. That's quite an idea, isn't it, Frank?"

"Quite an idea," Frank said numbly.

"He still sort of has this wife, but she throwed him out on account of the wreck. He was sad about that because she was sure enough well fixed. So, have I helped you?"

"Thank you, Junie-friend. You've helped me."

"For what it's worth, I never heard Gracie say she was in love with him."

Frank got up and went downstairs with June. He washed the dishes and she dried. Then they went out into the front yard and raised the American flag. He smiled up at it in his bathrobe as the cool mountain wind made it crack over the busy street. He arranged to have Darryl's truck repaired, and June said she'd find Darryl and set it up. Aspirin was helping his discomfort and he was building confidence. The sunlight angled against the sides of houses along the street. A man with a huge pockmarked nose led a pair of straining Irish setters, one from each hand, up the hill. He had his billed cap on backward as though anticipating a sled ride. Frank commented on June's beautiful yellow Buick in his driveway, its eventful curves shadowed by the dark arms of the old maple.

There seemed to be a slight visual vibration over everything. He thought of what June had said about the West. He knew Gracie used to feel that way too. The tone of the West had been set by the failure of the homesteads, not by the heroic cattle drives. The tone was in its bitter politics. But that wasn't the whole story. He knew it was a good place. He knew Gracie had been coming to see that. There was something in its altitude and dryness and distances that he couldn't have lived without; and it was a good time to remember that. When he was walking in the hills and could see sundown begin about forty miles away, or smell running water in the bottom of a sagebrush ravine, or watch the harriers cup themselves to the curve of earth and slash through clouds of meadowlarks, he felt that thankfulness. It was always a starting point. He went to the mirror and watched himself say, "I love it here."

37

Monday morning in the American West. J. P. Morgan was pissing off the securities firms by expanding its underwriting. Now I'm happy again, thought Frank. Dog eat dog. Stock prices higher, bonds surge, NASDAQ sets record for third day. Nervous investors looking for strong earnings records. John Deere is laying people off. Restructuring charges were producing a quarterly loss for United Technologies. Not a word about chickens.

On the hope that there is synergy even in failure, Frank had invited Orville Conway of Wilsall, Montana, to his office for a meeting. He had read over the weekend, between morose fits of bathrobe living, that Montana's ninth-biggest chicken farmer was facing bankruptcy. Frank thought this could be the missing portion of the synergy he dreamed of for his old hotel. Orville Conway's defeat implied that the seven-month winter canceled certain business opportunities. It was especially poignant in the case of Orville Conway, who was widely admired as a modern and skillful practitioner in the industrial multiplication of chickens. The very word "failure" made Frank reach out to Orville, and so he called him and told him he had an idea.

Orville got right past Eileen and presented himself in Frank's doorway. He had a rawboned, rural face with deep-set eyes and prominent enough teeth that it was quite a struggle for him to keep them covered with his lips. He also had a fashionably blow-dried hairdo that formed a kind of pouf just over his forehead, covered half his ears and came down over the collar of his buck-stitched blue western sport coat. The possibility of failure hung over Orville Conway like a soggy, impermeable cloud of desperation and defiance. Frank stood briskly and came out from behind his desk, thrusting his hand into Orville's big, work-hardened mitt. The weight and toughness of that hand in the context of the sartorial fancy and mushroom cloud of impending doom touched Frank. He could see that, imperiled as his own business life was, he had more edge left than Orville Conway. Still, they shared the prospects of financial desolation, and that was inspiring.

"Please sit down, Orville."

"Thank you."

"Can I have Eileen bring you some coffee."

"I'm all coffeed out," said Orville. Frank picked up the phone and asked Eileen to hold his calls.

"Orville, I learned about some of your business problems in the paper," Frank said, and Orville reddened right out to his ears. Frank had not seen such shame in a grown man before.

"We're talking about restructuring some debt," Orville murmured.

"That just slows things down, gives the bank a deeper choke hold on you." Frank was instantly dizzied by his wrath against banks.

There was a sustained quiet as Orville Conway took his time evaluating the moment. "I don't have a lot of choices. It's all I've ever done. This was my shot and I took it. I don't have a lot of information about other businesses. I got a wife and kids at home. And we done pretty good all along there, considering. It's not an excuse to talk about changing times. I'm way too far from the transportation. The bank's got a pretty good lien on the place. I done this all on the home place and it's about two thousand feet higher than here and it is just too darn cold. I already starved out there once, in the cow business. Feed costs are high, but really, it's bein' high and cold and too far from things. I hate like heck to go under and I'm not going to let it happen if I don't have to. I feel kind of bad about, you know, whoever might have been looking for me to go ahead and make it come out right."

Frank was thinking, This could be the birth of a new chicken kingdom. He felt a slight buzz, a familiar surge edging on gooseflesh. He and Orville were going to kick ass, Conway and Copenhaver (C & C), people ingesting chicken like bats in a cloud of houseflies.

"Orville, I have an idea."

Orville didn't look very hopeful. He had seen some heavy weather. Frank was moved by him and took a moment to reconsider; his own back was against the wall and he wanted to be sure he wasn't simply transferring some bad luck. He didn't think he was. Shooting fish in a barrel was not necessarily a universal business image either.

"Orville, do you own the property on which you raise chickens?"

"I have a large mortgage."

"So you are faced with a bank wishing to foreclose while there is something left."

"That's true."

"I am in a similar situation with a property I own here in town, a clinic. It is substantially leveraged. I have failed to get along with my tenants and they have moved out. I am trying to buy some time before the bank comes in, but I may not succeed."

"Sounds like we're in the same boat."

"Not entirely. I also own the Kid Royale Hotel on Main Street, which as you may know is a famous building from the Territorial era. It was the biggest hotel on the Montana frontier but I have never been able to do anything with it because the cost of renovating it would be prohibitive. Back in the seventies when I acquired it, there was a lot of money for that sort of thing, federal grants, floating around. But we never got it. Those funds were all spent back east, pilgrim stuff, whatever, the Civil War."

All through this summation, Orville developed a series of nervous and possibly impatient gestures: knitting and reknitting his fingers, biting the back of his right thumbnail, darting his eyes to the window and recrossing his legs. Frank could feel the pressure of the needy chickens. Finally, Orville spoke.

"I know that they have been real successful in the East and Midwest raising chickens in old hotels. But Mr. Copenhaver, I have to be honest. I can't afford to rent your hotel from you."

"I don't want you to. I just want you to move in. We'll joint venture. If this makes the difference for your business and moves it back into profitability, we will commence the payment of a lease at that time. But my part wouldn't kick in until you were in the black again."

Orville didn't have to think very long. "You want me to draw something up?"

"That'd be fine. I know we can find fair numbers. The main thing is, I own this building outright. Let the bank take back your chicken ranch. Let 'em raise a few eggs themselves. They're all talking about going back to basics. They can start with chickens."

"The cocksuckers," said Orville rather surprisingly.

"Exactly." Frank hesitated only a moment trying to imagine whether he meant the bankers or the chickens. Once again, Frank shook the powerful hand of Orville Conway. There was a very definite feeling about Orville, that he knew what he was looking at when he was looking at you. And this was the first little bit of accustomed movement Frank had felt in a long while. But he couldn't always expect June to come around and get him going.

38

Frank walked home from the office. He passed the irregular col-
onnades of Schwedler's maples — a fashionable tree of the twen-
ties — the cotoneaster hedges, the American lindens and, around
the bases of the turn-of-the-century homes, the bridal wreath
spirea. The street in front of his house was a marvel of retained
atmosphere, the permanence of settlers' hopes, a perfect scene for
the freewheeling newspaper boy coming along now, underhand-
ing the evening paper onto lawns; the blue sports car whining
along one gear too low; the plumbing truck with galvanized pipe
lashed to its roof rack; and the black Saab that swung, like a
wingless airplane, around the corner and parked in Frank's driveway. Frank stopped to watch. He was far enough away that he
could easily duck an unwelcome visit. Schoolchildren were starting to appear on the far side of the street, coats tied around their
waists, carrying bookbags, walking backward to talk to those
walking frontward.

It was Edward Ballantine. Frank took this anonymous moment
to size him up. Ballantine was wearing a topcoat over blue jeans and
NBA-style high tops. He had on a pair of orange reflective mountaineering glasses, and to hold them a leather thong that hung
partway down his back. He removed the glasses and dropped them
to his chest while he looked over the doorway. He seemed pretty

confident as he stepped up on the porch to knock on Frank's door. Frank walked as quietly as he could without seeming furtive, and crossed the street.

"May I help you?"

"Oh, Frank, hi," said Ballantine. He had a facial trait that Frank identified as vaguely out-of-town and which consisted of animating his eyes while leaving his lower face in a noncommittal state. An insincere approach, Frank concluded, allowing for sudden mood shifts depending on the politics of the moment. He thrust out his hand for a handshake, and without looking at it Frank declined to take it. "May we go inside and have a word?" Ballantine asked, starting to throttle down the tone, utilizing the deftly shifted expression toward coolness.

"No," said Frank, "we may not." Frank recalled that Ballantine had already quizzed his accountant about the state of his finances.

"Am I to understand that you will not speak to me?"

"Not at all. You just need to do it here on the sidewalk. That's my home. You know, a man's home is his castle."

"I think there are still some issues of joint tenancy there, Frank, with Gracie."

"Could be, but for now possession is nine tenths of the law. And is that why you're here, to discuss Gracie's divorce settlement with me?"

"No, I —"

"Because that's really not your job, is it, Edward? Though my accountant informs me you've been sniffing around."

"If you'll give me a chance to talk, I'll tell you why I'm here."

"It really is none of your business. I'm sure you can understand that, can't you, Edward? It's not a big concept. If it is to you, just let me know how far you got with it and I'll try to help you with the rest."

"Frank."

"?"

"Shut up."

Frank felt a violent impulse sweep through him, but it passed.

Then Edward said, "I think you're at the point where you might think of looking at your own life to find out what happened to your marriage. I mean, your wife wasn't stolen by the Comanches or something. She pretty much shot out of here."

"She did, didn't she."

"She sure did."

"Well, I'd sure like to see her."

"Just stop at the house. That's why I came by. I wanted you to know where you could find us."

"Where's the house?"

"One Twenty-one Third."

"Let me think about it first. But maybe I'll stop over."

"Nice place," said Edward. He lifted his hand toward Frank's house, let it fall.

Frank wondered why he had bothered. "You want to buy it?"

"I don't think so."

"That was sort of part of the fantasy at one time, that house."

"So I've heard," said Edward.

"I thought maybe it would be better if you and Gracie had it —"

"It's best if you see her."

"— than if I go on rattling around in it. I'd be happier in a hotel, frankly."

"I thought you owned a hotel."

"Yeah, but it's for chickens."

Edward gave him a puzzled look, then reminded Frank that he ought to speak to Gracie. Edward turned to go to his Saab. Frank could see that it was hard to know how to make the proper exit, and in fact, he himself turned fairly woodenly to go to his house. He heard the little aircraft whir of Edward's car, got the mail from his mailbox and went inside.

He put a Lean Cuisine in the microwave and turned it on. He switched on the radio, always set on the oldies station, and found, to his satisfaction, a Youngbloods retrospective in progress. The crooner Jesse Colin Young seemed to speak directly to him from the darkness while he opened his mail. What's this? Eastman

Kodak was going to buy the rest of Amerilite Diagnostics Ltd.? I didn't even fucking see that coming! Weren't these the pukes that said, 'Keep it simple, stupid'? Frank hated the sense that if he took his eyes off these birds for so much as a day, they pulled something on him.

The phone rang.

"Mr. Copenhaver?"

"Yes?"

"This is Gladys Pankov from the city planning office. I also represent the Preservation League in my capacity as planner and secretary."

"Right?"

"I was wondering — is this possible? — if you could clarify something for me about the Kid Royale Hotel. We had hoped that some program for its restoration were in place. But we've just received the oddest notice at the planning office."

"Okay, now I'm with you. My mind was elsewhere. Kodak is on some kind of acquisitions tear. Now, yeah, okay, uh . . . no, that's no longer the plan."

"It's not?"

Frank thought he knew what was coming. "Are you calling to tell me that exciting new grants are now available for this kind of work?"

"No, actually, I was running down a rumor."

"It's going to be a chicken ranch," said Frank sharply.

"Yes, that was it. Well, just a couple of questions, then. Did you know that one of the rooms was the suite of William Tecumseh Sherman?"

"Sure, the guy that killed all the Indians. That's a big room all right, hold a lot of chickens."

"Calamity Jane, Buffalo Bill stayed there, George Armstrong Custer, three of the original Vigilantes —"

"If I'm not mistaken," Frank interrupted, "they're all dead. So, there's plenty of room for the chickens. Look, I hate to be short with you, but I'm nuking a cannelloni." He got off the phone and felt his scalp. He thought about Gracie. It would be tempting to rage against women. Endless destruction around the world. Back to Helen, Cleopatra, Lady Macbeth. Mad scientists. He investigated his paper. Poinsettia white flies devastate two agricultural counties in California. Is it men who are so crazy about poinsettias that they want to mail them to friends in California? Blaming the victims? The victims are lovely California vegetables with lethal bugs lodged in their vitals. They and their consumers, people from — one of Frank's favorite phrases — all walks of life.

That night when he lay down, instead of thinking about his loneliness or the imminence of certain foreclosures, he thought about the gap between short-term and long-term interest rates, the yields on two-year Treasury notes. Frank Copenhaver was sinking into a chicken-driven destiny. If he could just get back on his feet, he was going wide open into biotech firms. Their names helped him drift off: Regeneron, MedImmune, Genentech, Alkermes, Glycomed, Isis . . .

39

Mike was there at daybreak. He brought Frank his paper and some breakfast from Hardee's in a nice white bag with a hot slick spot on its side. Frank was still in the shower, letting the hot water stream against the stiff back of his neck while he made several plans for the day. He could see out the window the swimming shapes of cars in the street, and when he finished his shower, he rubbed a small circle in the steam and looked below the house to see who was parked there. It was Mike's Country Squire. For some reason, looking out over the town from this perspective, he thought how much more interesting it would be if they were involved in a war here — tanks in the streets, partisans lobbing grenades into cellars or, best of all, the lust to wipe everything out and start over again. This need for a war was pretty basic, he suspected. His lousy little town had never had one. The closest it had come to a siege of Vicksburg were a few slapping matches around election time.

So, Mike was here. Mike had never taken a big chance and he would never take a big fall, but he had his virtues. He was a deeply loyal person, blindly loyal, a beautiful trait in a country whose salad bars sold lettuce by weight, a country whose true spiritual leader was Benedict Arnold. Frank could never get in a schoolyard fight when Mike was around; because if he should lose, Mike, big and fat and strong already, would jump on the victor and pound him to a pulp. At another time, Frank would have to have the fight all over again, this time collapsing under the blows of a deeply indignant adversary. Mike was straight and clear regarding Gracie. It was part of having an opinion about everything, and every opinion a function of team spirit. He was a Copenhaver and she was a treacherous flooze.

By the time Frank got downstairs, Mike had made bacon and eggs to go with the stuff from Hardee's and had put everything on the table. He was feeding himself with one hand and holding an open hand to the chair opposite him for Frank to sit down.

Frank sat. "My teeth are fine," he said. "I'm sure that's why you're here."

Mike gave him a mirthless grin as if to say, "Very funny, Frank." He dabbed his mouth with a napkin.

"They're a little sensitive to cold, but that's not so unusual."

"Frank —"

"I had that onslaught of cavities spring before last, and a little gum recession."

"Frank —"

"You let that flossing go for one day and it might be a long time before you get back to it. Then what do you have? Bleeding, sore gums, the prospects of —"

"Frank, please stuff something in your fucking mouth." Silence from Frank. "Thank you. Now, didn't I make you a nice breakfast?"

"Yes."

"Aren't I a nice brother, with your well-being always in mind as a fellow Copenhaver?"

"Yes, you are, Mike. And I have come to accept your dogged conservatism as a desire to build a world on the basis of those models we once shared together: Lego, Lincoln Logs and the immortal Erector Set."

"You've lost none of your acid wit, I see," said Mike. "The acid may be rising in proportion to the wit, but it's still pretty much all there."

"I appreciate that. Compliments haven't been showering of late."

"It's really no wonder. It's hard for people to look on at an innovative businessman who abruptly decides to commit economic suicide."

"Are you referring to risk management here?" asked Frank.

"I'm referring to the talk of the town."

"You haven't seen how it's going to turn out."

"How's it going to turn out, Frank?"

"A chicken in every pot, for one thing."

"Yeah, I just heard about that one. Frank, do you realize I love you?"

"Thank you, Mike."

"It occurred to me that perhaps you have concluded no one loves you."

"I suppose I had had that thought, Mike," said Frank. "But thank you for loving me."

"You know, just because some opportunistic whore sees a brighter light over somebody else's driveway doesn't mean you have to give up on having a coherent life."

"Mike, please."

"And think about your beautiful Holly."

"I do. But that's not simple either. You know she's been seeing Lane Lawlor."

"I knew that. But so what? She'll come around."

"I hope so. And so will I. Yes, my boy. Rest your little head. I'll come out of this thing in a blizzard of deposit slips."

"Frank —"

"I know."

"Frank —"

"I know, I'm doing what I can. There's a slight fog over the target, sure to clear."

"You can always slip out to the ranch. It's an easy commute. Might help to hear some birds."

"This is handier. I can walk downtown."

"But Frank," said Mike, his face clouding. "At the rate you're going, you'll be lucky to hang on to your house."

Frank hadn't heard that before. He went on wiping up the yolk with a wedge of toast. He thought he brought real insouciance to this moment. Take my house?

"Whatever blows their hair back, Mike. Some of these things are like weather. You just have to watch Willard and wait for another system."

"All I want you to know is, I'm down there among those guys, the bank, whatever. I'm doing what I can to slow the process. But what you have to do, Frank, is to try to have a change of attitude."

"Okay."

"And remember I love you."

"Okay."

Mike left and went to work. Frank wasn't thinking about anything but speaking to Gracie. He imagined it'd go something like this: "Hi, Gracie, good to see you again. No, no, no, I don't think we should do *that*. I think we should build up to *that*, if indeed we do *that* at all. Without question, you would like a reprise of my activities, my accelerated life story, *post* your departure but *pre* my, how shall I say, decline? You look pretty much the same, how do I look? I suppose there's been water over the dam but that won't prevent our talking. Is this your lawyer? I don't mind if he's here, he looks pretty stupid, some of this will be too much for him to absorb. You see, Gracie, I've had a failure of faith at some level. That pyramid called America, of which I was but a small stone, has inverted and is now resting on its point. As you see (you took physics), this makes for a wobblier arrangement than the one we grew up with, with the big part on the bottom."

He was now making an extraordinarily close examination of himself in the mirror: hairline, pores, teeth. He reminded himself not to compress his lips, which produced the effect of widening his face in a kind of, in a kind of . . . well, it was unattractive. He wasn't going to work, he decided; he would do this first. So what was he thinking, putting on these drab clothes, this I-am-sincere hopsacking blazer? Women don't want sincerity or any other foursquare merits. They want to look at a man and say, This animal is about to spring on me like a Bengal tiger, ease that big lever till it seats. With that stupid hopsacking sport coat she would assume he was about to fuck the lawyer or the lamp but not her in his vapid sincerity getup. Officer, he rolled in here doing sixty, and before you could say Jack Robinson, had his dick crosswired in the reading lamp. Do take him off, I'm trying to watch the news.

Frank sort of came to, still standing in front of the mirror. Slow down, hoss, he said to himself, whoa-up now, big fella. He put on his jeans and old cowboy boots and his nicest green sweater. He headed for 121 Third Street.

40

Third Street. A quiet neighborhood. The yards were orderly but not so well kept that plastic toy parts looked out of place. The lawns blossomed each year with campaign signs of one kind or another, from U.S. president to local county commissioners. Flats of petunias from local nurseries lined most entryways and, in warm weather, the smell of outdoor cooking reached the sidewalk.

Frank passed a young man playing his guitar and singing on a wooden porch. A mongrel bounced to a white fence alongside the sidewalk barking hoarsely, as though each time it landed on the ground the impact drove the barks from its lungs. Frank didn't react and the dog gave it up as a bad job. An old Dodge rested on flat tires alongside the curb. Its hood was up and two teenage boys rested on their elbows and chests underneath it, contemplating the engine with such absorption that neither felt the need to speak. When Frank was a boy he wanted a car so much, he tried to study how they worked. He memorized the four-cycle engine — intake, compression, power and exhaust — so that if he ever got a car, he would know how to operate it. What could recommend itself better to a pubescent youngster than a rolling love nest with its own music system? It explained the dreamy glaze of teenage drivers.

Now he was nervous. He was only a few houses away. In fact, there was the Saab. He stood in front of an English-style cottage with tall trellises covered with honeysuckle on either side of a narrow porch. Frank tried to understand exactly what he was doing here. He tried to remember who used to live here. He thought it was a piano teacher. He hesitated, and would have retreated if he had been sure he was unseen. Then Edward Ballantine came to the door and said, "Ah, I thought you might still come. Good." Gracie appeared behind him. Frank couldn't see her face well enough to glimpse her thoughts. "I think I'll just ease on," said Edward. "I really ought to be out of the way." He went out the door and, fixing Frank with a determined beam, down to the sidewalk. "Make the most of your visit," he called back. "It's for everyone's good."

Finally, Frank stood in front of Gracie in the doorway. The Saab went off with its airplane noise. Frank felt a little unsteady. He wished he'd brought something. Flowers would have been a laugh all right, but it would have been nice to do that anyway, nice and impossible.

"Hi, Grace."

"Hello, Frank." He must have looked blank because her face broke into a smile and she added, "Hi, I'm Gracie."

He felt a panicky numbness. He had not expected this and didn't feel he could be sure of anything he said. Gracie was wearing a pink cable-knit cardigan over her shoulders and her hands were clasped in front of her. She had her hair up and it emphasized the good way the years had firmed her face into a small strength. Her eyes were brown and deep-set, and there were times when she looked a bit Indian.

"Edward suggested that maybe we could talk," he said.

"I've been expecting you."

"I wonder, shall I come in?"

"I really don't know."

"I think you can trust me, Gracie."

"It's not that. I just don't want to watch you noticing how

we've furnished the place. I think you're well capable of making that the issue."

"I am curious. I suppose I'd say something. Well, we could sit out here. Or go somewhere to eat. It's almost that time. Honestly, I wouldn't make the furniture the issue. I'm not that bad."

Gracie pointed to the street. "Eat it is, then."

The Mine got a pretty good lunch crowd. It was an Italo-American restaurant featuring vaguely familiar Italian dishes with the usual local short cuts. It was designed to suggest a complicated grotto with lumpy white walls and dripping red candles in wall sconces. Despite the active clientele, the place seemed ripe for abandonment; but then it had seemed that way for more than a generation. On being seated by a distracted young man who pulled back Gracie's chair and blindly handed them two menus, they confronted the very specific moment of quiet.

"Well, we've already seen each other once."

"It was different, somehow," said Frank.

"How is that?"

"You were on your own. If only for the day. And we were there for Holly, weren't we."

Gracie looked into her menu. "It's unbelievable," she said. "Your life goes upside down. You travel around the world. Nations fall. Wars break out. But the menu here never changes. It's humbling to think your life could end, your family could move away, and this Lasagna Special would still be paper-clipped to the menu."

Frank sensed her in some palpable way that was different from seeing her there holding her menu, a strand of dark hair hanging in her face. She braced the menu one-handed with her thumb in the crease, freeing her other hand to move the hair back over her ear. He thought he was safe watching her study it, but her eyes floated up and engaged his. She smiled.

"What are you having?" he asked.

"I hadn't really looked."

"Better look. This place gives you one moving shot at the waiter and it's over."

Frank stared at the menu and thought, before he had found it: club sandwich. The first time he had eaten one, when he was a young caddy spending his fees at the country club patio restaurant and imagining that the club sandwich somehow expressed the social superiority of country club people, he sank the hidden toothpick into the roof of his mouth. He had always wondered why that teary moment, wagging his free hand in agony, had begun his long love affair with the club sandwich.

Gracie said, "You're having the club sandwich, right?"

"You got it."

"That's the summit of local cuisine, isn't it."

"Probably."

"Republicans have been able to evolve over a long period of time without disturbance," said Gracie. "I know they didn't invent the club sandwich but they have certainly made it their own."

"I just smile at these remarks."

"You were never really typical, except for your eating habits."

"Incidentally, I haven't ordered a club sandwich yet. And I don't feel absolutely locked into that choice."

"Where is the waiter, anyway?"

Frank craned around. "I'll try to flag him down."

"Now don't get on a tear. He'll be here soon enough. They're very busy. Besides, I'm having the lasagna. They never run out of that. Never."

Frank was looking over at a table of four businessmen he knew. One was a broker at D. A. Davidson, Bob Klane, great racquetball player. Two were guys at Century 21, Terry Simcross and Vance James. They'd done Quail Run, north of town, forty or fifty single-family dwellings. It had fascinated Frank because there were no quail in Montana. The fourth was Dr. Alioti, an ob-gyn formerly of his clinic, what Phil called a "cunt doctor," an active investor in local businesses. Frank didn't blame him, having built a fortune staring into all those multishaped, disembodied vulvas, for wanting an activity on a very broad scale. The point was, he had caught the four of them peering over at his table and then inclining toward each other to have a little discussion.

"Do you mind terribly if I find a waiter?" Frank asked.

"Yes, I do mind," Gracie said. "I want you to be patient and quiet. We have lots to talk about."

"Those four shits came in after we did and they're already eating."

"I want you to show repose and wait to be served."

A waiter glided under one of the arched grotto entries. He seemed to be headed their way. Gracie caught Frank staring and said, "Be patient." The waiter sailed right on past and out an archway on the other side. Frank elevated his eyes to the gondoliers in the shiny print beside their table and tried to stay calm. He wanted to talk to Gracie, but what seemed to him an abusive atmosphere was oppressing him. The four business acquaintances exploded into laughter. Frank aimed his eyes on them.

Gracie was watching him. Maybe she knew what they knew, that he wasn't doing well, that his careless capacity for earning money was backfiring, that events were overtaking him, that the man who had always been just ahead of events was now slightly behind them. He could soon seem to be a victim. Already, he had begun to notice a smiling attitude in people around him. He could try a leveling explosion somehow, but that would just be a matter of buying time. And people understood that. They knew what desperation was in others. They knew it as a prelude to bottom-feeding time. Frank could start right this minute by calming down about not being served. He would do as Gracie said: he would calm down. He would wait his turn. As far as he was concerned, the waiter could shove that club sandwich right up his ass if he wanted to.

"Are we okay?" Gracie asked. She was looking closely at him. She knew him thoroughly. No one else did, really. It was a damned shame that it was now apropos of nothing. Still, she had beautifully smooth round arms.

"So," said Frank, "I take it you've been traveling."

"Yes."

"Any place in particular?"

"Not really. A couple of places with mountains, one with cactus. One had a beach."

"Were the rooms comfortable?"

" 'Were the rooms comfortable . . .' Yeah, the rooms were comfortable."

He thought of the tall, hip, draping posture of Edward Ballantine. He thought about standing in a river when nothing was wrong, or sitting on some hill watching the weather change, smelling the south wind come across a rain-soaked prairie. He was tired of thinking. He wanted to get a box lunch and go watch a car wash in action.

"I'm really hungry," Frank said.

"It's the lunch hour. They're doing all they can. You have to take a more positive view of other people. Frank, I can tell you this. It's a major problem with you. You expect the worst of other people."

"I want something to eat." He knew it wasn't true. He perhaps expected the worst of her.

In a little while, the four business associates got up from their table, paused for a moment to chip in on the tip. The doctor turned with some apparent upper-body stiffness and acknowledged Frank with a nod. One of the realtors, Terry Simcross, raised a hand as if to say "How." The racquetball player placed his hands flat on the wall and did some limbering up, and they all went out under the low arch. There were now very few people in the restaurant. Frank wanted so much to begin talking freely to Gracie but he simply couldn't get it out of his mind that they had not been waited on.

"You know, I suppose that I have been having a rather glum spell in business."

"I had lunch with Lucy yesterday. She filled me in."

"I see," said Frank. Gracie tightened her eyes but said nothing. Maybe she had nothing further to say. He did a quick evaluation and concluded that Lucy probably didn't say anything to her. Still, he thought the eye-tightening represented an instant of being evaluated by Gracie. Call it a draw.

266

He remembered imagining his former home life: tasteful, spacious, comfortable, cheerily caught up in routines they devised themselves, routines they amiably pretended to wish to escape. They used to talk about foreign travel, second homes. He watched a couple at the table behind them pay their bill and get up to leave. He gazed at the gondoliers.

"We are not in a particularly good business era here in town, as you saw with Amazing Grease. And I haven't been paying attention the way I should have. There used to be a virtue in being so diversified, but it is now perilously close to scattered. And right now, I'm pretty scattered."

"Scared?"

"Scattered. I think I'm in a kind of adjustment period, you know? I think others might handle it better than I do. It just takes time."

Gracie leaned across the table until she was close to his face. His heart started to speed up because he thought he was about to be kissed. She said, "You shouldn't fuck Lucy so much if it doesn't mean anything to you." Then she leaned back.

"I know." What else could he say?

"Lucy was my friend."

"It takes a certain amount of gumption to find a stranger," Frank said. "You have to really mean it."

Gracie looked off, her eyes snapping. Frank tried to ease out of it by explaining the period when he relied entirely on self-stimulation.

"It was like being a jai alai player."

She didn't laugh.

The waiter came into the room, empty except for Gracie and Frank, and swiped at the empty tables with a cloth. He wore a white apron over a green-and-white-striped soccer shirt and pump-up basketball shoes with silver speed streaks on their sides. When he got close enough, Frank told him, as levelly as he could, that they would like to order. The waiter, with a voice much deeper than his youthful face would have suggested, said, "I'm sorry, but we're closed."

41

"*Oh, no you're not.*"

"Frank —"

"We've been in here an hour," said Frank.

"You should've asked for a waiter," said the waiter.

Frank got up in a way that caused his chair to skid across the room at considerable speed and bound around like some live thing.

"Frank, please."

The waiter jumped backward on his pump-up sneakers and spun toward the kitchen. Frank tried to pick an even gait in following him. When he got around the corner, the waiter had disappeared into the kitchen and the manager was standing at the swinging door, a small man in a sport jacket, dark-complected with a sharply outlined widow's peak. His full cheeks were stippled by a heavy beard.

"May I help you?" He smiled.

"Yuh, you may. My wife and I would like to have lunch."

"But we closed at two." He looked closely at Frank.

"This I realize," said Frank, picking this odd locution in an attempt to match the manager's reasonable tone. "But we've been in there waiting for over an hour."

"No!"

"Yes!"

"And you expect me to believe this?"

"I can prove it. Several acquaintances of ours were in here with us."

"I'm Federico," said the manager, holding out his hand.

Frank shook hands with him. He said, "Frank."

"This must be no treat for the missus," said Federico, "but we'll see if we can patch it up." He gripped Frank by the shoulders, tilted his own head and looked at Frank closely. "Is everything okay?"

Frank went into a loose Robert Mitchum posture. "What's not to be okay about except I can't get anything to eat here?"

"You looked pretty crazed there, Frank, when you come around that corner. You looked about a bubble and a half off plumb."

"It was getting to me," Frank allowed.

"Frank, I am going to prepare lunch for you and the missus. It'd be my great pleasure to cook for you. After that, you'll wonder how you ever ate that stuff on the menu."

Federico followed Frank back into the dining room, which was now completely empty. Well, it was no wonder and it was no surprise. Frank immediately realized that Gracie wasn't going to sit around while he caused a scene. Besides, he was doomed. His complete failure to control his impulses had again prevented him from doing what was most important to him. He was deeply shaken. He stared into the empty room until Federico moved around in front of him, spread his hands in inquiry and, with wide sparkling eyes, asked, "Where is the little woman of our earlier discussion?"

"She bugged out," said Frank, still defensively locked into his forties movie slouch. He didn't know how to go on to the next thing. This little Mediterranean type seemed maddeningly precise. It brought out the dormant galoot within him.

"Frank, I repeat my earlier question: are you okay?"

Frank decided to try something. He said, "No, I'm not okay." He let his face collapse. The hell with being okay.

"Was there really a wife?"

"There was. It doesn't matter if you believe me. We were just hungry. We were going to eat together." Then he added in stifled despair that could have broken out in a howl, "*We could never get a waiter.*"

"Frank, have a seat. I am going to cook for you. Don't panic, Frank. I believe you. Do not, I repeat do not, jump to your feet and chase the little wife around the town. Take some time out for a beautiful meal. You have to change your timing. You look like a lunatic. The little woman will run from such a face."

Frank sat down obediently.

"I am going to prepare you a meal and then I am going to sit down with you and tell you how to be with the woman."

It seemed a legitimate challenge not to blow sky high, not to race into the street in geekish pursuit, not to be so blatantly needy, though it was questionable what he might hope to conceal from Gracie. Eating mysterious food with this swarthy man, whose restaurant had given him such poor service that he lost a longed-for opportunity of contact with his estranged wife, was going to test his great desire for grace under pressure. He was jumping out of his skin. He didn't want to hear about the woman and how to be with her.

"And now," said Federico, "I am going to the kitchen."

Frank kept up the slouch and waved him on his way. The hand with which he waved, resting across the back of the chair so recently occupied by Gracie, swung idly at the wrist. Oh, this is good, thought Frank. He pursed his lips in an expression of leisure he had sometimes observed, eyes elevated into a middle distance. He had lost all sense of natural behavior. He found himself to be peckish and tried speculating on the approaching meal. He imagined that Gracie was somewhere nearby, expecting his footsteps at any time. That's not a crazy idea, he thought.

The sound system came on, Elton John singing "Daniel." A few moments later, Federico appeared and set a bottle of wine on the table, saying, "Valpolicella," pausing to listen to the music and singing along: "Must be the clouds in my eyes." Federico left the room and Frank checked his watch. He had a glass of wine. He was to do this several times and actually begin to perspire before Federico returned in triumph. "Il primo!" he said, and placed two dishes on the table. "Spaghettini al carrettiere." Some kind of spaghetti deal, Frank surmised, and began to eat. He was ravenous already, but this would have made him ravenous. He mumbled respectfully and moved his eyebrows up and down in appreciation. Nice little guy, thought Frank. I guess he's an Italian.

"I saw the pope on TV here a while back," said Frank amiably when he finally had an empty mouth.

"That Polack," said Federico, a sharp pinch appearing in his forehead. "Let's not talk about him. I mean, kiss my ring, please!"

"This is delicious," said Frank.

"Yes, it is," said Federico. He got up and went out to the kitchen. There was some shouting out there, dominated by Federico's voice. Evidently, he had someone still helping him in the kitchen. Frank shot his cuff and had another look at his watch. He'd been here a long, long time. He drank another glass of wine. He still hadn't heard how to handle the woman. The wine took the slipperiness off his teeth. He couldn't understand Federico, but somehow Federico had deprived him of his momentum. The pasta was delicious, but it was more than enough for lunch. It was a sunny day outside; he had really pressing things to do and somehow, increasingly against his will, he was imprisoned in this kitsch grotto waiting for more food. Time seemed to crawl.

At length, Federico reappeared with two more plates and another bottle of wine clamped under his arm. "Il secondo! Fagioli dell' occhio con salsiccia."

"I've never seen this before," said Frank, looking at the plate.

"You wanted a cheeseburger?"

"No, no, no. This looks wonderful." He took an appreciative bite. It *was* wonderful. Federico uncorked the second bottle of wine and refilled their glasses.

"The woman . . ." Federico mused as he raised his glass to his lips. "She is sitting on a fortune."

Frank felt a glow go through his head. "How can you be so vulgar?"

He looked down at the beautifully variegated textures of black-eyed peas, plum tomatoes and sausages in olive oil and garlic sauce. He didn't seem to have any problems and he had quit looking at his watch. He was having a wonderful experiment in sedation. Federico looked twisted all right, but twisted in a fanciful, harmless way, like a gnome.

"Little more vino," he said.

Frank poured. "Were you born in Italy?" he asked.

"Naw, Roundup."

"Roundup?"

"Yeah, they got everything in Roundup." The continental accent was gone. "Major Serb hangout since I don't know when. And . . . there was a time when Dean fuckin' Martin coulda run for mayor. *Hey!*" he shouted.

A voice came back from the kitchen.

"Put on Dean Martin!"

"Look, Federico —"

"Fred. Federico is just my restaurant name."

"Fred, this has been great —"

"And free."

"Oh, well, that's nice, good, thank you. But look, I've got to get going now. Really, I'm going to have to eat and run."

Fred was raising his forefinger in the air, the ball of the first digit now at eye level to Frank. "One thing, Frank."

"Yes?"

"Before the bank gets involved under a reorganization, why don't you discount the hell out of your clinic and sell it to me. You know they're coming. This leaves them holding the bag, what every red-blooded American boy desires."

Frank was horrified that this information was so general. "Do I know they're coming?"

"You know they're coming. I know who you are, Frank. I think you realize that."

Frank considered the light fog in his brain and decided he could rise above it. He cleared his dishes to one side of the table and felt things slow down gracefully. He looked across the table, mentally measuring Fred, and said, "Make me an offer."

Fred had his right elbow on the table and was leaning on his hand. He straightened up and turned the hand so that the palm faced the ceiling. "Where do I start?"

"With an acceptable price. That's the fastest."

Fred smiled. "What do *you* think it's worth?"

"Fred, I can't buy it and sell it at the same time. Make me an offer."

"Make you an offer . . ."

"Yeah, like pull up your Fruit of the Looms and go for it."

This was getting pretty close to what Frank and his friends in high school referred to as the family jewels. This would shoot right to the heart of a Dean Martin fan.

"I guess we could look at structuring a deal. How would you want this, Frank?"

"In American money."

Fred leaned on his fist for a moment and then said, "What about five hundred thou?"

Frank said nothing. It was an insulting offer. This guy was primitive. Frank's hand was rested on the table. He raised it slightly and pointed upward.

Fred smiled and said, "A little dish of spumoni?"

"No thanks. Fred, who told you I might need to sell the clinic?"

"Talk of the town."

Frank immediately related this to Gracie. That must be an interesting development to her, an antidote to the wearying predictability of the once brilliant businessman. El Floppo. For an instant, Frank saw failure as a way of dancing out ahead. Any creature that goes in a straight line is an invitation to predators. Except that old Fred here was sort of the predator.

"Did you see in the paper where Pepsi is coming out with a see-through cola?" Fred asked.

"They're gonna fall on their ass," said Frank.

"I agree," said Fred, "but you know, colas are naturally clear."

"Huh."

"Little known fact. They add the coloring. I saw this VIP from Coke, cornered by reporters. He was yelling, 'We have no plans to market a clear Tab!' He looked like the wolves had him. He was shakin' in his boots. I kinda felt sorry for him."

"How's anybody going to know this stuff's clear?" Frank asked. "They going to pour it out on the ground?"

"The product's gonna be in bottles, not cans."

"Oh."

Fred eased his checkbook out of his inside coat pocket. Frank smiled amiably, but it was camouflage. Fred had no way of knowing that this sale wouldn't even meet the mortgage. Frank was trying to remember how these things were cross-collateralized — the hotel, the mini-storage, the office equipment and so on. He remembered reading that the boa constrictor doesn't actually squeeze you to death but simply takes up the slack when you exhale or relax and never lets you get it back. Result? *Mort*. At the same time, contemplating the loss, Frank had the thought, This isn't quite registering. He tried to picture a soup kitchen. It was like dabbling in failure.

Fred said, "You want my guy to prepare the closing?"

"There isn't going to be a closing."

"That's where you're wrong, Frank. There's gonna be a closing."

It was happening. The snake was taking up slack. You could have whatever you wanted, but you couldn't take a breath.

42

As Frank walked up Main Street, he reflected that recent history had shown that business failure and political disgrace were reliable preludes to spiritual awakening. Maybe I have that to look forward to, thought Frank. He was standing in front of a shop that sold stereo systems. They had Vivaldi and Tina Turner in the window and a display showing a man slumped in a large armchair, holding on for dear life, his hair blown back, all by the power of his sound system. He wondered why everything was crazy juxtapositions, cartoons or exaggerations these days. He wondered why his career was up in the blue and he was running around trying to field it like a pop fly.

There before him was Karl Hammersgard, the baseball coach, who had a cigarette centered in his teeth. He was shorter than Frank, but he bent back from the waist to talk rather than bend his head at the neck. This was one way short people looked up to taller people without appearing like they were looking up a stovepipe. A car pulled alongside them and parked. Frank caught the blue oval and the word "Ford" in the corner of his eye.

"Where've you been, anyway?" said Karl Hammersgard.

"I've been around."

"You have? Maybe I just haven't been paying attention. I saw Gracie. Is there . . . what."

"Is there what?"

"Anything cooking?"

"Not with me, Karl. Alas."

"Alas, huh?"

"Well, semi-alas."

"I think it's alas, old pal."

"Maybe it is, Karl. I'm one of those guys you read about who's not really in touch with his feelings."

"Hey, me either. I don't want to be in touch with my feelings. What a can of worms!"

"You said it. Say, what about Dick Hoiness? You see Dick Hoiness?"

"Frank, I seen Dick Hoiness about four days ago. Dick has really took off, got his own office, got a new car. I'm proud of him. Isn't it something? He was the worst of all you hippies."

After Frank continued down the sidewalk, he thought about Fred. It was Fred's turn to hoard. And Dick Hoiness's. I'm not going to hoard anymore, he told himself, no matter what.

He used the side door of his office to avoid any awkwardness with Lucy at the travel agency. There was a note from Eileen saying that she had quit and asking him to call. He called and got a recitation of events in which Eileen tried to be fair-minded, but she spoke in a sardonic tone about her need for a predictable atmosphere, a world that was not changing daily. She said that she would be willing to work on a contract basis, some bookkeeping and some typing, if that was needed. Frank thought that it might well be. He thanked her for many years of service, and when he got off the phone, he felt immediate relief to have the office to himself. He began to work at his desk. The bills and letters were hopelessly mixed up; so were the incomprehensible wads from the tax assessor, who was just now coming into season. He found himself reading the unsolicited mail; not just Victoria's Secret but also ham catalogues, tool catalogues, garden catalogues, sporting equipment catalogues, video catalogues, salmon products catalogues, fun things for kids catalogues, self-help catalogues. There were many things to buy. It was desolating.

He was surprised that, in view of his personal problems, he was so interested in the slowed sales growth of diet colas. He remembered 1982 as the year Diet Coke came on line, and 1984 as the year Diet Coke went to NutraSweet. His life must not have been perfect then, but now it was seriously imperfect and he focused on Clearly Canadian as the first beverage to identify some of the new energies out there, with mountain blackberry and orchard peach sodas sold in blue glass bottles that were heavy in the hand. A Pepsi spokesman stated in the *Wall Street Journal* that his company was not going to sit on the sidelines and watch the New Age go by without their participation. Besides, Pepsi was trying to find the right spin for their spokesperson Michael Jackson's relentlessly grabbing his dick in his latest video. In a surprise move, Kraft, a division of Philip Morris, was testing canned cappuccino in Arizona. Frank sighed at these national battles, thinking of his reduction to hotel keeper for chickens. He didn't feel that visiting these chickens with dick in hand would produce a national news conference and exploding chicken sales or he would have headed on over there and gotten down to business.

Someone was stirring around in the front office. Frank folded his paper and called out, "Yes? Can I help you?"

"Dad?"

"Holly? Hol, is that you?"

Frank went into the front office, once occupied by the hugely appreciated Eileen. Holly was standing there with her old high school girl grin. She was wearing a snap-button shirt and jeans with a scarf through the belt loops. The effect of the costume was a bit more "western" than Frank was accustomed to. He gave her a hug. Then she followed him into his office and allowed him to pull up a chair for her.

Holly had moved back into town. She was taking a semester off to be with Lane Lawlor. This was better for Lane's contacts in the range livestock industry, and Lane felt he had timber products well covered. He was working as a lobbyist for "some people." Frank tried to ask mildly, "Which people?" but it came out a little strong. They settled for "people." Frank was seething.

"Have you seen Mama?"

"I have seen Mama," said Frank.

"And?"

"We were, well, we had an unsuccessful luncheon."

"An argument?"

"No, we just couldn't get waited on. Then I got annoyed, and you know how she is about me being annoyed."

"But that touches me."

"What does, Hol?"

"You blowing your stack, Mama annoyed."

"Oh, yeah. Well, in that sense it was like old times."

Frank tried to make a couple of stacks of paper on his desk.

"Do you miss those times, Dad?"

"Every day," Frank said.

"You do?"

"I do. I miss a lot of things. I miss you. My life is not in very good order."

"I know."

"Well, see, that embarrasses me too."

"Don't let it."

"Some things get out of reach." He was thinking that her proclivity for Lane Lawlor didn't help.

"We read in the paper about your putting chickens in the Kid Royale Hotel."

"Desperate strokes for desperate folks."

"But Dad, where did that idea come from?"

"I didn't originate it. They've done it in the East for years with old hotels. They're really perfect chicken coops on an industrial scale. We think we can make money. It was a partnership I needed. I can't really afford to restore the place." Frank was conscious of talking too much. He could scarcely depict his pleasure in covering romance, from honeymoons to the Old West, with a thin layer of leveling chickenshit. He didn't want to burrow around in all this anyway. He wanted to go fishing with Holly. He thought that if he couldn't, he would suddenly die.

They stopped by the house to gather their tackle. Holly's was still there. Lane didn't fish; he was an elk hunter and in fact had made a bit of a name for himself through his marksmanship, picking off infected buffaloes on the border of Yellowstone Park. Frank, seeing Lane's picture in the paper, thought that, in his knee-high lace-up boots, his broad Stetson and his red plaid coat, he had rather anticipated the photographer. Cuddling his rifle, he had made several articulate statements about the Constitution and its bearing on gun ownership. Lane knew his stuff, that was for sure.

It was a cool, pretty day and it seemed but a jaunt to get through the subdivisions, the more spacious acreages north of town with horses and, here and there, llamas in the yards. They passed low gumbo hills and wandered along the east branch of the Bridger River, then turned up the road to the creek where Holly had had such a triumph. Frank thought how much better it was to have done something together than to have spent all their energy in discussions. Today he hadn't wanted to discuss his life, his marriage, his record as a parent. He had wanted to do something with Holly. Anything would have done — throwing a Frisbee, making chili, fishing.

They pulled into the brush so as not to make their poaching more conspicuous than necessary. Frank drew the old bamboo shafts of his Paul Young rod from the rod tube and smelled the varnish in the rod sack. He had owned the rod for thirty years and it had become too valuable to fish with, probably, but he fished with it anyway. Frank felt good standing next to Holly and rigging up. She doubled her fly line and ran it through the guides faster than he strung his rod, running the point of his leader through the guides. He opened the battered aluminum fly box that had been a gift from Gracie twenty years before and they looked into the compartments.

"We could wait and see if anything is hatching," said Holly.

"I think it's best to be prepared to cast upon arrival."

"Give me a size sixteen blue-winged olive."

"Hackled?"

"Please."

He handed her a fly and said, "I know you've got your own, but I'll spot you one."

Frank tied on a 1930s Blackfoot River favorite called a Charlie's special, which a friend in Missoula had tied for him. A note had come with the flies: "Excuse the sloppy job on these flies. The hackle was horrific. Every piece had a spiral stem. Must've come from some poor Indian chicken mutated by Bhopal."

By the size of her trout on their last trip, Holly was entitled to lead the way. They pushed through the woods, Frank gingerly carrying his bamboo rod butt-first. There wasn't the number of wildflowers there had been previously, but a splendid stand of bear grass revealed itself on an open hillside. They were almost head deep in the streamside grass before they broke through and found that the creek was gone.

In its place was a fetid mud channel beginning to crack in the sun. Where they stood in the middle of the channel, the banks rose high over their heads.

"Are we lost?" Frank asked.

"I don't think so."

They walked a short distance in the direction of what had been upstream, and Frank stopped. He said, "Right here is where you caught that fish." He could see the deeply undercut bank, a cavernous space that had been an ideal chamber for a big fish to live in secretly. The ferns were dying on the banks, and here and there were the remains of fish, picked over by birds and raccoons. From the mud came an intense smell, undoubtedly from the millions of watery invertebrates that had lived there.

They walked on and reached a fence that now crossed above their heads. Passing under it, they came to the heart of a farm. They could make out the upper parts of barns and granaries and electrical poles. They climbed out onto the bank. From here, Frank could see what had happened. The Caterpillars with which the farmer had built up a broad dyke to impound the stream were parked nearby. The ruptured earth on the face of the berm still bore the blade marks; and the impoundment behind it continued to fill, so that the serviceberry bushes and aspens that were now half submerged were still alive. Bright new aluminum pipes for an advanced irrigation system were pyramided on low wagons. Frank had a brief impulse to put a good face on this. "Looks like we'll have to find someplace else to fish." Holly nodded. "Is this fella a friend of Lane's?"

"Dad, I don't think you can lay this one on Lane. And if the water was leaving the state, I'm for this."

"He's the sort of fascist windbag that produces this kind of activity."

"I'm going home."

"I'm sorry."

"I'm sure. And yes, this might be one of our followers. We believe in-stream storage is the basis of our future." She was talking in a curiously rhetorical way, a recitation. The tone was, Take it or leave it.

Frank drove Holly to her apartment. They talked very little on the way back. Frank thought that it was pretty unlucky to go fishing and find the stream had been stolen, particularly when you needed the stream for more than just fishing.

43

The phone rang in the dark. He had a feeling it might be Gracie, who got up about two hours before dawn. She was always worried about missing something. Frank was able to reach over to the bedside table and get it without turning on his light. It was Gracie.

"Shall we try again?"

"I'm willing to try again, if you are," he said.

"I'm talking about lunch."

"That's what I mean," he lied, "lunch. What did you think I meant?"

"Lunch, I guess."

"No, let's not have lunch. It's too structured. Let's go to the library."

"When?"

"When does it open?" Frank asked.

"I think nine."

"I'll meet you in front," he said.

"Okeydoke."

"Well, good night."

"Goodbye."

Frank got up at daylight. From his bedroom he could see a blush on the houses along the street. A car went by and he looked down at its empty ski rack. A leisurely dog appeared and lifted his leg against the base of a stop sign, then circled it slowly, scratching with stiff legs. A magpie flew down onto a laurel branch and shifted its head back and forth for balance while the oscillations of the branch slowly came to a stop.

In the shower, Frank thought about how he had always believed the ridiculous adage about how if a nail were lost, the shoe would be lost, the horse lost, the battle lost and so on to an avalanche of failure. He accepted these things as an aborigine accepts the airplane, as the poor accept Republicans. He knew that this was a useful thought process that would cease when he ran out of hot water. Since the house had only a thirty-gallon tank, his capacity for fruitful contemplation was limited.

As the water cooled, and as he realized he had to save a little for shaving, he homed right in on this new loneliness which came not simply from solitude but from ambiguity about his everyday activities, activities that had long been a source of comfort. It was clear that beyond meeting living requirements, the only joy in business lay in humiliating the neighbors. Frank didn't even know who they were! He probably ought to observe them again soon. In his present state, the bristling quest for humiliation by people in their big new cars and sprawling houses seemed healthy, a formula for happiness, a spiritual elixir, a sovereign to the hot-blooded in their pointy shoes.

The sun was just up and hardening its light for the day when Frank got downstairs, where he found Phil Page making himself a pot of coffee. "You eat breakfast?" Frank asked. He always took the tone of immediately continuing some previous conversation.

"I had some doughnuts."

"I'm going to make something. You want something?"

"Sure, I'll eat it."

Frank beat some eggs in a bowl and got out a loaf of bread. "Can you eat French toast made with raisin bread?"

"Sounds great."

"So what's going on?"

"A lot."

"Really. Well, let me get this on first. You want to grab the OJ out of the fridge? Just put the carton on the table."

"Man," said Phil from the refrigerator, "you need to clean this baby out. This shit is growing some blue fur. Fucking penicillin nightmare."

Frank put their breakfast on the table and sat down. When Phil sat, after dramatically washing his hands, Frank said, "Okay, go ahead." He was checking out Phil's long beard. It made him look like an old Appalachian miner. Phil had to pull it to one side while he ate, and it looked like a lot of trouble. Frank couldn't imagine it helped his love life, unless women liked something like that waving around on their tits. It seemed unlikely. One hardly knew what they wanted. He remembered the sense of terror he had had when a woman psychiatrist he met at the Big Sky Ski Resort told him, democratically illustrating how she was human too, that there was nothing she enjoyed more than a cold bottle of Kristal champagne and a good spanking.

"It was on the radio last night," Phil said. "Some rancher said he wanted to shoot a wolf. He said he wanted to get caught so he could say his piece in court."

"That's too bad but it's no surprise. I heard the only one left was a male, but that was from my secretary and I don't think she cares."

"There's only one left. A big silver female."

"How do you know there's even one left?" Frank asked.

"She's got a radio collar on her. That's the one the Fish and Wildlife is tracking. They're hoping she doesn't get killed. She's the last one. But that rancher said there's lots more like him and they're gonna get that wolf one way or the other."

"Is this going to be enough French toast for you?"

"Yeah, it's real good."

"It's easy to make."

"Just dip the bread in there, right? And fry it?"

"That's it. So, we're talking about Smokie, right?"

"Right," Phil said. "I'm thinking she must be trying to follow that wolf around, trying to keep it from getting shot." Frank offered him the last of his French toast. "No thanks, you eat that. I've had plenty. Take a look at this." Phil picked up what looked like a portable radio with a wide antenna on its top.

"What is it?"

"It's a radio direction finder. I stole it from the Fish and Wildlife truck."

"Oh, Phil. What are you going to do with it?"

"I'm going to find where the wolf is hanging out, and that way I'll find Smokie," said Phil. "Maybe it'll keep something from happening to her."

"Huh. Good luck. Hey, you know what? I think I'm drinking too much."

"Is that right. Do you think it's got you?"

"I was reading in the *National Geographic* about the Bay of Fundy, where they have these thirty-foot tides. You can walk out for miles on the bottom of the bay at low tide and pick up fish and clams and lobster. But you better know when the tide is coming back in. If you wait till it reaches your ankles, you'll never reach the shore alive. I think maybe that's the way booze works. I'm thinking I better watch it."

"I let it get to my ankles," Phil said. "I know that." He got up and walked over to the window, drew the curtain back and looked into the next yard. "I already know that. But anyway, look, here's what I'm thinking. Maybe we better find her. Who knows what some of them cowboys are liable to do if she gets between them and the wolf, which is what she's trying to do."

"Where's this last wolf supposed to be?"

"Over in the Tobacco Root Mountains."

"That's not the easiest place in the world to get around."

"I want you to go in there and help me find her," said Phil. "I can't do it alone."

"Can you give me till tonight to figure out when I can go?" Frank knew that this high-minded notion would soon blow over. "Because you know what I'm doing today?" He was standing now. He straightened an imaginary bow tie, as though he were headed for the moment that would turn his life to dream.

"What are you doing today?"

"I'm going to see Gracie."

"Gracie," Phil said as his face helplessly darkened. "What's she doing back in town?"

"How the hell should I know? What's Smokie doing in Montana? What's June doing on a Buick lot?"

"What's my wife doing fucking the doctor?"

"And so on. Exactly."

44

The library had a room that housed the papers of several early Montana governors. It had a long table meant for research, and beside it a tall south-facing window that framed the shape of a terrific maple that stood within a low-walled court. The maple fractured the intense southern light and filled the room with a blue, green and silver glow. Frank loved to imagine the contemplative people whose horizons were undiminished by a thirty-gallon hot water tank and who would let this fine and eternal light accompany the life of the mind.

"How's this?"

"This is fine," said Gracie. She set her bag on the table and took the back of her chair in her hands. Frank knew what would be in that bag: a Walkman and tapes, an apple, a plastic rain parka, an address book, a wallet, a paperback and at least one complete anomaly: once it was a New Orleans phone book, once a field guide to spiders.

"So, let's sit down," he said. They sat on either side of the table, as though they were at a meeting. Well, this *was* a meeting. Frank felt a sweeping comfort. Something near his center was entering repose. His head retired. He knew it was only a matter of time before the center boiled over and the head was back in charge.

"Just so I can understand, Grace, Edward realizes that we are meeting?"

"He does." Gracie had her hair tied up with a piece of yellow silk. A few strands fell across her forehead and temples.

"I just don't understand why that is acceptable to him. I know there're plenty of weird new males out there. But are some of them completely unpossessive?"

"You would hope so, wouldn't you? I think in Edward's case it's important for him to know that my . . . amorous past is erased. If I can freely meet with you, I think that would satisfy that requirement."

" 'Requirement.' "

"Yes."

"It would seem that Edward is a completely healthy new man, then."

"He doesn't think so. He believes that he has an addictive personality."

"Addicted to what?"

"Money."

"You can be addicted to money?"

"Edward thinks so. He thinks that it is every bit as addictive as cocaine or alcohol. His wife is very rich and he worries he will go back to her because of his addiction."

"He's already spoken to my accountant about my financial health. Maybe he's having a little slip."

"Haven't you reached the point where you've lost interest in scoring off other people?"

"My testosterone levels are about where they've been. Anything with warm blood makes my trigger finger itch."

Gracie dug around in her purse until she found her Carmex. She opened the lid and swirled the surface inside with her forefinger, then applied some to her lips. "Look Frank, I'm going to be honest with you. Edward feels his relationship with me began in deception and typified the behaviors he associates with his addiction. He says that if you don't actually make something, the acquisition of money has to be based in deception. For example, in sales, the money you make is the difference between what the thing you sold is worth and what you have deceived someone into believing it is worth. On the other hand, everything Edward does turns to gold."

"Is it true he buys the life insurance policies of AIDS victims?"

"Yes," said Gracie, unmoving. "But it's not what you think. The sick person needs some cash and gets it. In this case, they deceive themselves because they think if they get the money they can keep from dying. Whereas Edward knows he's soon going to have the insurance settlement. Or if they don't deceive themselves, then it's the insurance company who are kidding themselves by never realizing that people would understand the idea of being doomed and that those people would go on ahead and discount their policy to a complete stranger."

"It's depressing."

"I think so too," said Gracie. "But so much is depressing. It's depressing that Holly has grown up."

"Isn't it."

"It seems like yesterday she was fingerpainting in her room," Gracie said.

"Yup. Or how about at her piano recital when she stood up and said, 'I cannot play "Streets of Laredo" because I have a sore G-finger'?"

"No more. She's a cheerful right-wing fanatic with her own life now."

"Wipe your eyes, Gracie."

"Give me a sec."

"So, where were we?"

"These chairs are hard, aren't they?"

"You sit in my lap?"

"Stop it, Frank."

"I still love you, Gracie."

"No you don't, and if you do, shut up about it."

"Why?"

"You make all these statements. I'm not real big on statements these days."

"Okay."

"So, like, can the statements."

"Okay!"

Gracie paused to blow her nose. Frank noted happily that she was comfortable making a loud, unselfconscious honk. He bet she didn't do that around Edward of the Money Problem.

"Anyway," she said, "I much preferred it when we were younger. I suppose it's a good thing that most of the world has no idea about what fun hippies had. Otherwise, nothing would work. It's necessary for most of the world to be deceived. That's where Edward and I differ. He is now addicted to the idea that he can put an end to deception."

"For the whole world?"

"He says it's little steps for little feet."

"Does this mean that when Edward gets his way, I'm going to have to pump my own septic tank?"

"Maybe."

"Pull my own wisdom teeth?"

"Could be."

"This is not a world I'm looking forward to, Grace."

Gracie got up from her chair and went to the window. Frank looked at her, remembering that he liked the way she held her shoulders back so that her back seemed concave and her shoulder blades disappeared even under a thin dress. He liked that the dress still gathered at the top of her buttocks.

"Anyway, I'm going to try to help Edward with what he thinks is his problem. I owe him that."

Frank thought that the concept of this debt had a conclusive note that he was not sure he was correct in hearing. Any relationship between men and women was a mounting debt. Why would she single this one out?

"So, I won't be seeing you . . . ?"

"That's why I asked you to meet me this morning."

"To say goodbye?"

"Not at all. Edward wanted me to find out if you would be

willing to meet with him in some sort of therapeutic way. Do you think you would?"

This was like hearing from your draft board during a national emergency. He could be as frightened as he wanted to be but he could hardly decline.

"Uh . . . sure."

45

He got back to the office, let himself in and turned on the lights. There were several messages trailing out of the fax machine but the phones were silent. There was the *Journal, Barron's, The Economist.* He enjoyed the otherworldly atmosphere of a modern office after hours. He tried his secretary's chair; it had an extraordinary flexibility of movement and she had had no view to distract her from the possibilities the chair offered. He ripped off the fax messages and noted that two of them were from the bank and were rather firm. They were far from summonses but they were certainly firm. The last message was from Jerry Drivjnicki at Reed Point, reminding him of their pig partnership. Frank had forgotten the pig partnership, but in this message Jerry asked him to please come to the stock show in Bozeman and show some interest in at least their *show* pigs. Jerry's message was relatively firm too.

Maybe Frank would have to go. He knew this particular walk-through: in a stockman's hat and camel's hair coat, you stood next to your pigs and stared into their genetic future while waiting for the judge. He realized that this small investment notion had put him somewhere he had no business being. But even as he smiled at the picture of himself in his big hat at the pig show, he realized he'd better not miss it. He remembered that when he had partnered with Jerry, the bank had said they "had trouble seeing money for him." He didn't know how he had gotten into so much action with cows, pigs and chickens. If he got the little dish he could play the commodities on the satellite, but that was too fast, too dangerous. He'd seen many a good man taken down by one of those dishes, Old MacDonalds of the microchip.

Frank parked well beyond the show barns, among the stock trailers. He climbed out of his car, pushing his big lizard cowboy boots out ahead of him. Several 4-H kids had tied their animals to the sides of their trailers for a final grooming. There was a beautiful slick steer, half asleep, being painstakingly brushed by a girl in her teens; there was a self-important ram having his forelock combed by a boy in a cowboy hat, several unattended horses under blankets and hoods like big ghosts, all out in the parking area. The stall barns were dark and smelled of straw bedding and dung. Here and there people were grooming their animals inside the stalls and portable radios played next to plastic trays of brushes, combs and hair spray. He felt first rate in his topcoat and big hat, eager to be among the pigs he co-owned, grand red Durocs he'd held to his chest as babies, now avatars of swine genetics the size of ponies, squinting with wiliness. He shot his coat cuff to look at his watch: he was just in time for the theoretical heart of pork belly futures as understood in the northern Rockies.

He stepped into the main hall with a gasp: clusters of hogs of truly exaggerated size stood with their handlers under powerful overhead lighting. Men and hogs were several inches deep in cat litter. There were bleachers all the way around and these were almost full of hog fans. A judge wandered among the hogs, speaking in a clandestine manner to an assistant who made notes on a clipboard. The judge was a small-faced man in a Stetson hat with a tight, permanent scowl. Frank spotted Jerry Drivjnicki, who grinned and waved him over. He stood next to a gleaming, mighty red Duroc, Tecumseh. It was like standing next to a spaceship.

"This must be Cump," said Frank.

"This is him," said Jerry, stepping to one side presentationally so Frank could admire Tecumseh. "He ain't like you remembered him, is he?"

"He was a suckling, Jerry."

"That whole litter was good ones," said Jerry.

Frank looked toward the bleachers and there was Gracie holding a pair of opera glasses. Next to her was Edward, her male companion, looking none too well. Frank's dismay at seeing her was set against the rather dissolute appearance of Edward.

"But Cump," Frank heard Jerry say, "he just jumped out at a guy. I knowed he was headed for the big time."

Gracie hadn't spotted Frank. Then Frank saw Holly, and Lane next to her, a real family tableau. He didn't for a moment think they would recognize him, but he saw Lane pointing down toward him and the four chatting among themselves. Frank felt body heat rising within his camel's hair topcoat and around the perimeter of the heavy, wide Stetson. He felt his posture fail slightly, a deadness of flesh and purpose. And some of the pigs didn't seem completely under control, skidding their handlers a bit as they tried to keep the animals in line while they awaited the judge. Feeling something against his rump, Frank turned to head off the interest of a half-ton boar hog. He caught the eye of the handler, a big vacant farmer with huge flat hands wrapped around his staff. Frank looked off and caught Gracie's eye and, he thought, her faint smile. He knew he was probably rising in Lane Lawlor's estimation, out here playing the stockman.

"You need to feel part of this," said Jerry. "I'm gonna let you handle showing this pig. Hell, he shows hisself. He knows he's making history."

Frank wanted to ask that Jerry not leave him. But it was too late and he couldn't think how he might say it anyway without expressing his sense of outlandish solitude. Several of the hogs were now squealing across the arena at one another, which brought a stir of concern from their showmen. They knew how to deal with it, but Frank could only hope Tecumseh stayed put.

Jerry gave Frank his staff, eased off and found himself a place to lean against the wall. The hog in back of Frank gave him another shove and Frank instinctively slipped his gaze up to Gracie, who was pointing her rolled-up program toward an animal that had gotten her attention. It was just as well; he wasn't eager to have this butt-rooting observed and was thinking of flogging the farmer if he didn't get it stopped. A few rows up sat Frank's hired man, Boyd Jarrell, who politely moved his eyes away once Frank had seen him. Frank was wondering if he was just being paranoid to be so startled at seeing all these people here. He supposed he was glad to have Boyd watch him taking an interest in the pigs. He thought they would all have to understand the costume he was wearing, but he wasn't sure. He really was dressed for Chicago or the National Western in Denver. He just couldn't have an outfit for every place a pig or a chicken or a steer with his name on its papers turned up. Frank hoped they would accept that. He did feel overdressed, though, as if he already expected to win the grand championship. He felt ridiculous.

He began thinking about the approach of the judge. He really had no idea what his role might be. He could only observe that the others were standing next to their hogs by way of establishing their ownership, he guessed, or responsibility. The judge with his mean little face seemed not to occupy any plane with his eyes that could be crossed by any other eyes. He simply went from hog to hog, seeing no humans, then making extremely brief remarks to his assistant, an effeminate teenage boy in a royal blue Future Farmers of America jacket who licked the end of his pencil before writing anything down. All power rested with these two, and since he did not understand his situation, Frank began to elaborate a stone-faced concern to go with the topcoat and the Stetson and the very distinct sense of being evaluated from the bleachers. He was relieved to notice that the showmen and the judge did not exchange words of any kind. For Jerry's sake he wanted their hog, Tecumseh, to do well; but he concentrated most on quietly handling his own part, however it turned out for the hog.

Frank felt proud of his big, well-behaved animal, who stood motionless and refrained from even joining in the squealing around the hall. There was certainly some sort of communication emanating from the judge, something nonverbal, because a middle-aged woman showing a vivid Hampshire gazed at the ceiling with tears shining on her cheeks the minute her hog was judged. Perhaps she had overheard the judge's remarks to the little farm sissy, thought Frank. Or perhaps she had never before faced the fact that she had a bum pig.

Now the judge was before him, looking right into the face of Frank's hog, as though he could read the mind of the pig and know whether or not he would transmit intelligence to his progeny. Frank knew that judges often looked for "femininity" in cattle, and maybe some such trait was sought here. Frank's hog ignored the judge but the brute behind Frank gave him another shove. He hitched his shoulders within the camel's hair topcoat and stared into the middle distance, feeling the hot breath of the other hog rise through his shorts. He rose on the balls of his feet but found himself trapped between the judge and his own hog. He strongly felt he must keep silent just now as befitted the demeanor of a stockman, but the butt-snuffling had become unbearable. He turned enough to take in the face of the farmer behind him and thought he detected a faint smile. That did it.

He swung around and gave the hog a good crack. It was a mistake. The brute squealed and dove forward between Frank's legs. Frank was astraddle the pig, looking into the sour but amazed face of the judge, and then the animal broke into a wild heaving gallop around the arena with Frank on its back, scattering other hogs and the contestants who tried to hold them back. Frank was trying to stay on in the hope that the hog would soon stop, but every time the pig looked back and saw him, it energized him into further squealing stampede.

There was a loud response from the bleachers that did not sound supportive. For a while, Frank felt that people and pigs were racing past him, but it was the marvelously steady and rapid gait of his own mount that swept him through a coliseum of obstacles. Coming around for another circle, he noticed showmen racing for the exits and the pop of flashbulbs. Frank was still trying to look his best. The crowd streamed past on the side. The rotation of the ceiling was no help and he was beginning to list, which put him in a better position to view the outthrust muzzle of the runaway pig. A very worried Jerry Drivjnicki appeared in front of him, arms outstretched like a traffic policeman. He was run over; and indeed, it was only another moment before Frank watched the plane of cat litter slant up at him and suddenly rotate, and the pig bounded away.

Frank sat up. Everywhere, shavings and animal droppings clung to the camel's hair, and the front of his Stetson was bent back against the crown like Yosemite Sam's. Instinctively, his eye sought the bleachers. Gracie and Ed, Holly and Lane, were hustling for an exit, fleeing from this disgrace as from a fire. Close by, legs stick-like in front of him, massaging a hoofprint in his scalp, Jerry Drivjnicki stared at Frank with anger. There were distinct veins in his cheeks and his lips were flattened against his teeth.

"I raised the pig that was supposed to be champion here," Jerry said. "All you had to do for our partnership was stand next to that pig. It didn't seem like a whole lot. I guess I got ahead of myself. But let me ask you this: how would you like a kick in the ass?"

"I think I'll hold off."

"You think you'll hold off."

Jerry walked away. The other contestants kept their distance from Frank. Whatever it was he had, they seemed to think they could catch. Frank was dismayed. He always liked Jerry. Jerry was a good guy. Jerry should have been a steady beacon to him and he was disgusted. Frank was interested in people who could throw a switch like Jerry just had. His father had that capability. He could cross his legs, grimace at something in distaste and make a waving-throwing gesture of his hand to indicate he was all through with this or that, whatever it was. Frank was always hung up in some gray area. He admired the way Jerry walked off. Jerry was all through with him. It was the last straw. Pretty good, thought Frank, the last straw. At that, Boyd Jarrell appeared before him.

"Well, what do you think, Boyd?"

"You rode the tar out of him, Frank. I believe you can ride anything you can get your leg over."

"Thanks, Boyd."

"Frank, I've got to talk to you."

"This is a good time," said Frank. He hoped Boyd had something nice and clear on his mind. Frank needed to discuss some objective thing.

"I thought you was a hell of a guy to overlook our differences and let me come back to work. I just wanted you to know I'll stay as long as you and Mike hang on to it."

"I appreciate that very much," said Frank, thinking, There goes one more source of revenue. "I guess I owe you an apology for the car wash, Boyd."

"It's covered," said Boyd, gesturing around the small coliseum where Frank's disgrace lingered. "More than covered. I didn't have an audience. I imagine you feel pretty bad."

Frank looked up to see the last of the pigs crowding the exits. He wondered who won and felt a little gypped. They'd hardly had a chance to judge his beautiful red boar. Then a vision of his wild gyration through the hog show at the base of the bleachers came back to him and he felt the heat radiate from his skin again. His mind wandered.

"I'm all right."

46

He went back to his house and stood in the kitchen opening mail in his topcoat while canned chili heated on the stove. There was some junk mail for expectant parents that he threw across the room. He stared through the cooking steam to think. He was still embarrassed. Worse than embarrassed — humiliated. Yes, that was it, humiliated. He took off the topcoat but momentarily retained the hat. Noticing a smell from the coat, he took it into the next room. He was wondering about Gracie. He started to feel a little crazy, so he turned the heat down on the stove, made himself a drink and sat at the kitchen table with his mail. Wearing the hat gave him the feeling he could jump up and run outside if he so desired. He started with the financial forecasts. He wanted to rise above the day. The drink was good in every way, a warm fun-bomb with great healing powers.

Nothing all that wrong with the market, really. People were definitely looking for yield, as who could blame them. Frank was starting to unwind. He was going from live pigs to more of a macro picture. It was certainly the day of bond mutual funds. And nobody seemed to give a flying fuck if it was municipal or global. There was plenty to cheer in today's gasoline futures. All sorts of signals out there that the Fed was easing rates. The ever exciting General Mills was bringing out a four-grain version of Cheerios, with the usual motive of kicking the shit out of Kellogg's Rice Krispies. Good luck: this was the fourth tune-up of a serviceable fifty-year-old idea and Rice Krispies was still around. Try to get it into your heads, boys.

The chili was done and Frank removed his hat. There was then a ring at the front door. Frank thought, This could be good. He plunged his hands deep into his pockets and walked around the bottom of the staircase to the hall. He just knew it was going to be Gracie.

He looked out the window beside the front door. It was Phil, stroking his beard with one hand and ringing the doorbell with the other. Frank had a moment's thought, which immediately struck him as unworthy, that he might pretend not to be home. Ignoring his friends would be a sign of total collapse and he wasn't going to let it happen. He went up and opened the door. Recalling a habit of their high school days, they made deep Chinese bows and Phil came in.

"Want some chili?" Frank said, leading the way down the hall. "I just got in from a pig show."

"Okay, if you got enough. A pig show?"

"I got enough. Yeah, I had to ride a pretty big one. I stayed on, made the whistle."

Phil didn't know what Frank was talking about. He didn't like anything to do with farming, ranching, agriculture. His assumption was that every pig was a government rip-off, a harmless creature that occasioned subsidies and price supports and had no reality of its own. Until now, though, he didn't seem to realize people rode them.

In the kitchen, Phil looked into the cooking pot. "You got a salad or anything?"

"Look in the fridge."

Phil got some tired-looking vegetables out of the refrigerator and began paring away the bad spots. "My old lady finally flew the nest for good," he said.

"I didn't realize she was still technically around."

"We were legally separated, but I finally decided to tell her about Smokie."

"So, what's going to happen?"

"I'll make it."

"That's good," said Frank, keeping it small. He didn't know if he wanted to get into this. He thought Phil was a little premature on the Smokie issue. "Couples seem to be a thing of the past, which should help the housing market. Although I see new home starts are down."

"What did you think about Clarence Thomas and Anita Hill?"

"I wasn't smart enough to follow it. I wouldn't exactly call them a couple."

"Look at what I've salvaged," said Phil of the neat pile of salad ingredients.

The phone rang and Frank answered while gesturing approvingly at the vegetables. It was Jerry Drivjnicki calling to say that he realized that what happened wasn't Frank's fault.

"What's past is past," said Frank philosophically, yet wondering if his regular dry cleaner would take umbrage at the pigshit embedded in the camel's hair.

"Olav Finberg won the darn thing," said Jerry. "That's when I began to think. He had two pigs in it and one was no good. In fact, that one pig was out of control. That was the one that took you for a ride. That pig couldn't have won nothin'. After the wreck was over, Olav was standing there with his good pig, and the judge was so rattled he let Olav win."

"Was Olav that farmer standing right behind me?"

"That's Olav."

Frank sighed. "Well, I tell ya, Jerry, I'm all pigged out. They seemed to fit when my life was in a different place, but that time is gone."

"Frank, if the pigs ain't doing for you what you want, I'll get you back out. Just say the word."

"I took it from you that it was over with today, Jerry. Let's keep it that way."

"Okay, Frank."

Jerry hung up, then Frank hung up. Frank could tell by the way Jerry signed off that he was miffed. He hoped the next pig he saw was at a barbecue.

Phil said, "You got anything to drink?" This was clearly about the drink itself and also about need in general. The request was accompanied by a brief, solemn gaze that was made forlorn by Phil's long beard. Frank knew what to make Phil, a simple bourbon and water; and he made himself one too. He was glad to see Phil, glad to take a moment out with a friend, a moment away from the linearity of his recent life to just do some simple drinking.

Phil wore a shirt that seemed to be made out of pillow ticking and Frank was reminded how he often thought Phil looked like a Gallatin County pioneer, maybe a small stock farmer or someone who sold whiskey to the Indians. He had that blank look he associated with local frontiersmen in photographs, which probably had more to do with the instructions of the photographer to not move and spoil the portrait than it did with the actual personalities of the subjects. From that, Frank, like most people, had surmised that a bleak view of the world prevailed a hundred years ago. If it weren't for their written materials, which revealed a new Eden, this great technological breakthrough would have maligned them for all time. Phil looked like a victim of photography; Frank knew he was full of enthusiasms but he didn't let them show very much.

"Frank, I didn't have a great week." They were in the front sitting room, one of the fussy, semi-formal spaces in this Victorian house that Frank and Gracie had bought out of a piety about the olden days. It had one inconvenient room after another. They had never known where to put Holly, from infancy through childhood and high school years. It was an atmospheric setting for some thoroughly ersatz elements of their life as a family: tall-ceilinged rooms with heavy-metal band posters, a sewing room filled with sporting gear, family recipes on the word processor, microwave Cajun cookbooks, mountain bikes in the front hall. This evening, you could see the place eating at Phil in the form of discomfort as the poor bastard tried to find a soft spot in a seventy-two-year-old wing chair.

"Smokie left too," he said.

"How are you taking all this?"

"I'll live," said Phil.

Frank saw a tremor in his face. "Phil, is there anything I can do?" he said after a moment. Abruptly, Phil began to weep. Frank felt an ache go through him, a helpless surge, and it was awkward. Through the racking sobs and streaming tears, Phil must have perceived Frank's discomfort. He began waving at him. Frank thought he was being told to do something but he couldn't make out what. The phone began to ring. Frank decided not to answer it. Phil clamped his hands on the arms of the chair and sank into it. His whole body was jerking while the phone rang. "Turn on the radio," Phil moaned. "I gotta get out of this."

Frank turned on the country station. A reverent interview with Dolly Parton from Dollywood, her theme-park home, was in place. The two men began to listen. Phil had difficulty but he was paying attention. Evidently, "country" was where "family" counted; references to the Mama figure and the Daddy figure. You could feel her dimples come over the airwaves. And now for the vibrato that built it all, sassy and dramatic, equally at home in Appalachia and Rodeo Drive: "The Coat of Many Colors." As though each man were assigned one of Dolly's big breasts, the room grew calm. They gazed off in comfortable friendship, the ghastly weeping now subsided into tolerable ungainliness. They sucked down the bourbon.

"How did we get in so many wrecks, Frank?"

"Jeez, Phil, I'm stuck. How's the chili?"

"It's good. I feel better. I mean, I feel like an asshole but I feel better. I didn't mean to get so upset. I guess I figured I could. We been in a lot of corners before. I guess I had it coming. Before Kathy, I turned some nice kids into whores. Course, I had to be one too, to do it. Used to take them in the caboose all the way to Forsythe, supposed to be watching for fires along the track, and we'd be rolling numbers and having us a big old time. Lucky old Smokie didn't give me the chance to do it to her. Part of me is proud of it. So, if you're never gonna grow up anyway, might as well have a good cry."

"I've been reading where it's supposed to be good for you," said Frank. "Men are starting to get into it. All around the country."

"Do you do it?"

"Not much."

Phil sighed. "I'm gonna get me a big, grateful, coyote-ugly type of gal one of these days and settle down for the long haul."

It was quiet for a moment.

"I suppose we ought to eat something at some point."

"I don't know about this chili. You can sort of taste the can."

Frank set two fresh drinks on the table with a significant clunk. A sudden light from passing cars shuddered on the walls. There was a pile of newspapers he hadn't gotten to. These sorts of things acquired a strangeness when you were living alone. Your sense of adventure goes into your marriage, and when the marriage is gone you're stuck with a hundred versions of a road map when you're not planning a trip. Frank bobbed his ice cubes with his forefinger and smiled to himself. A lot of men in the news these days blubbering. It was supposed to be the sign of a real man, but it just didn't look right to Frank. Although with Phil it seemed okay.

Phil had been talking: ". . . Plus — plus — shit."

"What?"

"I don't know."

"Do you think it's hopeless with women, Phil?"

"Yes, I do."

"Any women?"

"That's been my experience."

"Is your wife going to live with that doctor?"

"I doubt it. She's just graduated to one of his little somethings on the side. That's a hell of a category, isn't it? But that's what she wants to be."

"You care for some of these newspapers?"

"Naw."

"I don't know what my wife is up to either. She just seems to be circling the airport. She's sort of around again, and to be perfectly honest it makes me nervous."

"I don't know what the fuck they want," Phil said.

"Nervous and sad and crazy. I don't know quite what it means. I was going to think about it tonight. I always figure these things out just before I go to sleep. But with men and women, it seems everyone wants the authorities to intervene. You sort of picture lawsuits being the ideal relationships of the future. At least you can kind of let it happen."

"Run up some bills."

"I'm not saying it's a way to cut costs in a relationship."

"My wife and I don't have that kind of money," Phil said. "We're old-fashioned. We'd just like to kill each other."

"The last time I felt really close to Gracie, well, we were going to open a burger joint, something different, something with a slogan, and what it was going to be about was volume sales. I was just thinking numbers. But Gracie, who's a great cook, thinks whatever you do should be good for the world, whereas I just like business. And I honestly mean it when I say that when Amazing Grease went upside down I didn't gloat because she did serve really distinctive food while it lasted. And it was like anything she did for good reasons was doomed and anything I do for my usual money-grubbing motives would succeed. It was really humiliating to Gracie. We never actually said it. It was like her view of life was nowhere because she couldn't face what a paltry, hopeless deal it was and I could. But the funny thing is, since she withdrew in defeat and just let the lesson speak for itself, I haven't been able to do as well either. Or I don't want to. Or I fail to see what it means. Or, whatever."

Phil wore a pinched, inward look. He had both hands around his drink. He seemed to be watching something inside himself. He lifted the drink up and finished it. "I gotta go," he said.

"Phil, is everything okay?"

Phil was up and next to the door. "I really can't answer that question."

Frank knew better than to follow him out the door. Instead, he brought the television in so he could see it while he ate. The Broncos. Elway goes back, back, uncorks a Hail Mary . . . incomplete. He finished his drink and made one more because he could just begin to feel that good old mellow feeling: the coexistence of life's elements as so successfully seen through the bottom of a glass. He smiled at the wholesome chili. He thought with sweet sadness of his pain and Phil's pain, all the while knowing they were learning something important. He forgot the overpowering sense that nothing is learned, that this is a circle and a headache in which the nerves of the abdomen are counterweighted by the capacity for remorse. For example, he contemplated with a faint, annunciatory smile the idea that nothing really was important.

47

The wind had swung around to the northwest and the bright summer clouds were replaced by the slanting, lead-shot systems of somewhere over the Divide. It was still warm, but for the first time they were getting other people's weather. Frank wondered if he was imagining a bustling, slightly worried quality of people in the street. For his own part, he craved to be out in the country.

He might only have wished to escape. The bank had begun proceedings against him and had suggested that he might "opt for the quiet alternative" and hand over several things that they had identified, including his house. The house's value increased suddenly to him. It had belonged to his grandfather. His father had sold it and Frank bought it back twenty years later. In the meanwhile, it had become a duplex. Frank and Gracie converted it back into a single-family home and raised Holly in its multiplicity of steam-heated rooms. The old house had seen some unhappy moments, but Frank thought there was a chance that things would change, and he still wanted to hang on to it in case they did. He did not necessarily hope that he and Gracie would get back together but that he would find some accommodation with his situation and that would approximate happiness, or absorption in something, maybe a renewed absorption in business. But the bank going after his home affected him viscerally.

His success had once consisted in an ability to mix himself in the throng wholeheartedly while maintaining a kind of detachment that told him what the general currents were in what seemed to be pure Brownian movement. For example, he long knew where people were getting ready to move to. When they got there, they'd find he owned much of the land and would have to buy it from him. He had built the clinic before there were enough doctors to fill it. They were still coming to ski or fish from their homes and practices in Texas, California and New York. He knew they were getting ready to move; they didn't. As people relatively exalted in their own minds, they resented his having foreseen this. A few tried renting offices or practicing out of private dwellings. It didn't last. They ended up renting from him.

Something about professionals made Frank enjoy gouging them, a quality in himself that explained the popularity of people like Lane Lawlor. It was interesting to see what it would take to get the doctors to band together and build their own clinic. Now the bastards were gone. Still, it was zoned light industrial over there. He was thinking of moving a little electronics thing in from its dismal headquarters in Three Forks; they made position-indicating radio beacons to be worn by skiers in avalanche areas, a little like the one worn by that poor old wolf. It was a good product, but he just didn't care right now. He had no idea where people were headed or what they wanted. He was like a hawk that was losing its eyesight.

He tried an experimental weekend at the ranch. He fully expected to find ghosts there, of his family and himself; but what he found was that it was empty except for Boyd Jarrell, who was back at his old job. Boyd actually waved to him, though it was a dismissive wave, as he dragged a set of tractor chains from the barn. Everything was familiar but it was without any further resonance. He could locate, room by room, scenes of important early events, but they not only failed to enhance those memories, they reduced them. The room off the kitchen with the ironing board mounted to the wall, where his father had had his first heart attack, was just a cold, empty room. It seemed insufficiently inviting to accommodate a heart attack. The front room, where as a family they had watched Sid Caesar and Imogene Coca, failed to bring back memories. To Frank's dismay, it only brought back memories of Sid Caesar and Imogene Coca.

The attic contained two Flexible Flyer sleds and the camping equipment that had gotten such complete use. Frank's father was a skillful packer of horses and the outings with his sons were lessons in diamond hitches and squaw hitches, demonstrations of the driving of a picket pin and of jackknife cookery, mantying gear, Decker versus sawbuck pack saddles and the language of trailblazing. Frank recognized his gratitude now. How much better to recall a parent in action than in statements. In fact, most of the statements Frank remembered from his father, he remembered unhappily. The actions he remembered were among his treasures.

Mike had sold off the timber. He had that right under their partnership agreement: Frank had the grazing, Mike had the timber. Frank had leased his grazing and Mike was now irrevocably cutting down the trees. Through the long weekend, Frank listened to the hot-rod snarl of the chain saws. It took many years for those trees to stand up like that and just a minute to be killed. From the house, Frank could see parts of the bristled surface of forest above the ranch folded over flat. He could hear the skidder making its terrible sound in the living trees and he could see smoke from the trucks. He could even see the safety orange of the hard hats. More than anything, he heard the doleful howl of the saws in the shattered forest. He knew how the soil would be rent in hauling off the trees and decided to skip that part and go back into town. It was probably time, he thought, for Americans to learn to love pavement with all their hearts.

48

Tonight, finally, was the Branding, featuring Lane Lawlor. Seven people called and made sure Frank didn't miss it.

Frank wore the old belted Aquascutum overcoat that had belonged to his father, for the simple reason that he, Frank, was never seen in it. He wore his new Air Jordan high tops and his John Deere billed cap pulled low over his forehead. He was in disguise. He paid his admission to one of the five women seated behind a low folding table and got his hand stamped with the image of a spur. Then he entered the already crowded Earl Butz Kiva, a room that had once filled with the cries and ecstasies of an audience in actual physical sight of the gleaming head of James Watt, who had taken to the lecture trail with the fallen warriors of Watergate and Iran-Contra. Frank thought of an earlier generation, when Billy Sol Estes, born too early, languished in prison instead of traveling the rubber chicken circuit. "All you need is love," said the Beatles. "Love is all you need."

This was a high-spirited crowd, though. People stood up in their seats to call across to neighbors. There were hundreds of cowboy hats and gimme caps like Frank's that formed a rich carpet sweeping toward the stage. Frank knew many hardworking ranchers and farmers, but he saw none of them tonight. Overhead projected a steel frame that suspended the lights for the stage, empty now except for a piano and a standing microphone before the curtain. For almost twenty minutes, nothing happened except people looking for their seats. Frank surmised that some subtle change in the lights, some infinitesimal fading or brightening, which caused rock-and-roll audiences to explode like plankton, must have occurred because the audience began to stamp its feet and shout. The noise increased like a volcano. Frank felt fear, felt it in gusts as something rolled over him that he did not quite understand. Could these people really be from around here?

The slit in the curtain opened as in giving birth, and out trotted not only Lane Lawlor but Frank's own child Holly. She twirled in her white cowgirl boots and ten-gallon hat. A roar went forth from the audience. Frank had no idea Lane was so popular. Where have I been? he asked himself as the crowd around him began to flow upward into a standing ovation. Frank stood too. He didn't have the nerve to leave his arms at his sides. Instead, he raised his hands and held them, palms in proximity as if clapping. Lane patted the air in downward motions of his arms to ask shyly for quiet. The fact that he was a big clumsy man seemed to help him. For a moment the audience was having none of it. They defied his request and cheered louder. He let his arms hang at his sides and dropped his chin modestly. At length, the noise subsided and everyone settled into their chairs. Holly darted everywhere, keeping the energy high. To Frank, she seemed to be having a fit.

As Lane moved to the microphone and made a few practiced adjustments, Holly softly played "The Streets of Laredo" behind him on the piano. She faded out as he began to speak. Very quietly he said, "Montana is not a zoo." The audience boomed its response. Frank looked around in alarm. One large man behind him was pulling his mouth apart by the corners and emitting a terrifying whistle. There were numerous gimme caps flung into the air, though as of yet none of the more expensive cowboy hats.

About six rows over, Frank spotted Sheriff Hykema. Lane muttered away as if talking to himself, about how it was not our obligation to provide comfortable housing for animals that had lost the talent for survival in our modern world. "Hey," he said, "if you can't hack it, here's the door!" This produced general, respectful applause. Then Lane stepped back from the microphone and, profiling himself to the audience, tossed his head back and howled like a wolf. They knew what he meant by that! A roar of laughter blended imperceptibly with more applause. "Fern-feelin' prairie fairies gonna getcha!" he said, then joined their good-natured laughter, tried to get serious and dropped his forehead to the microphone helplessly. He lifted his head and aimed his mouth at the ceiling and called out, "God, can you tell me, 'cause no one down here can: why do these out-of-staters want us to have a system in Montana *which has failed in Russia?*" The pandemonium produced by this question was slow in subsiding. "And as far as the federal government goes, there's more gunfire in a Washington, D.C., playground on a good day than there was in a month in Dodge City in eighteen hunnert and seventy-five!"

"Yeah!" they shouted back at him.

"Read your history!"

"Yeah!"

"Listen to your conscience!"

"Yeah!"

"Let me make it simple for them sonsofbitches: we're the *good* people; they're the *bad* people!"

"That's right!"

"I wanta tell you. The cold, cool waters of the West are flowing from her wounds. They are leaving Montana while I'm talking to you. What wouldn't I give to dam the smallest one, that creek a little child jumps across. If you are unlucky enough to run into someone who wants those rivers flowing elsewhere"— here Lane took a suspenseful pause —"gut-shoot them at the border." A roar went up. Holly struck thunderous chords on the piano. "Gut-shoot them at the border!" Another roar, another howl from the piano. "*Gut-shoot them at the border!*"

Some crazed-looking woman was climbing up over the front of the stage. She struggled to her feet. "Hey, lady, the evening is still young," Lane sang into the PA system. He inverted his palms near his face like Jack Benny. The audience laughed out a kind of encouragement. The crazy woman staggered for balance across the stage while Lane backed away in mock terror. Then Frank saw: it was Gracie! Was she in on this too? Gracie strode across the stage to the piano and yanked Holly to her feet. A sound from the indignant crowd swept forward.

Frank stood up. Holly was struggling with her mother under the cones of light from the overhead grid. Lane was doing a ringside commentary: "You've got to choose sometime, Holly . . . Folks, I'd like you to meet Gracie Copenhaver, owner-operator of the now defunct left-wing hot-tubbers' hangout Amazing Grease. Remember, the Constitution guarantees your rights even when a parent tries to abrogate them. Folks, what's happening to my piano player? Looks like Mama's in a world of hurt. You call that an excuse? Holly, you're younger and stronger. You have the Bill of Rights on your side! You have the Fifth Amendment! Don't let your mother drag you down into the kind of life she has created for herself!"

Frank was on his feet, shoving people out from in front of him. One rancher seized his arm and Frank knocked it loose, hard. He climbed up and over the stage's apron, gripping the nonskid carpeting on the stage, the shadow of the microphone across his back. As soon as he had his feet under him, he dove straight into the middle of Lane Lawlor, pummeling him as they went down. The sound from the crowd was like that from a provoked animal. It rolled over Frank like a gust or an ocean wave. That was all he saw. In the flooding darkness, he remembered the long-ago trip to Utah when he'd argued with Gracie and Holly played dead in the pool. They were together again. "Holly!" he called into the mountain of denim. "Gracie!"

49

He felt his lips. They had become objective facts, cracked and swollen. He made a squeamish perusal of his head with his fingertips: nothing really horrible, no stitches, but a dull ache at the very back of his head, a traditional boot target.

There was a breakfast tray beside him. Who brought it? It looked wonderful. He thought, Some nice person brought me my breakfast. He felt love just sort of leaving him and going into space. There was the *Journal* rolled up beside it. How good. There were three codeine tablets with water; someone had anticipated his present headache. He swallowed them. And now for the world.

The news of the world was full of failure and miscues. Ford was recalling 641,562 Aerostar minivans. Currency traders were dumping the pound. Japanese trust banks' pretax profits plunged. The criminal investigation of Salomon Brothers continued. Bond prices slipped again. The usual remedies for jump-starting the economy were not succeeding. I know why, thought Frank. It's because we're disheartened. We bought all the stuff, we shit in the nest, we don't believe in anything. How dare you jump-start us with reduced interest rates! We're the folks who butt-fucked the goose that laid the golden egg! We can no longer be jump-started!

There was a strong tread on the stairs. "Mr. Copenhaver?" came a voice in the pause between audible steps.

"Yes, who is it?"

"It's Brad Taylor, Mr. Copenhaver. I'm with Security Merchant Bank." There was no further sound.

"That's my bank," Frank called back suspiciously. And this, he thought, was what was known in my father's day as a young whippersnapper.

"I have Dr. Jensen down here with me. Who would you like to see first?"

"How the hell should I know? I don't know why I would need a doctor and I don't know who you are."

There was a pause.

"Dr. Jensen said I should go ahead. May I come up?"

"Come on."

Brad Taylor stood in the doorway with a file folder in one arm, dressed in a gray suit with a silver-and-red-striped tie and his hair combed so that it fell to one side. "How do you do, Mr. Copenhaver."

"How do you do."

"How are you feeling?"

"Fine, considering I received the combined weight of two hundred corn-fed farmers and ranchers united in the service of world fascism. How old are you?"

"Twenty-four."

"Your whole life ahead of you. What an appalling prospect."

"Thank you."

This one was in a fog, thought Frank. "Ordinarily, I deal with George Carnahan. I've seen him in a few tight spots over the years, and given what a spineless puke he is, I take it you're bringing me bad news."

"I'm afraid I am."

"I see you're a shy boy."

"I'm nervous."

"Don't be. This isn't your fault."

"I know. Still, I hate to be in on this kind of thing."

"What kind of thing?" asked Frank, his suspicions further aroused. You run with the pack for years, then one day you note a circling tendency and find yourself in the center.

"Well, there was a tremendous shortfall on those cattle we floated. And we've seen the clinic and the condition it's fallen into. We've been very troubled —"

"Don't be. The Japs just bought a painting for six million. At least somebody's gonna eat these critters. It's more than just blue sky."

"But is it?"

"What are you getting at?"

"We're concerned with the reaction of our examiners."

"Piss on 'em. Besides, that's banker double-talk. This imaginary figure called the examiner. The most ordinary people reject this bullshit. Banking is nothing but a pyramid scheme. You're an apprentice swindler. George Carnahan is a more polished swindler. That's why he's not here today. Brad, it's a bleak thing that an attractive young man like you should already be making references to the examiners."

Brad Taylor looked completely dazed. He held up the file folder and said, "Why don't I leave these for you to go through. George thought it was only fair, given the long relationship we've enjoyed with you, to let you know the remedies we're seeking to cover our losses on the cattle."

"You going to try to take the clinic?"

"I'm afraid we are."

"I'm afraid you aren't."

"We'd let you try to sell it, but our position takes all there is."

"What about this house?"

Brad nodded.

Frank told him, "Over my dead body. This motherfucker has been the site of my hopes, dreams and failures ever since that day in October long ago when I gave up being a hippie and set out to make a fortune. I brought this house back into our family. Tell you what, explain to George I've got several show pigs over in Reed Point. They need a new home. We're deep discounting them all and several of them kiss pretty good by George's standards. Tell him I said so. Take the file folder with you and goodbye."

Frank rolled over and waited for the exit steps of the young man and the sound of Dr. Jensen's ascent. I require that these rich scenes occur in my own unencumbered home, Frank mused, with its deed in the cupboard. Here I have farted, cooked, dealt and procreated coequally, enriching its thousandfold oak boards with my own life. If there are to be dramatic scenes of my decline, let them take place in this fine Montana home.

Now comes before us Dr. Jensen, wishing to know if Frank is comfortable. Frank said that he was, and asked if the doctor had examined him before he regained consciousness. The doctor said that he had, and concluded that Frank suffered a concussion. Frank thanked this young doctor for making a house call while still in his spandex bicycling shorts. The doctor said that he was welcome. He said this idly because he was checking out the house, taking in the oak floors, the depth of crown molding, the swirling shapes of the staircase, the fancifully paned windows, the ice-cream, deep, hand-troweled, perfect plaster with its frieze of tangled roses 'round the top. Frank gazed at him, seeing right into this, and thought, In a moment he will pant like a coyote hazing jackrabbits into traffic on the interstate.

Dr. Jensen took Frank's wrist between his thumb and fore-finger, raised his arm to drop his sleeve away from his watch, then studied its dial. "What's the fate of our old clinic?"

"Why do you ask?" Frank said. "You're not there anymore." He smelled something.

"Er, well, because this could be a good time to open com-munications again. Various efforts at resettlement in other spaces have been less than perfect."

"So, you guys might want back in?"

"Might."

"Gets pretty dicey when you can't co-op the electronics and stuff." Frank figured out the smell, an old college favorite, a men's cologne called Canoe.

"Absolutely."

"Well, you're too goddamn late. I'm selling it to a Wop for a noodle factory."

As Frank said these things, he wondered whether he meant any of it or if a desire for a dark-sided fulfillment at the expense of his adversaries had given him a lingo of revenge that he donned like a disguise. He hoped this wouldn't be the birth of a new, obnoxious Frank Copenhaver, but in his present wooze, he wasn't sure. He just felt that, out here alone, he had to fight his battles stylishly because in his failing greed there was an errant valor in complicating the lives of well-paid white people.

"Phil tells me you made off with his wife for good."

"I'm afraid she got a taste of the good life and kept on rolling. Got her a car dealership in Great Falls."

"So the pressure is off everybody."

Dr. Jensen smiled at him mildly. Not patronizingly. To him, Frank seemed to be a lawn ornament, perhaps, or a float in a small-town parade. He was reaching Frank a piece of paper, which Frank perceived, with a bit of cynical closure, as a bill. But it was a citation for disorderly conduct from Sheriff Hykema.

"I asked him not to wake you up," said Dr. Jensen.

Frank fell asleep again after the doctor had gone, and thought he was dreaming when George Carnahan stood at the foot of his bed and said, "How dare you talk to my impressionable young associate as you have." Frank flowed along with the dream, enveloped in its unfolding. "How dare you take any position other than that we have treated you with inordinate flexibility and kindness, unwavering Christianity and goodheartedness, in your many years of reckless wheeling and dealing. For reasons none of us can understand, you have ceased entirely paying attention to business. Several of my older colleagues have suggested that you have reverted to being the fog-bound hippie we remember you to have been, as though it were some sort of debility that must one day surface. And finally, how dare you call me a spineless puke and a pig-kissing swindler. I am your old friend and business acquaintance who hates to bring you bad news. If in avoiding doing that personally I sidestepped a painful moment, so be it. And now I would like you to examine these." By now Frank's eyes were open and he knew it wasn't a dream.

"George, get my glasses off the mantel."

George brought Frank his reading glasses and Frank examined a stack of identical checks on which someone had signed his name and wrote "1st payment," "2nd payment," down to, ten months later, "last payment." The funds were used to buy a small filling station. Frank looked up at George and studied him in his checked tweed jacket. George had loose jowls and a tiny, disapproving mouth.

"Who owns the filling station, George?"

"I'm afraid it's Eileen."

"What do you know about that?"

"I'm waiting to hear."

"Do you know this station?"

"Yes."

"Is it a good one?" Frank asked.

"I'm afraid it is. Out on an empty stretch of road toward Whitehall. I mean, there's about one living in it, but it's doing eighteen percent, pretax. She runs it tight as bark on a tree and makes damn sure she preserves her margins."

"I taught her to speak and now she curses me."

"She will when you turn her in."

"Who said I was turning her in? Did I say to you, George, that I was turning in my old secretary?"

"Frank, you're not yourself. This head thing. At your worst, you'd always have been able to spot someone bending over backward to save you."

"Unlike others in the business community, I've taken a pause to relocate some meaning."

"You took a pause when Gracie left, Frank, and now your pause is jammed. When I get back to the bank, the VPs are going to be on me like flies on shit. They're gonna ask me. And what am I gonna answer? I'm gonna answer, It's irreversible."

"You can read about it in the papers, George. Consumer pessimism is on the upswing. Besides, I am not going broke. I'm just relinquishing day-to-day responsibilities."

George had had enough. He left. Frank rolled up in the covers, forming a tube with just his face sticking out. He looked out at the big blue sky. It made a pleasant abdication to think of himself as an atom compared to outer space. He had a sense no one was buying his reevaluation of his life. Soon it would be time for him to ask if he was buying it himself.

50

"You'll have to sit up." He opened his eyes and there was Lucy with his dinner on a tray. He was woozy from codeine but glad to see her. She was wearing a pure white linen blouse and skirt. It seemed a miracle to find the only person he knew who lived in this peculiar zone.

"It's like being in the hospital," he said with a puzzled smile. He hoped he would seem to be referring to something far larger.

"You might as well be in the hospital."

"Where's your nurse's costume?"

"Very funny." She pinched his cheek. "Very funny."

She put the tray on his lap. It looked appetizing: a breast of chicken encrusted with some herbs, butter beans, half a roasted yam, a little salad, quite nice indeed.

"Are you eating?" Frank asked.

"I already ate. I've got stuff to do."

She moved as if to go. Mouth full, Frank raised his hands to stop her. He tried to say "Stay for a moment," but the yam caused it to come out very differently. A crease of annoyance appeared between Lucy's eyebrows, partly concealed by her extraordinarily precise bangs. He plucked orange specks of yam from his blanket and swallowed with an audible gulp. "I was hoping perhaps you might stay and visit for a moment." He was conscious of a sluggish spasm moving the yam down his gullet while he tried to suavely murmur a few niceties.

"Gracie said I could bring your dinner because no one else planned to. But she said that if I hung around for quote a little tête-à-tête unquote, she would quote tear my fucking face off unquote."

Frank's spirits were careening wildly. He considered himself completely recovered except for the small matter of the blinding headache and faint codeine buzz. He was ashamed to realize that it was but a matter of time before his crooked heart was consoled by Lucy finding a way to have sex with him. They seemed to have an odd lack of control over this. Waiting for the inevitable, Frank marveled druggily at the curious way women betrayed each other. It seemed wildly at odds with their stated policies. His sluggish perceptions took this in voluptuously.

Lucy was fussing with the curtains now. Soon she would be carried toward him by an invisible conveyor belt. She had raised Gracie as a menace not to herself but to both of them. Lewd conduct, like teenage love, required abstract opponents to reach full flower. Frank allowed his silence to become loaded silence. With hieratical signification he moved the tray, with its burden of pimpled chicken skin, rind of yam and sheen of salad dressing, to the table beside the bed. Moronic speechlessness found its counterpart in a faint smile of Lucy's. Frank thought, I have won the toss and elected to receive.

The blast of a car horn outside seemed to announce the beginning. Vague and adrift, Frank permitted the uncoiling of his cock until its jaunty presence was visible through the sheet. He put his hand up Lucy's skirt with a boardinghouse reach. Lucy was like a tree shedding its leaves in the fall. She stood naked beside the bed knowing he was now helpless. I suppose she's having a good time, he thought absently; and now comes the "tally me banana" part. She mounted him in reverse, a position that enabled her to watch the street. She was shivering, then hooting faintly like an owl in the brush. He held her buttocks so as to participate in their motion. By spreading them slightly, he was able to take a more precise measure of their activity, concluding that the vertical travel of the asshole, which seemed so dramatic, was actually only a matter of inches. Then came her voice. He couldn't make heads or tails of it. It was not the dragonish bellow that sometimes announced the onset of her orgasm. It seemed to be a call-and-response thing, more than one voice in spirit, high and low or, more properly, *here* answered by *there*. Then Lucy shouted without much of what Frank took as conventional passion, "I'm coming!" But before Frank could join her in ecstasy, she had climbed off him and was standing next to the bed, getting back into her clothes in a hurry. There had indeed been two voices: Lucy's and, from the bottom of the stairs, Gracie's. "I'm coming as fast as I can!" Lucy yelled down to the first floor in a fearful rage.

Gracie appeared in the bedroom doorway and, fixing Frank with a metallic smile, said, "How could you?" Lucy finished dressing, staying well out of Gracie's reach, and they both went downstairs. He felt unwilling to breathe.

There was an immediate uproar from below. For several moments, Frank was certain that it was composed entirely of voices; then he wasn't so sure. Worse, he felt it was getting closer, possibly moving up the stairs. He sensed that this emotional violence favored his situation, if he lived through it. But this ill-construed tone seemed to follow him everywhere like a pox. He knew the two women were in pain, but the only thing he thought he could offer was the suggestion that they ought to dump their growth stocks and get in on these tax-free Montana highway bonds while there was still time. He saw right away that there was no chance they'd listen. They'd probably just get madder.

"It is typical of the situation we held on to for so long," Gracie was saying, "that anything we try turns into chaos." She was working her way down the clothesline at the side of the house on Third, clothespins under her chin, hanging out sheets, towels and Edward's voluminous boxer shorts. "I have not been back for long, but *all* the harrowing scenes of my recent history have taken place in that short time and they have *all* involved you in one way or another."

"Did I tell Holly to accompany Hitler on the piano?" Frank said.

"He's not Hitler. He's not good, but he's not Hitler."

"Sorry. I know what you're saying. Honey, you were great out there."

"Gee, thanks. I especially wish that we could do as Edward suggests: meet in a civilized way and make sure we have left clean wounds so that the healing process can begin."

"I'm very suspicious of this 'healing' concept," Frank said. "I've heard a good bit about it lately and it always leads into a discussion of some unbelievably tedious 'inner journey.' I'm afraid I've grown much too old for that sort of thing. The messages of my formative years all came from Little Richard, who has never soiled himself with an inner journey."

Gracie was unwarmed by these genial maunderings. "I wouldn't know. I'm the bimbo who tried to sell Creole cuisine to the locals, remember?"

"You just fell down on your market research. Trail mix is the local soul food."

Frank kept on watching Gracie hang her wash. Did this mean she didn't own a dryer? Maybe Edward liked the smell of fresh air in his linens. These days people would do such things out of a vision of a simpler America.

Frank was looking at the clothespins, wondering how much longer they would last. He watched Gracie with endless appreciation of her concentration, her standing on tiptoes and, almost unbearably, the way, when she finally finished what she was doing, she used her thumbs to move her hair back behind her ears; that, or the way she saw him noticing. There was a momentary sense of everything else having stopped, a kind of silence, breathlessness.

Then it all came back: who he thought he was, who he thought she was, who she thought she was, who she thought he was; how, in the best case, it might well be mostly behind them, the flat earth on which much is irrevocable. Even the bad years, he thought, even the years of psychobabble and attacking each other with the previous night's dreams. He had despised all those poetic nature books she read with topics like "impromptu clamming" as a spiritual exercise. And she had said he had no values, not even hippie values, that he came from the world of Grain Belt beer, novelty sex and car worship, from a hick town in a hick state. We are not people, he thought, we are envoys. Seek a postponement.

Yet, when she was in front of him, close, close enough to touch, she asked him, without raising her eyes to his, "Frank, if I asked you to do something, would you consider it?"

"Yes, I would."

"Anything?"

Frank felt his heart lock. "Anything," he said. Gracie lifted her face and looked into his eyes. Anything, he thought.

"I've got to go," she said.

"Wait a minute, what do you want me to do?"

"You already said you would."

"But what is it?"

"Frank, I want you to meet with Edward. I think you need to fill in all the blanks. I think you're losing it, Frank. I think you better find out what's what and go from there. You already gave me your reply," said Gracie with a little curtsey. "Bye for now." She went into the house, stopping in the doorway to say, "Remember what a good sport I've been about you fucking that sorry whore in my old spindle bed."

Frank was going to speak but the door was now closed. Instead of an arch that embowered their conversation, it was now the bald front of a house. And the road to finality was clear as daylight.

The Kid Royale Hotel and chicken farm was being picketed by the Preservation League. It was a beautiful day for picketing, with a bright sky filled with bright nimbus clouds and a gentle breeze from the west that carried a smell of lawns, a superb day for protest. Frank had known it was only a matter of time until they got here. One young woman walked up and down in front of the hotel in a sandwich board while she read a book. The sign said:

> STOP FRANK COPENHAVER
> FROM BURYING OUR PAST
> IN CHICKEN DROPPINGS

"I'm Frank Copenhaver," he said as he passed her by. "Why don't you put a group together and buy me out? I could use the money."

"Yeah, right. You're a tycoon, mister."

"I was getting there all right, but my bank says I've failed. Now I want to join you in the granola underworld."

Without looking up from her book, she said, "This is harassment. Another word and I'll turn your ass in."

A blast of odor greeted Frank when he opened the door. He held it open long enough so that he could picture the invisible progress of the smell onto the sidewalk. There were few pedestrians but they reacted physically to its arrival with shrinking movements and rapid gaits. Here comes your regional heritage, Frank thought, on the wings of a dove. The picketers might well decide to do their work in the form of meditative petitions issued from fern-filled quarters in another part of town.

Frank was thrilled to step into the lobby and hear the racket of Orville Conway and his family, two tall boys and his big freckled wife with a scarf tied over her head. They greeted him and kept working; as he wandered through the building, he saw them nailing up chicken wire, running PVC pipe in the hallways to water the birds, rigging doors and corner roosts. One boy was hauling chicken feed and oyster shells in heavy sacks that hung from his broad shoulders while his mother guided a push broom down the corridors. The younger boy, wearing a Walkman, ran a nail gun as he secured the wire with lath strips. Over the din of their work, a cultivated voice chanted outside through a bullhorn a rhyme about it being no mystery what chickens do to history. The second floor, meanwhile, was completely up and running.

Orville took Frank down the chicken-wired, doorless rooms filled with genial chickens greeting Frank with a wave of complaisant clucks. Orville looked upon them with admiration, a few strands of blond hair spilling from his wide head.

"I believe we're to where we can see it might work," he said.

"I'm excited about this, Orville."

"The wife and I, we was hoping."

"You're all working so hard, I'm just glad to be in partners with you."

"Them folks in front ain't no bother. They'll get tired pretty quick. We used to sell them organic chickens at the farmers' market. One old gal pulled this dressed chicken's legs apart and give it a sniff and told the missus it wasn't fresh. The missus said, 'Hell lady, Marilyn Monroe couldn't pass that test.' Us, we don't get tired. Me, Shirl, nor them boys. We call them folks out front died-again Christians."

Frank wandered around and tried to convey his enthusiasm to the Conway family and walked back outside through the picketers.

"It's a changing world," said one wise male picketer in long dreadlocks.

Frank told him, "It's a fact, Jack."

Then he got in his car and drove out to the town of Impact to pick up his scale receipts for his yearlings. He never had gotten them and it looked as if he'd need a mountain of paper to slow that bank down. On the narrow paved road, he passed a small buck that had been hit by a car, its head angled back sharply; its antlers lay on the pavement about fifteen feet away. There were several vertical, ribbed white clouds in the blue sky that looked like the afterimages of spinning tops. A truck went by with a license plate that read, "44 MAG."

He picked up his receipts from the woman who ran the general store. He bought the *Sun* because of its interesting headline, BABY STOLEN FROM MOM'S WOMB WHILE SHE SLEEPS, and the *Enquirer,* which reported that Bill Cosby was working on his own test tube baby, and which revealed that Sonny Bono's memoirs stated several important things about Cher: *A,* she was a lousy lover; *B,* she was so stupid she thought the moon was part of the sun; and *C,* she had been unfaithful with certain members of his band.

Frank remembered being out here long ago, grossly loaded, having to follow "Lewis and Clark Trail" signs the state had erected just to get home. He drove through the low, undulating hills covered with sagebrush and serviceberry bushes. Lightnin' Hopkins sang on the radio, "You know my little woman ain't no Mexican . . . ," making Frank daydream of his own true love, now connected to him by a thread. His mind was in ribbons thinking of all their trials on this lonesome road. White hair in five minutes.

But out there, all around, was his god of handsome land. As it leveled off before the car, other country flowed into it from his past: the cedar breaks and cotton fields of Texas, the big sun there and softer clouds, cotton wagons behind tractors, little caliche roads, senderos, heading off to pumping stations in the distance . . . twenty-four-year-old Gracie next to him, trying to find something good on the radio. The old man in the service station looked affectionately at the two of them and said, as a kind of invitation, "If you ever wear out a pair of boots in west Texas, you'll never leave." Now Frank's tear ducts clamped like little fists and tears poured down his cheeks. He rested his teeth on the steering wheel and tried to see the road through swimming eyes. It had been so good.

51

Judge Elvin Blaylock, his T-shirt showing at the neck of his judi-
cial robes, gazed for a moment at the accused, announced that he
found him guilty of disturbing the peace and fined him one
hundred dollars. The clerk of the court was the only one present,
but nevertheless the judge was circumspect in asking Frank to
come to his bench so that he might speak to him *sotto voce*. He
said, "I would like to see you in my chambers." He got up,
declared that court was adjourned and exited through a door
behind him. Frank waited for a moment and followed.

He closed the door behind him. Judge Blaylock was standing in
boxer shorts and T-shirt. Frank asked, "Is that what you had on
under the robe?"

"What's it to you, big boy," lisped the judge.

"Just asking."

"Frank, asshole. May I call you asshole?"

"Another time, Elvin. I'm not strong just now."

Blaylock came up close to Frank and cuffed him lightly in the
head and then, seeming contrite, smoothed his hair back for him.
"Frank, you and I have known each other all our lives. Your old
man did pretty well. You and Mike got a little start. My old man
ran a snow plow for the county when he wasn't drunk. We had
zip, okay? That's why I worked to get where I am. It's no big deal

to anyone but me, okay? But you, Frank, you're heading the other way. You just believe that anything you throw away you can always get again. I just want to be the one guy you know from way back to tell you that if that's what you think, I want to wish you all the luck in the world. Kind of like, 'So long, it's been good to know you.' "

Frank rocked his head, exhibiting a cheery dismay at taking this in. Inside, he felt a chill.

"Edward, do you mind that I have called your house?" Frank had made himself hold off for one full day.

"Not at all, Frank."

"I've got to ask Gracie one or two things. I —"

"Come on over! We're just a hop, skip and a jump."

Edward let him in the door, asking, "Shall I make myself scarce?" It was Sunday and church bells rang across the town.

"No need. I won't be long." This was so brittle that Frank could feel all his back muscles clenching. He noticed that Edward had a small ponytail held in place with a rubber band. Was that new?

"Tell you what," Edward said, "I've got bromeliads to mist and this is a good time for it. Before I go, may I say in all sincerity that I am really looking forward to our meeting."

"I thought I'd get into that with uh —"

"Gracie!" he boomed in high mellifluousness.

"Exactly."

Gracie appeared in the doorway to a side room through which shone a subaqueous light. "Hi, Frank." Both Edward and Lucy were present in this brief remark.

"Hello, Gracie."

There was such deep-seated fraud in these plain greetings that Frank had an instant of looking forward to his part in the war on deception.

Edward seemed to take in this bracing moment of awkwardness before flailing his arms out in a gesture that declared he was leaving. "I don't know about you guys," he said, "but I wish things were more normal."

Frank followed Gracie into a glassed-in room with a floor made of large slate flags, greenish in color. There was a row of potted plants, some in flower, some climbing like vines up the redwood lattice that had been provided for them. Here and there were white wicker chairs and chaise longues with striped canvas seat covers. It was a pleasant room that reminded Frank of what semi-lousy taste he and Gracie had. They weren't quite the avocado Formica people who had increased so in numbers, but compared to homosexuals and Episcopalians, they were remarkably tasteless; or if in their life together they had ever had anything good, they failed to take care of it. It was a genuine case of not being very well bred. Fishing tackle in the living room, wet towels drying out on the handlebars of the stationary bicycle, sanitary napkins on an open shelf in the guest bathroom — Frank and Gracie had, at their best, strengths elsewhere.

Gracie stretched out on a chaise while Frank sat in an armchair that flexed under him as he sat. He scooted over a foot or so to get the tip of the Amazon pitcher plant out of his shirt collar. There was a hazy green glare from the windows, and when Frank looked off to his right, he could see the cool glow of the sun illuminating the yard.

"I'm glad you came over," she said.

"I am too, though I feel a little awkward," Frank said. She was wearing a man's gray-striped dress shirt and jeans. He thought she was beautiful. He always thought she was beautiful, even when he was angry at her and discovering a surprisingly instantaneous hatred embedded in his love. Looking at her, he took account of his being in love with her and recognized that it was irrevocable; it had no negotiating value. In that sense, it may have been neither here nor there. Frank acknowledged that true love made people, if not autocratic, then cruel. It was the source of barbarism. People around those who were in love were innocent bystanders, combatants in the way of friendly fire.

"Holly came by," she said. "She wanted to apologize. It didn't turn out the way she'd planned. The whole thing made me feel horribly guilty and reminded me that we have an obligation to bring this whole business to a swift and clean end."

"I'm not following."

"Well, let me fill you in. Do you have any idea what Holly was doing with Lane Lawlor?"

"No."

"Think about it. In your opinion, is he her type?"

"No."

"But we never questioned it, did we?"

"Love is blind. Isn't that our basic training? Aren't we taught that we're traitors if we don't believe that?"

"I don't know, but it's not true. It's the opposite of blind."

"I'm stuck. What's she doing with him?"

"She wanted to cause a crisis," Gracie said. "The crisis should have happened a long time ago. But she was forced to escalate it. Then she said it got out of control. She never thought you'd attack Lane Lawlor and start a riot. It was like pretending to drown in Utah all over again."

"Wait a minute, wait a minute, wait a minute. What was the point of the crisis?"

Gracie looked at him. It amused her that he was so stupid. But this was too important to let her enjoy his stupidity. "The point of the crisis was to bring you and me together."

"Oh."

Frank's heart ached. They were twisting their child. The self-hatred rose like a tide of sewage. He looked at Gracie. She seemed pathetic. He could barely speak. He managed a faint smile and he said with an aching throat, nodding madly all the while, "Our little kid," causing tears to stream down both their faces. Frank could see no way out.

52

Eileen was working out of her home, which hardly implied a hobby. The front room of her neat house on Cree Street was a smartly arranged office of gray filing cabinets, desk and a copying machine that Frank thought, but was not sure, looked familiar. She welcomed him with a warmth that verged on high-pitched.

"May I sit down?"

"Of course! Will you have anything? Tea? Coffee?"

"Not a thing. But bless your heart, you're always thinking of me, aren't you?"

"I tried, I think, Mr. Copenhaver. For a good many years. But we hit a fork in the road when Mrs. Copenhaver, when Mrs. Copenhaver —"

"Yes, it was Fork City all right. But conditions weren't so bad."

"They were erratic."

"But *exactly*. You had very little response from me by which to measure your efforts. What could be clearer? I had been an attentive businessman. And suddenly you were there rather pointlessly shuffling papers, gathering things for my signature which would remain unsigned for months. You had many hours in which to contemplate your retirement fund and the very negligible contributions of our profit-sharing plan. You took phone numbers from people who would never be called back. You might well have begun feeling almost deceptive having to pretend that you worked for someone who was actually trying to do something with his business. It was your unlucky job to have to dignify my gyrations with a lot of empty words."

"It wasn't easy." She smiled with that peculiar smile which was predicated on the lips either hiding or holding the teeth.

"It wasn't easy."

"It wasn't easy," she repeated a bit more emphatically. "I did what I could."

"Of course you did. You were there all day and you did what you could."

"Yes," she said. The atmosphere was cooling.

"But the mind tends to run in those circumstances."

"Not mine!" said Eileen.

"I should have said, 'The list of options seems to lengthen.' "

She decided to listen and see where this was headed.

"It lengthens and lengthens until it is like a long old diamondback rattlesnake that starts way over here and goes *wa-ay* over there where its head is, slowly raring up to about eye level and saying, 'Eileen, I've got a good idea.' "

Frank fell silent. Eileen said nothing. Next to a filing cabinet, the curtain stirred as a car passed the window. Frank placed photocopies of the bad checks in Eileen's lap, a copy of the statute on fraud and embezzlement, and a set of sentencing guidelines. "All things considered," he said quietly, "I think we'll let you keep the gas station. Monday around nine be okay?" He got to his feet and, as orotund as Edward Ballantine, intoned, "Back to rule and regulation," stretching out the *u* sounds and elevating the eyebrows. This whole thing was less hearty in tone to Frank than he was letting on. But he was taking charge.

Earlier in the day, he called Holly and they talked for a long while. One thing she had said stuck in his mind:

"Mama pointed out that because you're my parents, I make the assumption that you're a unit and that's not necessarily how you see it. I can't imagine wanting to be a part of a unit. I mean, I'm not waiting for the door to open so Mr. Right will come and help me form a unit. But I got off on the wrong track with you and Mama. I just looked up and saw: unit. I think you always presented yourselves to me that way. But it's not your job to set an example."

"But I'm afraid it is," said Frank, feeling heat go up the back of his neck. "I know I didn't do it well. Anyway, I'm sorry your crazy plan didn't work."

"You are?"

"Well, I say I am. You know, you can never really go back, sugar."

"Oh," she said. "Oh, I know."

Frank didn't want to make any such statement. He hoped Holly didn't take so withering a remark seriously but recognized it simply as a rumor from another country, and that with any luck she'd find herself a fine young anarchist with orange hair, a watercolorist or a Basque separatist, a pretender to the throne of all the Russias, a Suriname hotelier, anything but the ideologue of private property rights she had used so effectively to frighten her parents, which, for what it was currently worth, they would always be.

Edward Ballantine called Frank at his office. His was actually the first call Eileen patched through on her return. It was a small thing, but it gave Frank a sense of welcome regularity to hear her voice identify the caller. He fingered his Dictaphone while he took this call, vowing a blizzard of replies to unanswered mail.

"Frank," said Edward, "I'm trying to establish a spot for our meeting that doesn't contain too many unwelcome associations for anybody."

"Eat shit," said Frank, tired of all this phony politeness.

"Save it for the meeting, sport. I'm really not hearing you out of that context, except for picking a venue."

"I thought we were doing this for you in your widely publicized war on deception."

"It's not just for me. People need to be able to go on with their lives. We don't want the setting to be too exceptional. We want it to partake of the everyday."

"What've you come up with so far?" Frank asked, not really knowing what Edward was talking about, relieved to not have to go someplace he associated with uranium or hang gliding or the new spirituality.

"I think I've got a great little spot. The Friends Meeting Hall."

"You mean the Quakers?"

"Yup."

"We'd have it to ourselves?"

"For as long as we want," said Edward.

Frank thought this was remarkably like a real estate deal. In some ways, it was also the sort of thing his mother was always putting together on behalf of her book club or canasta group, or a "drive" for caddy scholarships, or the improvement of the rodeo grounds. He didn't like dignifying their talk with all this emphasis on its location.

He and Edward must have been talking about the schedule because they rang off on Edward's remark, "See you tomorrow morning, then. At nine."

Frank drew all the curtains in the office so that his desk lamp illuminated a large circle, as though it were nighttime. He slumped down in his chair, the microphone in his hand, and began flicking mail toward himself and answering it in the most perfunctory manner. He was conscious of the speed at which he was working, challenged even to go faster. He answered several letters with the word "no," and several others more discursively with the statement "The answer is no." Each letter he replied to he threw on the floor, and a pile soon grew next to his chair. He said no so often that it occurred to him that someone in the next room might conclude he was being tortured. Documents calling for his signature he threw onto another pile. He took all bills at face value and threw them into the first pile unreviewed. He used to enjoy this, sorting everything into a network of streams; there had been a movement of information between himself, Eileen and the U.S. Postal Service that was like breathing, a cadence that could rise and fall with his business activity. No more. This was like sweeping dead flies out of an abandoned house. Nevertheless, and despite the presence of dividends and rentals and even a token first payment from the chicken hotel, there was a sense of things flowing, generally, in one direction: out. He thought of someone in a deep tub of water who, having opened an artery well below the surface, notices that the water is steadily changing color.

He didn't really care! Something important was coming up and this wasn't important. "Easy come, easy go!" he cried out with a chilly laugh. Well, that wasn't true either. He had worked hard, but it was like childbirth: when it was past, you didn't remember the pain. In this case, he was indifferent to the child. And yet it was boring to join the millions deploring success. He had, over the predictions of his father, been successful. Since his father was now dead, he could hardly rub his nose in it. And if his father had been alive, he might have enjoyed it. He had lived to see the beginning of Frank's success and seemed to be pleasantly surprised. It would be nearly impossible for a son to credit to his father such a simple reaction as "pleasantly surprised." But with several years to contemplate his father's actual reaction to his business activity, Frank was forced to conclude that his father had been pleasantly surprised. Perhaps suspicion was a father's obligation to a son — to say equably, "You look like a bum to me," and remain congenial when junior insinuates the murder in his heart. Anyway, as Frank's farmer grandmother used to say, "It's all in the Bible."

Frank returned from lunch and resumed his dictation. Eileen came in and picked up a tape from him at one point, brought letters for signatures and, at what seemed an arbitrary moment, announced she was going home. Frank looked at his watch: it was five. "Ah, so it is," he said. "See you in the morning." She departed with a wry smile. She had fallen from a high place only that week as the owner of her own business and seemed a bit like a captured officer in a POW camp.

And just a minute after Eileen left, Lucy, who must have been stationed nearby, came into his office. This was somehow frightening. He tried to defuse his alarm by tracking it down. He could already see she was conscious of it. He worried that a demand was headed his way and pretended to be groggily emerging from his work instead of what he really was, excessively focused on the moment.

She led with "I see you're starting to put in full days again."

"Yeah, I've got to."

"Inspired by what? Embarrassment?"

He tried honesty. "We'll just have to see." She was wearing a dark, dyed silk dress that came all the way to her calves, riding boots and a light cotton jacket with pockets so big their tops hung open.

"Did Gracie say anything about the other day?" Lucy asked.

It was pleasant to take this light, inquiring tone, as though that sweaty inadvertence were easily tamed in memory. "No, she didn't. There really hasn't been an opportunity."

"We used to be friends."

"Well —"

"I thought you had broken up. But this is just one more instance of 'A stiff prick has no conscience,' right?"

"Please, Lucy, these phrases."

"Not ladylike?"

"I don't know, harsh, I guess."

"Harsh," she said, leaning across his desk to slap his face. "I'll give you harsh."

"Off we go," he said, pulling his chin in but not raising his hands to protect himself.

"I'm a travel agent."

"I know."

"I'd like to leave it at that."

"It's understandable that we try to reach out and have other things in our lives," he said, but this brought on another ringing slap. He wasn't quite sure why.

"Write some tickets, go home, eat, go to bed. I was going with a really nice guy, a developer. But Gracie wanted to know how I could cooperate with the degradation of the environment. Who does this big Louisiana cunt think she is?"

"I don't know, Luce, really I don't. I'm supposed to find out in the morning."

"Ah-ha! We're having a what, a heart-to-heart?"

"I don't know what to call it. It's Ed Ballantine's idea. It's more their deal than mine. I just said I'd go. My real goal right now is to keep my head above water. I've been sort of neglecting things."

"*Neglecting* things — you've been out of control! You ought to tell Miss Louisiana you can't live without her and you're going around causing a lot of harm to other people. Thank God I saw the light and called Jerome."

"Jerome?"

"The developer! He just did a hundred forty-one single-family dwellings in Salt Lake and he loves me. He loves *me*. And I'm getting ready to reciprocate my ass off! Why? Because he loves *me, me, me*."

He wanted to tell her that he hoped she found a great new life in opportunism. He felt threatened by all this raving and slapping. He didn't want Gracie so described and he was disgusted with himself to suspect he enjoyed being fought over. And on second thought, he really didn't; it was like being a meatball thrown into a kennel.

"Anyway," Lucy said, "I shouldn't be so tough on you. You don't have much in the way of a personal life. Maybe you don't have the capacity. And inside, you may be about as squirrelly as anyone I ever met. But you know, I looked at my little agency. It's nothing great. I ship bodies. But I do okay and it's well run. I had to make a decision about my goals. I decided that I'm going to dedicate myself to money. How does that sound? Money, money, money! I can't change the world. I'm just a little speck. I have to do what everyone else does. I bet I'll be good at it. I may try to marry that guy and get all the single-family dwellings. I'll be the queen of the suburbs and everyone will have to do as I say. Things are great. I don't have cancer that I know of and I have learned several valuable lessons from you. I'm saying hello to everything you're saying goodbye to. I'm out of here, I'm gone, thanks for the memories." She pulled her dress up over her hips and pointed to the wedge of white silk over her crotch. "This goes too," she said, and left the room.

Frank was not at all prepared to leave for home. One of these days soon the bank was going to make its move on his house, maybe even put the notice on the door. There was getting to be some suspense about that. He was still dazed by Lucy's speech and the sense of having deserved the accusations. But everyone deserved a lifetime of accusations, he believed. Where did this assumption of agreed-upon rules come from? How archaic, he thought. It was like being assaulted by someone in a dirndl. It was like firing a Scud missile into a Christmas parade because you didn't believe in Santa Claus. He went on like this in faint indignation until that too passed and he mused on his several detachments from any succor that ever came his way. He hadn't had feelings of fellowship since he was a hippie, or any familial warmth since Gracie hit the road. He felt like a cooling asteroid in an ocean of darkness. And the humiliations were becoming ritualistic. God only knew what the occasion at the Friends Meeting Hall would bring.

He tore through the papers on his desk, hungry for a brainstorm. Michael Milken would be eligible for parole in just three more years owing to possible sentence reductions for his cooperation with prosecutors. Would he be seen as a hero returning from exile at Drexel Burnham Lambert, with possible unseen synergies in the junk bond market? A man who was the equivalent of ten thousand bank robbers would be back in the thrilling soup of American business; and presumably Mr. Frank Copenhaver would have a buck or two to throw into the game. So, there was life. There still was life! He said several more "no"s into the Dictaphone, advising Eileen to use them as she saw best, and called it a day.

53

A small flagstone walkway led from the sidewalk on Grant Avenue to the honeysuckle-embowered entryway to the Friends Meeting Hall. Frank thought that there must be very few Quakers in town, but he was comforted by their vague reputation for peacefulness, and hoping, above all, that this fucking thing didn't turn into a slimefest. He just had to get the poison tide stopped. Gracie would meet him at the house later.

He let himself in and found that Edward was already there. Edward was wearing a tropical-looking white shirt with short sleeves that hung outside his baggy cotton slacks. His shock of brown hair stood up from the center of his head like a cockscomb. He rushed up to Frank and welcomed him with a double-handed handshake and a deep look. Frank found himself suddenly shy. A sissy smile bloomed on his lips, and incomprehension expressed as a little puff of air through his nose. He felt a gust of overpowering conventionalism. He wished to look past the insulting horrors of his situation and be well bred in every way.

Edward abruptly left the room. Against the wall were several old brown folding chairs with white stenciled codes on their backs. Frank took it upon himself to set two of them out. They were of some patented design, and at first he couldn't figure out how to get them open. He tried to think of a proper arrangement for them, then gave up, placing them across from each other. He looked at the tall, double-paned windows that revealed the trees and sky, and he longed to fly away; in fact, sitting down in one of the chairs he had unsuccessfully tried to arrange, he escaped into thoughts of migrating birds, wheeling southbound flocks gazing down at the gentle curves of the planet.

Then Edward returned. "Shall I get a pitcher of water and some glasses?" he asked.

"No. In fact, I've got to use the bathroom before we have our talk."

Frank locked the bathroom door and stood for a long time looking at his face in the mirror. He couldn't understand why he was going to enter into what would have to be a grotesque discussion. Not so long ago, he could have done one of several drugs and come out filled with wit and leadership, an overview even. Without any expression at all, he projected all sorts of histories and motives on this bland face. In one story, he was an extra playing a youthful tar in *Wake of the Red Witch;* in another, he was Lincoln freeing the slaves. He went back out into the hall, then into a kitchenette with its Mr. Coffee and paper towels and under-the-counter refrigerator. He made up a pitcher of ice water and found two glasses. He placed these on a tray and returned with dread to the meeting room.

For some reason, just now, he feared that his covenant with Gracie had run out of time. Frank's romantic streak never accounted for time. When he was a boy, a sparrow sang at his window every morning for a whole summer, but it always quit at exactly eight forty-five. His father had said it was nothing but a union sparrow. Frank wanted that bird to sing without reference to time. Maybe he could face that his life with Gracie had just been time-bound and now it was her fate to be a moving target. Still, it was hard not to feel that they were trapped by other people and situations. It was hard not to look for something to blame because the stakes were so ominous.

Edward said, "I think that it is important that we try to be orderly about this. I have to tell you my story, Frank. Let me just get on with it. When I was up at the college museum, designing the Trail of Tears exhibit —"

"Wait a minute," said Frank, "I'm lost. What do you do?"

"I'm an anthropologist," said Edward. "That's my first love. Which doesn't pay so great. Which is why I have gone into other things."

"Oh. And what's this thing you were designing?"

"An exhibit for the museum showing the retreat from Nebraska of the Northern Cheyenne Indians. It's a gold-plated consciousness raiser if ever there was one, and we had a grant to do it up right, no short cuts and no compromises. We built almost full-size models of one of their typical camps, with a big blue sky overhead, a real firmament, and a religious feel to everything that would help us sense that this was a holy story, which of course it was. We needed models for some of the life-size sculptures of the Indians. These we found very easily from among the Native American students at the college." Edward was settling into his amiable narrative. "And I put up a little notice in the health food store for a well-preserved fortyish woman with dark complexion and hair."

Frank felt panic sweep over him. "And Gracie answered the ad?" he asked.

"Gracie answered the ad. Look, we just have to get the facts. We don't need to drag this out. But Gracie arrived in the evening while I was bolting together a sagebrush. And one thing led to another."

"In the museum?" Frank cried. "One thing led to another!"

"Well, not just baldly in the museum. In . . . one of the historical reconstructions of an Indian dwelling."

An image of the dwelling seemed to scorch Frank's mind. "My wife? In a fake tepee?"

Edward seemed to try politely to take in all this turmoil. "That's one way of putting it, Frank."

Frank just held his face and moaned. With unwelcome irony, he reflected that Edward wasn't just whistling Dixie when he said "Trail of Tears." He wished for details yet found himself repelled. The alternation of these impulses was maddening.

His first thought was that it was now final that he could never feel the same about her again. This was sort of an assertion. Another desperate assertion was that he would never feel the same about anthropologists or museums or Indians; and as for tepees, anything that even remotely suggested their conical shape would be too much to contemplate. He was plunging into an unbearable misery. For one acute wave, he thought his limbs would fly off in agony.

"How did you ever find out Gracie was seeing me?" Edward asked.

Well, of course it was a good question. Frank *had* found out, hadn't he? "Gracie told me."

"Why?"

"I was suspicious," Frank said. Really, who else could he tell this to? He remembered Gracie weeping, remembered all their tears. What was this ghastly need to say all this? It felt disgraceful. Maybe disgrace was more comfortable than holding it in. "I always loved to fish. I fished with my father. I fished with my daughter. I pleaded with Gracie to fish with me." Frank leaned forward in his folding chair and looked into the middle distance. He wanted to see a healthy outdoorsman out there, insouciant, above the fray, but he saw a big sap instead. "One day she said she was going to learn how to fish, but she didn't want me standing over her, telling her what to do. Okay, so I don't stand over her and tell her what to do. I was really happy about that. I mean, how far is minding your own business from abdication? I thought, We could fish together. We could go to New Zealand and catch lunkers together under the Southern Cross. To me, this presents a very romantic picture."

In his agony, Frank leaned farther forward and the folding chair snapped shut on his buttocks, propelling him onto his knees, the chair retaining its grip like an alligator. He struggled to his feet, reopened the chair and sat down again. Resisting a keening tone, he addressed his remarks to Edward, as though he were entitled to an explanation of this chain of events. "She left the house several times a week with her rod and reel, waders and tackle vest. I wanted to go with her but she wouldn't let me. Which makes me, what, a nice guy? an asshole? Do they have a book on this? It went on for months. She said she was improving but she wasn't ready. She was improving. She wasn't ready. So far, so good. When I told my friend June that Gracie was fishing, June said, 'So, that's what she's calling it.' Finally, the season was almost over. I absolutely insisted on going with her. I got my tackle together. We drove to the Madison, a spot I have there, a great spot where two channels come together, a long gravel bar with willows along its banks —"

He could see that he didn't need this much detail. It was as if he were making sure Edward caught lots of fish. "I parked the car and watched Gracie get her stuff together. It became pretty obvious that she didn't know what she was doing. She didn't know how to put the reel on the rod, or the line through the guides, or tie on a fly, or anything. She knew absolutely nothing about fishing! I looked at her waders. They had never been in the water. Suddenly, I had this stab, this recognition, that she was up to no good. I was silent. She must have known I saw through this. I kept thinking: we're middle-aged, we're pathetic, this shouldn't be the occasion for a lot of accusations. But I had to know." He paused and blew his nose. "So I asked her."

"And?" said Edward.

"She told me."

"She told you the truth?"

"Yes." Frank was thrilled to realize that Edward had never heard this story from Gracie, never heard it at all. Talk about anthropology! The fact that Edward had corrupted his marriage had somehow shrunk beside the fact that Gracie had withheld this tale of his moronic deduction. It was personal.

Edward chuckled a bit, maybe grimly, but chuckled. Frank felt the pain of absurdity. He had been happier among the Eskimos. His eyeballs felt dried out by helpless rage and sadness.

He looked around again. He didn't see much chance of getting out of this. He wasn't accusing himself of wanting to get out of this, but he wanted some sense he wasn't falling into the hole he felt opening in the middle of himself. He tried imagining a time in the future when they were all gone and none of this mattered. And it didn't help. Gracie once accused him of making her feel invisible. What if Holly had said, "You made my mother invisible"? What would there have been to say after that? "I'm going to make you invisible"? Frank remembered Gracie's cry:

"I always was able to stand it, able to stand you making fun of my dopey little restaurant, able to watch the side of your head buried in the *Wall Street Journal,* even though it was the same head that was once buried in Carlos Castaneda, the *I Ching,* Baba Ram Dass, Richard Flanagan —"

"Richard Brautigan," Frank had corrected.

"Because you had such a wonderful relationship with Holly," Gracie had said, "and I could always remember you with hair down to your back and Holly sitting on your shoulders. But then, it seems unbelievable, Holly grew up and left. And I couldn't lie to myself anymore."

As though her cry from the heart had been nothing but a performance, Frank had said, "Let's not take our eyes off the applause meter, folks!"

I hate myself, he thought. He had accommodated his tribe by living as he had. He found out too late that that wasn't good enough. It was like one of the new-style muggings where you wake up and they've stolen one or more of your internal organs.

"I still don't know what you want from me," Frank said to Edward. He felt flat and hopeless. Edward looked a bit deflated himself. It was not a meeting between kings. Maybe this was the dreaded bankruptcy.

"I had to talk to somebody who'd know how it felt," Edward said.

This artificial claim tripped something in Frank. He had had enough. Blank and murderous, he asked, "Who'd know how *what* felt, Edward?"

Edward seemed to examine Frank's face for intention, sincerity, something. "To be left by Gracie," he said.

What? Frank tried to hold it down. He wasn't going to give this guy anything. He leaned back in his chair. Perhaps he could accommodate Edward a little, hands across the abyss. After all, it was something Edward would have to live with. But Edward seemed to be awaiting some payoff, a rare moment. All Frank wanted was verification. He still wasn't sure.

"You got the gate, huh?"

"I'm afraid I did," Edward said. "I guess I was just wanting some confirmation that this had anything to do with me in the first place."

With a new pride and the sense of a pathway perceived at last, Frank told him he was the wrong person to ask. It was enough to know that Edward suspected that he might have been used.

Frank's mind was racing. He had to find Gracie right this very minute. He wondered if he was getting ahead of himself. It was as if he were making notes for something he wanted to happen, defying postponement. Suddenly, Frank got to his feet. Edward looked on, open-mouthed. Frank ran outside and continued running until he was half a block from his house. He slowed to a walk and caught his breath. He found Gracie walking around the front lawn.

"What a funny house," she said.

She barely let him talk. He thought they might gaze on the place together. But she was thinking about something.

"Let's try to find Holly," said Gracie. "She's gone back to the one with a ring in his nose. She took down the douche bag and the picture of the *Enola Gay*." Gracie seemed to be going right on to the next thing. Frank reluctantly saw this as a sign of strength. "Let's put in an appearance." She chattered on about the missing piece of time. She'd been to Europe! She'd been back to Louisiana! He lagged behind in one of the gray areas that subtended all his emotional changes of state. That, he was prepared to admit, was a weakness. But if he admitted all the things that got him out of bed in the absence of strengths, wouldn't he lose what little footing he possessed? He should have taken that chance, he knew, back when Gracie stood solidly beside him. It was now a distinctly less propitious time for such a housecleaning.

"Gracie, if I had ever really thought about you going off with someone, I wouldn't have picked Edward particularly as your type."

"He's not my type."

"I guess I'm missing something," said Frank. Gracie unlocked the Buick and they both got in. She gripped the wheel and looked down the road as though she were already driving.

"You guess you're missing something! Well, that's a start."

Frank said nothing. His head seemed to be enlarging from the unmoving diameter at his shirt collar. He craned around behind the windshield, not even driving, not even knowing Holly's address.

"I understand your business is falling apart," Gracie said. "Wouldn't that be a miracle?"

"I can fix it."

"Can you." It wasn't quite a question.

"Yes, I can."

"Have I nearly ruined you?" Gracie beamed. Frank didn't reply. Then she said, wonderingly, and to no one in particular, "Who would have thought?"

They drove down an empty street lined with the fiefdoms of small homes in which discord over colors, shapes and roofing materials, fences, breeds of dog and shrubbery, seemed to end the westward movement in its provisional neighborhoods.

Gracie said, "I had the funniest idea. It was about children, I guess, and how bringing them up causes this sadness. Almost as if their life tells you you're going to die? I mean, I know it's love, but it sure is kind of a lonesome thought. You know what I mean? While I was gone, I went back home and paid a little visit to my old indigo plantation, quote unquote. You remember that? And where I used to think about vanished glory, this time I was just in mind of all those people gone. Frank, you know what I figured out?" She looked at him to give him a chance to answer. When it was clear he wasn't going to say anything, she said,

"There's nothing crazier than picking up exactly where you left off." Then she smiled.

Finally, the houses thinned out and dropped away, and the street turned into a long, twisting road, and if there was a stop sign anywhere, it must have been hidden behind the curves.

VINTAGE
CONTEMPORARIES

___ **I Pass Like Night** by Jonathan Ames	$8.95	0-679-72857-0
___ **The Mezzanine** by Nicholson Baker	$9.00	0-679-72576-8
___ **Room Temperature** by Nicholson Baker	$9.00	0-679-73440-6
___ **Vox** by Nicholson Baker	$8.00	0-679-74211-5
___ **Gorilla, My Love** by Toni Cade Bambara	$9.00	0-679-73898-3
___ **The Salt Eaters** by Toni Cade Bambara	$10.00	0-679-74076-7
___ **Violence** by Richard Bausch	$11.00	0-679-74379-0
___ **Chilly Scenes of Winter** by Ann Beattie	$10.00	0-679-73234-9
___ **Distortions** by Ann Beattie	$9.95	0-679-73235-7
___ **Falling in Place** by Ann Beattie	$11.00	0-679-73192-X
___ **Love Always** by Ann Beattie	$10.00	0-394-74418-7
___ **Picturing Will** by Ann Beattie	$9.95	0-679-73194-6
___ **Secrets and Surprises** by Ann Beattie	$10.00	0-679-73193-8
___ **What Was Mine** by Ann Beattie	$10.00	0-679-73903-3
___ **A Farm Under a Lake** by Martha Bergland	$9.95	0-679-73011-7
___ **The Revolution of Little Girls** by Blanche McCrary Boyd	$10.00	0-679-73812-6
___ **The Planets** by James Boylan	$10.00	0-679-73906-8
___ **Dream of the Wolf** by Scott Bradfield	$11.00	0-679-73638-7
___ **The History of Luminous Motion** by Scott Bradfield	$11.00	0-679-72943-7
___ **A Closed Eye** by Anita Brookner	$11.00	0-679-74340-5
___ **Brief Lives** by Anita Brookner	$11.00	0-679-73733-2
___ **The Debut** by Anita Brookner	$10.00	0-679-72712-4
___ **Fraud** by Anita Brookner	$11.00	0-679-74308-1
___ **Latecomers** by Anita Brookner	$8.95	0-679-72668-3
___ **Lewis Percy** by Anita Brookner	$10.00	0-679-72944-5
___ **Providence** by Anita Brookner	$10.00	0-679-73814-2
___ **Big Bad Love** by Larry Brown	$10.00	0-679-73491-0
___ **Dirty Work** by Larry Brown	$9.95	0-679-73049-4
___ **Harry and Catherine** by Frederick Busch	$10.00	0-679-73076-1
___ **Sleeping in Flame** by Jonathan Carroll	$10.00	0-679-72777-9
___ **Cathedral** by Raymond Carver	$10.00	0-679-72369-2
___ **Fires** by Raymond Carver	$9.00	0-679-72239-4
___ **No Heroics, Please** by Raymond Carver	$10.00	0-679-74007-4
___ **Short Cuts** by Raymond Carver	$10.00	0-679-74864-4
___ **What We Talk About When We Talk About Love** by Raymond Carver	$9.00	0-679-72305-6
___ **Where I'm Calling From** by Raymond Carver	$12.00	0-679-72231-9
___ **Will You Please Be Quiet, Please?** by Raymond Carver	$10.00	0-679-73569-0
___ **The House on Mango Street** by Sandra Cisneros	$9.00	0-679-73477-5
___ **Woman Hollering Creek** by Sandra Cisneros	$10.00	0-679-73856-8
___ **I Look Divine** by Christopher Coe	$5.95	0-394-75995-8
___ **Dancing Bear** by James Crumley	$10.00	0-394-72576-X

VINTAGE CONTEMPORARIES

VINTAGE
CONTEMPORARIES

VINTAGE
CONTEMPORARIES

____ **Soft Water** by Robert Olmstead	$6.95	0-394-75752-1
____ **Sirens** by Stephen Pett	$9.95	0-394-75712-2
____ **Clea and Zeus Divorce** by Emily Prager	$10.00	0-394-75591-X
____ **Eve's Tattoo** by Emily Prager	$10.00	0-679-74053-8
____ **A Visit From the Footbinder** by Emily Prager	$10.00	0-394-75592-8
____ **A Good Baby** by Leon Rooke	$10.00	0-679-72939-9
____ **Mohawk** by Richard Russo	$13.00	0-679-75382-6
____ **Nobody's Fool** by Richard Russo	$13.00	0-679-75333-8
____ **The Risk Pool** by Richard Russo	$13.00	0-679-75383-4
____ **The Laughing Sutra** by Mark Salzman	$11.00	0-679-73546-1
____ **Mile Zero** by Thomas Sanchez	$10.95	0-679-73260-8
____ **Rabbit Boss** by Thomas Sanchez	$12.00	0-679-72621-7
____ **Zoot-Suit Murders** by Thomas Sanchez	$10.00	0-679-73396-5
____ **Anywhere But Here** by Mona Simpson	$12.00	0-679-73738-3
____ **The Lost Father** by Mona Simpson	$12.00	0-679-73303-5
____ **The Joy Luck Club** by Amy Tan	$10.00	0-679-72768-X
____ **The Kitchen God's Wife** by Amy Tan	$12.00	0-679-74808-3
____ **The Five Gates of Hell** by Rupert Thomson	$11.00	0-679-73571-2
____ **The Player** by Michael Tolkin	$10.00	0-679-72254-8
____ **Many Things Have Happened Since He Died** by Elizabeth Dewberry Vaughn	$10.00	0-679-73568-2
____ **Myra Breckinridge and Myron** by Gore Vidal	$13.00	0-394-75444-1
____ **All It Takes** by Patricia Volk	$8.95	0-679-73044-3
____ **Birdy** by William Wharton	$10.00	0-679-73412-0
____ **All Stories Are True** by John Edgar Wideman	$10.00	0-679-73752-9
____ **Philadelphia Fire** by John Edgar Wideman	$10.00	0-679-73650-6
____ **Breaking and Entering** by Joy Williams	$6.95	0-394-75773-4
____ **Escapes** by Joy Williams	$9.00	0-679-73331-0
____ **Taking Care** by Joy Williams	$5.95	0-394-72912-9
____ **The Final Club** by Geoffrey Wolff	$11.00	0-679-73592-5
____ **Providence** by Geoffrey Wolff	$10.00	0-679-73277-2
____ **The Easter Parade** by Richard Yates	$8.95	0-679-72230-0
____ **Eleven Kinds of Loneliness** by Richard Yates	$8.95	0-679-72221-1
____ **Revolutionary Road** by Richard Yates	$12.00	0-679-72191-6

Available at your bookstore or call toll-free to order: 1-800-733-3000.
Credit cards only. Prices subject to change.

VINTAGE ☀ BOOKS

Available at your local bookstore
or

To order by mail, please fill out or copy the form below and send to:
Random House Order Department,
400 Hahn Road, Westminster, Maryland 21157.
To order by phone, call 1-800-733-3000 (credit cards only).

- If you wish to pay by check or money order, please make it payable to Vintage Books.
- If you prefer to charge your order to a major credit card, please fill in the information below.

Charge my account with
☐ American Express   ☐ Visa   ☐ MasterCard

Account No. _____ Expiration Date _____

(Signature) _____

Name _____

Address _____

City/State/Zip _____

Title	ISBN	Quantity	Price	Total
The Bushwhacked Piano	0-394-72642-1	_____	x $11.00	= _____
Keep the Change	0-679-73033-8	_____	x $11.00	= _____
Nobody's Angel	0-394-74738-0	_____	x $11.00	= _____
Nothing but Blue Skies	0-679-74778-8	_____	x $12.00	= _____
Something to Be Desired	0-394-73156-5	_____	x $10.00	= _____
To Skin a Cat	0-394-75521-9	_____	x $10.00	= _____

Shipping/Handling* = _____

Subtotal = _____

Sales Tax (where applicable) = _____

Total Enclosed = $_____

In addition to the price of the books, enclose shipping and handling: $2.00 for the first book and $0.50 for each additional book ordered.
Prices subject to change without notice. Please allow 4–6 weeks for delivery.